DISNEP

MICKEY MOUSE

THE QUEST FOR THE MISSING MEMORIES

Facebook: **facebook.com/idwpublishing**
Twitter: **@idwpublishing**
YouTube: **youtube.com/idwpublishing**
Tumblr: **tumblr.idwpublishing.com**
Instagram: **instagram.com/idwpublishing**

ISBN: 978-1-68405-485-5   22 21 20 19   1 2 3 4

COVER ARTIST
MARCO GHIGLIONE

COVER COLORIST
EDIZIONI BD

LETTERS and DESIGN
TOM B. LONG

ASSISTANT EDITOR
ANNI PERHEENTUPA

EDITOR
CHRIS CERASI

MICKEY MOUSE: THE QUEST FOR THE MISSING MEMORIES. AUGUST 2019. FIRST PRINTING. All contents, unless otherwise specified, copyright © 2019 Disney Enterprises, Inc. All rights reserved. The IDW logo is registered in the U.S. Patent and Trademark Office. IDW Publishing, a division of Idea and Design Works, LLC. Editorial offices: 2765 Truxtun Road, San Diego, CA 92106. Any similarities to persons living or dead are purely coincidental. With the exception of artwork used for review purposes, none of the contents of this publication may be reprinted without the permission of Idea and Design Works, LLC. Printed in Korea.

IDW Publishing does not read or accept unsolicited submissions of ideas, stories, or artwork.

Chris Ryall, President & Publisher/CCO
John Barber, Editor-in-Chief
Cara Morrison, Chief Financial Officer
Matthew Ruzicka, Chief Accounting Officer
David Hedgecock, Associate Publisher
Jerry Bennington, VP of New Product Development
Lorelei Bunjes, VP of Digital Services
Justin Eisinger, Editorial Director, Graphic Novels and Collections
Eric Moss, Sr. Director, Licensing & Business Development

Ted Adams and Robbie Robbins, IDW Founders

Special thanks to Stefano Ambrosio, Stefano Attardi, Julie Dorris, Marco Ghiglione, Jodi Hammerwold, Behnoosh Khalili, Manny Mederos, Eugene Paraszczuk, Carlotta Quattrocolo, Roberto Santillo, Christopher Troise, and Camilla Vedove.

Written by FRANCESCO ARTIBANI

Chapter 1: The Memory Box
Art by GIORGIO CAVAZZANO
Colors by EDIZIONI BD

Chapter 2: The Carnival Mystery
Art by MARCO GERVASIO
Colors by EMANUELE ERCOLANI

Chapter 3: The Treasure in the Old Tree
Art by ANDREA FRECCERO
Colors by GIULIANO CANGIANO

Chapter 4: The Heroes of Mount Rattmore
Art by MARCO MAZZARELLO
Colors by VINCI CARDONA

Chapter 5: The Spring of Time
Art by STEFANO INTINI
Colors by EDIZIONI BD

Chapter 6: The Queen of the River
Art by CLAUDIO SCIARRONE
Colors by GIULIANO CANGIANO and LUCIO ROVIDOTTI

Chapter 7: Threat from the Future
Art by LORENZO PASTROVICCHIO
Colors by EMANUELE ERCOLANI

Chapter 8: The Memory Machine
Art by CORRADO MASTANTUONO
Colors by EMANUELE ERCOLANI

Art by GIORGIO CAVAZZANO
Colors by EDIZIONI BD

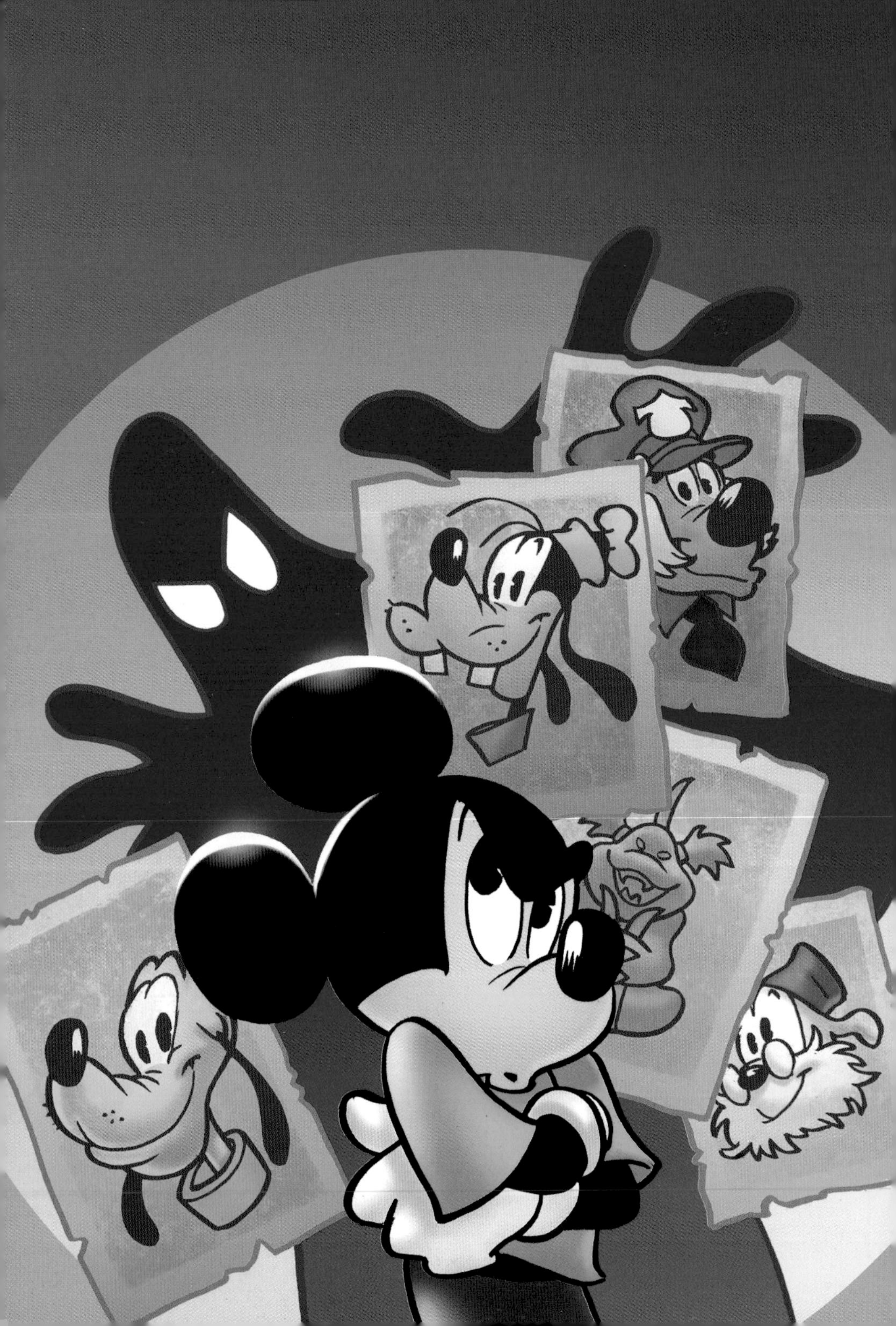

CHAPTER 1: THE MEMORY BOX

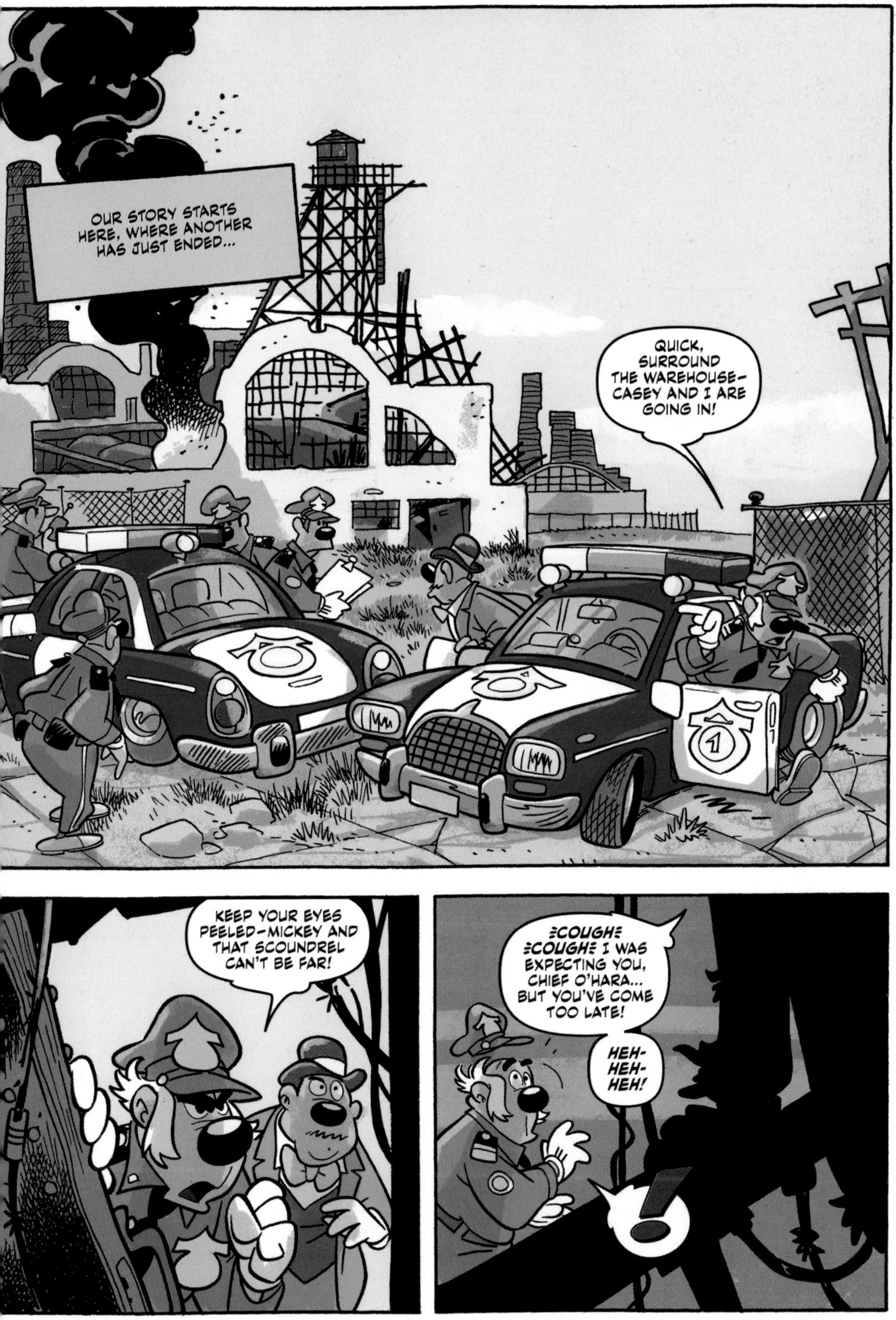

OUR STORY STARTS HERE, WHERE ANOTHER HAS JUST ENDED...
QUICK, SURROUND THE WAREHOUSE-CASEY AND I ARE GOING IN!
KEEP YOUR EYES PEELED-MICKEY AND THAT SCOUNDREL CAN'T BE FAR!
≡COUGH≡ ≡COUGH≡ I WAS EXPECTING YOU, CHIEF O'HARA... BUT YOU'VE COME TOO LATE!
HEH-HEH-HEH!
!

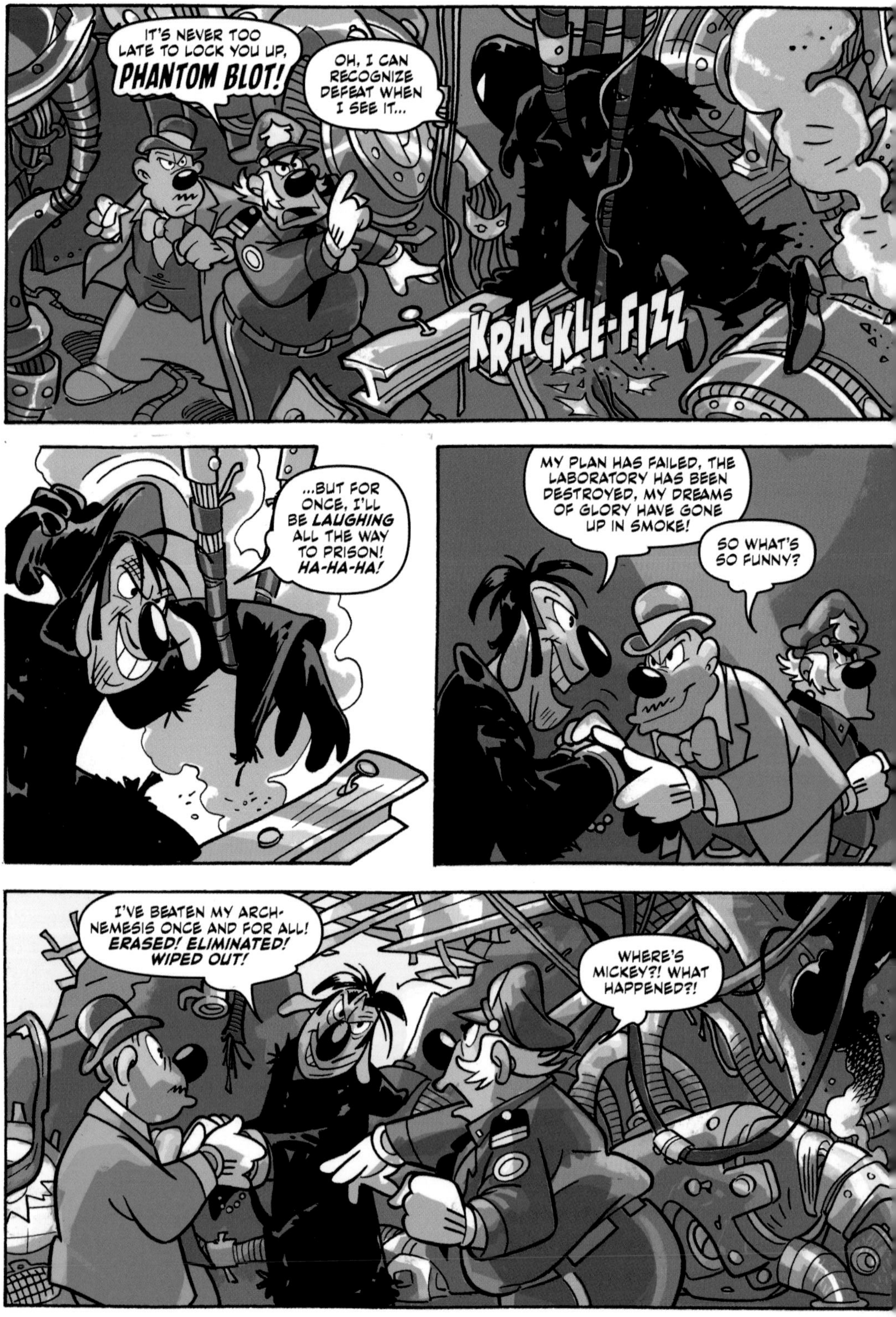
IT'S NEVER TOO LATE TO LOCK YOU UP, PHANTOM BLOT!
OH, I CAN RECOGNIZE DEFEAT WHEN I SEE IT...
KRACKLE-FIZZ
...BUT FOR ONCE, I'LL BE LAUGHING ALL THE WAY TO PRISON! HA-HA-HA!
MY PLAN HAS FAILED, THE LABORATORY HAS BEEN DESTROYED, MY DREAMS OF GLORY HAVE GONE UP IN SMOKE!
SO WHAT'S SO FUNNY?
I'VE BEATEN MY ARCH-NEMESIS ONCE AND FOR ALL! ERASED! ELIMINATED! WIPED OUT!
WHERE'S MICKEY?! WHAT HAPPENED?!

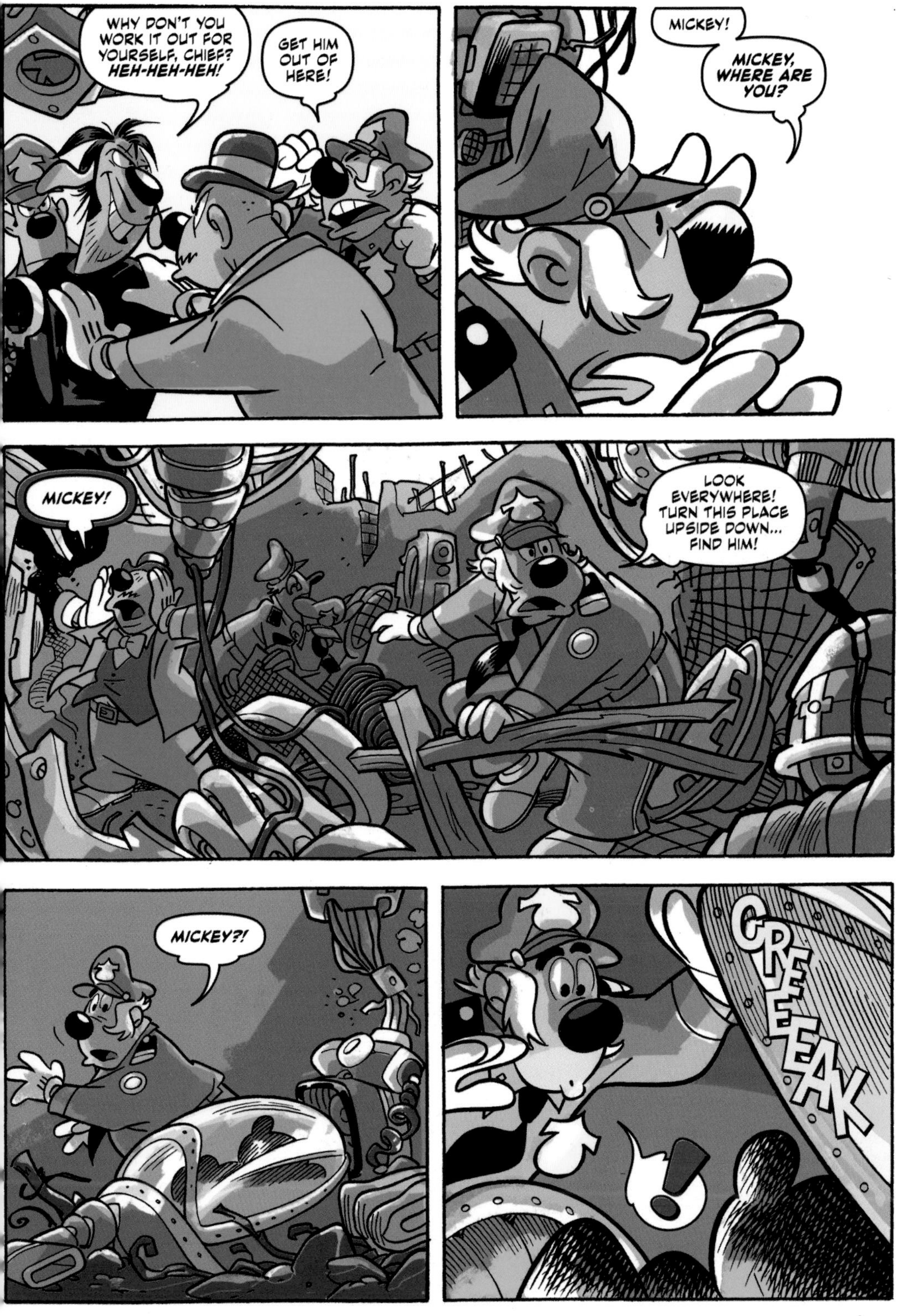
WHY DON'T YOU WORK IT OUT FOR YOURSELF, CHIEF? HEH-HEH-HEH!
GET HIM OUT OF HERE!
MICKEY!
MICKEY, WHERE ARE YOU?
MICKEY!
LOOK EVERYWHERE! TURN THIS PLACE UPSIDE DOWN... FIND HIM!
MICKEY?!
CREEEAK
!

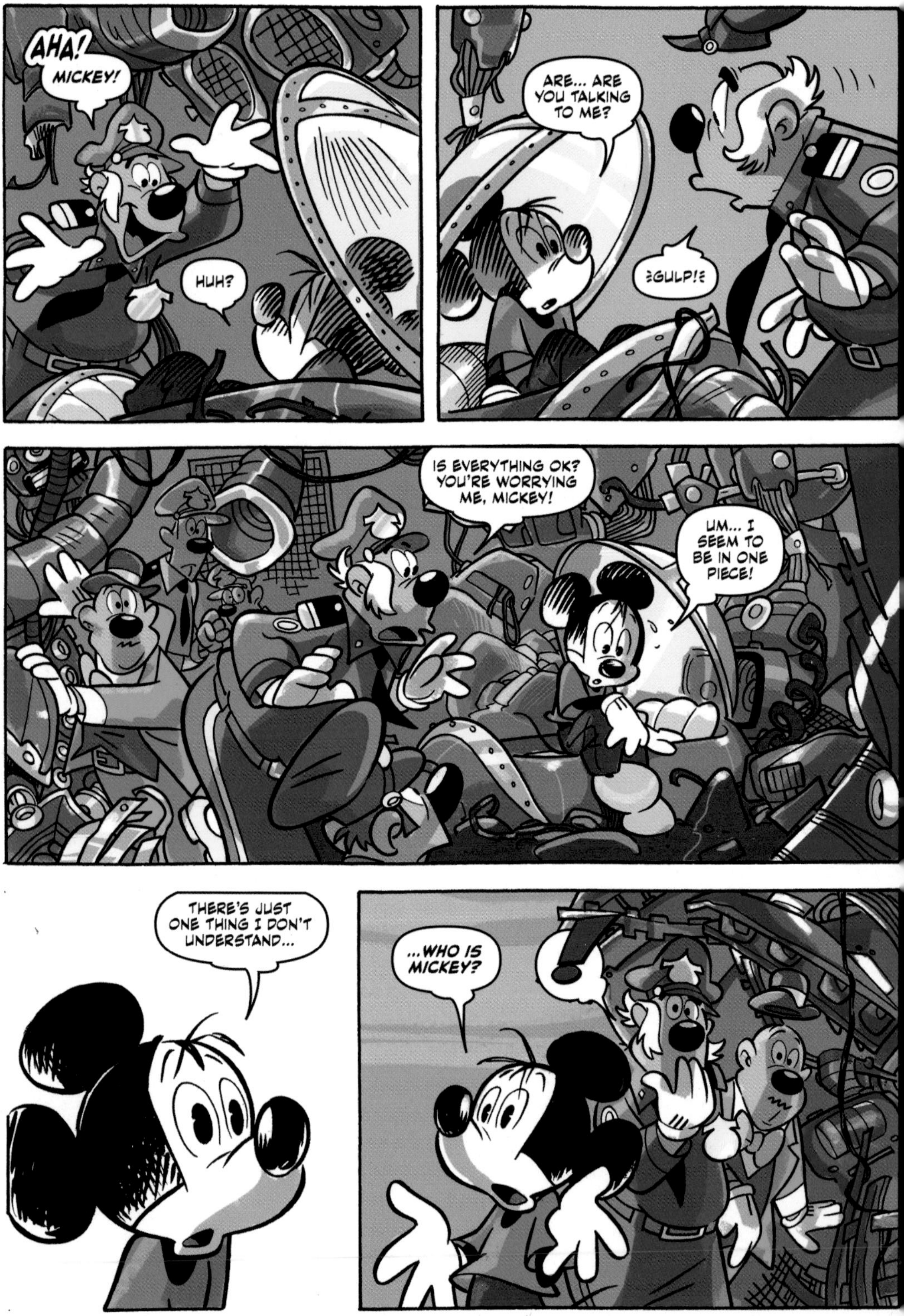
AHA! MICKEY!
HUH?
ARE... ARE YOU TALKING TO ME?
GULP!
IS EVERYTHING OK? YOU'RE WORRYING ME, MICKEY!
UM... I SEEM TO BE IN ONE PIECE!
THERE'S JUST ONE THING I DON'T UNDERSTAND...
...WHO IS MICKEY?

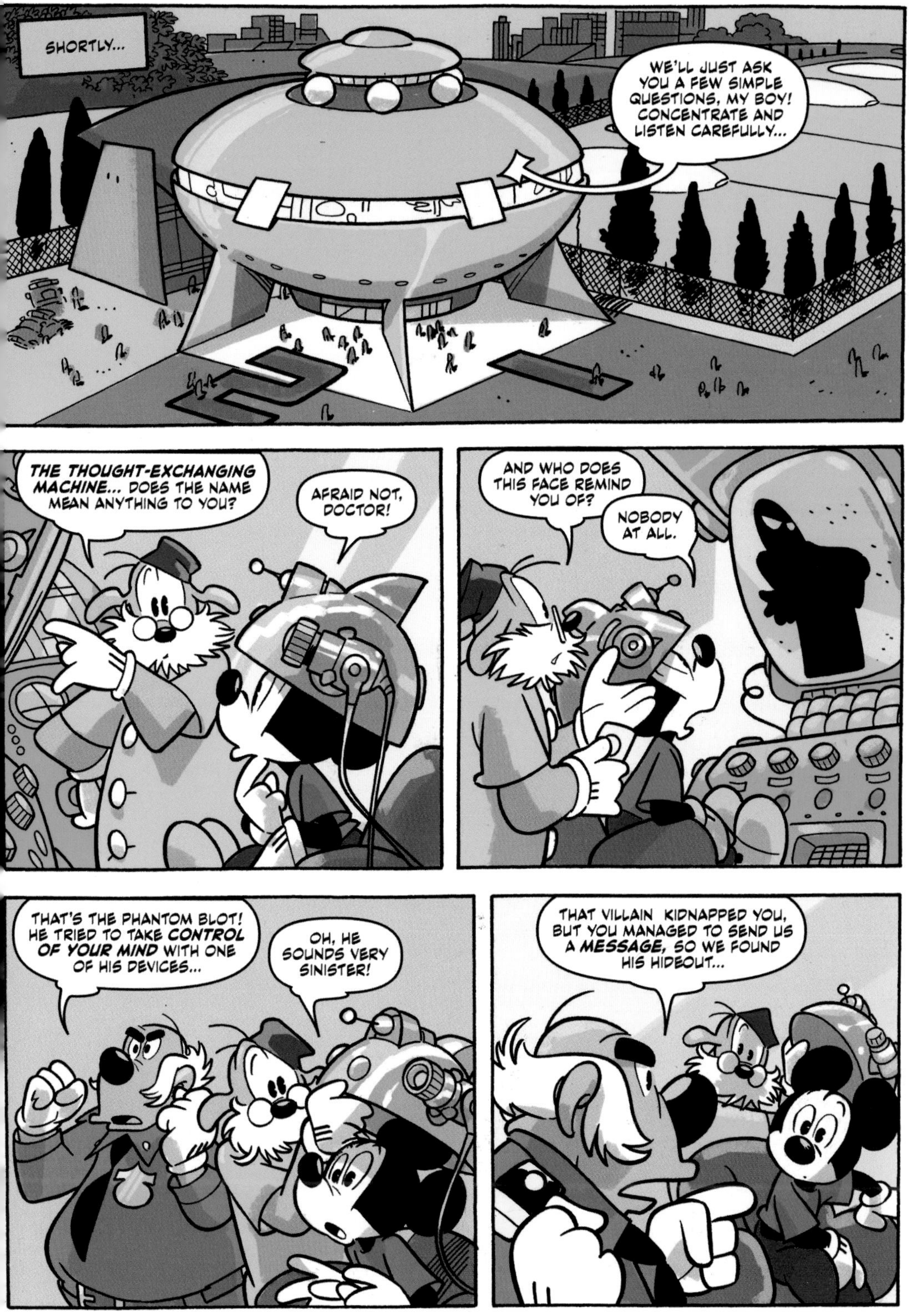
SHORTLY...
WE'LL JUST ASK YOU A FEW SIMPLE QUESTIONS, MY BOY! CONCENTRATE AND LISTEN CAREFULLY...
THE THOUGHT-EXCHANGING MACHINE... DOES THE NAME MEAN ANYTHING TO YOU?
AFRAID NOT, DOCTOR!
AND WHO DOES THIS FACE REMIND YOU OF?
NOBODY AT ALL.
THAT'S THE PHANTOM BLOT! HE TRIED TO TAKE CONTROL OF YOUR MIND WITH ONE OF HIS DEVICES...
OH, HE SOUNDS VERY SINISTER!
THAT VILLAIN KIDNAPPED YOU, BUT YOU MANAGED TO SEND US A MESSAGE, SO WE FOUND HIS HIDEOUT...

...HOWEVER, BEFORE WE GOT THERE, YOU *SABOTAGED* HIS EXPERIMENT, BLOWING UP THAT EVIL CONTRAPTION!

I DID THAT ON MY OWN? *WOW!*

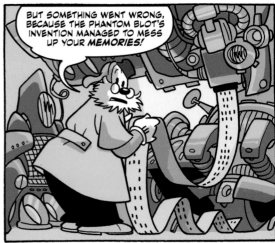

BUT SOMETHING WENT WRONG, BECAUSE THE PHANTOM BLOT'S INVENTION MANAGED TO MESS UP YOUR *MEMORIES!*

ITS *TURBOCEREBRAL WAVES* PENETRATED THAT POD YOU WERE IN AND CAUSED *GREAT DAMAGE* TO YOUR MIND!

≥GASP!≥

YOUR PERSONALITY, YOUR CHARACTER, EVERYTHING THAT MADE YOU MICKEY... *IS NO MORE!*

PERHAPS IT'S JUST *HIDDEN SOMEWHERE* INSIDE YOU, BUT THE FACT IS, YOU ARE NOW A *DIFFERENT* PERSON!

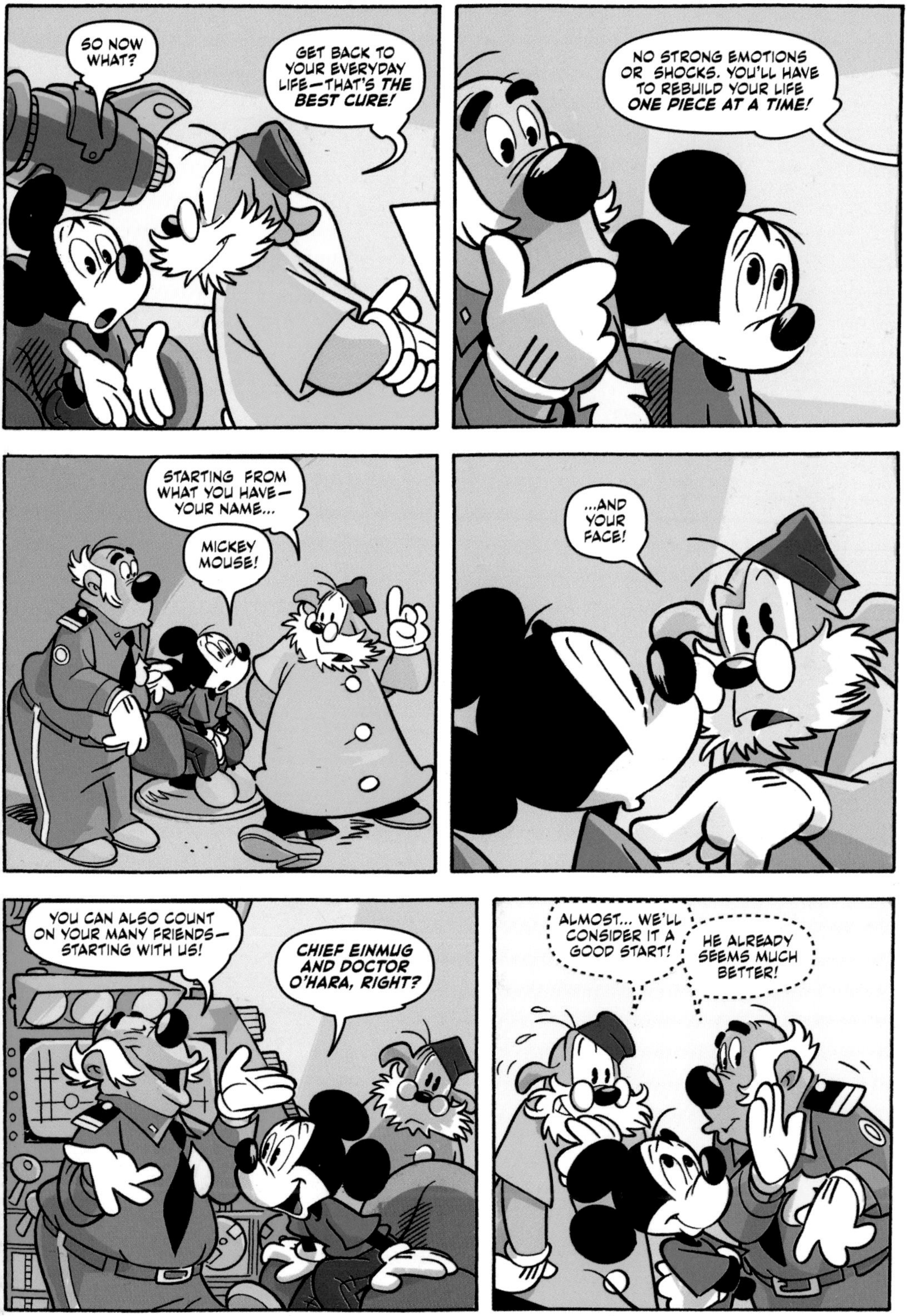
SO NOW WHAT?
GET BACK TO YOUR EVERYDAY LIFE—THAT'S THE BEST CURE!
NO STRONG EMOTIONS OR SHOCKS. YOU'LL HAVE TO REBUILD YOUR LIFE ONE PIECE AT A TIME!
STARTING FROM WHAT YOU HAVE— YOUR NAME...
MICKEY MOUSE!
...AND YOUR FACE!
YOU CAN ALSO COUNT ON YOUR MANY FRIENDS— STARTING WITH US!
CHIEF EINMUG AND DOCTOR O'HARA, RIGHT?
ALMOST... WE'LL CONSIDER IT A GOOD START!
HE ALREADY SEEMS MUCH BETTER!

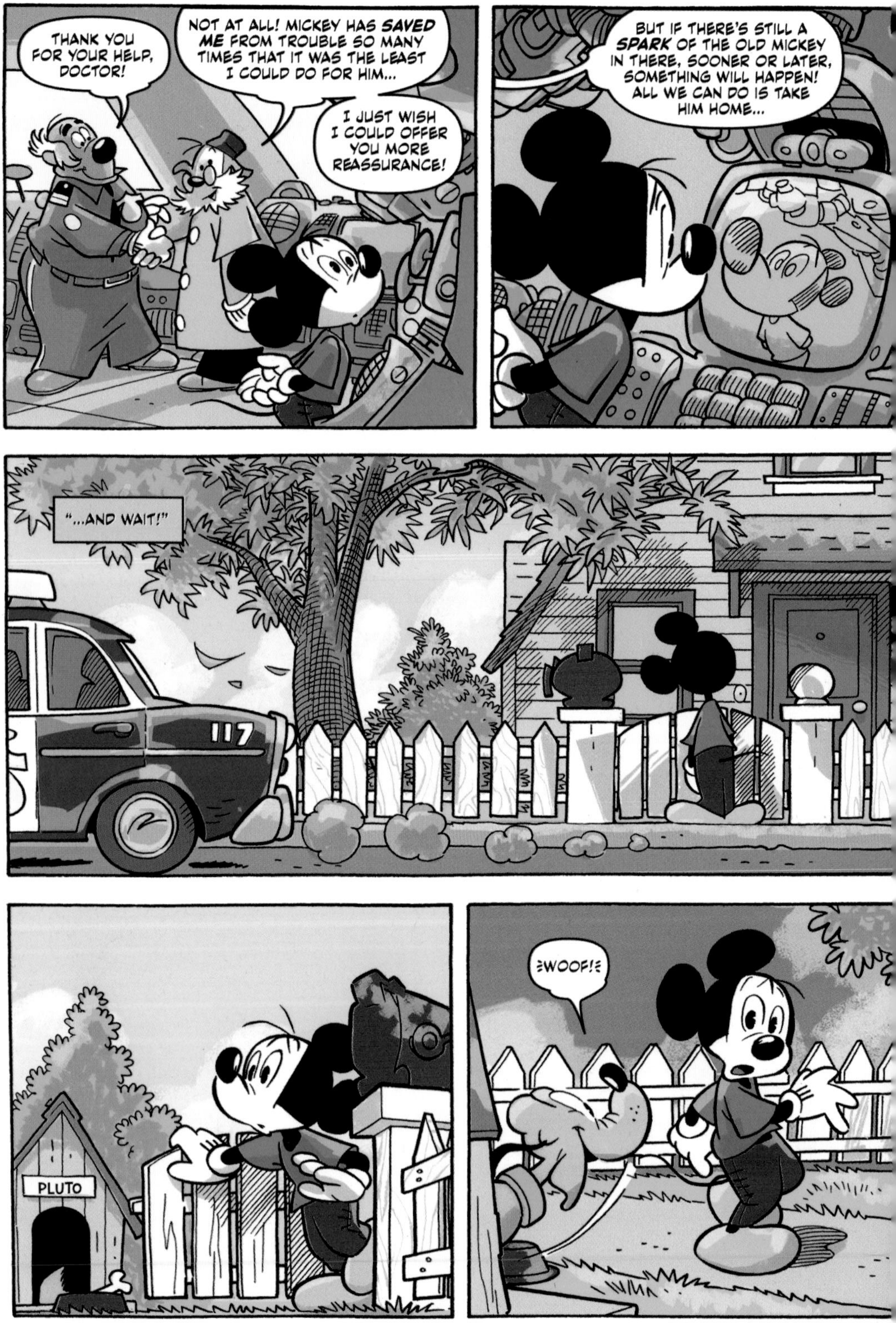
THANK YOU FOR YOUR HELP, DOCTOR!
NOT AT ALL! MICKEY HAS **SAVED ME** FROM TROUBLE SO MANY TIMES THAT IT WAS THE LEAST I COULD DO FOR HIM...
I JUST WISH I COULD OFFER YOU MORE REASSURANCE!
BUT IF THERE'S STILL A **SPARK** OF THE OLD MICKEY IN THERE, SOONER OR LATER, SOMETHING WILL HAPPEN! ALL WE CAN DO IS TAKE HIM HOME...
"...AND WAIT!"
117
PLUTO
WOOF!

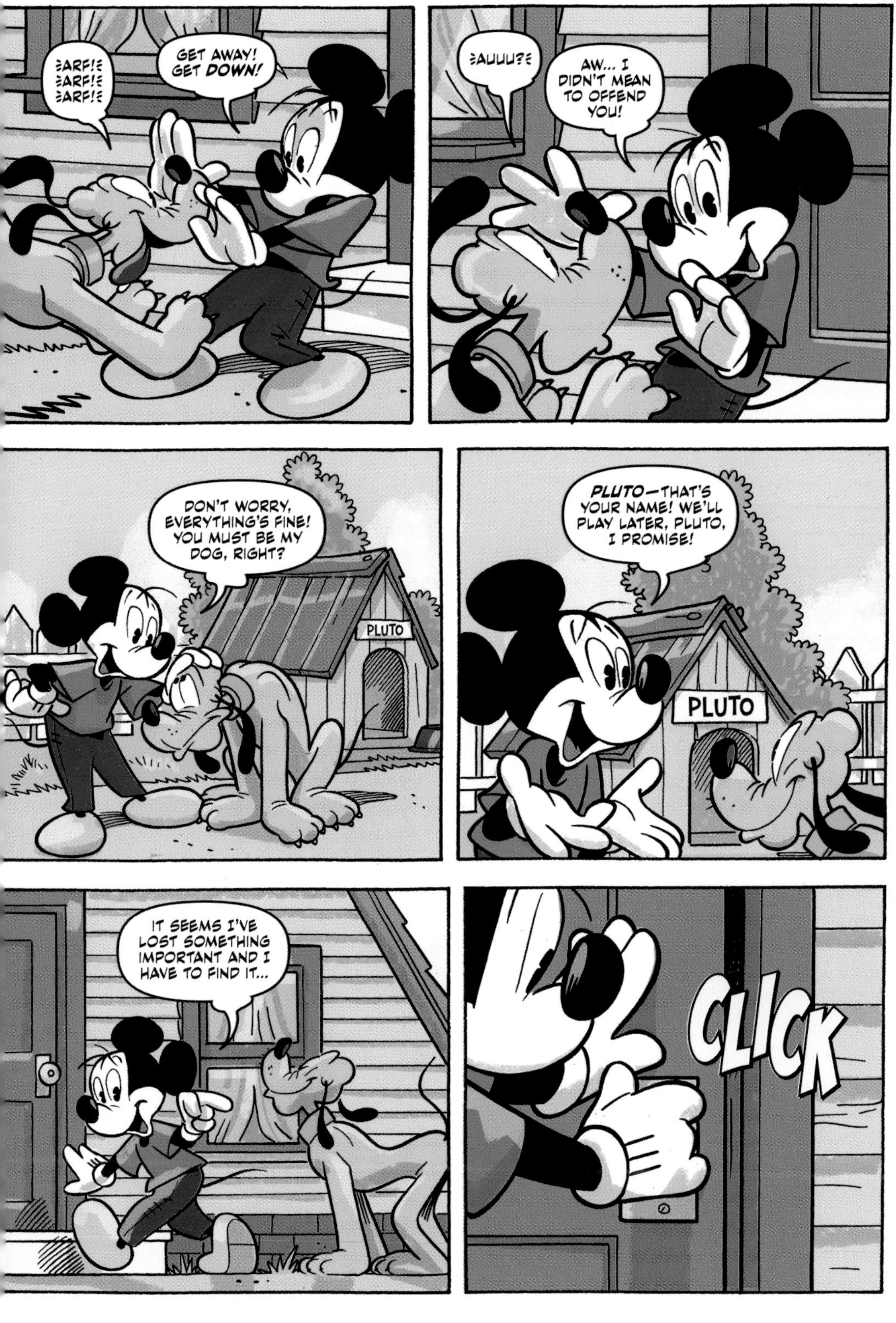
ARF! ARF! ARF!
GET AWAY! GET DOWN!
AUUU?
AW... I DIDN'T MEAN TO OFFEND YOU!
DON'T WORRY, EVERYTHING'S FINE! YOU MUST BE MY DOG, RIGHT?
PLUTO
PLUTO—THAT'S YOUR NAME! WE'LL PLAY LATER, PLUTO, I PROMISE!
PLUTO
IT SEEMS I'VE LOST SOMETHING IMPORTANT AND I HAVE TO FIND IT...
CLICK

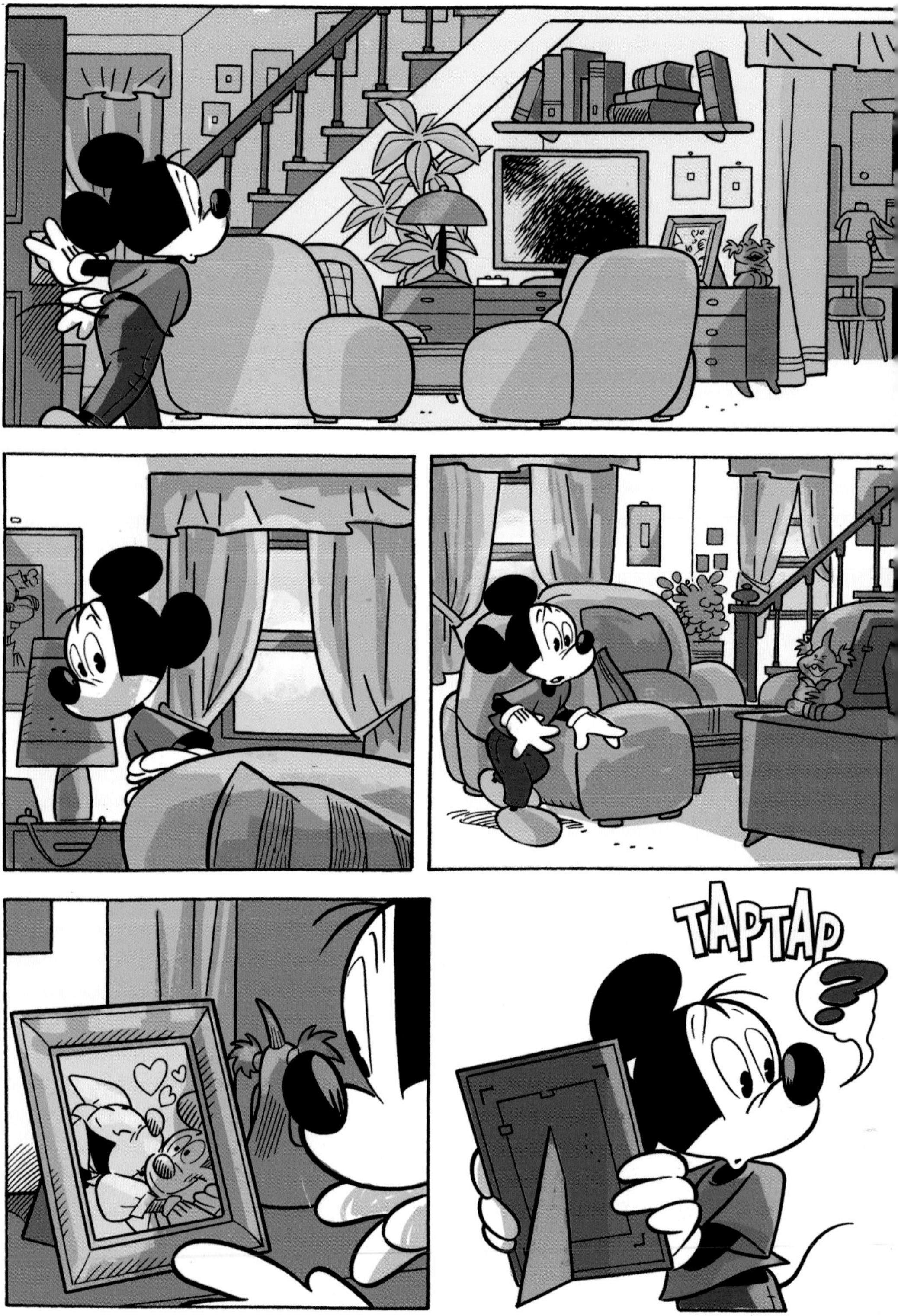
TAPTAP
?

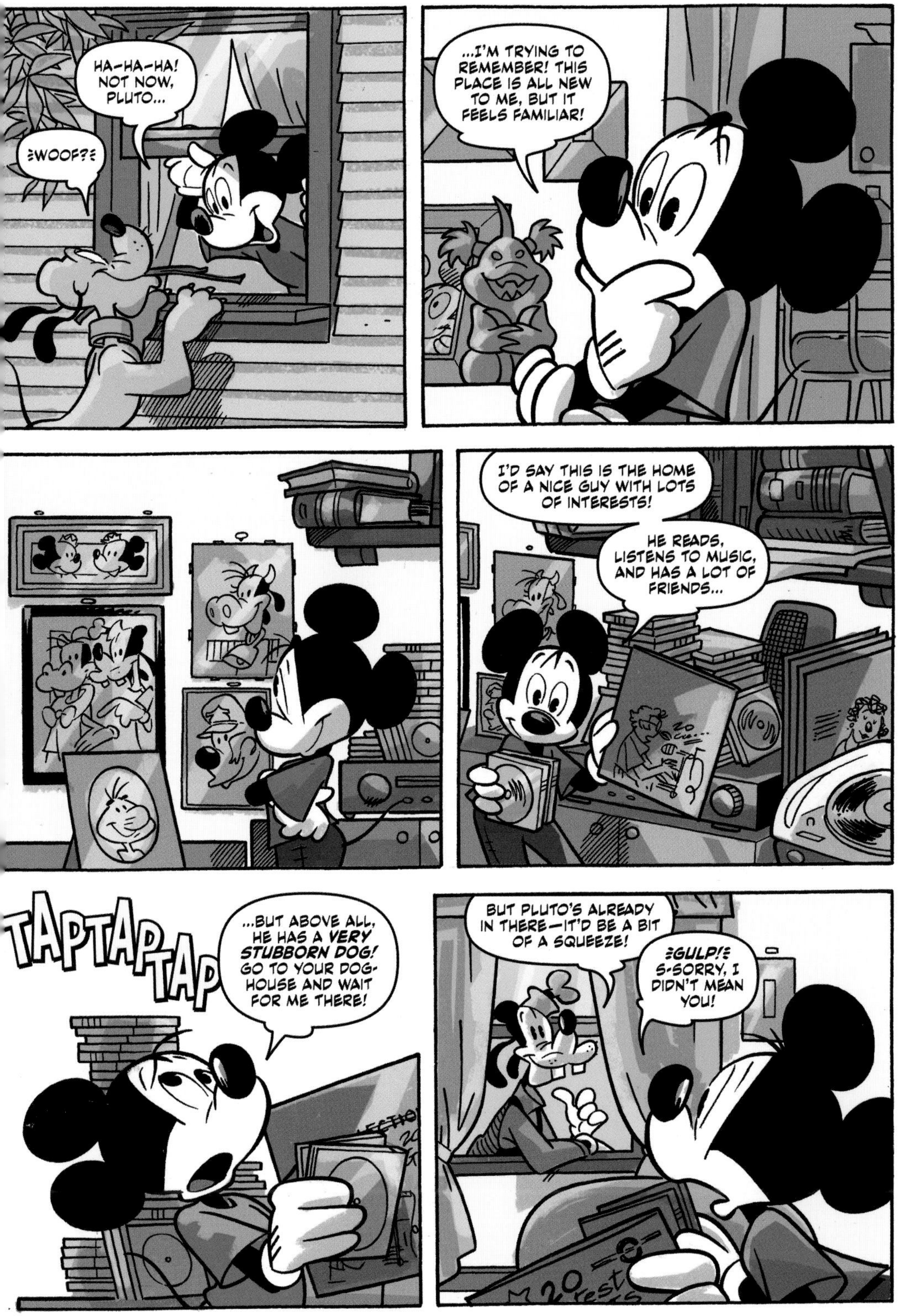
HA-HA-HA! NOT NOW, PLUTO...
WOOF?
...I'M TRYING TO REMEMBER! THIS PLACE IS ALL NEW TO ME, BUT IT FEELS FAMILIAR!
I'D SAY THIS IS THE HOME OF A NICE GUY WITH LOTS OF INTERESTS!
HE READS, LISTENS TO MUSIC, AND HAS A LOT OF FRIENDS...
TAPTAPTAP
...BUT ABOVE ALL, HE HAS A *VERY STUBBORN DOG!* GO TO YOUR DOG-HOUSE AND WAIT FOR ME THERE!
BUT PLUTO'S ALREADY IN THERE—IT'D BE A BIT OF A SQUEEZE!
GULP! S-SORRY, I DIDN'T MEAN YOU!

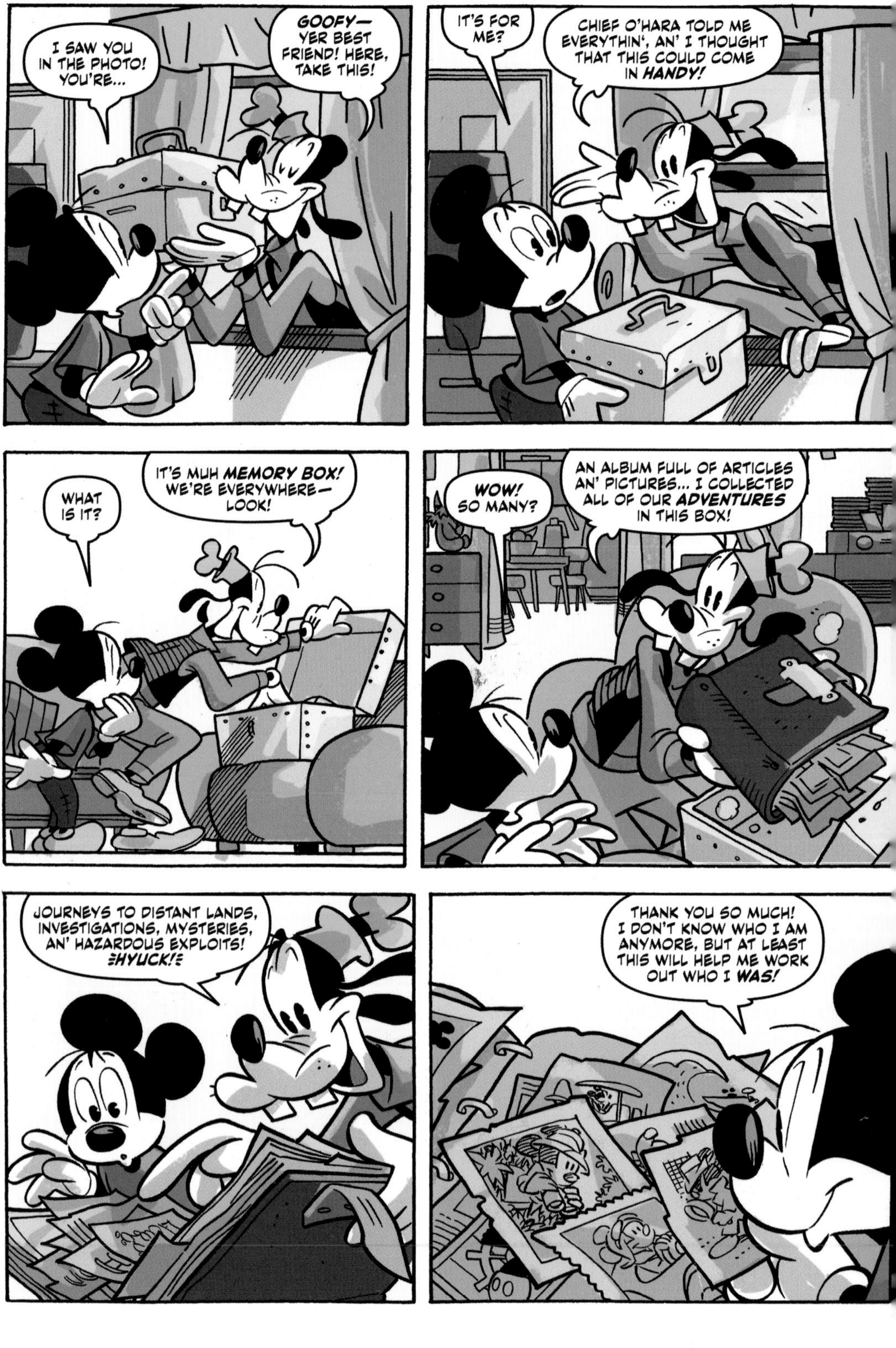
I SAW YOU IN THE PHOTO! YOU'RE...
GOOFY— YER BEST FRIEND! HERE, TAKE THIS!
IT'S FOR ME?
CHIEF O'HARA TOLD ME EVERYTHIN', AN' I THOUGHT THAT THIS COULD COME IN HANDY!
WHAT IS IT?
IT'S MUH MEMORY BOX! WE'RE EVERYWHERE— LOOK!
WOW! SO MANY?
AN ALBUM FULL OF ARTICLES AN' PICTURES... I COLLECTED ALL OF OUR ADVENTURES IN THIS BOX!
JOURNEYS TO DISTANT LANDS, INVESTIGATIONS, MYSTERIES, AN' HAZARDOUS EXPLOITS! HYUCK!
THANK YOU SO MUCH! I DON'T KNOW WHO I AM ANYMORE, BUT AT LEAST THIS WILL HELP ME WORK OUT WHO I WAS!

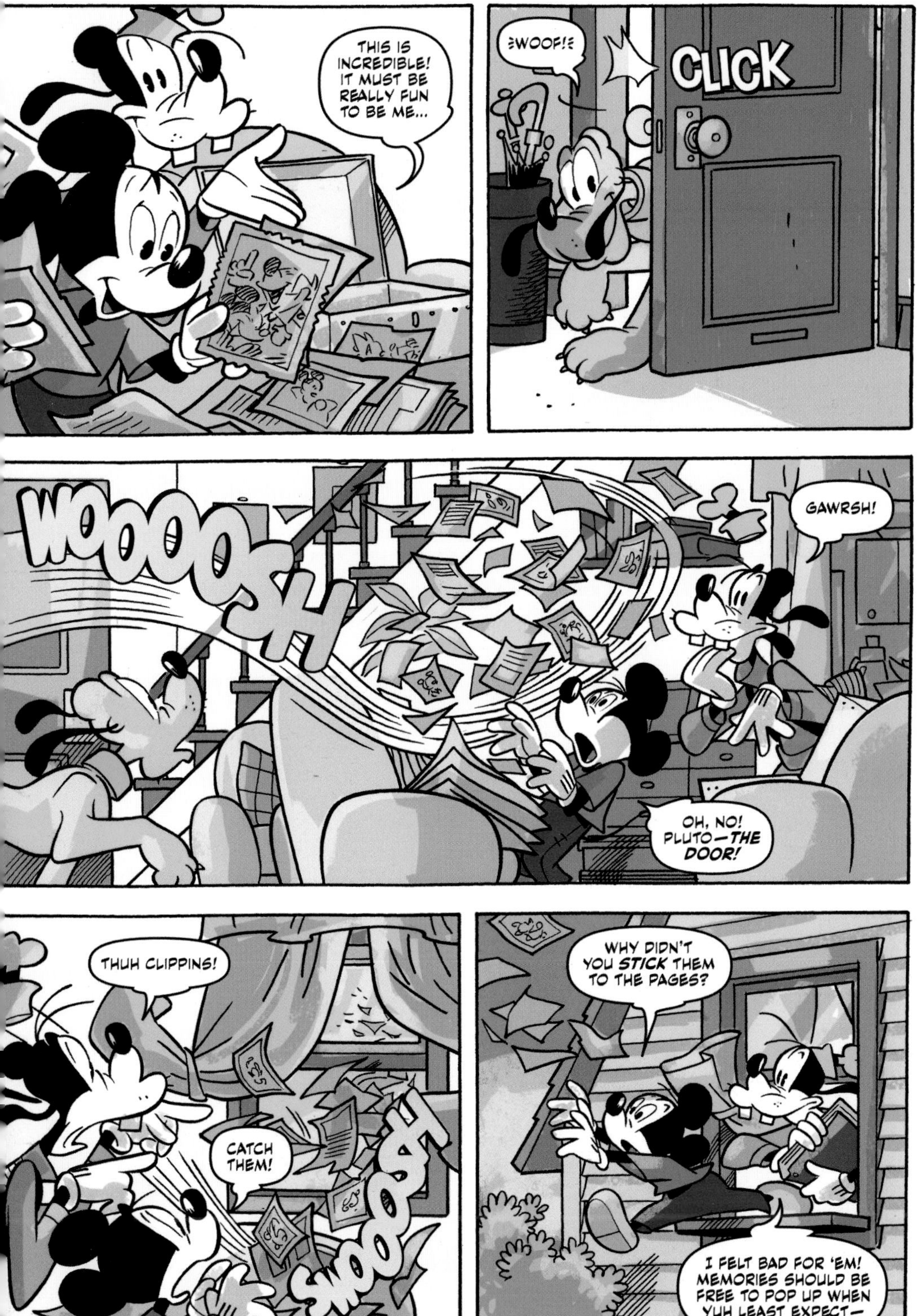
THIS IS INCREDIBLE! IT MUST BE REALLY FUN TO BE ME...
WOOF!
CLICK
WOOOOSH
GAWRSH!
OH, NO! PLUTO—*THE DOOR!*
THUH CLIPPINS!
CATCH THEM!
SWOOOSH
WHY DIDN'T YOU *STICK* THEM TO THE PAGES?
I FELT BAD FOR 'EM! MEMORIES SHOULD BE FREE TO POP UP WHEN YUH LEAST EXPECT—

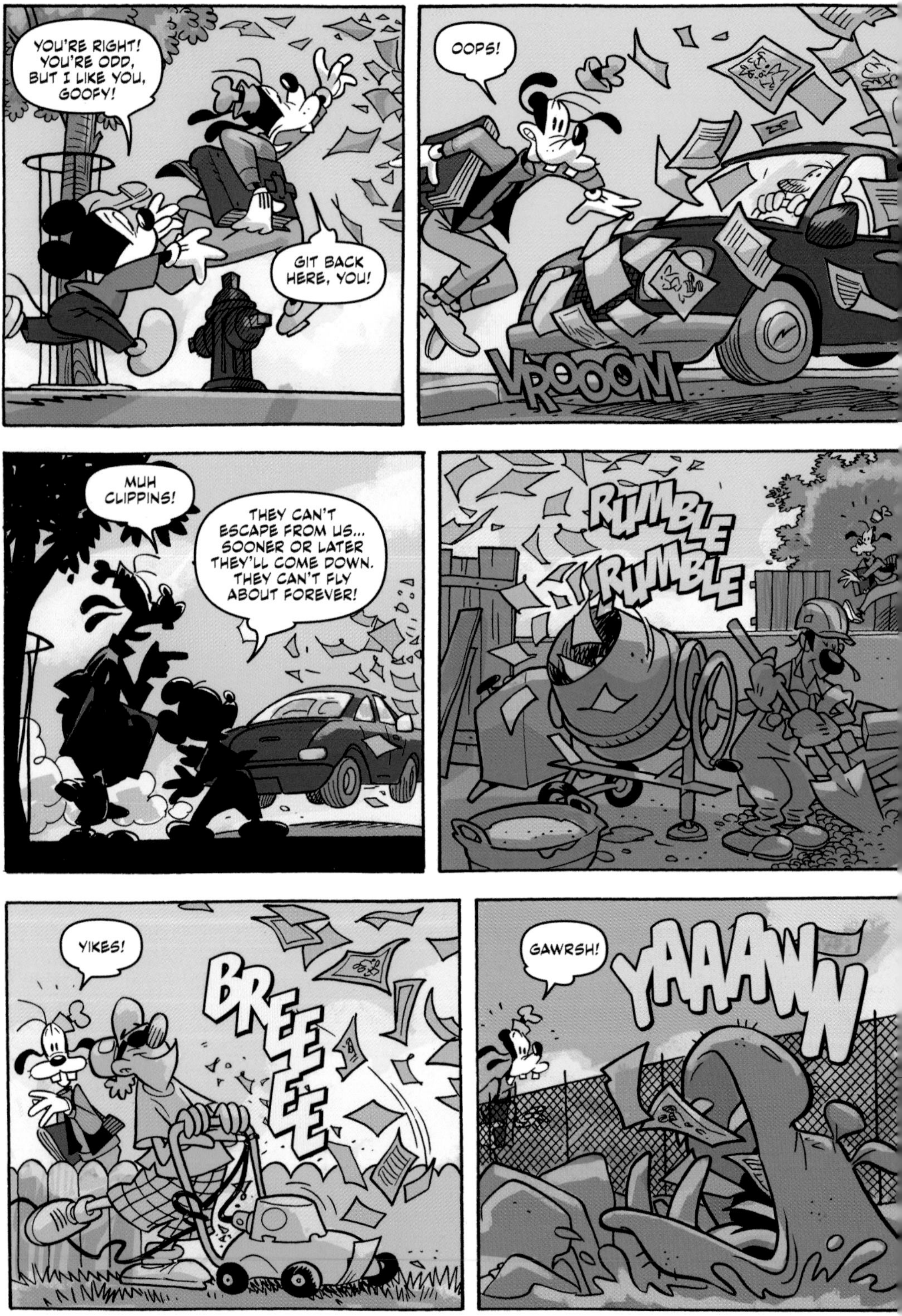
YOU'RE RIGHT! YOU'RE ODD, BUT I LIKE YOU, GOOFY!
GIT BACK HERE, YOU!
OOPS!
VROOOM
MUH CLIPPINS!
THEY CAN'T ESCAPE FROM US... SOONER OR LATER THEY'LL COME DOWN. THEY CAN'T FLY ABOUT FOREVER!
RUMBLE RUMBLE
YIKES!
BREEEE
GAWRSH!
YAAAWN

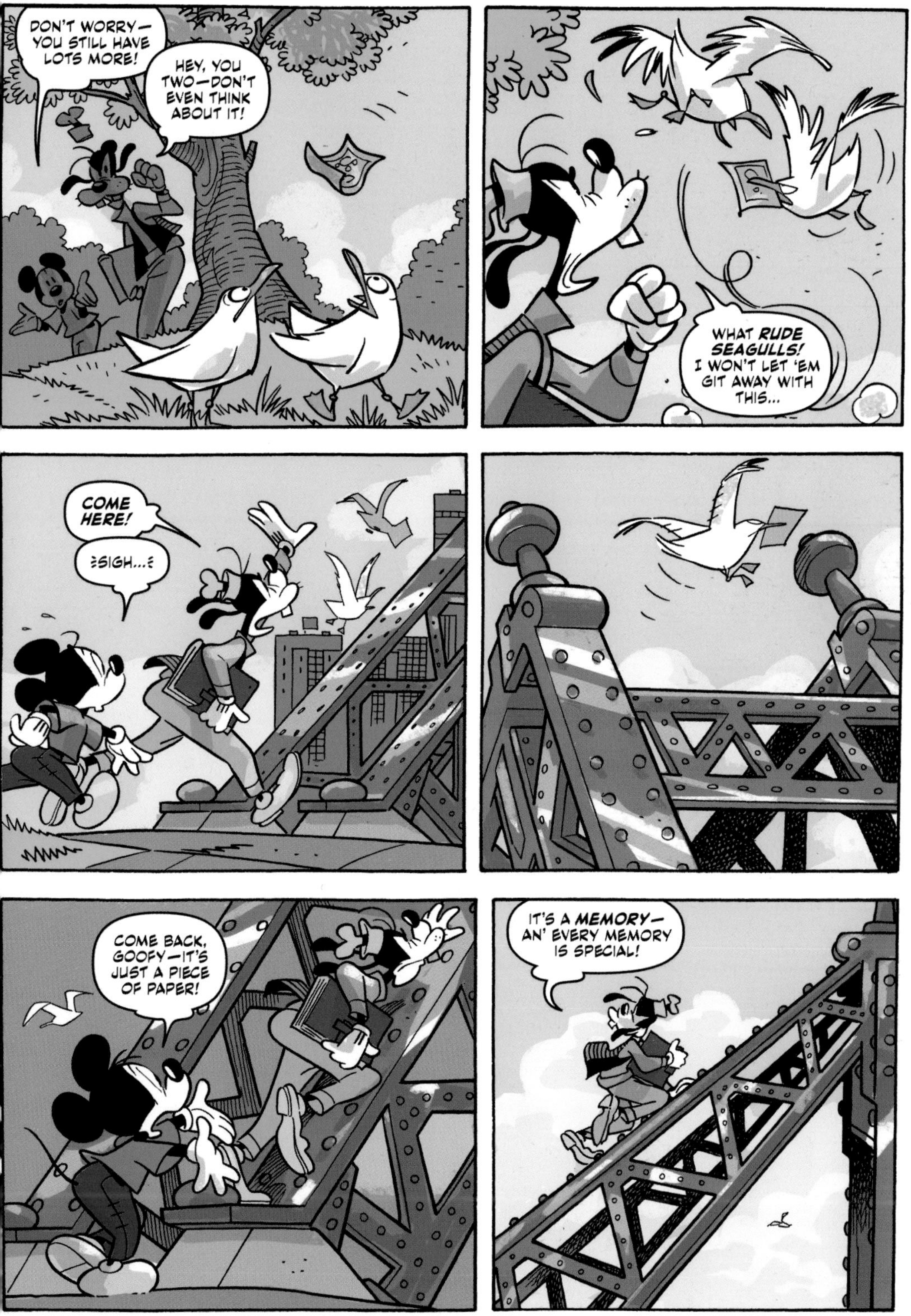
DON'T WORRY—YOU STILL HAVE LOTS MORE!
HEY, YOU TWO—DON'T EVEN THINK ABOUT IT!
WHAT RUDE SEAGULLS! I WON'T LET 'EM GIT AWAY WITH THIS...
COME HERE!
SIGH...
COME BACK, GOOFY—IT'S JUST A PIECE OF PAPER!
IT'S A MEMORY—AN' EVERY MEMORY IS SPECIAL!

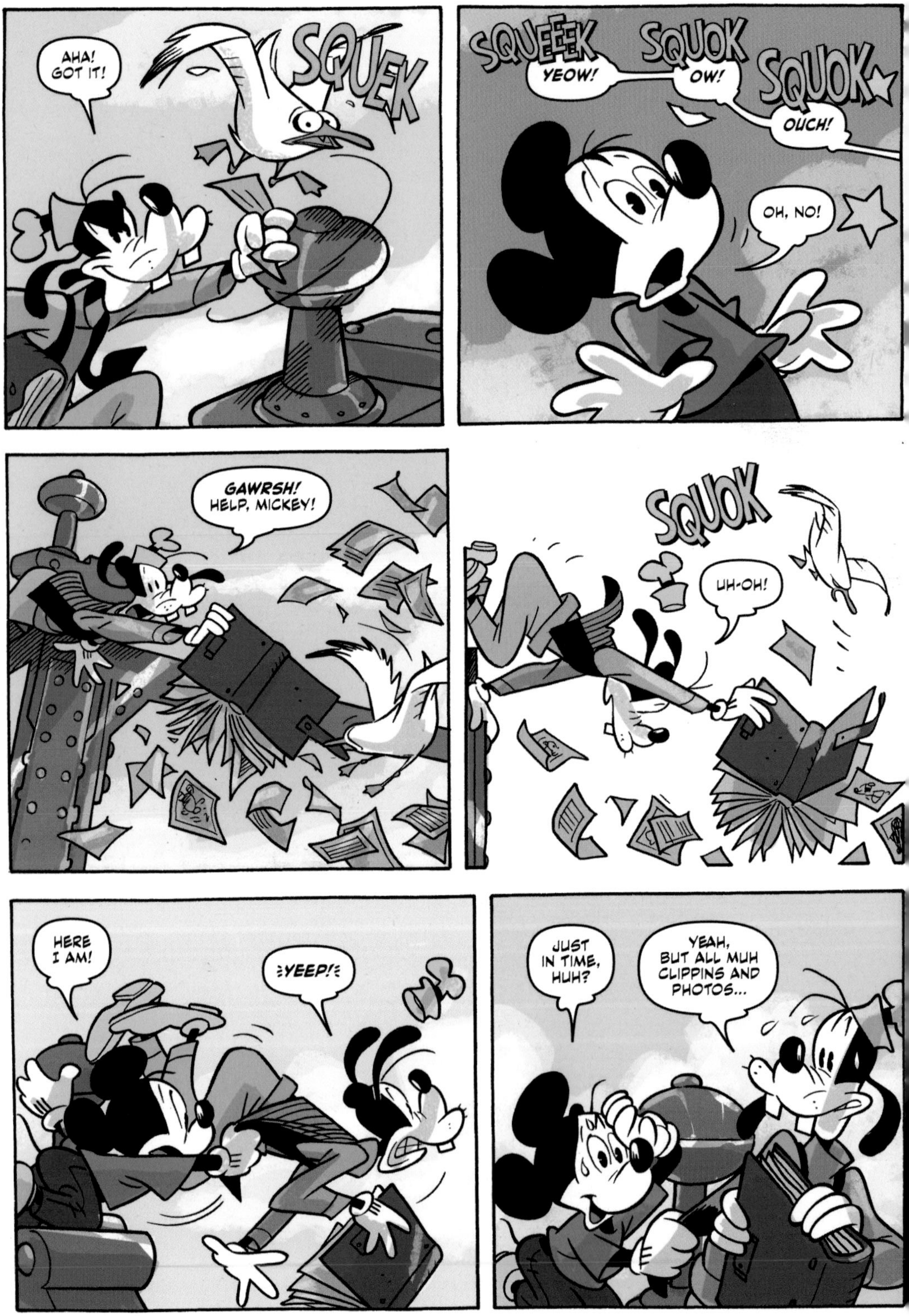
SQUEK
AHA! GOT IT!
SQUEEEK
YEOW!
SQUOK
OW!
SQUOK
OUCH!
OH, NO!
GAWRSH! HELP, MICKEY!
SQUOK
UH-OH!
HERE I AM!
YEEP!
JUST IN TIME, HUH?
YEAH, BUT ALL MUH CLIPPINS AND PHOTOS...

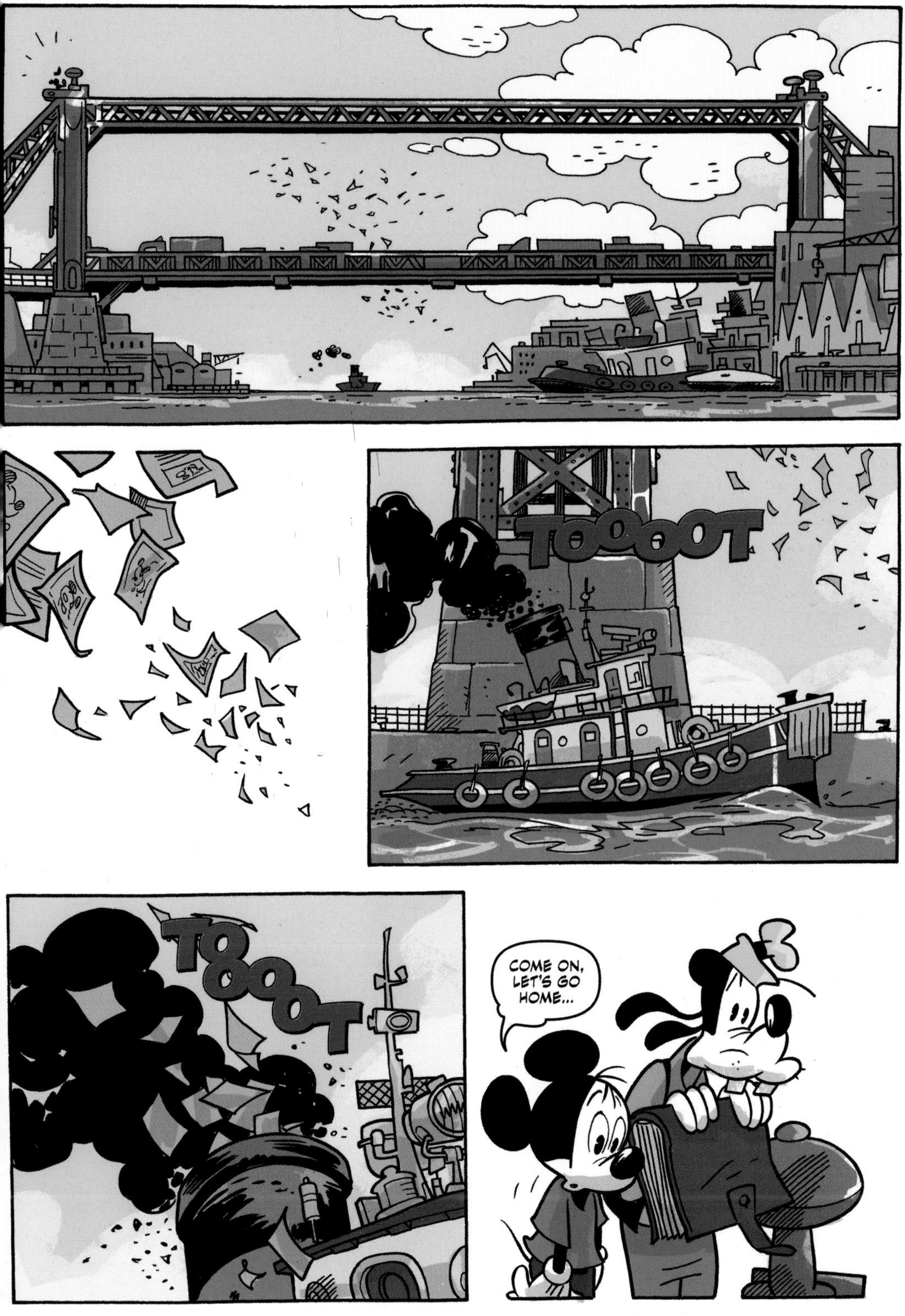
TOOOOT
TOOOT
COME ON, LET'S GO HOME...

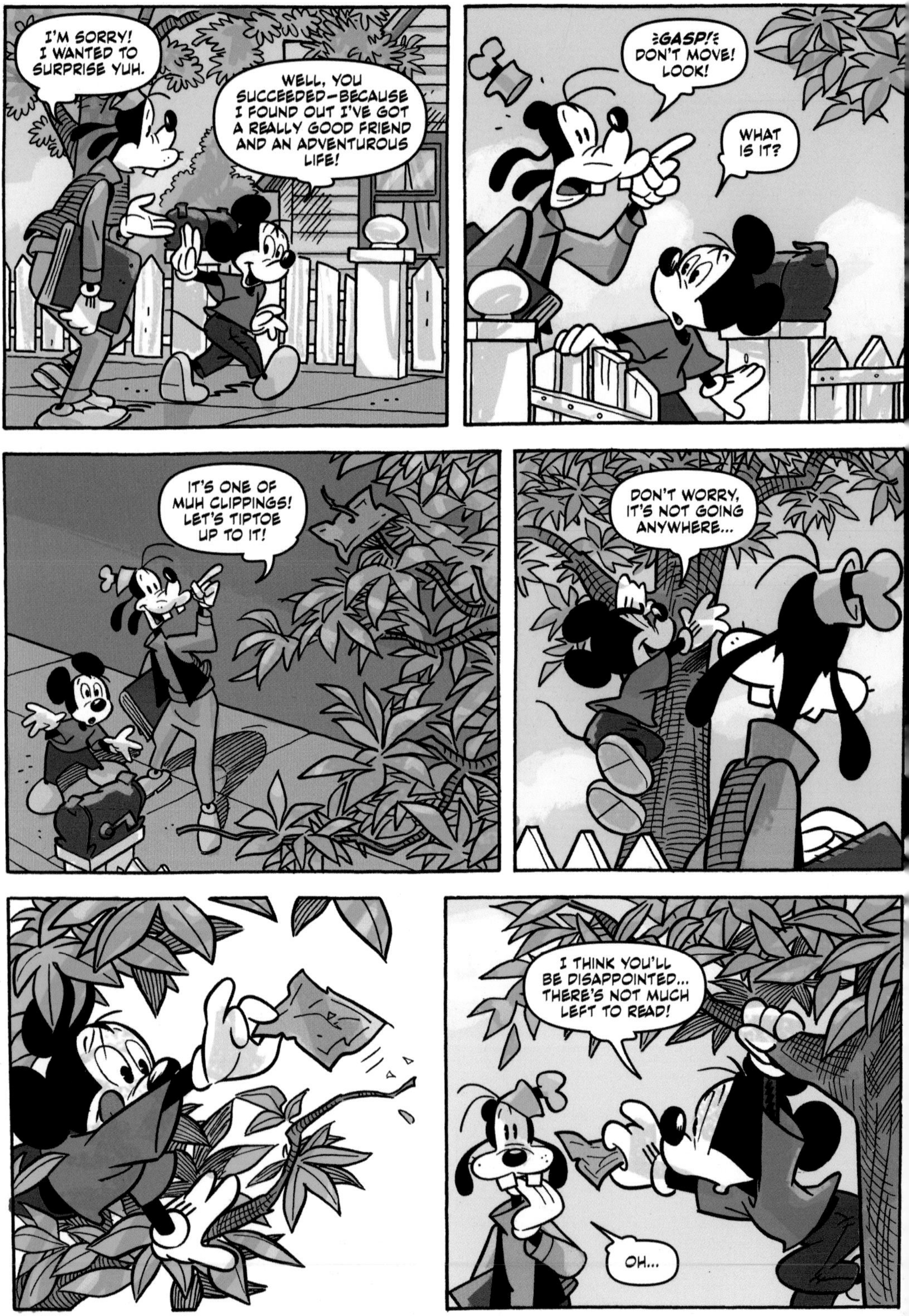
I'M SORRY! I WANTED TO SURPRISE YUH.
WELL, YOU SUCCEEDED—BECAUSE I FOUND OUT I'VE GOT A REALLY GOOD FRIEND AND AN ADVENTUROUS LIFE!
GASP! DON'T MOVE! LOOK!
WHAT IS IT?
IT'S ONE OF MUH CLIPPINGS! LET'S TIPTOE UP TO IT!
DON'T WORRY, IT'S NOT GOING ANYWHERE...
I THINK YOU'LL BE DISAPPOINTED... THERE'S NOT MUCH LEFT TO READ!
OH...

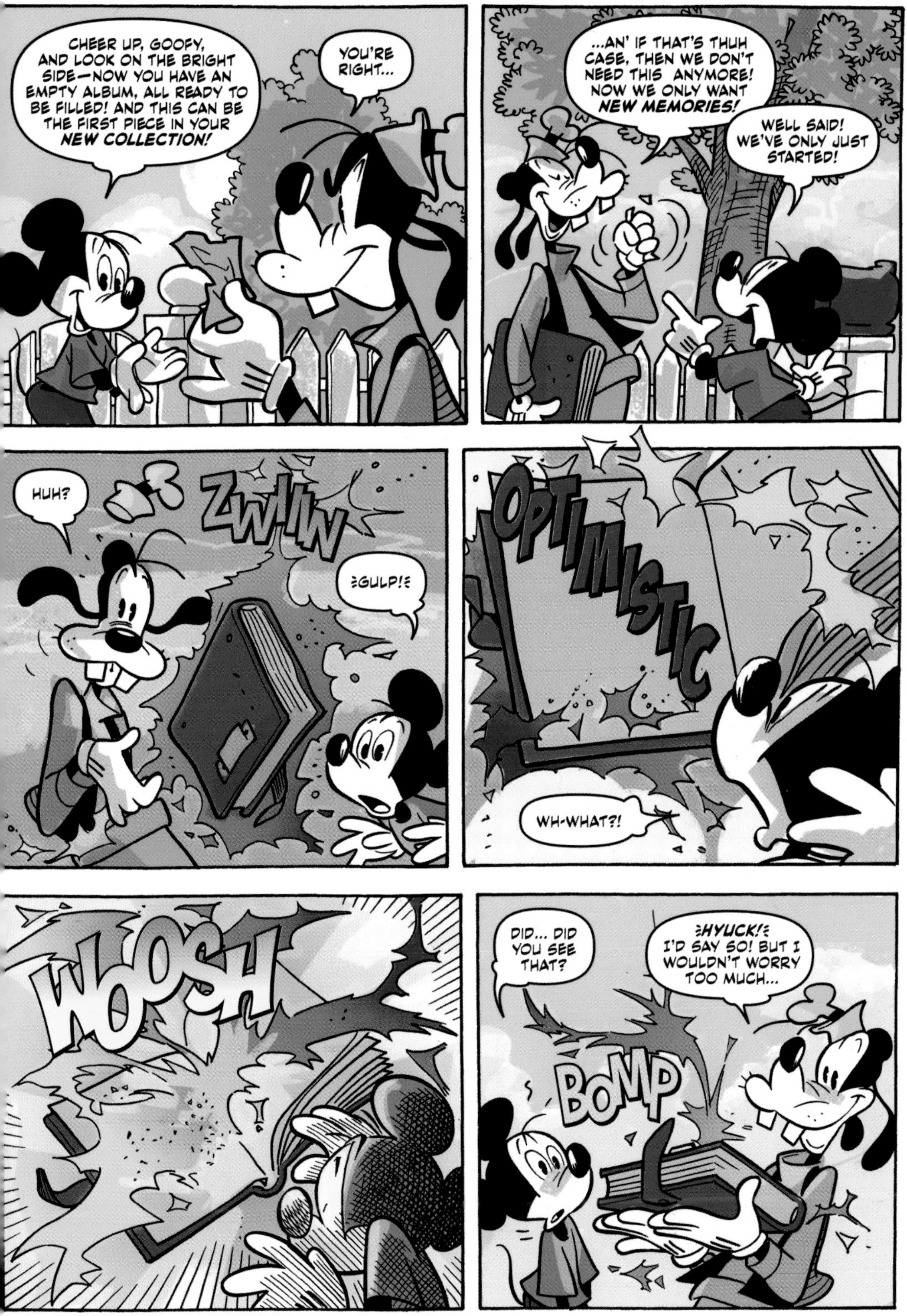
CHEER UP, GOOFY, AND LOOK ON THE BRIGHT SIDE—NOW YOU HAVE AN EMPTY ALBUM, ALL READY TO BE FILLED! AND THIS CAN BE THE FIRST PIECE IN YOUR ***NEW COLLECTION!***
YOU'RE RIGHT...
...AN' IF THAT'S THUH CASE, THEN WE DON'T NEED THIS ANYMORE! NOW WE ONLY WANT ***NEW MEMORIES!***
WELL SAID! WE'VE ONLY JUST STARTED!
HUH?
ZWIIIN
GULP!
OPTIMISTIC
WH-WHAT?!
WOOSH
DID... DID YOU SEE THAT?
HYUCK! I'D SAY SO! BUT I WOULDN'T WORRY TOO MUCH...
BOMP

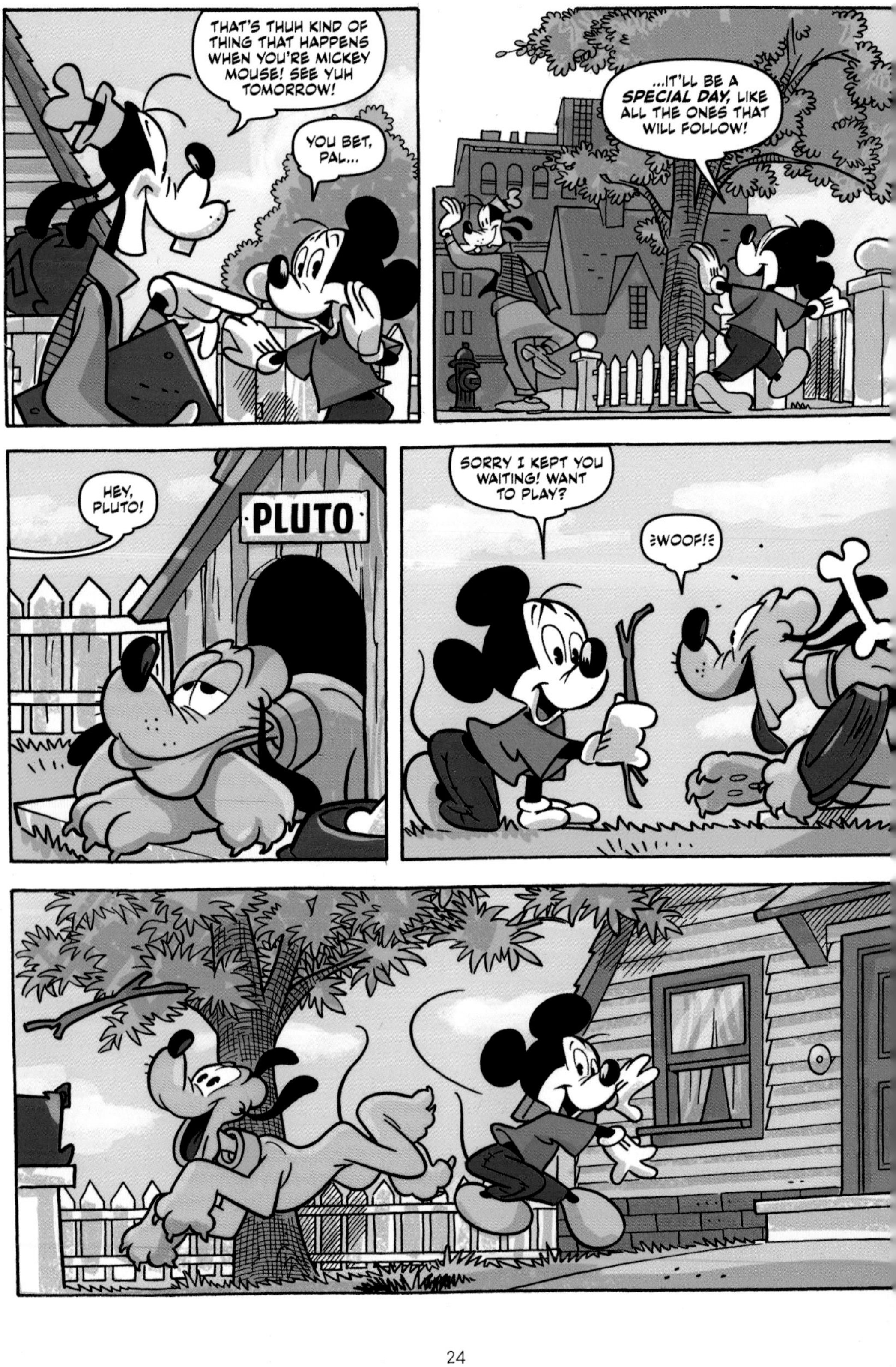

THAT'S THUH KIND OF THING THAT HAPPENS WHEN YOU'RE MICKEY MOUSE! SEE YUH TOMORROW!
YOU BET, PAL...
...IT'LL BE A SPECIAL DAY, LIKE ALL THE ONES THAT WILL FOLLOW!
HEY, PLUTO!
PLUTO
SORRY I KEPT YOU WAITING! WANT TO PLAY?
WOOF!

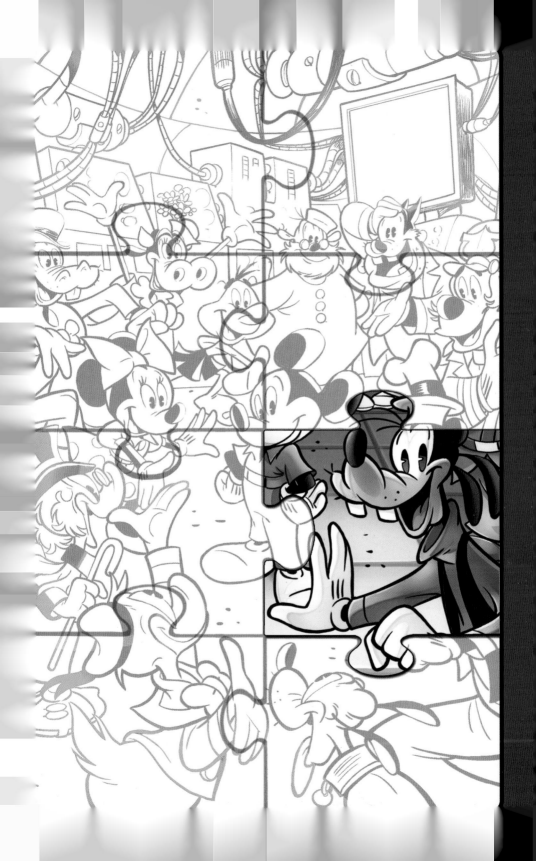

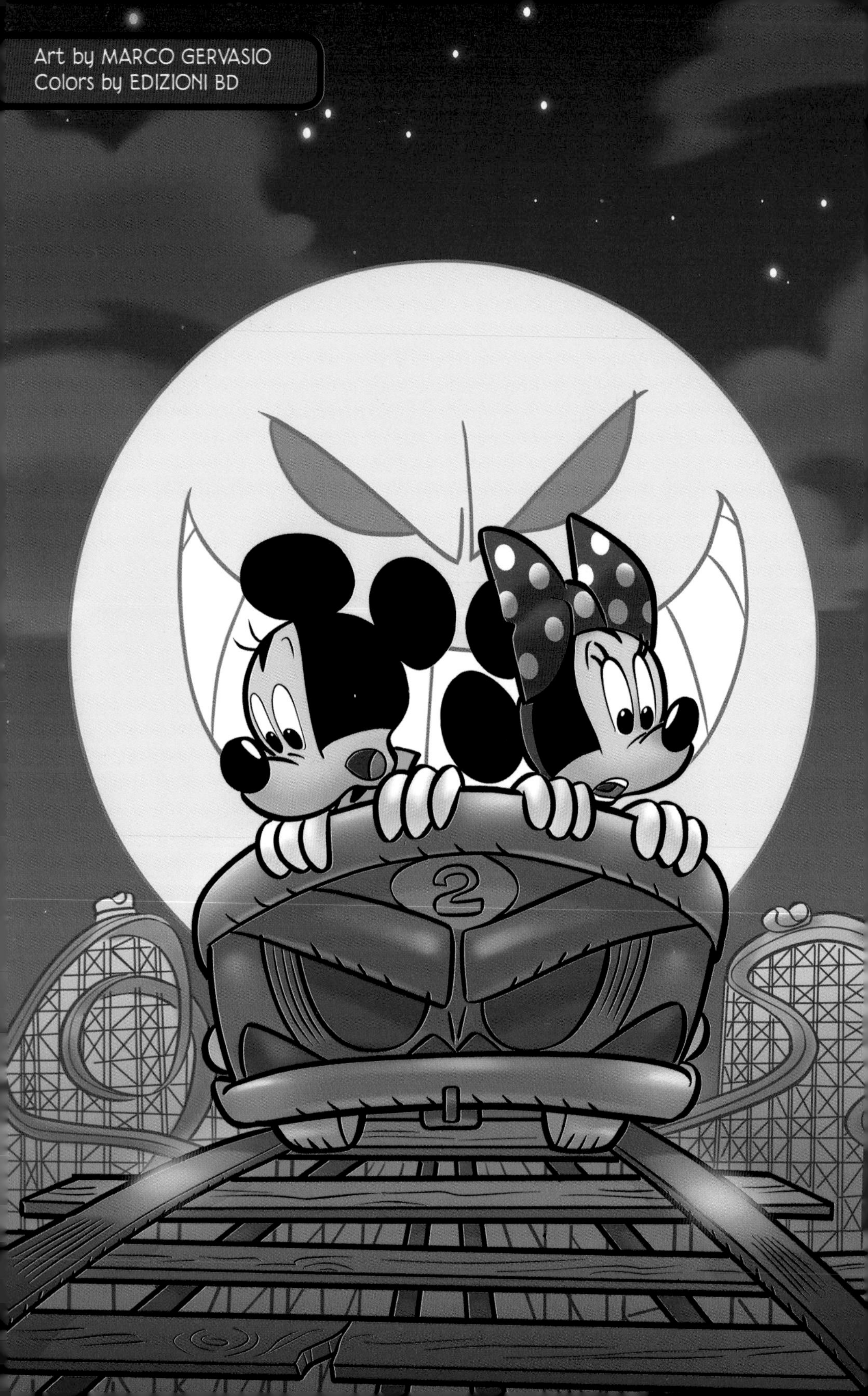
Art by MARCO GERVASIO
Colors by EDIZIONI BD
2

CHAPTER 2: THE CARNIVAL MYSTERY

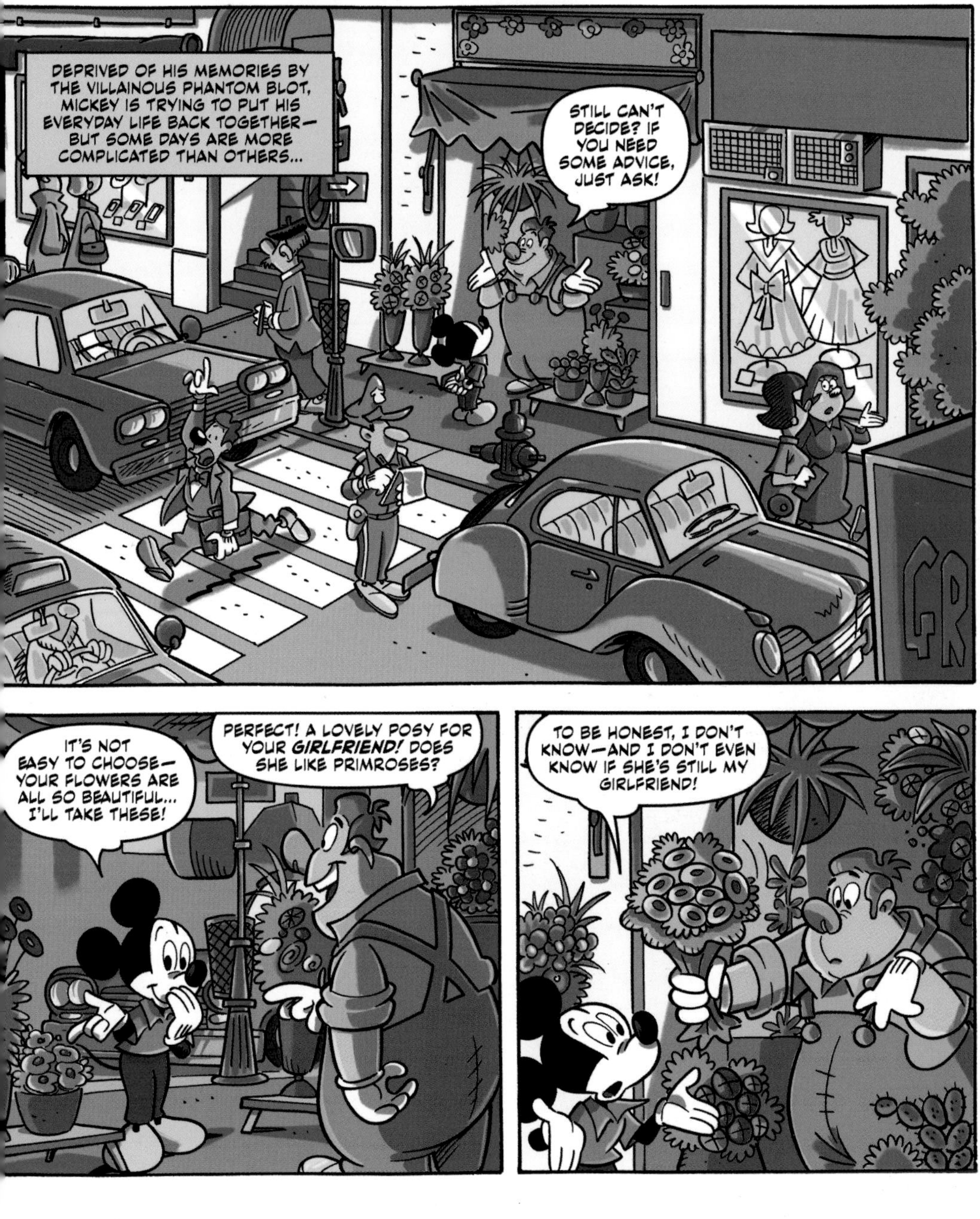
DEPRIVED OF HIS MEMORIES BY THE VILLAINOUS PHANTOM BLOT, MICKEY IS TRYING TO PUT HIS EVERYDAY LIFE BACK TOGETHER—BUT SOME DAYS ARE MORE COMPLICATED THAN OTHERS...
STILL CAN'T DECIDE? IF YOU NEED SOME ADVICE, JUST ASK!
IT'S NOT EASY TO CHOOSE—YOUR FLOWERS ARE ALL SO BEAUTIFUL... I'LL TAKE THESE!
PERFECT! A LOVELY POSY FOR YOUR *GIRLFRIEND!* DOES SHE LIKE PRIMROSES?
TO BE HONEST, I DON'T KNOW—AND I DON'T EVEN KNOW IF SHE'S STILL MY GIRLFRIEND!

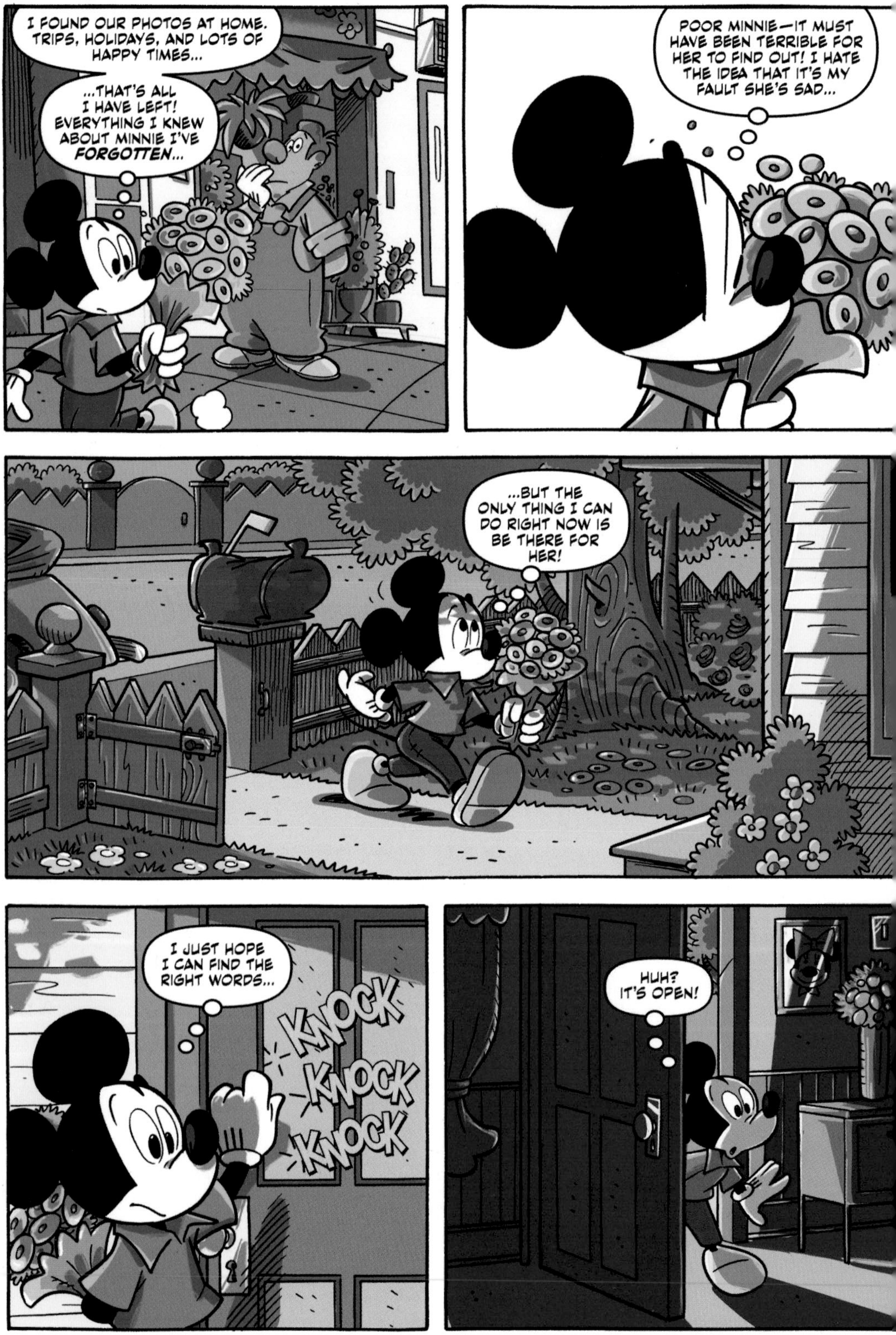
I FOUND OUR PHOTOS AT HOME. TRIPS, HOLIDAYS, AND LOTS OF HAPPY TIMES...
...THAT'S ALL I HAVE LEFT! EVERYTHING I KNEW ABOUT MINNIE I'VE *FORGOTTEN*...
POOR MINNIE—IT MUST HAVE BEEN TERRIBLE FOR HER TO FIND OUT! I HATE THE IDEA THAT IT'S MY FAULT SHE'S SAD...
...BUT THE ONLY THING I CAN DO RIGHT NOW IS BE THERE FOR HER!
I JUST HOPE I CAN FIND THE RIGHT WORDS...
KNOCK
KNOCK
KNOCK
HUH? IT'S OPEN!

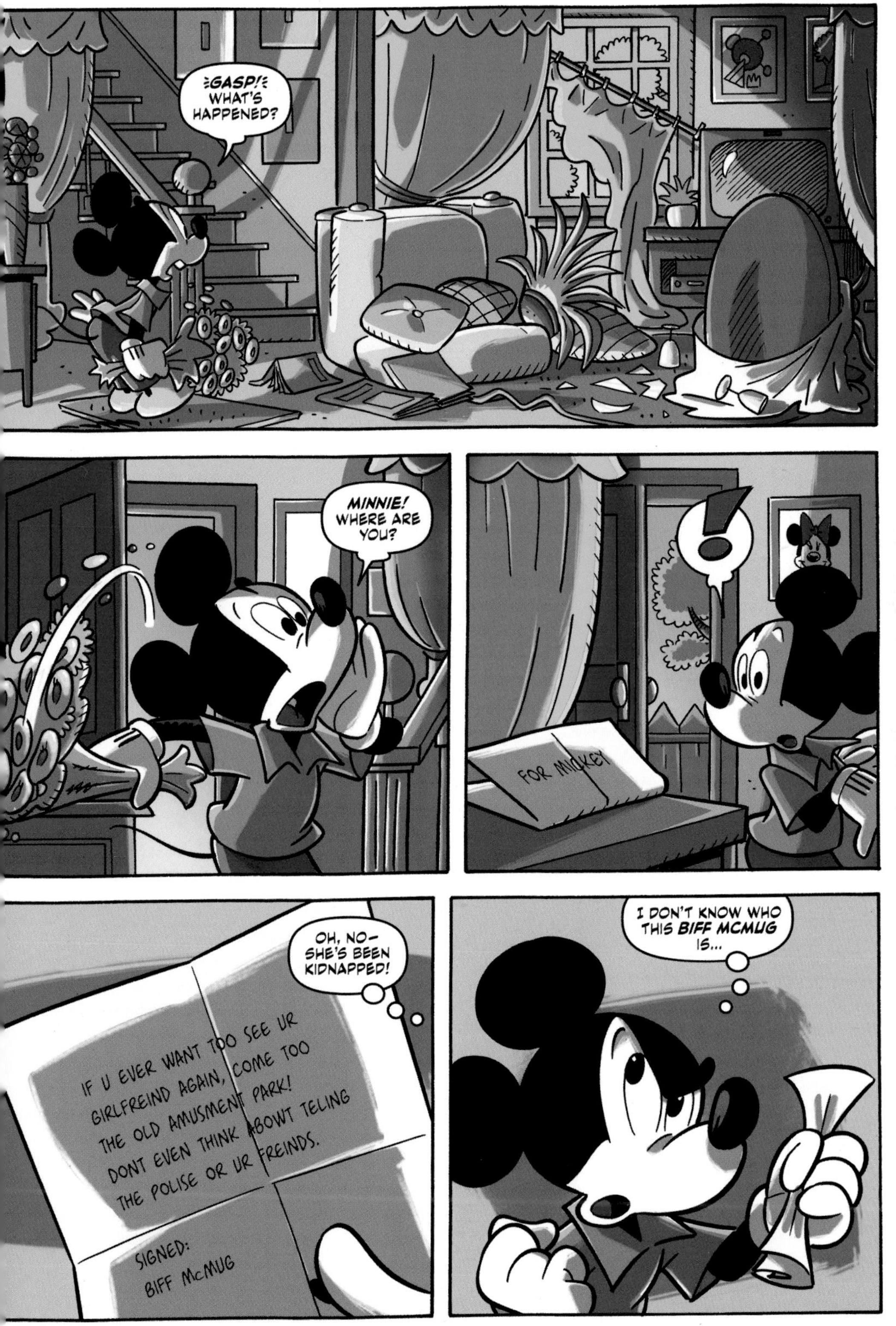
GASP! WHAT'S HAPPENED?
MINNIE! WHERE ARE YOU?
FOR MICKEY
OH, NO– SHE'S BEEN KIDNAPPED!
IF U EVER WANT TOO SEE UR GIRLFREIND AGAIN, COME TOO THE OLD AMUSMENT PARK! DONT EVEN THINK ABOWT TELING THE POLISE OR UR FREINDS.
SIGNED: BIFF McMUG
I DON'T KNOW WHO THIS BIFF MCMUG IS...

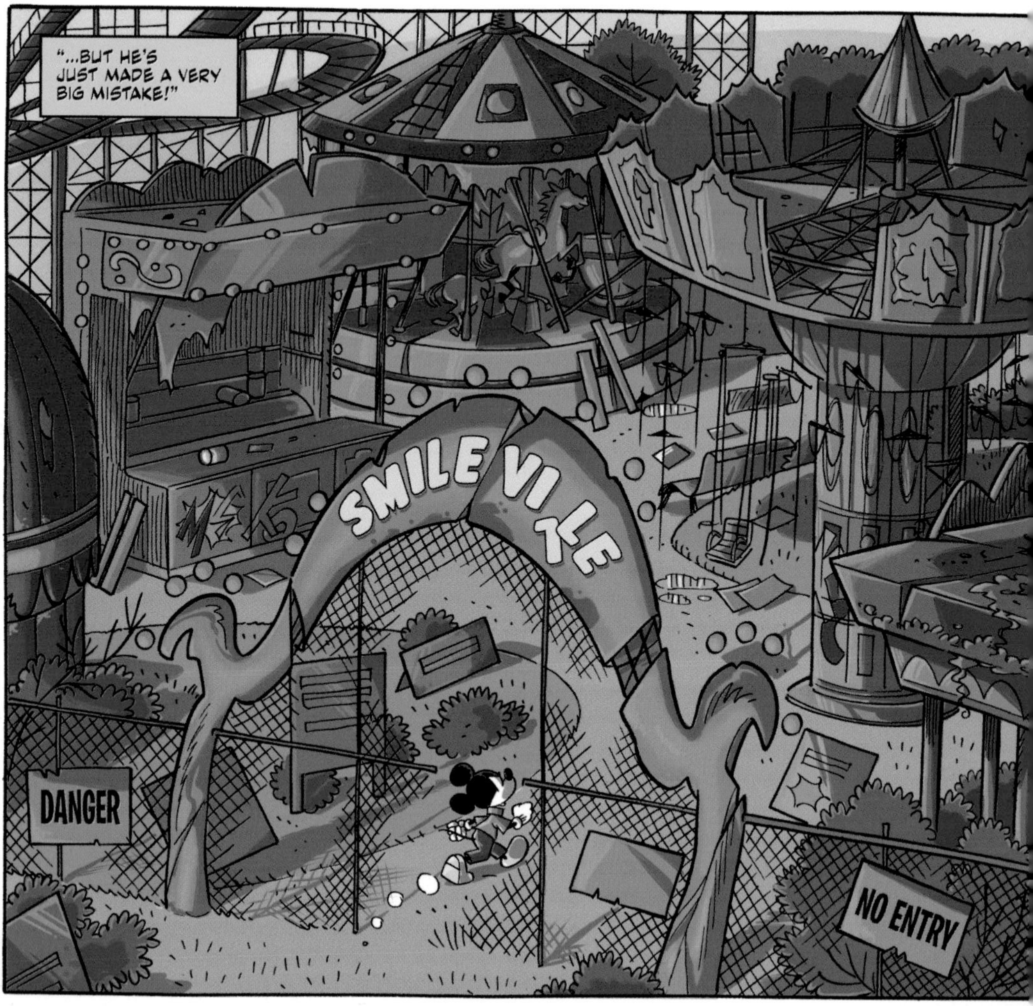
"...BUT HE'S JUST MADE A VERY BIG MISTAKE!"
SMILE VI LE
DANGER
NO ENTRY

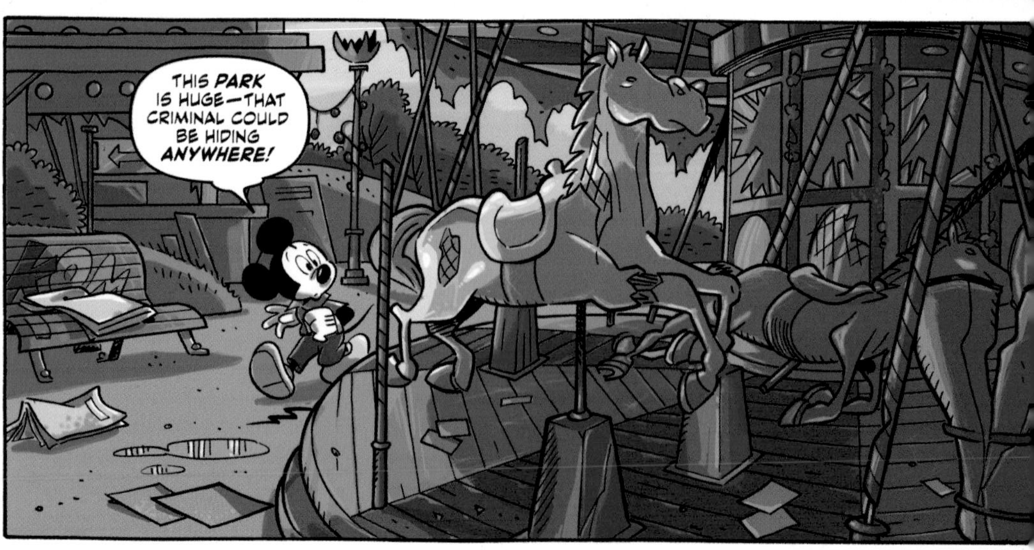
THIS PARK IS HUGE—THAT CRIMINAL COULD BE HIDING ANYWHERE!

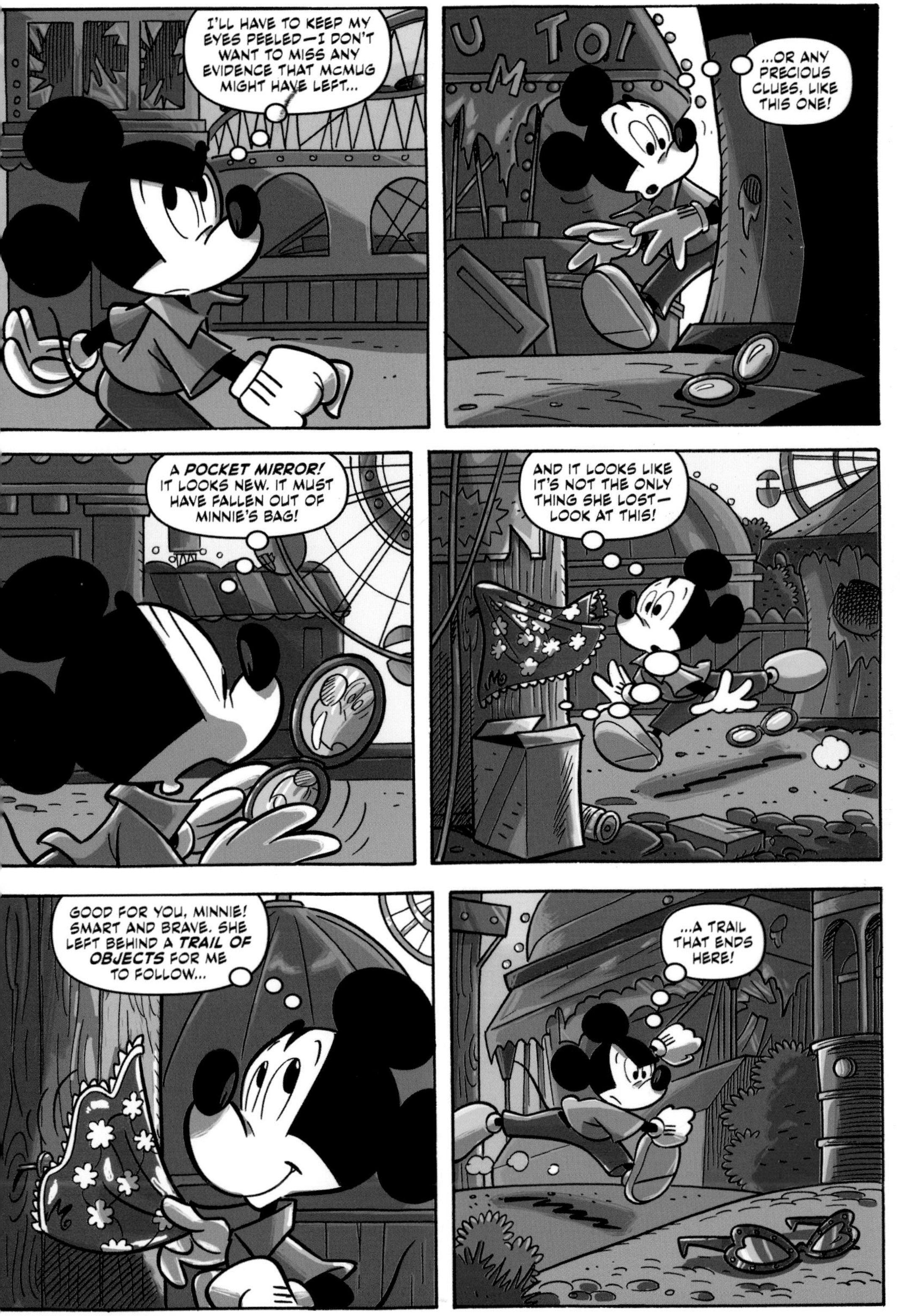
I'LL HAVE TO KEEP MY EYES PEELED—I DON'T WANT TO MISS ANY EVIDENCE THAT MCMUG MIGHT HAVE LEFT...
...OR ANY PRECIOUS CLUES, LIKE THIS ONE!
A *POCKET MIRROR!* IT LOOKS NEW. IT MUST HAVE FALLEN OUT OF MINNIE'S BAG!
AND IT LOOKS LIKE IT'S NOT THE ONLY THING SHE LOST—LOOK AT THIS!
GOOD FOR YOU, MINNIE! SMART AND BRAVE. SHE LEFT BEHIND A *TRAIL OF OBJECTS* FOR ME TO FOLLOW...
...A TRAIL THAT ENDS HERE!

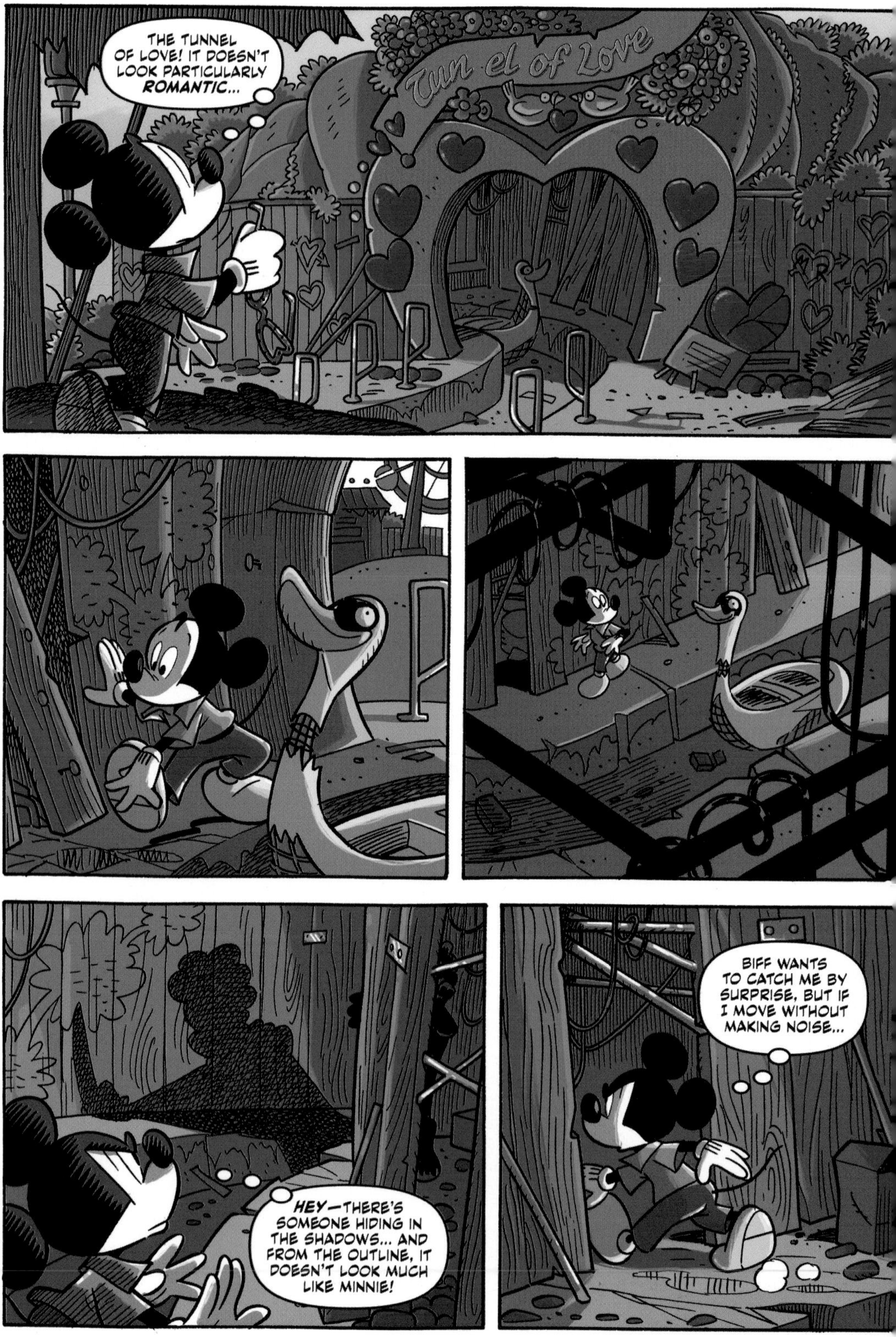
THE TUNNEL OF LOVE! IT DOESN'T LOOK PARTICULARLY ROMANTIC...
Tun el of Love
HEY—THERE'S SOMEONE HIDING IN THE SHADOWS... AND FROM THE OUTLINE, IT DOESN'T LOOK MUCH LIKE MINNIE!
BIFF WANTS TO CATCH ME BY SURPRISE, BUT IF I MOVE WITHOUT MAKING NOISE...

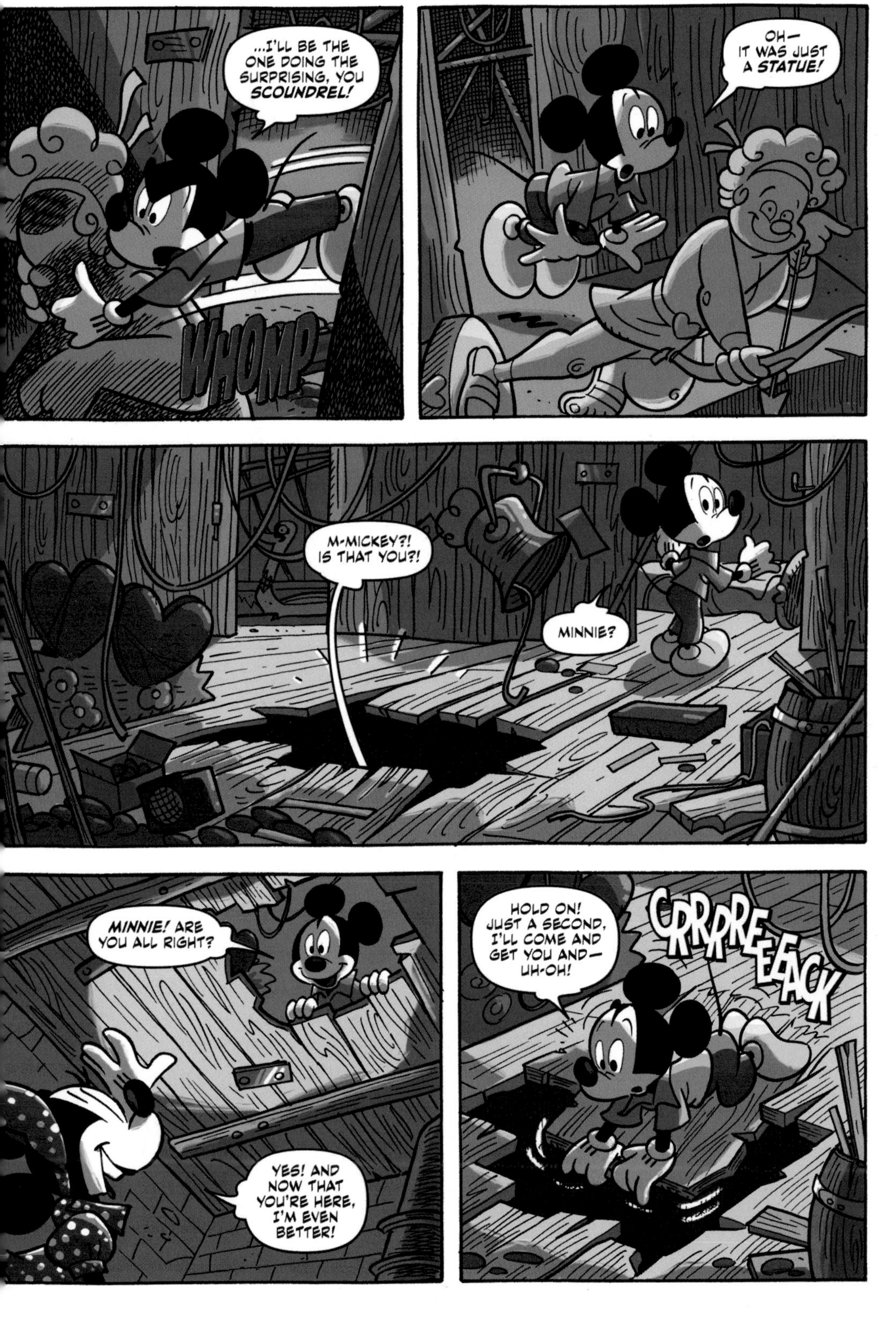
...I'LL BE THE ONE DOING THE SURPRISING, YOU SCOUNDREL!
WHOMP
OH— IT WAS JUST A STATUE!
M-MICKEY?! IS THAT YOU?!
MINNIE?
MINNIE! ARE YOU ALL RIGHT?
YES! AND NOW THAT YOU'RE HERE, I'M EVEN BETTER!
HOLD ON! JUST A SECOND, I'LL COME AND GET YOU AND— UH-OH!
CRRRREEEACK

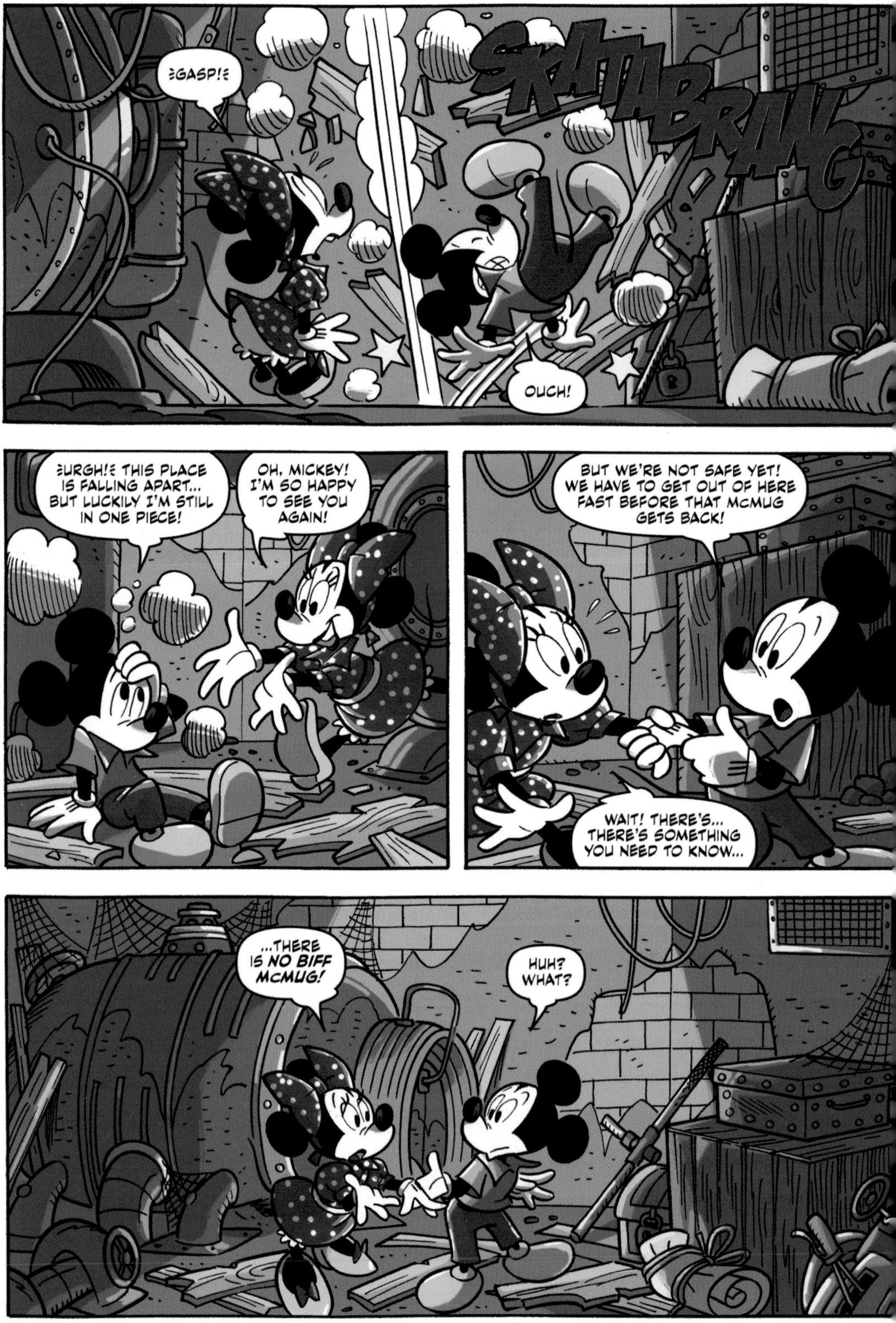
GASP!
SKRATTABRANG
OUCH!
URGH! THIS PLACE IS FALLING APART... BUT LUCKILY I'M STILL IN ONE PIECE!
OH, MICKEY! I'M SO HAPPY TO SEE YOU AGAIN!
BUT WE'RE NOT SAFE YET! WE HAVE TO GET OUT OF HERE FAST BEFORE THAT McMUG GETS BACK!
WAIT! THERE'S... THERE'S SOMETHING YOU NEED TO KNOW...
...THERE IS NO BIFF McMUG!
HUH? WHAT?

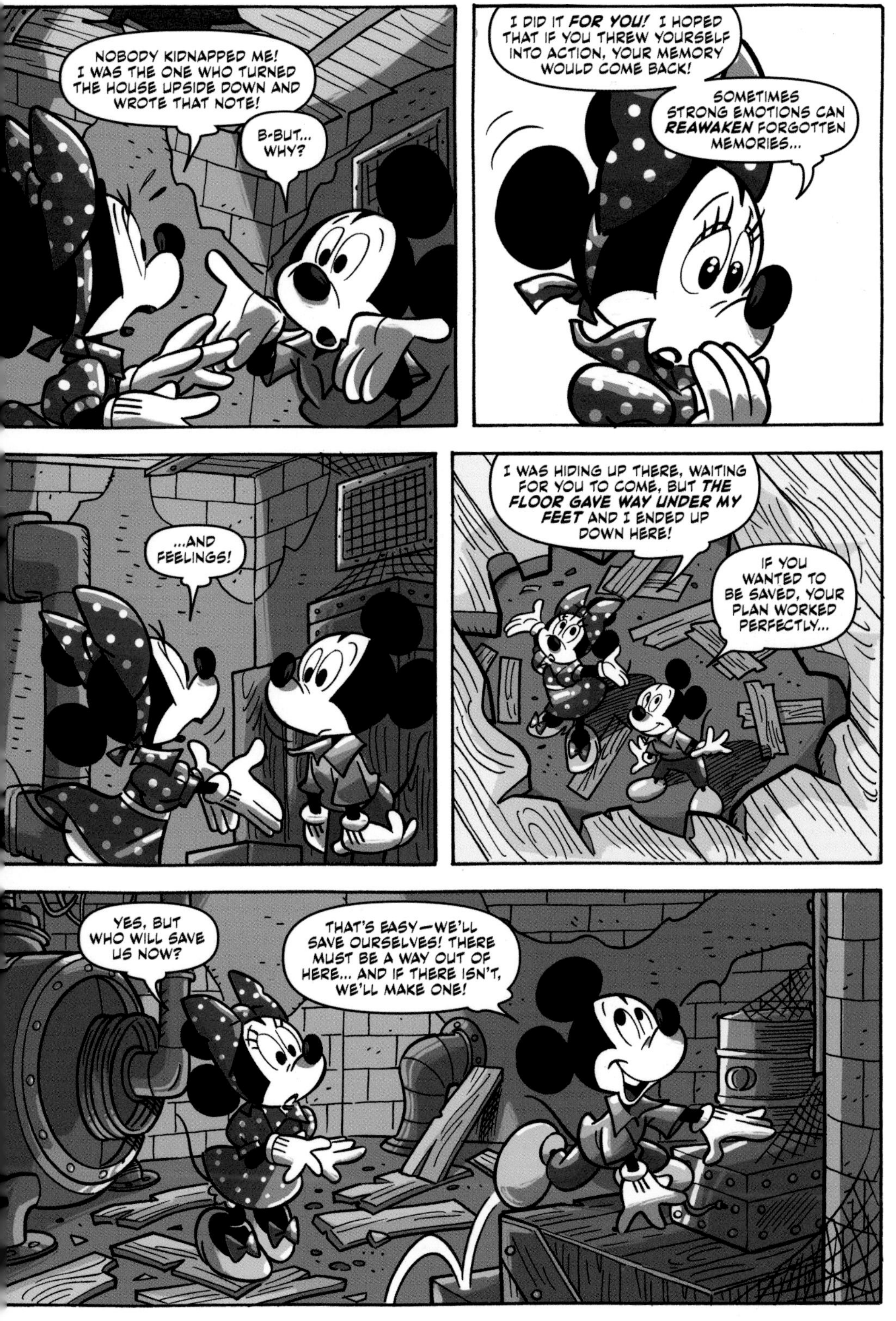
NOBODY KIDNAPPED ME! I WAS THE ONE WHO TURNED THE HOUSE UPSIDE DOWN AND WROTE THAT NOTE!
B-BUT... WHY?
I DID IT FOR YOU! I HOPED THAT IF YOU THREW YOURSELF INTO ACTION, YOUR MEMORY WOULD COME BACK!
SOMETIMES STRONG EMOTIONS CAN REAWAKEN FORGOTTEN MEMORIES...
...AND FEELINGS!
I WAS HIDING UP THERE, WAITING FOR YOU TO COME, BUT THE FLOOR GAVE WAY UNDER MY FEET AND I ENDED UP DOWN HERE!
IF YOU WANTED TO BE SAVED, YOUR PLAN WORKED PERFECTLY...
YES, BUT WHO WILL SAVE US NOW?
THAT'S EASY—WE'LL SAVE OURSELVES! THERE MUST BE A WAY OUT OF HERE... AND IF THERE ISN'T, WE'LL MAKE ONE!

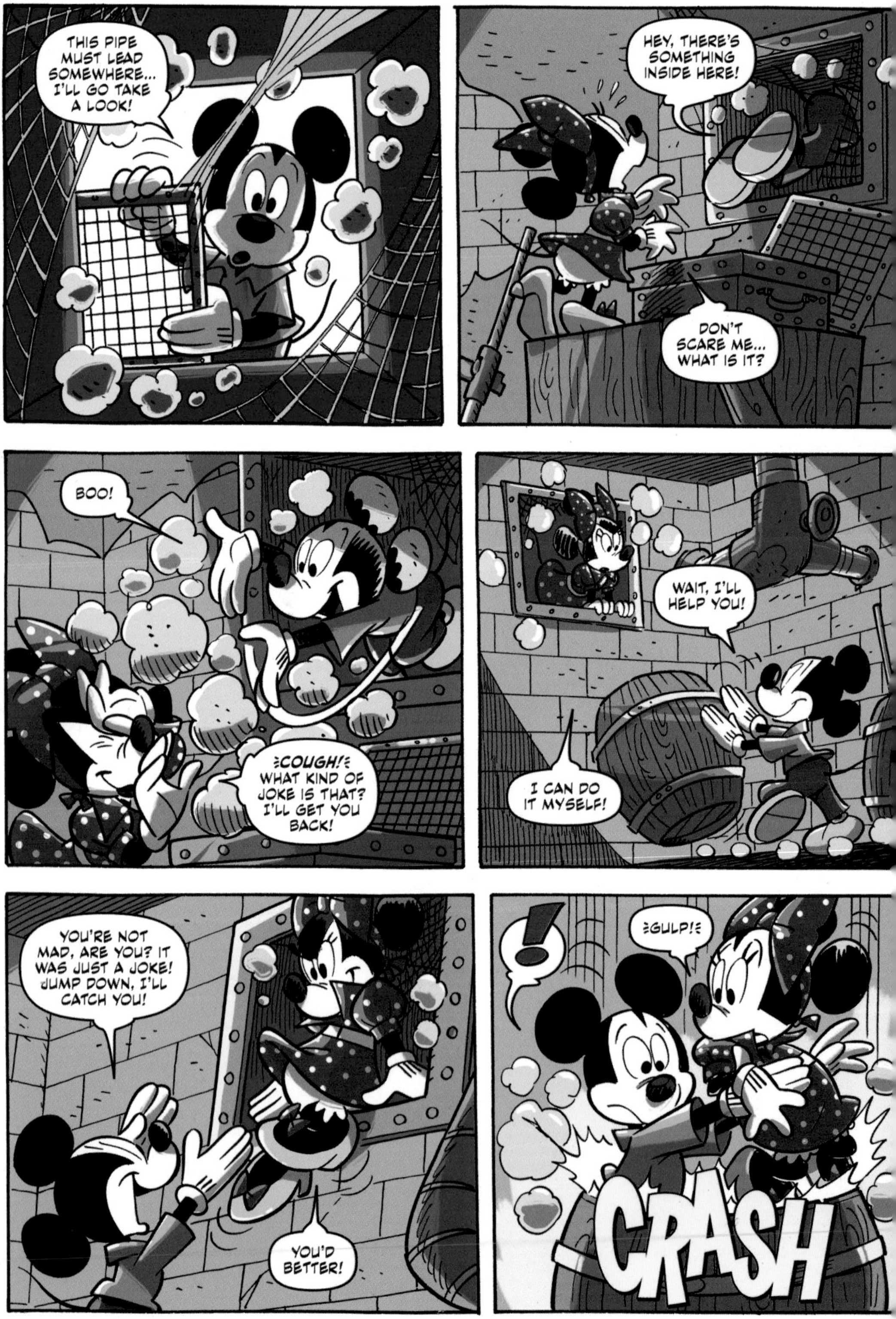
THIS PIPE MUST LEAD SOMEWHERE... I'LL GO TAKE A LOOK!
HEY, THERE'S SOMETHING INSIDE HERE!
DON'T SCARE ME... WHAT IS IT?
BOO!
≷COUGH!≶ WHAT KIND OF JOKE IS THAT? I'LL GET YOU BACK!
WAIT, I'LL HELP YOU!
I CAN DO IT MYSELF!
YOU'RE NOT MAD, ARE YOU? IT WAS JUST A JOKE! JUMP DOWN, I'LL CATCH YOU!
YOU'D BETTER!
!
≷GULP!≶
CRASH

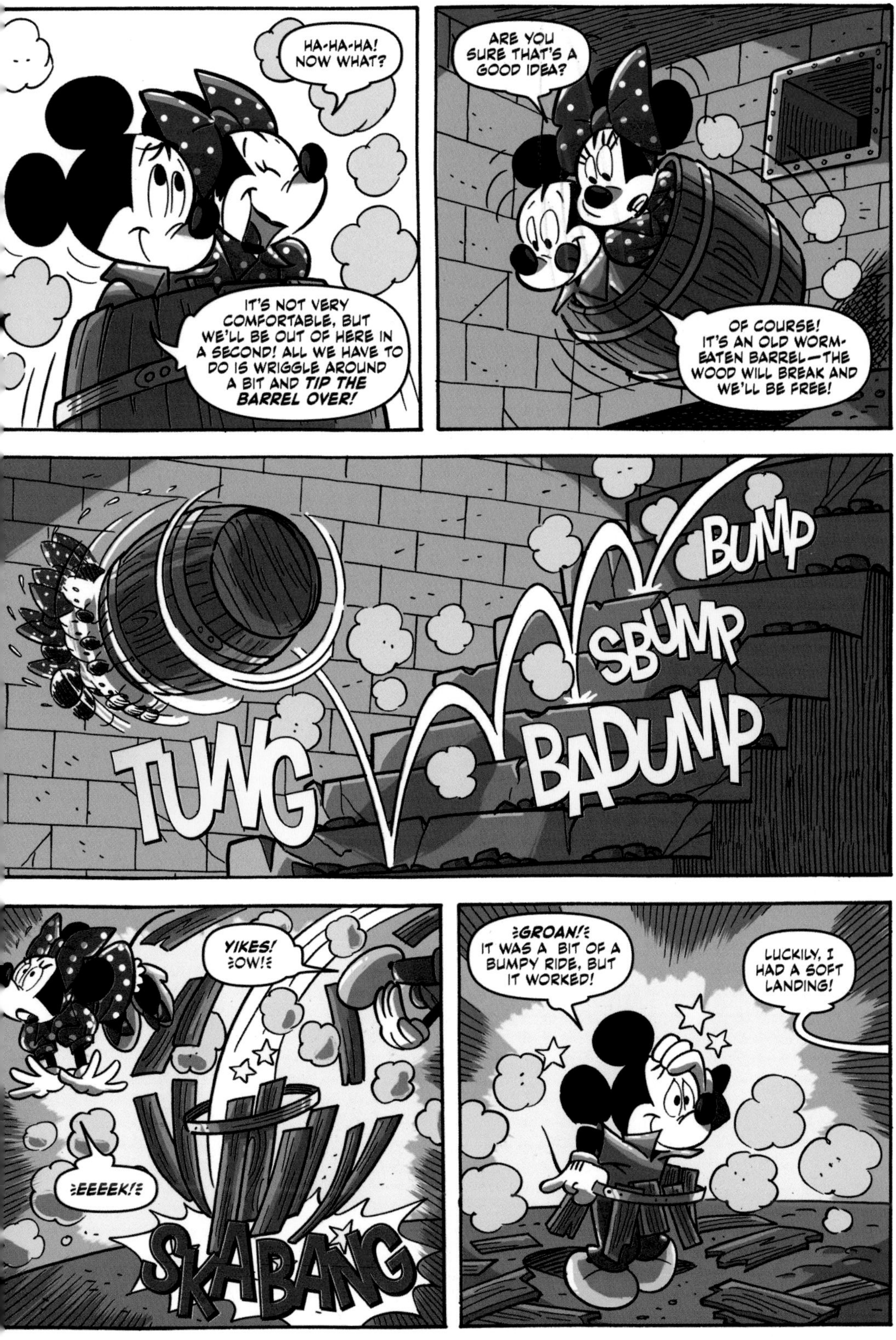

HA-HA-HA! NOW WHAT?
IT'S NOT VERY COMFORTABLE, BUT WE'LL BE OUT OF HERE IN A SECOND! ALL WE HAVE TO DO IS WRIGGLE AROUND A BIT AND TIP THE BARREL OVER!
ARE YOU SURE THAT'S A GOOD IDEA?
OF COURSE! IT'S AN OLD WORM-EATEN BARREL—THE WOOD WILL BREAK AND WE'LL BE FREE!
TUNG
BUMP
SBUMP
BADUMP
YIKES! ÷OW!÷
÷EEEEK!÷
SKABANG
÷GROAN!÷ IT WAS A BIT OF A BUMPY RIDE, BUT IT WORKED!
LUCKILY, I HAD A SOFT LANDING!

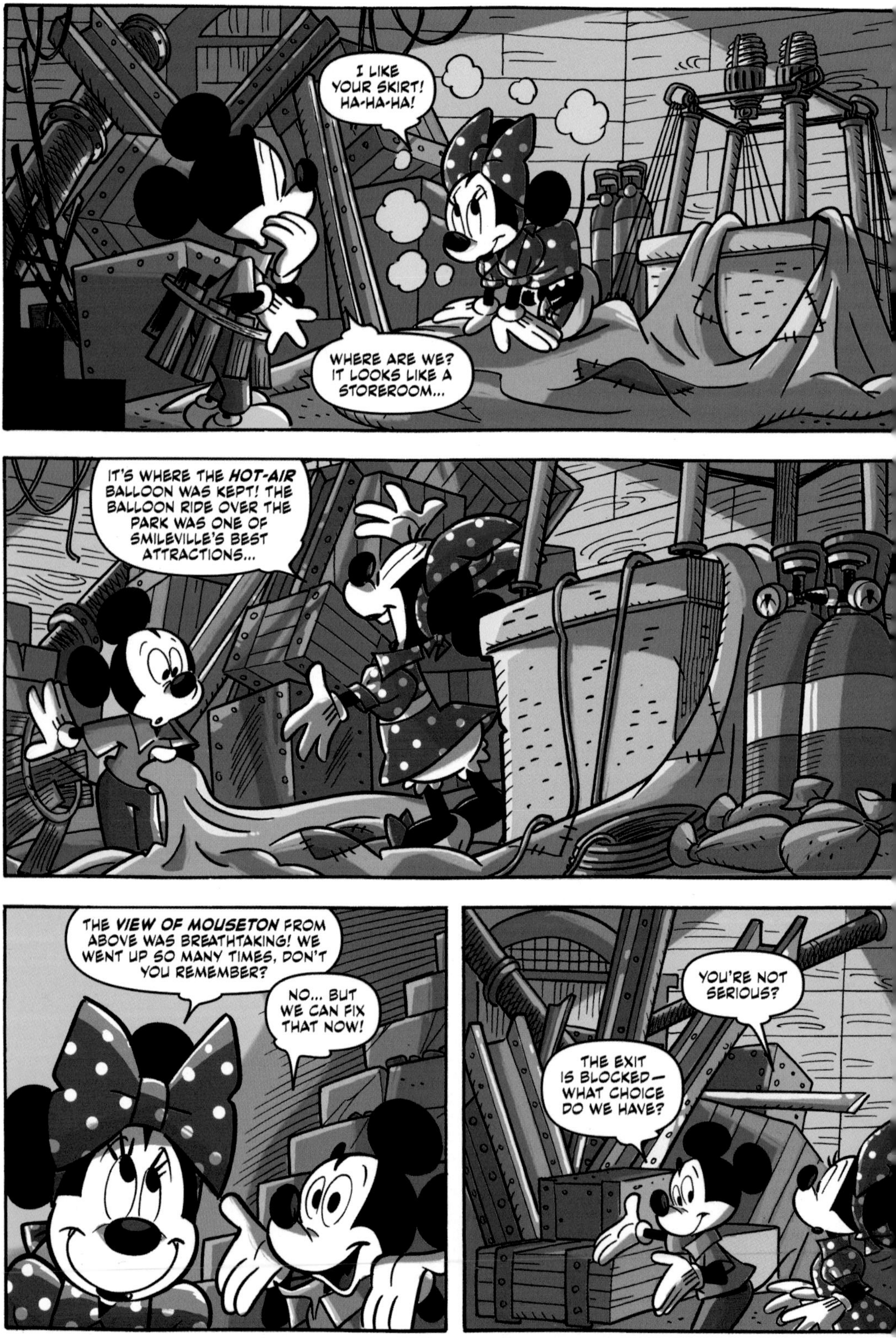
I LIKE YOUR SKIRT! HA-HA-HA!
WHERE ARE WE? IT LOOKS LIKE A STOREROOM...
IT'S WHERE THE HOT-AIR BALLOON WAS KEPT! THE BALLOON RIDE OVER THE PARK WAS ONE OF SMILEVILLE'S BEST ATTRACTIONS...
THE VIEW OF MOUSETON FROM ABOVE WAS BREATHTAKING! WE WENT UP SO MANY TIMES, DON'T YOU REMEMBER?
NO... BUT WE CAN FIX THAT NOW!
YOU'RE NOT SERIOUS?
THE EXIT IS BLOCKED— WHAT CHOICE DO WE HAVE?

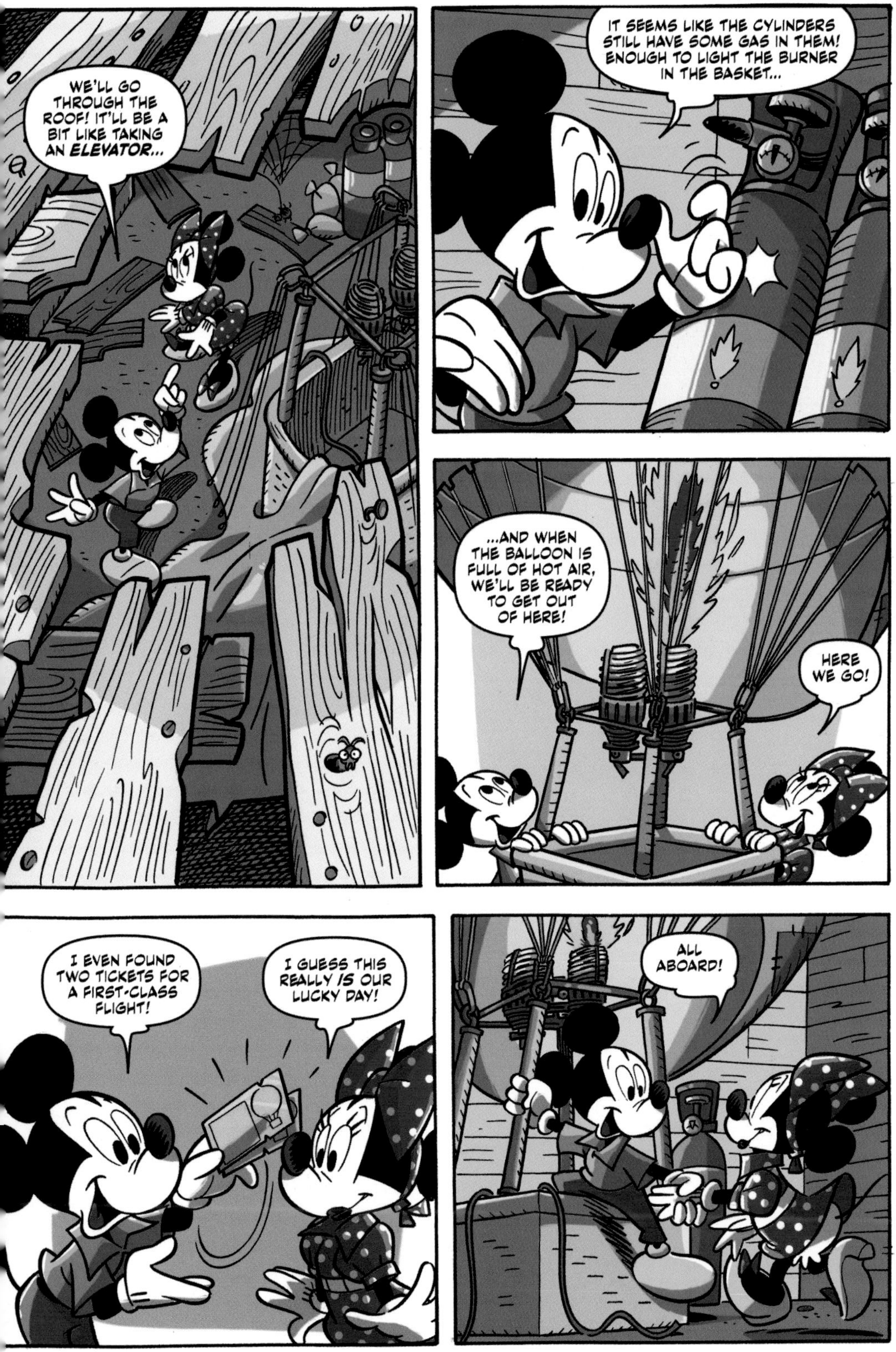
WE'LL GO THROUGH THE ROOF! IT'LL BE A BIT LIKE TAKING AN *ELEVATOR*...
IT SEEMS LIKE THE CYLINDERS STILL HAVE SOME GAS IN THEM! ENOUGH TO LIGHT THE BURNER IN THE BASKET...
...AND WHEN THE BALLOON IS FULL OF HOT AIR, WE'LL BE READY TO GET OUT OF HERE!
HERE WE GO!
I EVEN FOUND TWO TICKETS FOR A FIRST-CLASS FLIGHT!
I GUESS THIS REALLY *IS* OUR LUCKY DAY!
ALL ABOARD!

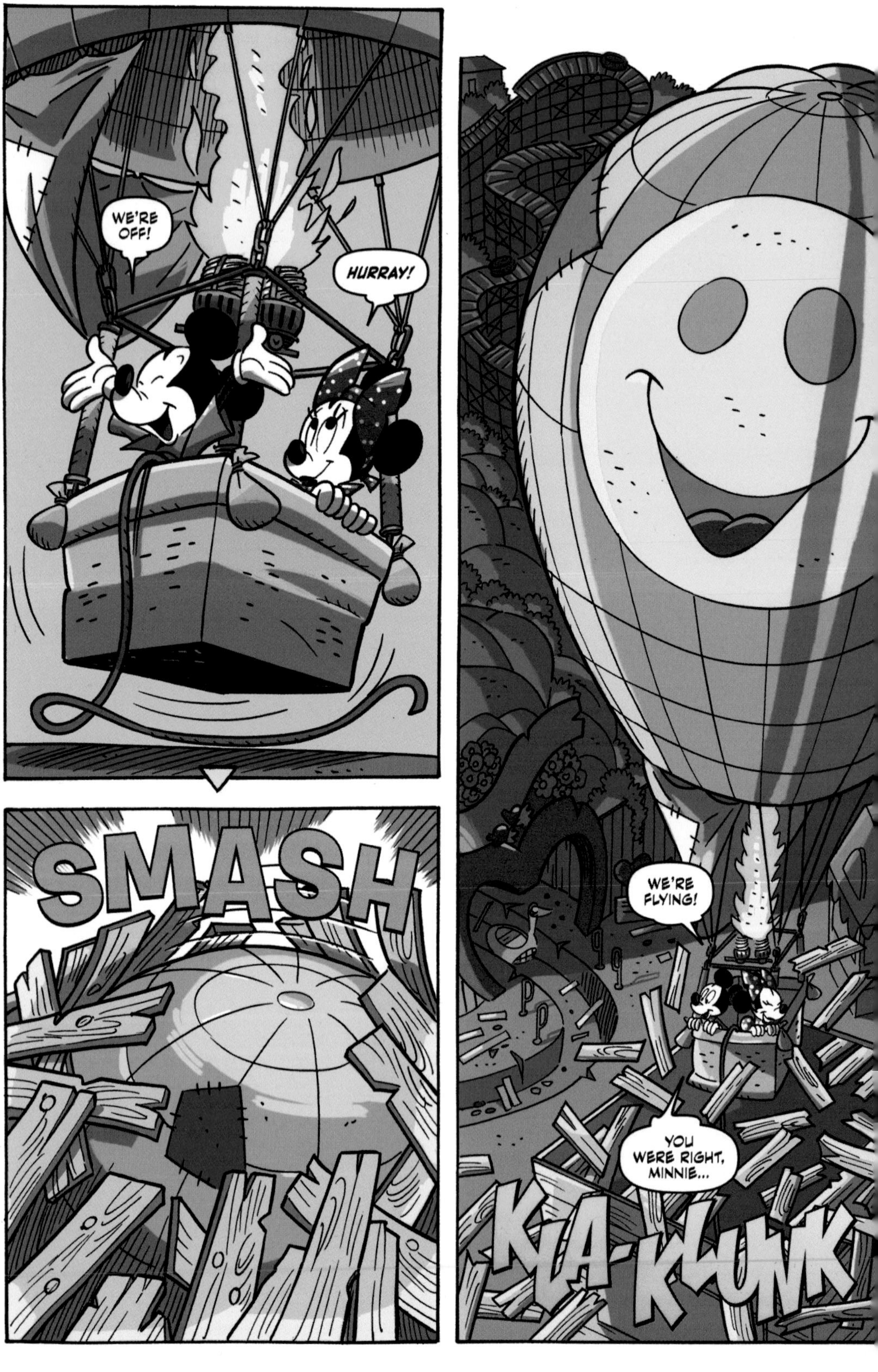
WE'RE OFF!
HURRAY!
SMASH
WE'RE FLYING!
YOU WERE RIGHT, MINNIE...
KLA-KLUNK

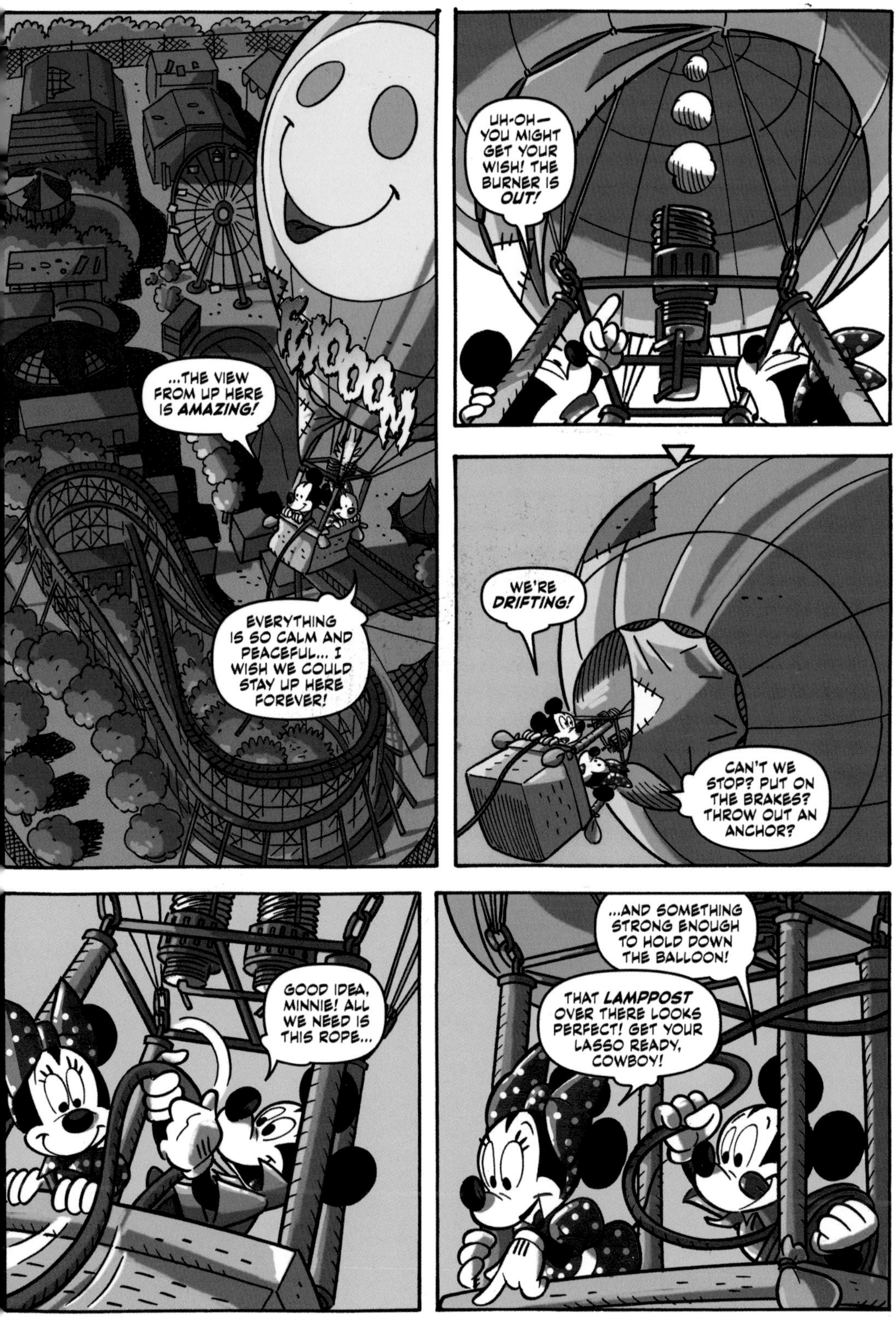
...THE VIEW FROM UP HERE IS *AMAZING!*
FWOOOM
EVERYTHING IS SO CALM AND PEACEFUL... I WISH WE COULD STAY UP HERE FOREVER!
UH-OH— YOU MIGHT GET YOUR WISH! THE BURNER IS *OUT!*
WE'RE *DRIFTING!*
CAN'T WE STOP? PUT ON THE BRAKES? THROW OUT AN ANCHOR?
GOOD IDEA, MINNIE! ALL WE NEED IS THIS ROPE...
...AND SOMETHING STRONG ENOUGH TO HOLD DOWN THE BALLOON!
THAT *LAMPPOST* OVER THERE LOOKS PERFECT! GET YOUR LASSO READY, COWBOY!

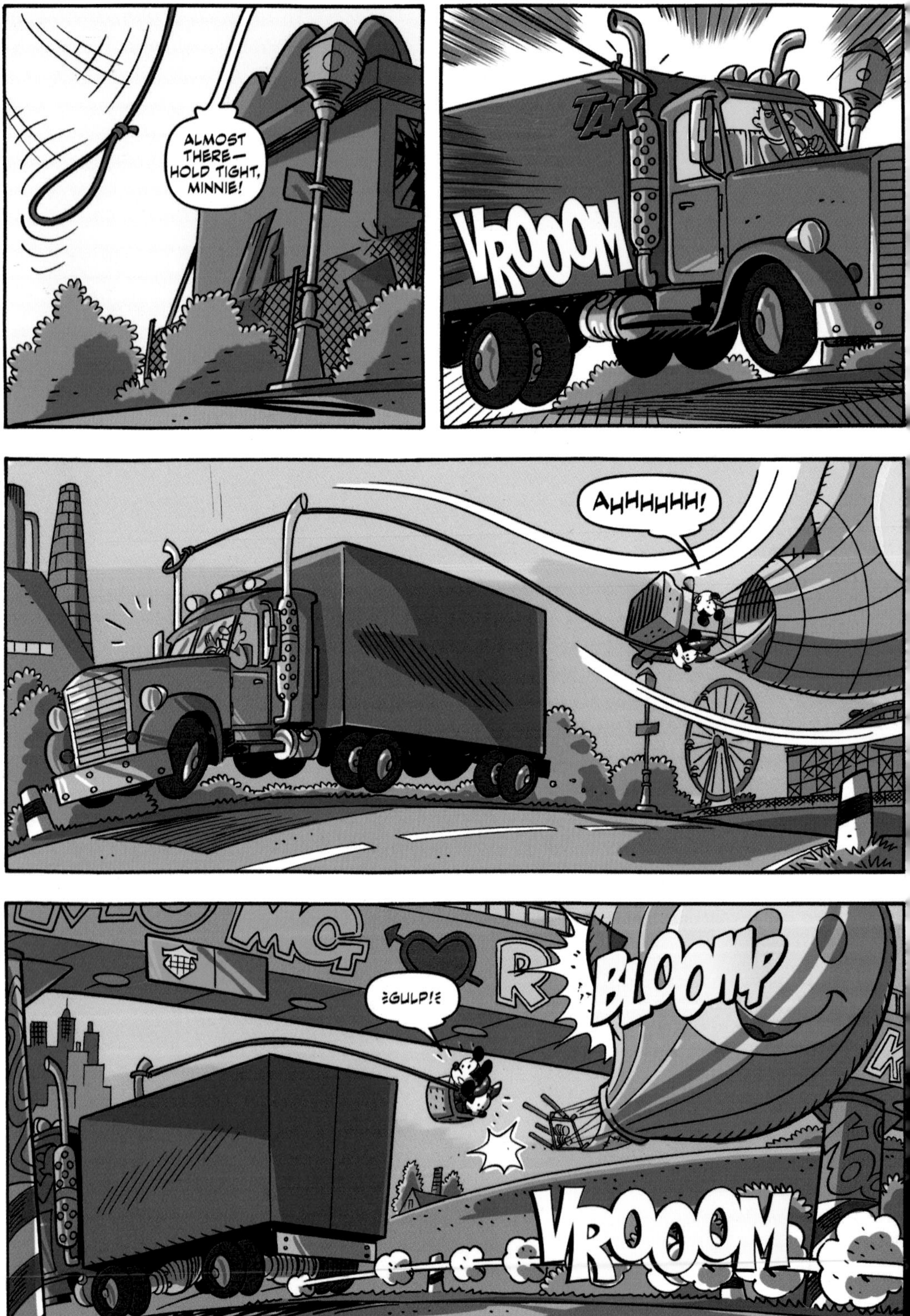
ALMOST THERE— HOLD TIGHT, MINNIE!
TAK
VROOOM
AHHHHHH!
GULP!
BLOOMP
VROOOM

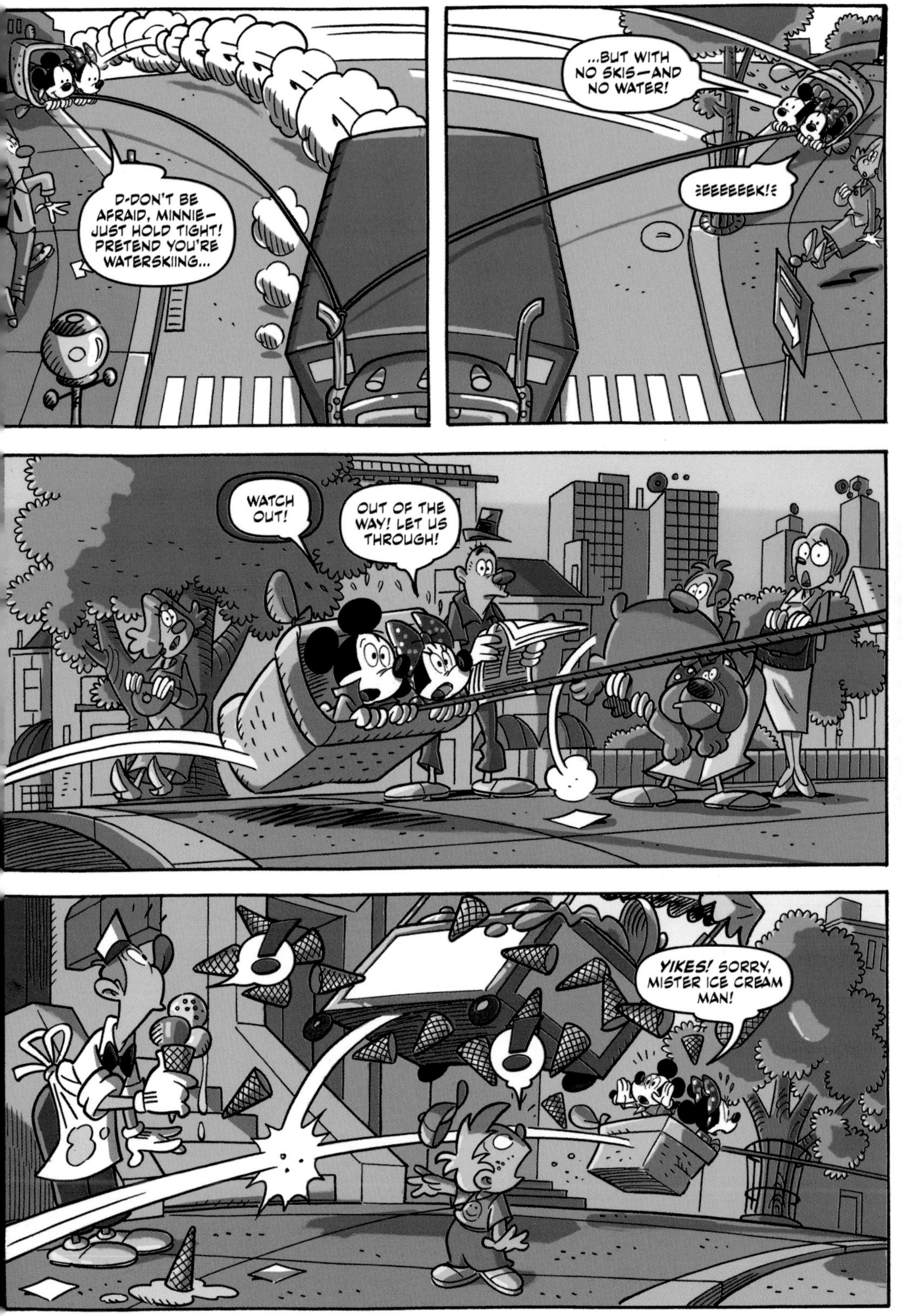
D-DON'T BE AFRAID, MINNIE— JUST HOLD TIGHT! PRETEND YOU'RE WATERSKIING...
...BUT WITH NO SKIS—AND NO WATER!
EEEEEEEK!
WATCH OUT!
OUT OF THE WAY! LET US THROUGH!
YIKES! SORRY, MISTER ICE CREAM MAN!

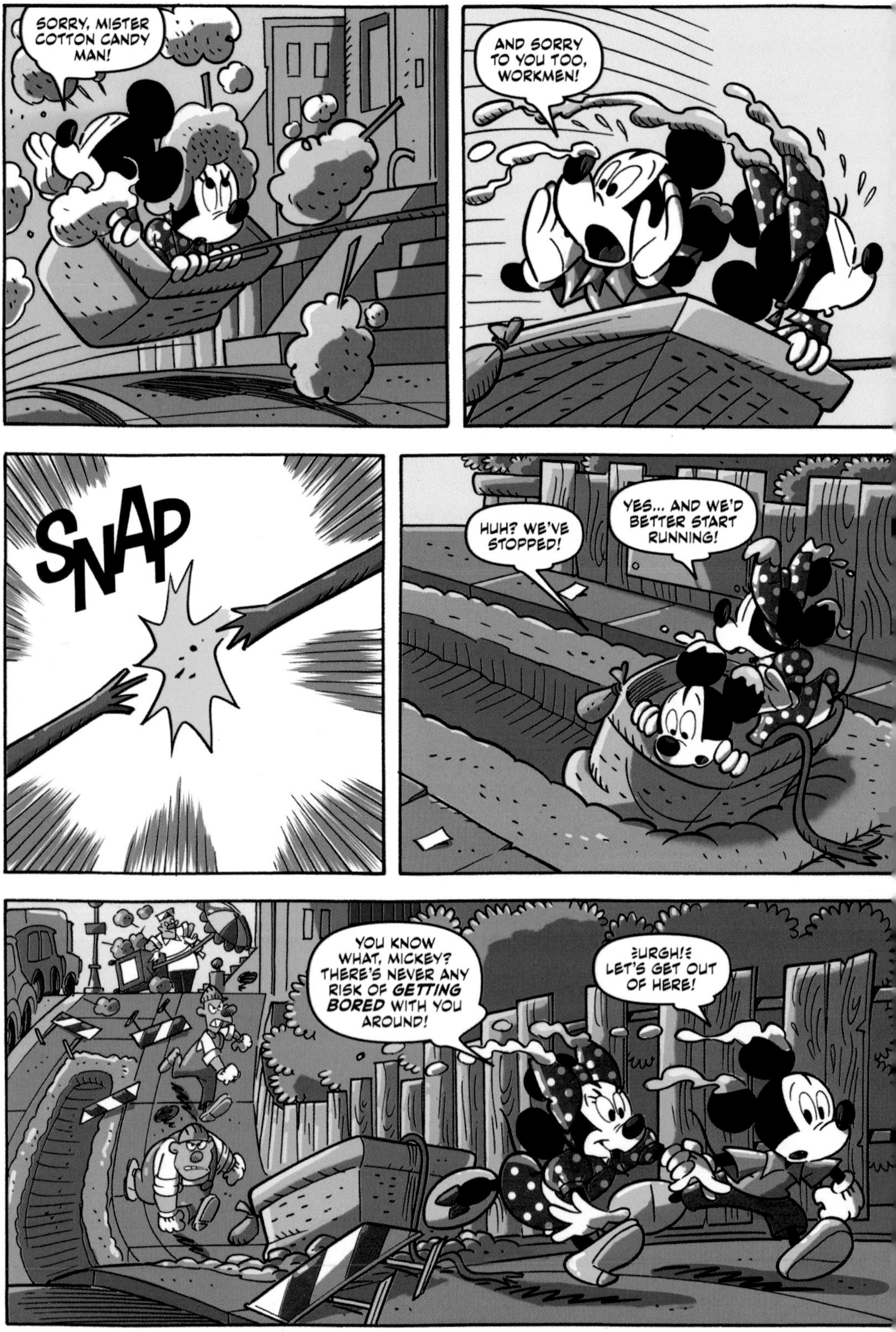
SORRY, MISTER COTTON CANDY MAN!
AND SORRY TO YOU TOO, WORKMEN!
SNAP
HUH? WE'VE STOPPED!
YES... AND WE'D BETTER START RUNNING!
YOU KNOW WHAT, MICKEY? THERE'S NEVER ANY RISK OF GETTING BORED WITH YOU AROUND!
URGH! LET'S GET OUT OF HERE!

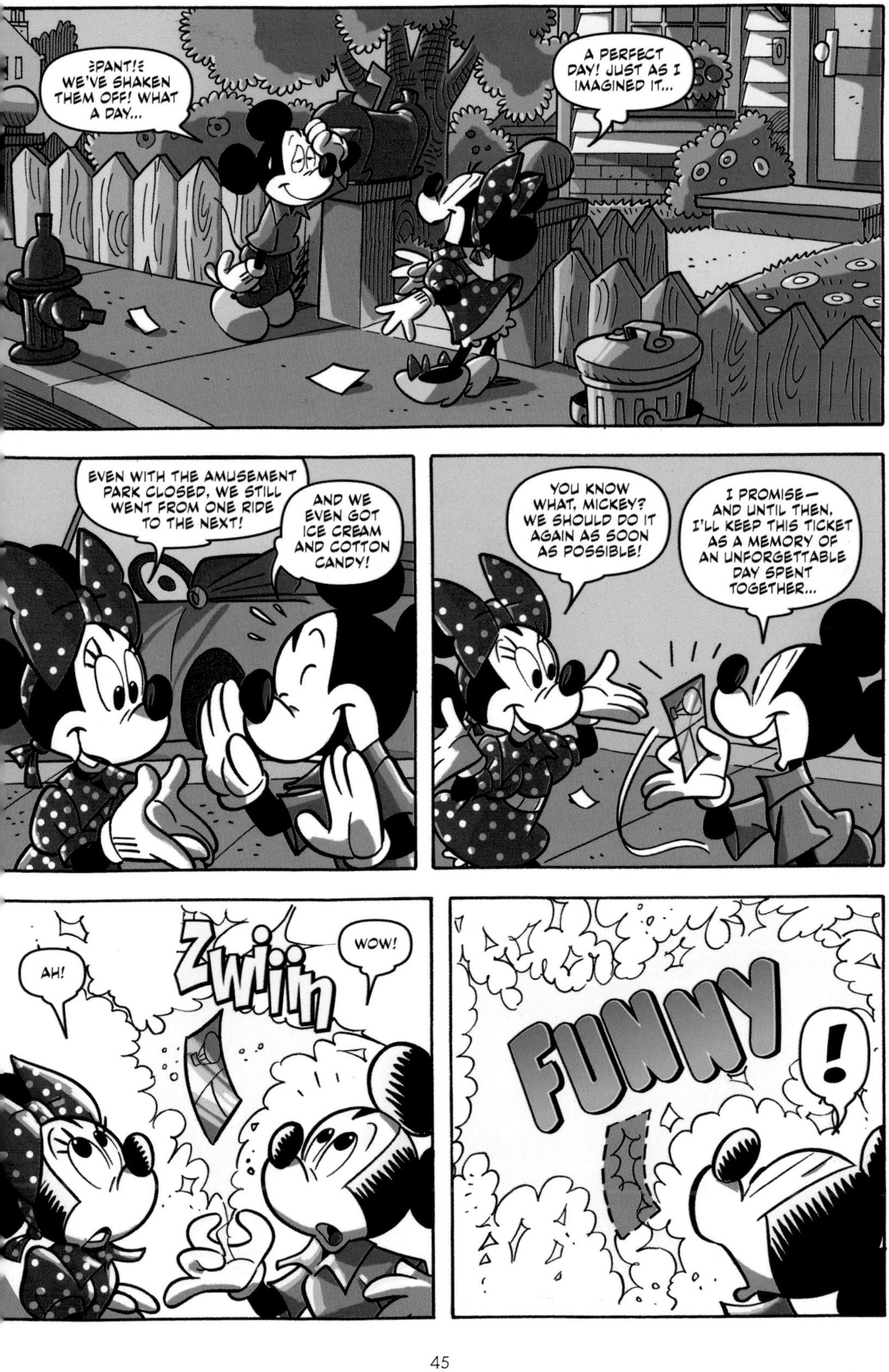

PANT!
WE'VE SHAKEN THEM OFF! WHAT A DAY...
A PERFECT DAY! JUST AS I IMAGINED IT...
EVEN WITH THE AMUSEMENT PARK CLOSED, WE STILL WENT FROM ONE RIDE TO THE NEXT!
AND WE EVEN GOT ICE CREAM AND COTTON CANDY!
YOU KNOW WHAT, MICKEY? WE SHOULD DO IT AGAIN AS SOON AS POSSIBLE!
I PROMISE— AND UNTIL THEN, I'LL KEEP THIS TICKET AS A MEMORY OF AN UNFORGETTABLE DAY SPENT TOGETHER...
AH!
ZWIIIN
WOW!
FUNNY
!

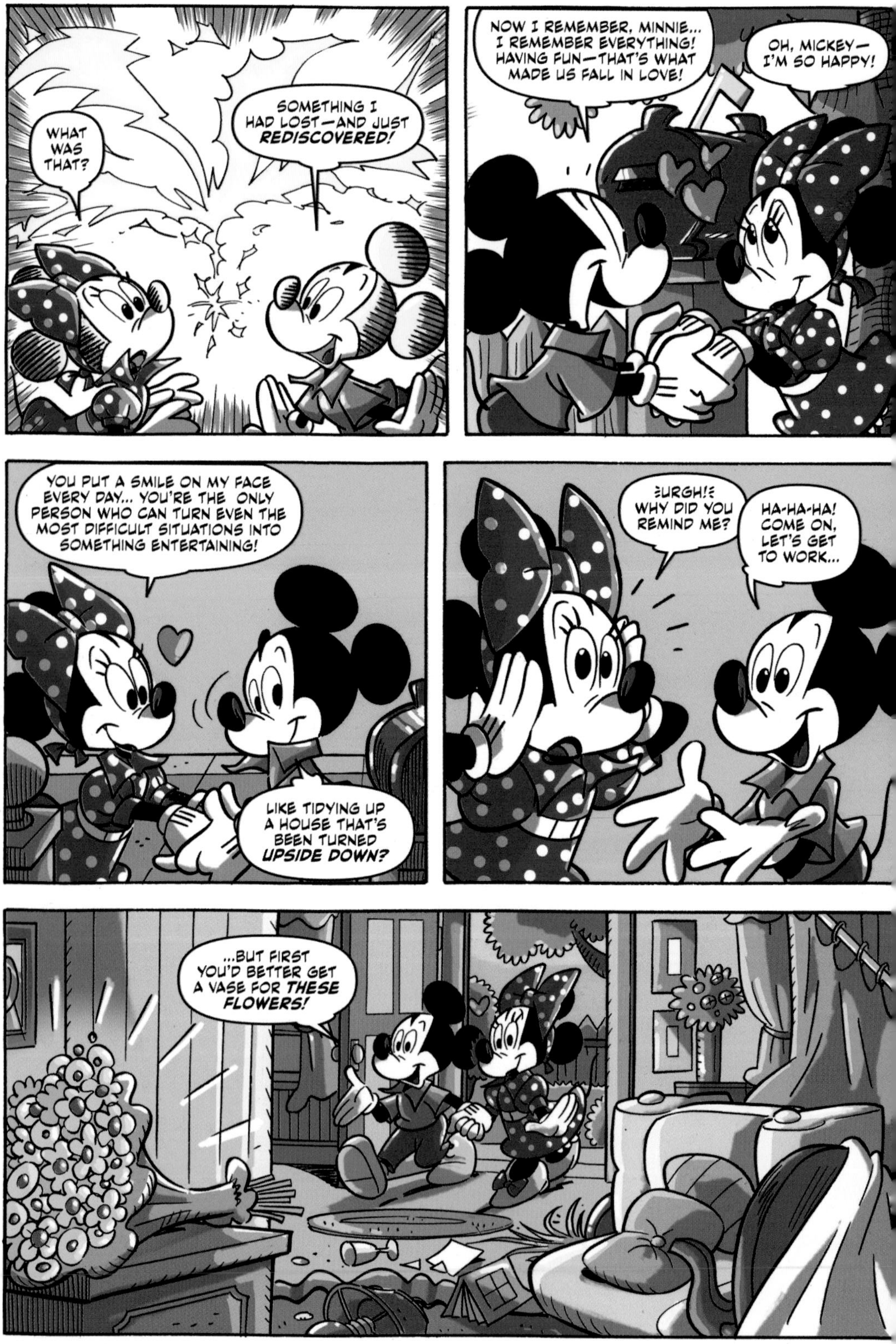
WHAT WAS THAT?
SOMETHING I HAD LOST—AND JUST REDISCOVERED!
NOW I REMEMBER, MINNIE... I REMEMBER EVERYTHING! HAVING FUN—THAT'S WHAT MADE US FALL IN LOVE!
OH, MICKEY— I'M SO HAPPY!
YOU PUT A SMILE ON MY FACE EVERY DAY... YOU'RE THE ONLY PERSON WHO CAN TURN EVEN THE MOST DIFFICULT SITUATIONS INTO SOMETHING ENTERTAINING!
LIKE TIDYING UP A HOUSE THAT'S BEEN TURNED UPSIDE DOWN?
URGH! WHY DID YOU REMIND ME?
HA-HA-HA! COME ON, LET'S GET TO WORK...
...BUT FIRST YOU'D BETTER GET A VASE FOR THESE FLOWERS!

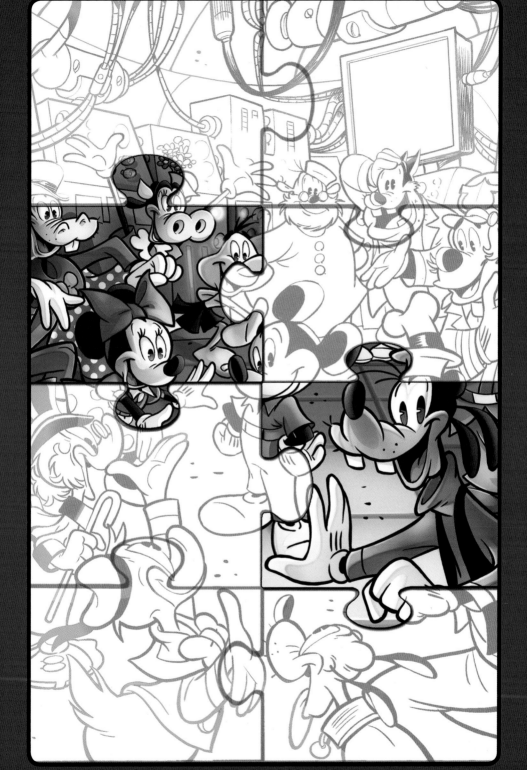

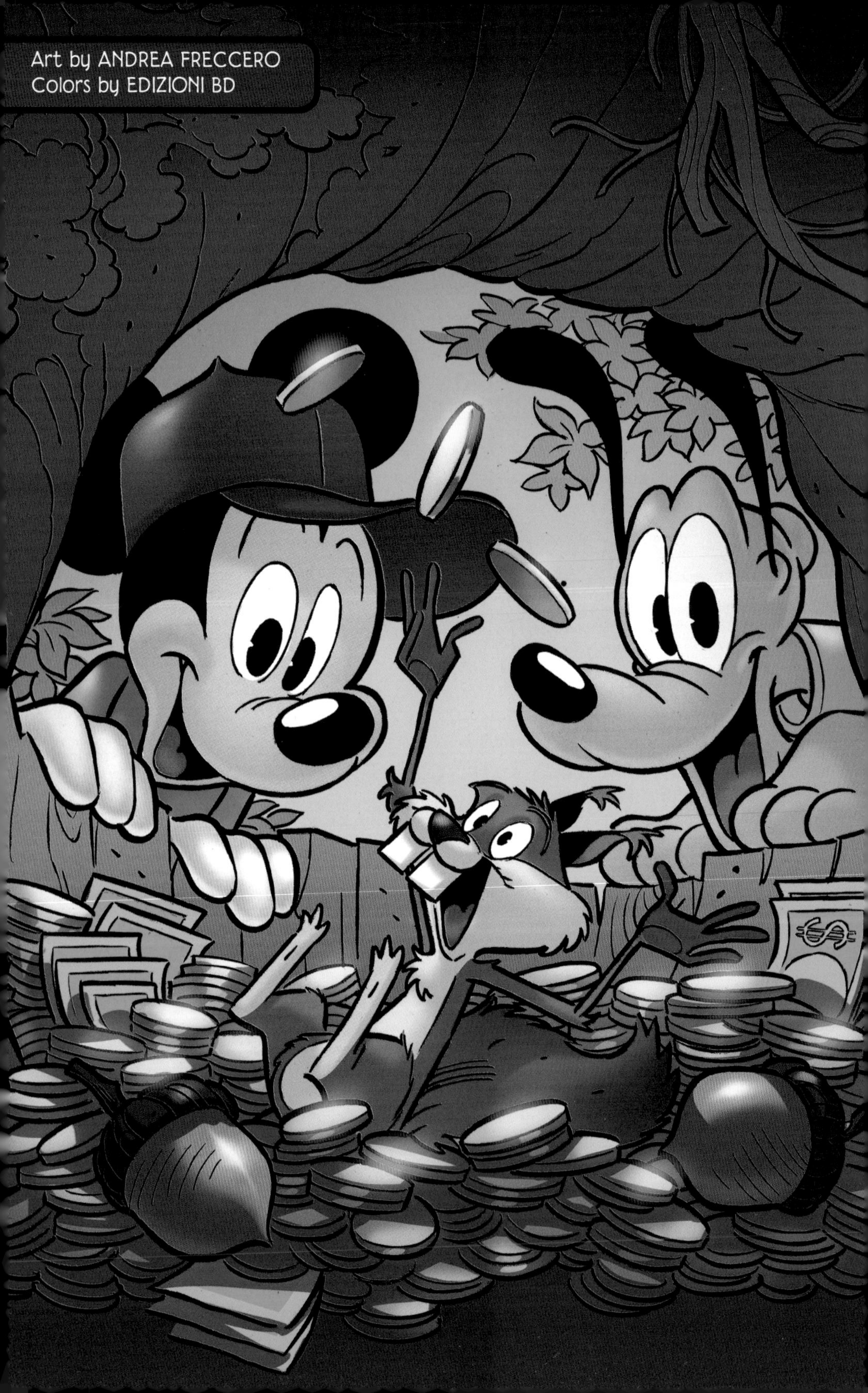
Art by ANDREA FRECCERO
Colors by EDIZIONI BD

CHAPTER 3: THE TREASURE IN THE OLD TREE

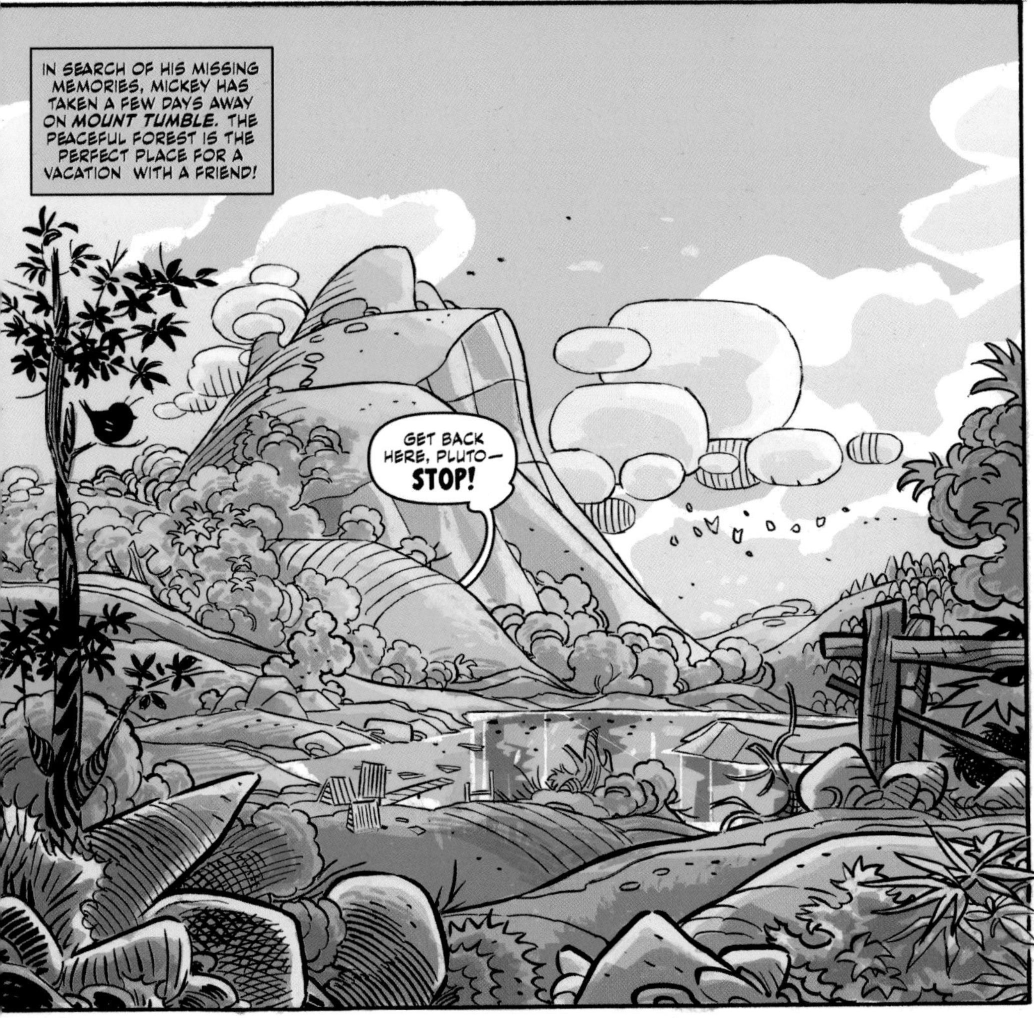
IN SEARCH OF HIS MISSING MEMORIES, MICKEY HAS TAKEN A FEW DAYS AWAY ON *MOUNT TUMBLE.* THE PEACEFUL FOREST IS THE PERFECT PLACE FOR A VACATION WITH A FRIEND!
GET BACK HERE, PLUTO— **STOP!**

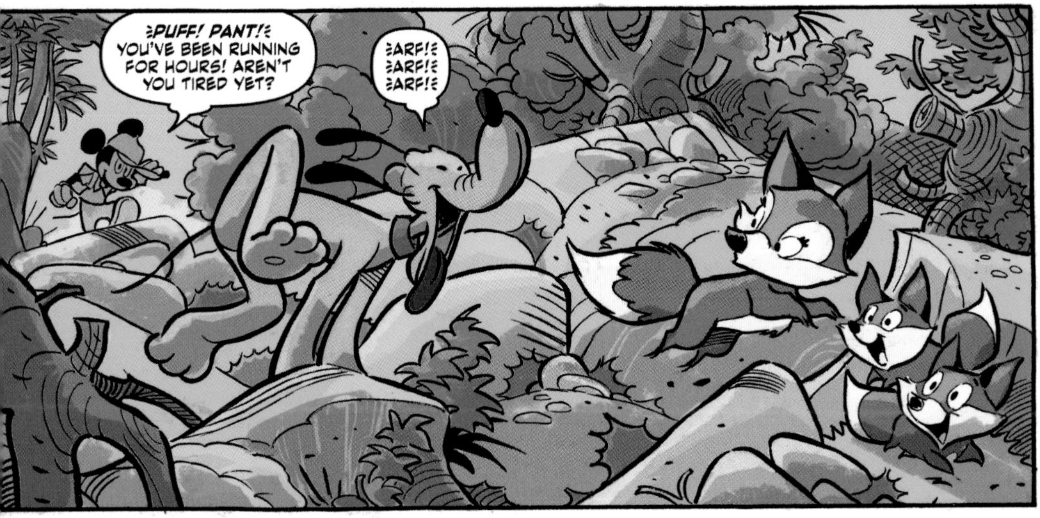
PUFF! PANT! YOU'VE BEEN RUNNING FOR HOURS! AREN'T YOU TIRED YET?
ARF! ARF! ARF!

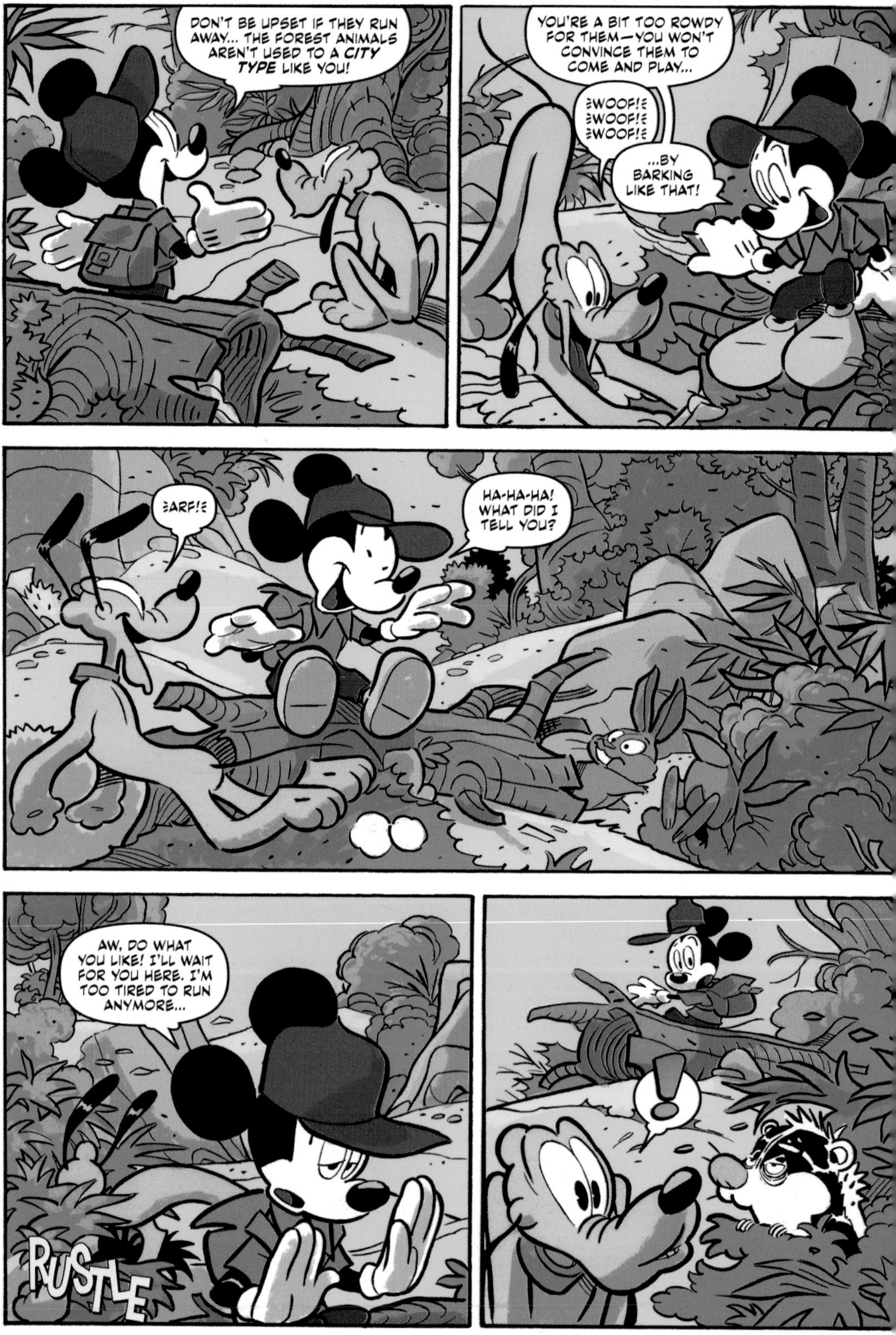
DON'T BE UPSET IF THEY RUN AWAY... THE FOREST ANIMALS AREN'T USED TO A *CITY TYPE* LIKE YOU!
YOU'RE A BIT TOO ROWDY FOR THEM—YOU WON'T CONVINCE THEM TO COME AND PLAY...
WOOF! WOOF! WOOF!
...BY BARKING LIKE THAT!
ARF!
HA-HA-HA! WHAT DID I TELL YOU?
AW, DO WHAT YOU LIKE! I'LL WAIT FOR YOU HERE. I'M TOO TIRED TO RUN ANYMORE...
RUSTLE
!

...THOUGH ON SECOND THOUGHT, A LITTLE *STRETCH OF THE LEGS* ON THE WAY HOME WOULDN'T BE A BAD IDEA!

≷SNORT!≷ ≷SNARL!≷

≷*PHEW!*≷ WE'RE OUT OF DANGER, OLD FRIEND— NO SKUNKS IN SIGHT!

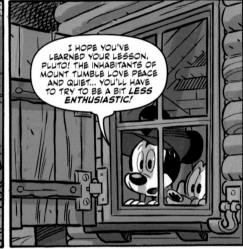

I HOPE YOU'VE LEARNED YOUR LESSON, PLUTO! THE INHABITANTS OF MOUNT TUMBLE LOVE PEACE AND QUIET... YOU'LL HAVE TO TRY TO BE A BIT *LESS ENTHUSIASTIC!*

PLUS, WE'RE HERE FOR A REST! YOU DON'T REALLY WANT TO RUN AFTER EVERYTHING THAT MOVES IN THE FOREST, DO YOU?

≷ARF!≷ ≷ARF!≷ ≷ARF!≷

≷SIGH!≷ WHY DO I EVEN BOTHER ASKING SOME QUESTIONS?

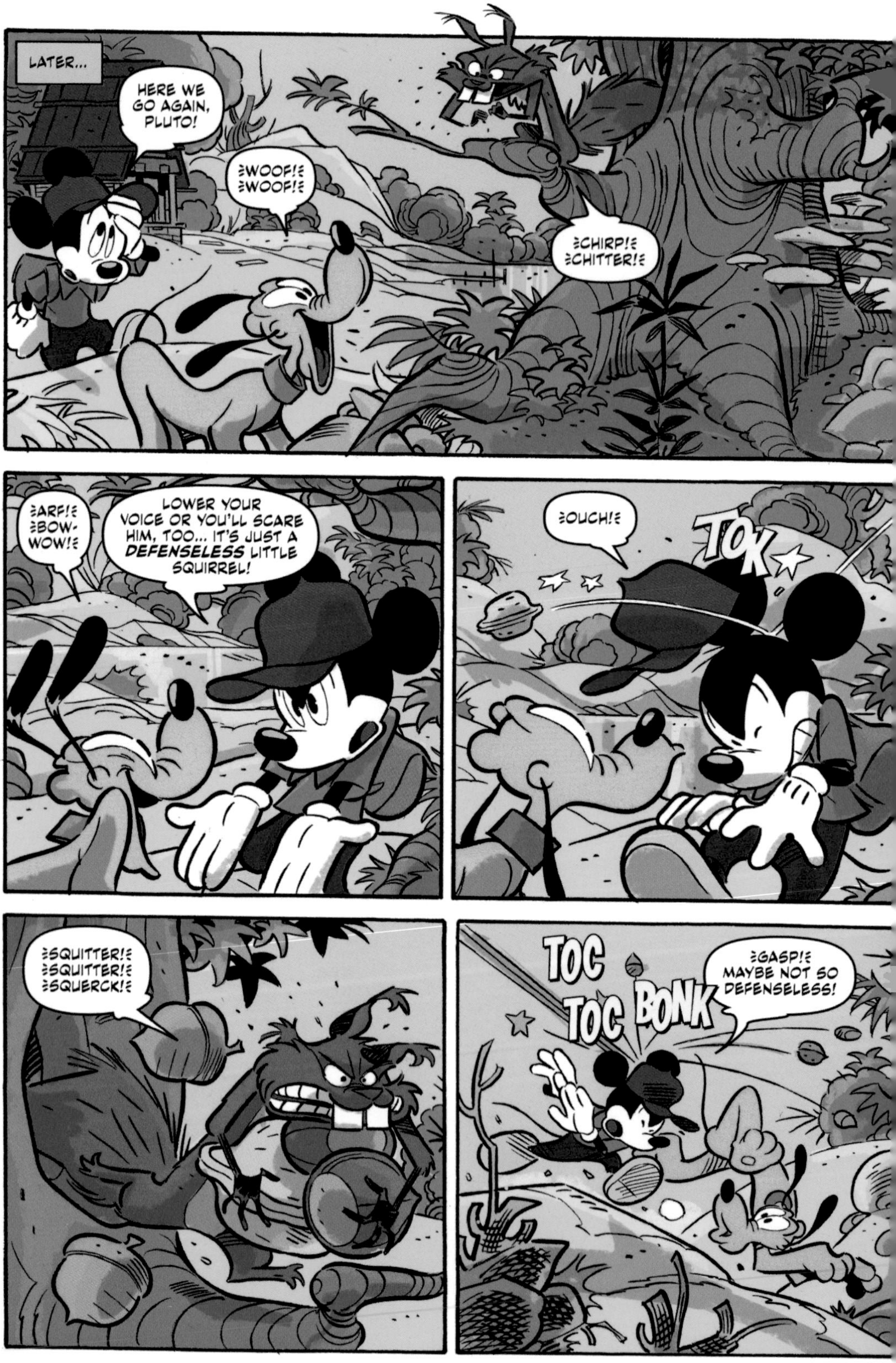
LATER...
HERE WE GO AGAIN, PLUTO!
WOOF! WOOF!
CHIRP! CHITTER!
ARF! BOW-WOW!
LOWER YOUR VOICE OR YOU'LL SCARE HIM, TOO... IT'S JUST A DEFENSELESS LITTLE SQUIRREL!
OUCH!
TOK
SQUITTER! SQUITTER! SQUERCK!
TOC
TOC
BONK
GASP! MAYBE NOT SO DEFENSELESS!

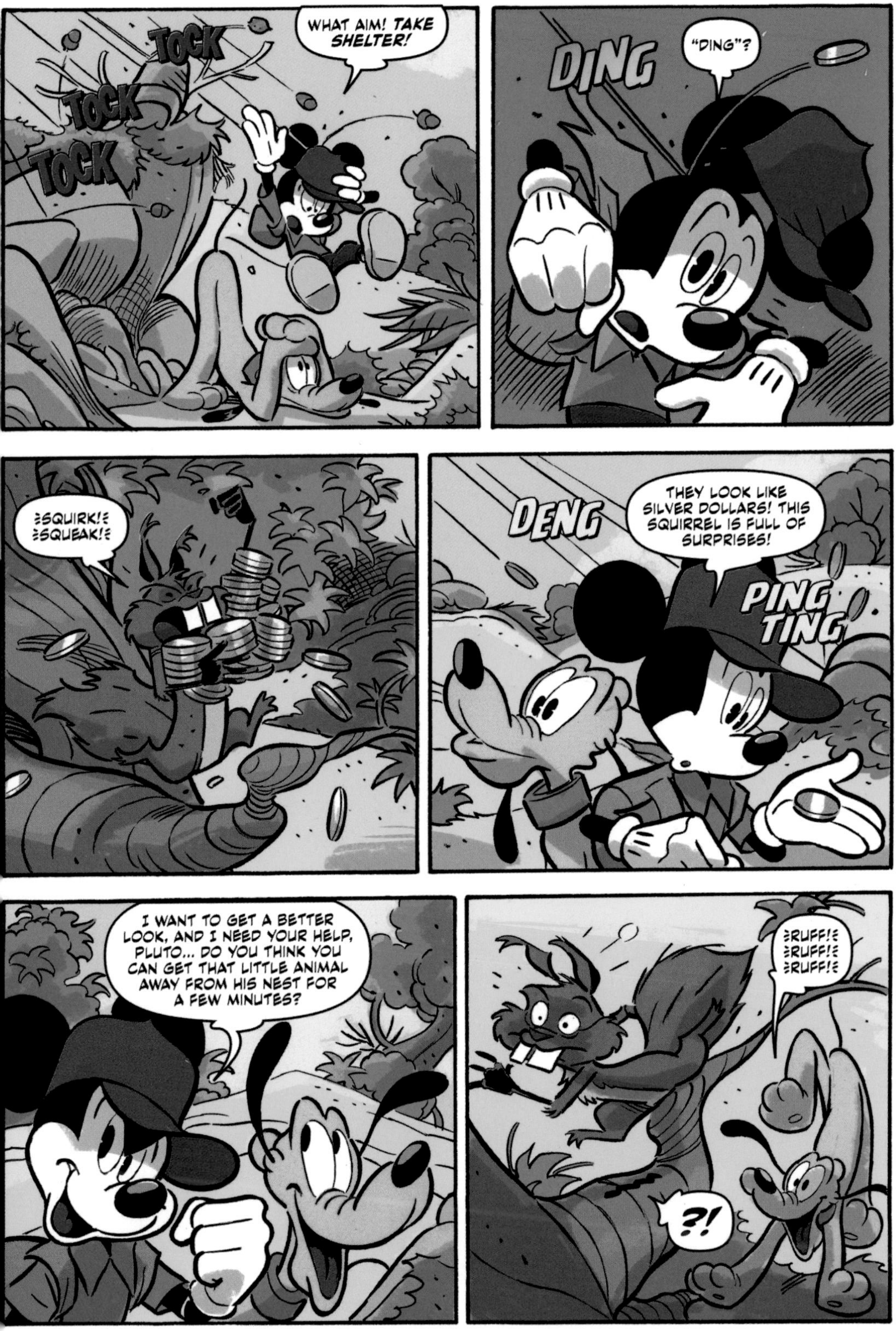
TOCK
TOCK
TOCK
WHAT AIM! TAKE SHELTER!
DING
"DING"?
SQUIRK! SQUEAK!
DENG
THEY LOOK LIKE SILVER DOLLARS! THIS SQUIRREL IS FULL OF SURPRISES!
PING
TING
I WANT TO GET A BETTER LOOK, AND I NEED YOUR HELP, PLUTO... DO YOU THINK YOU CAN GET THAT LITTLE ANIMAL AWAY FROM HIS NEST FOR A FEW MINUTES?
RUFF! RUFF! RUFF!
?!

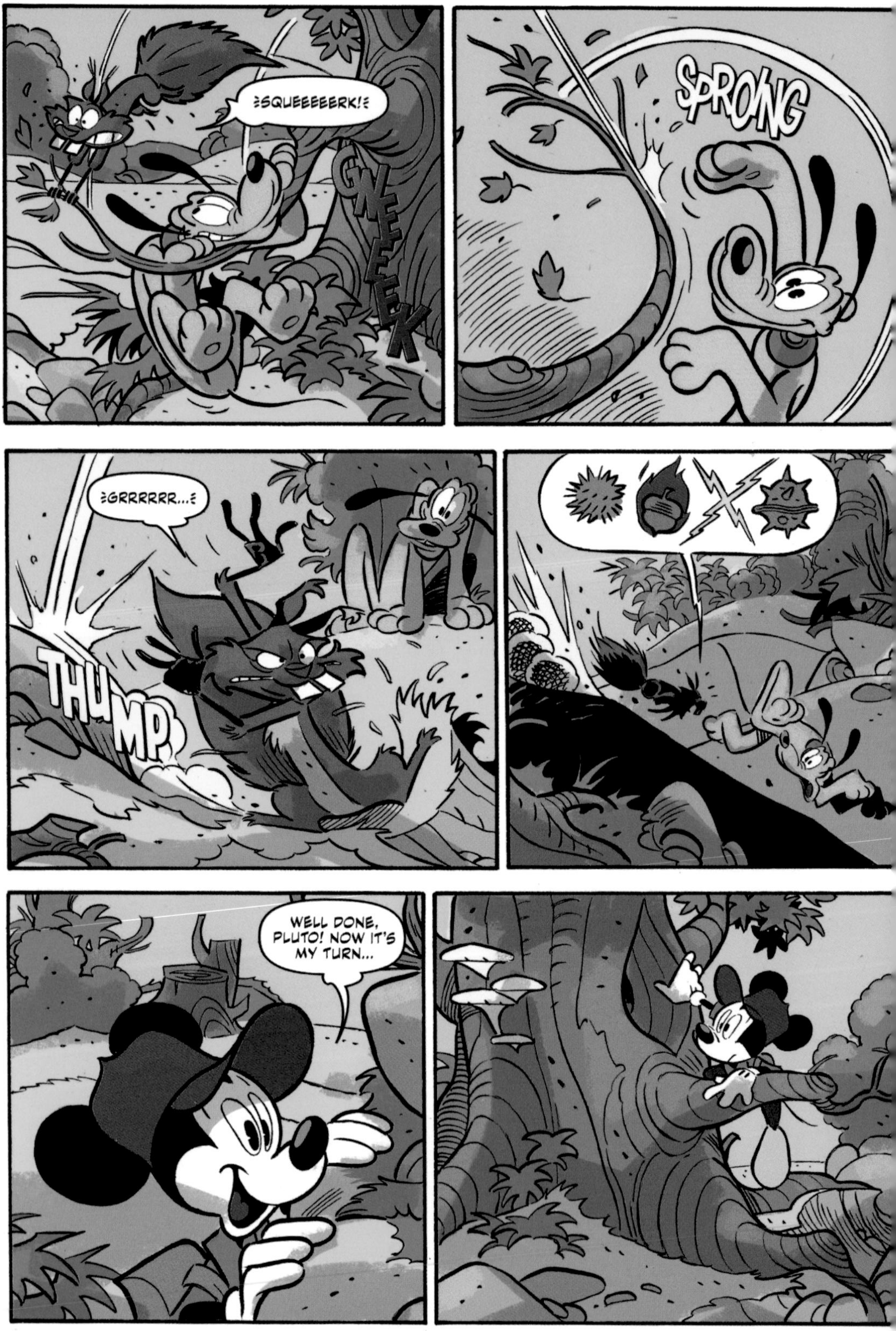
SQUEEEEEERK!
GNEEEEK
SPROING
GRRRRRR...
THUMP
WELL DONE, PLUTO! NOW IT'S MY TURN...

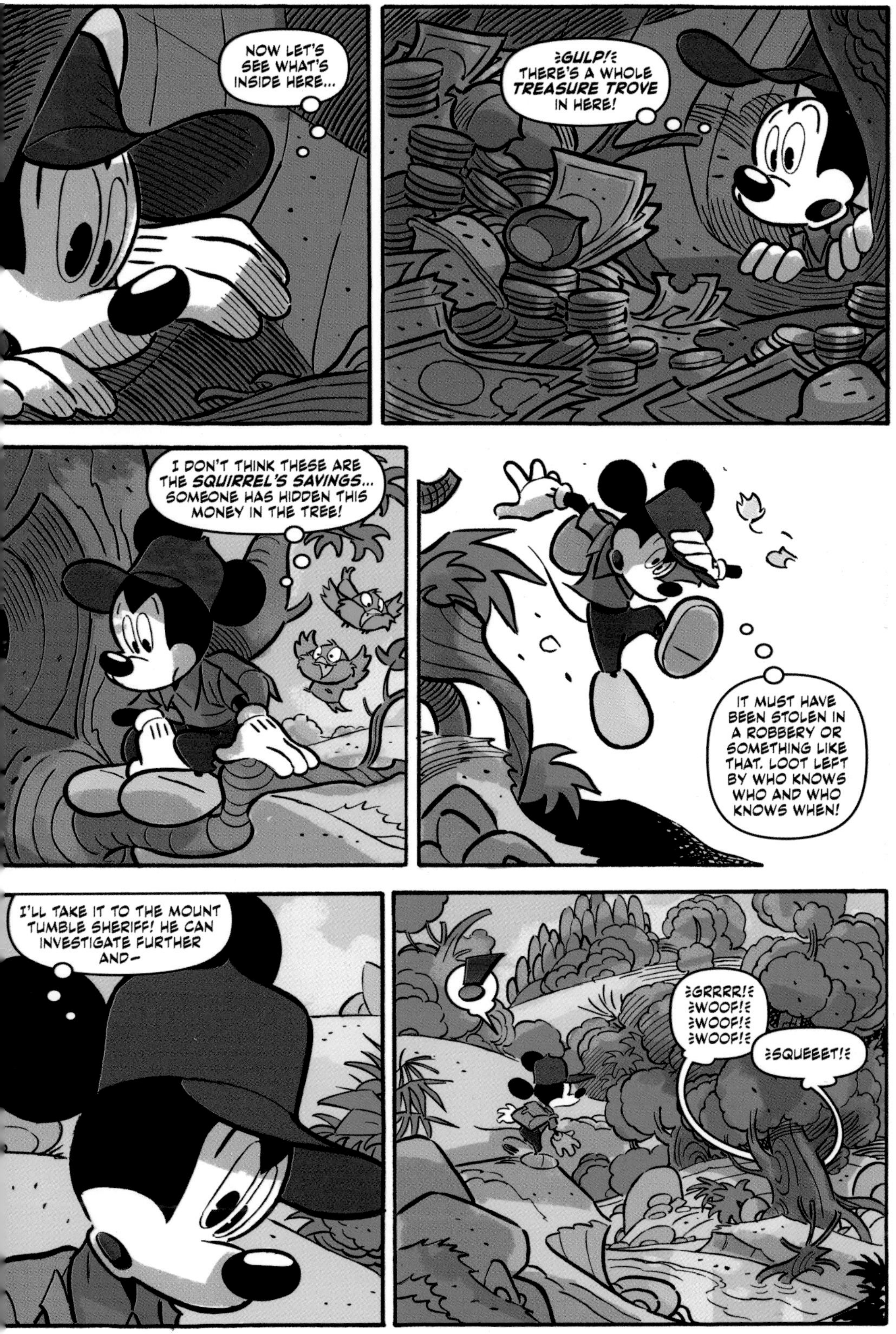
NOW LET'S SEE WHAT'S INSIDE HERE...
GULP! THERE'S A WHOLE TREASURE TROVE IN HERE!
I DON'T THINK THESE ARE THE SQUIRREL'S SAVINGS... SOMEONE HAS HIDDEN THIS MONEY IN THE TREE!
IT MUST HAVE BEEN STOLEN IN A ROBBERY OR SOMETHING LIKE THAT. LOOT LEFT BY WHO KNOWS WHO AND WHO KNOWS WHEN!
I'LL TAKE IT TO THE MOUNT TUMBLE SHERIFF! HE CAN INVESTIGATE FURTHER AND–
!
GRRRR! WOOF! WOOF! WOOF!
SQUEEEET!

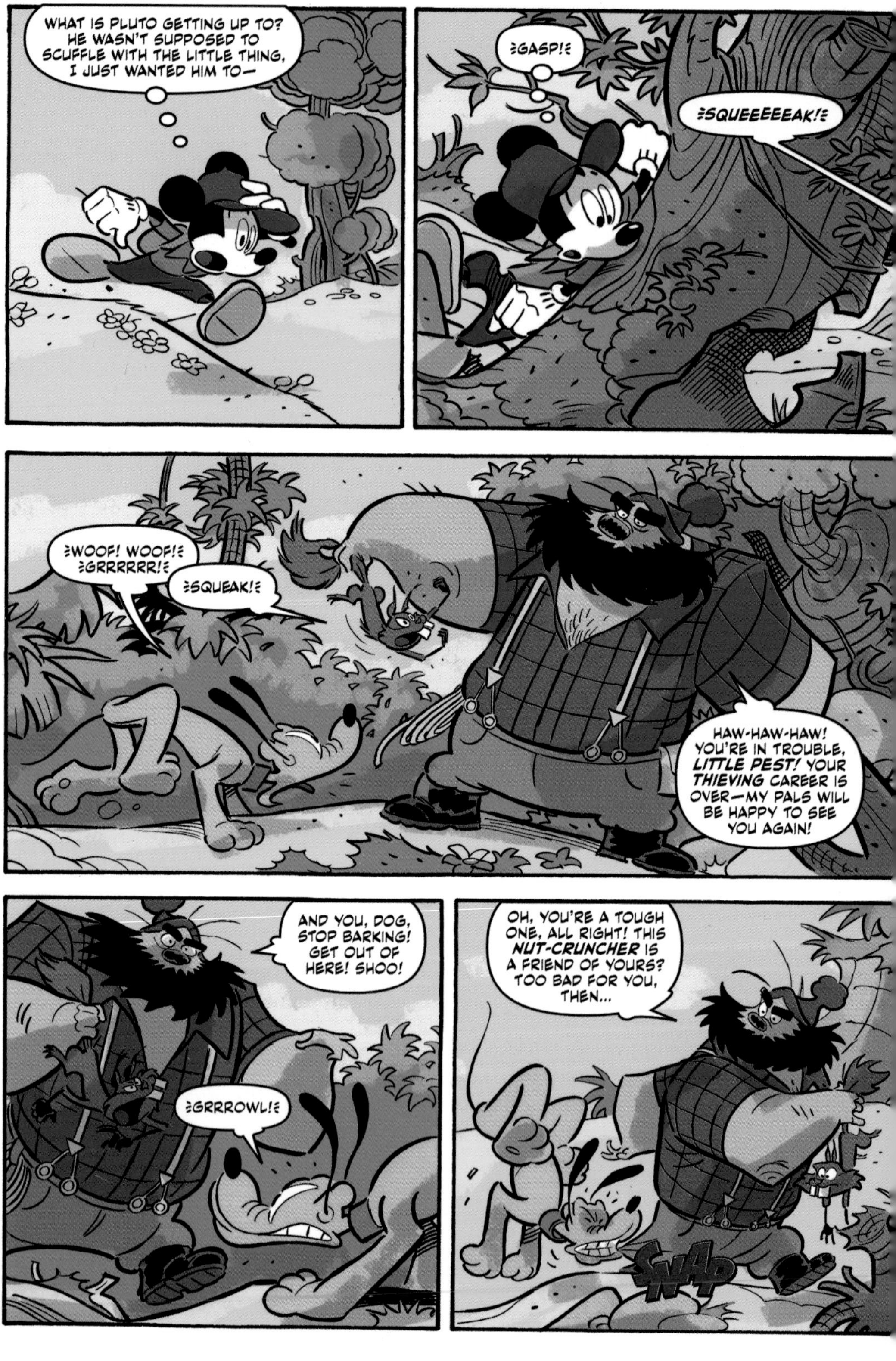
WHAT IS PLUTO GETTING UP TO? HE WASN'T SUPPOSED TO SCUFFLE WITH THE LITTLE THING, I JUST WANTED HIM TO—
GASP!
SQUEEEEEAK!
WOOF! WOOF! GRRRRRR!
SQUEAK!
HAW-HAW-HAW! YOU'RE IN TROUBLE, LITTLE PEST! YOUR THIEVING CAREER IS OVER—MY PALS WILL BE HAPPY TO SEE YOU AGAIN!
AND YOU, DOG, STOP BARKING! GET OUT OF HERE! SHOO!
GRRROWL!
OH, YOU'RE A TOUGH ONE, ALL RIGHT! THIS NUT-CRUNCHER IS A FRIEND OF YOURS? TOO BAD FOR YOU, THEN...
SNAP

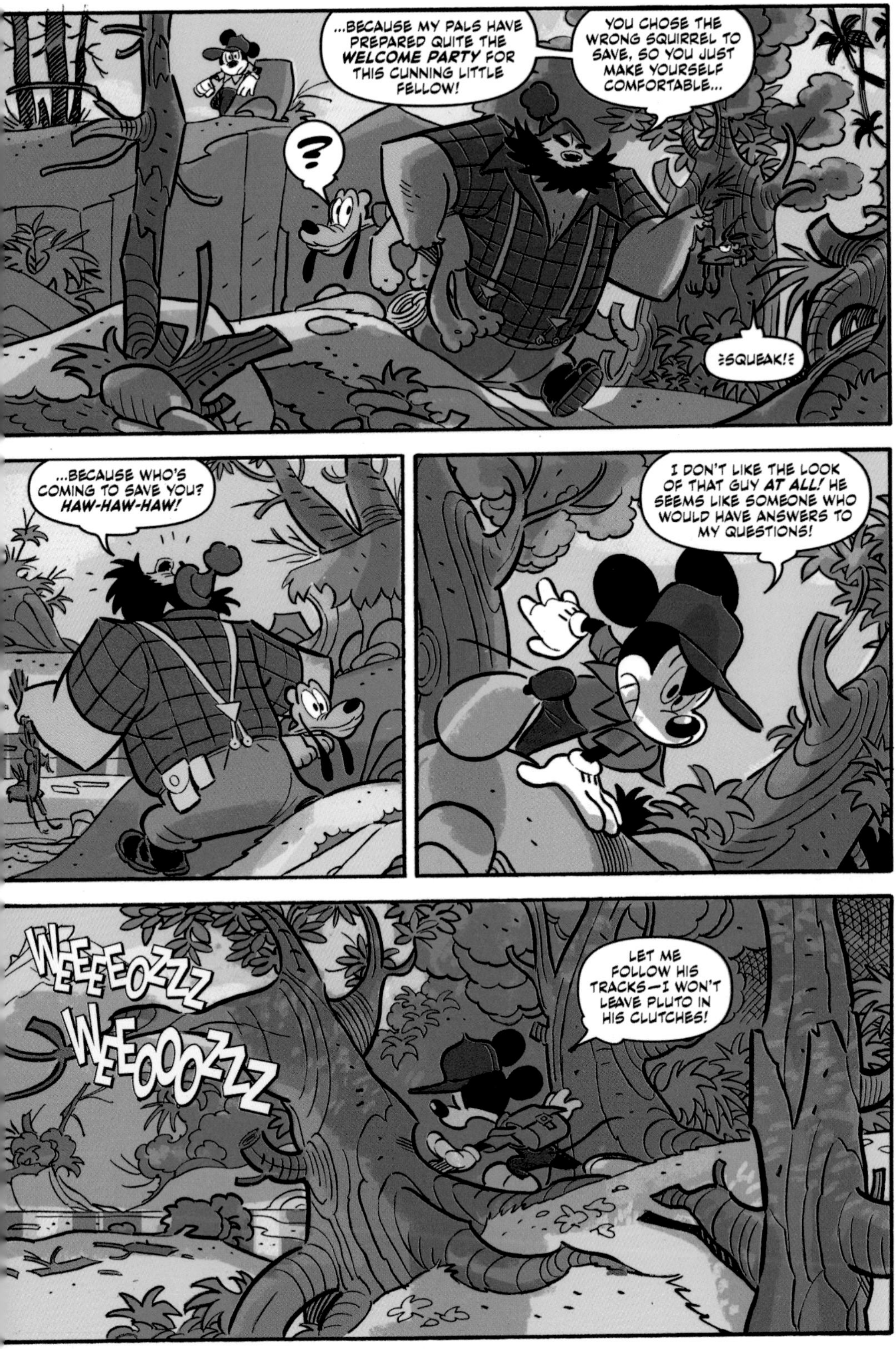
...BECAUSE MY PALS HAVE PREPARED QUITE THE *WELCOME PARTY* FOR THIS CUNNING LITTLE FELLOW!
YOU CHOSE THE WRONG SQUIRREL TO SAVE, SO YOU JUST MAKE YOURSELF COMFORTABLE...
?
SQUEAK!
...BECAUSE WHO'S COMING TO SAVE YOU? *HAW-HAW-HAW!*
I DON'T LIKE THE LOOK OF THAT GUY *AT ALL!* HE SEEMS LIKE SOMEONE WHO WOULD HAVE ANSWERS TO MY QUESTIONS!
WEEEEOZZZ
WEEOOOZZZ
LET ME FOLLOW HIS TRACKS—I WON'T LEAVE PLUTO IN HIS CLUTCHES!

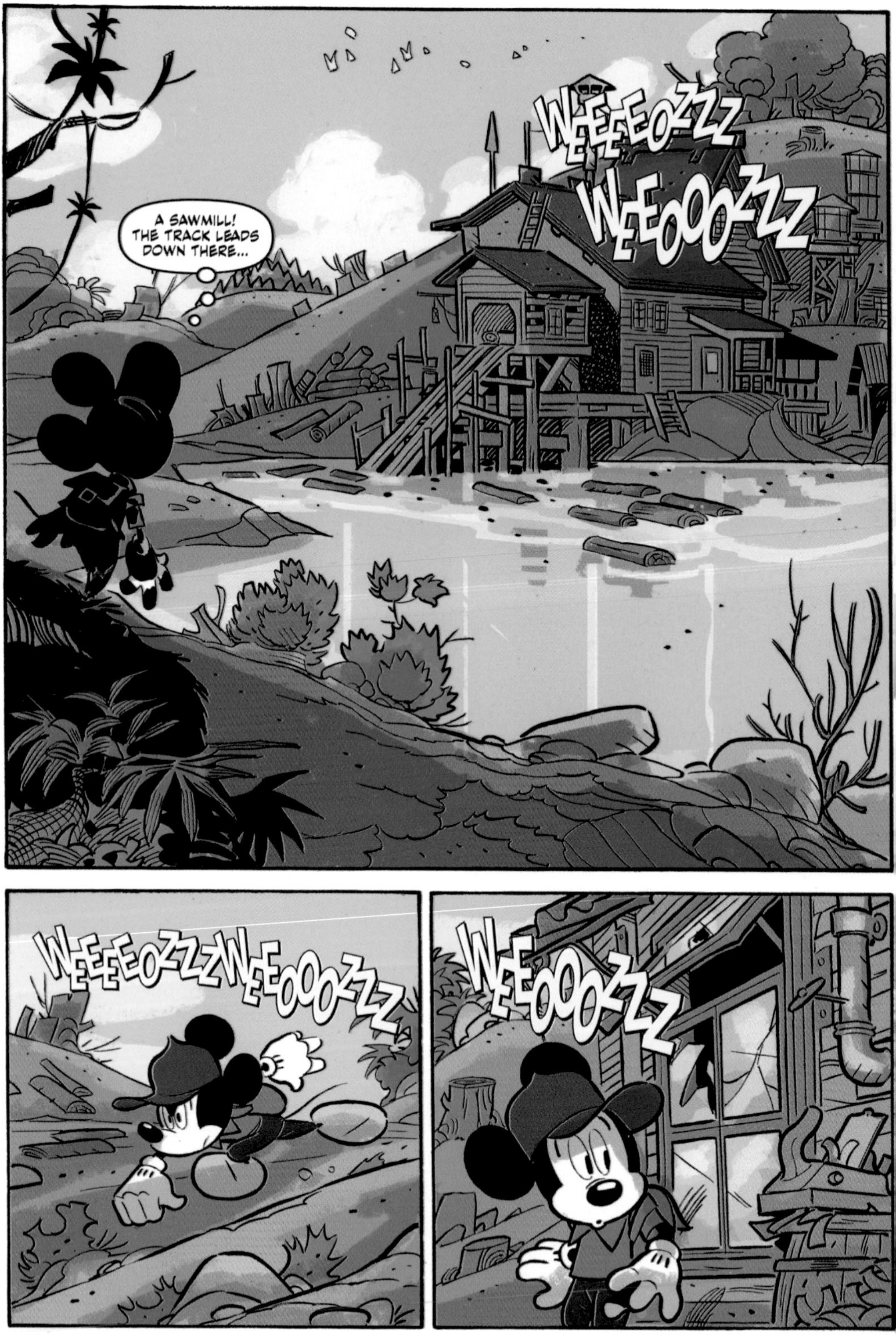
A SAWMILL! THE TRACK LEADS DOWN THERE...
WEEEEOZZZ
WEEOOOZZZ
WEEEEOZZZWEEOOOZZZ
WEEOOOZZZ

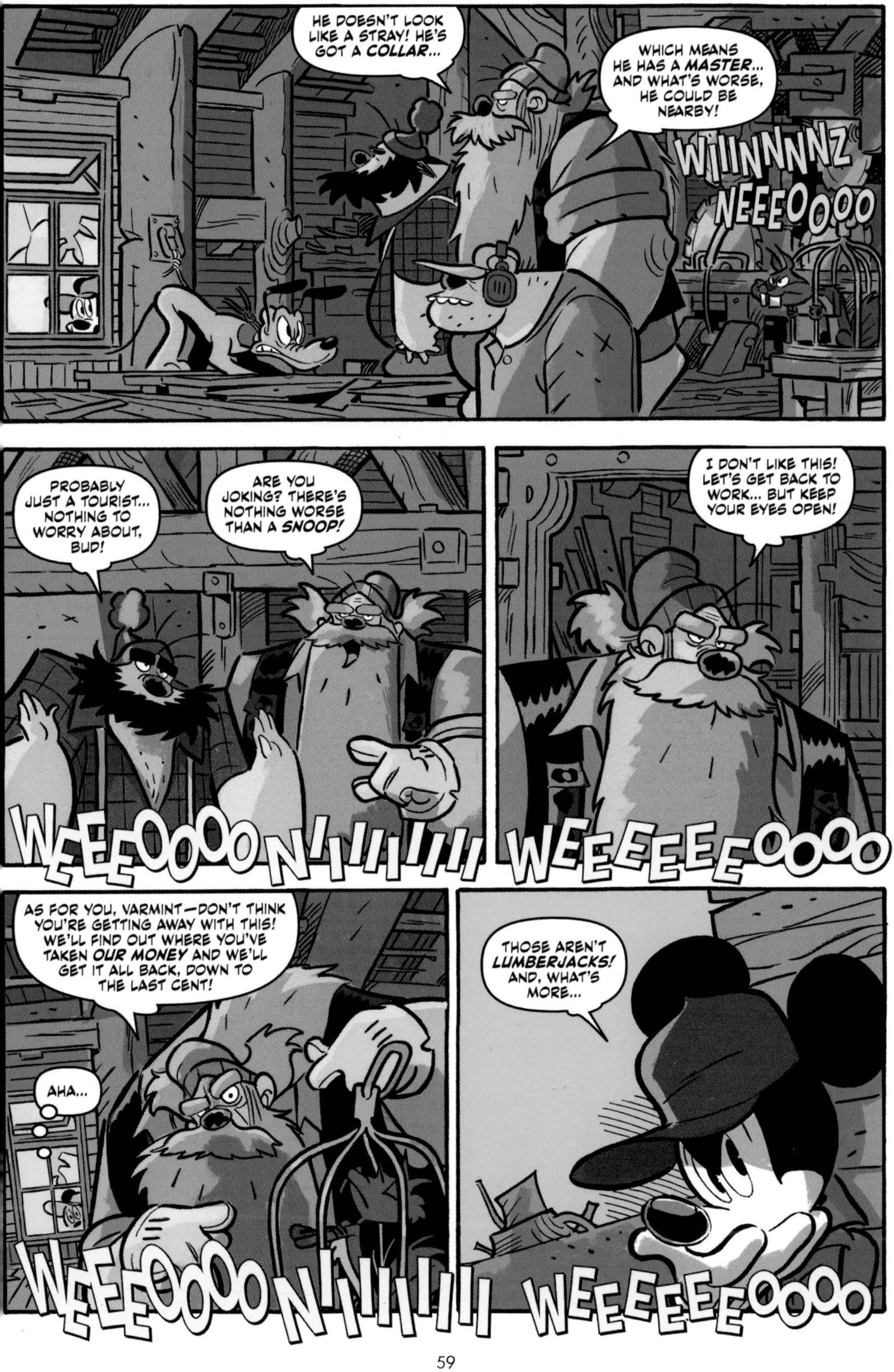
HE DOESN'T LOOK LIKE A STRAY! HE'S GOT A COLLAR...
WHICH MEANS HE HAS A MASTER... AND WHAT'S WORSE, HE COULD BE NEARBY!
WIIINNNNZ NEEEOOOO
PROBABLY JUST A TOURIST... NOTHING TO WORRY ABOUT, BUD!
ARE YOU JOKING? THERE'S NOTHING WORSE THAN A SNOOP!
I DON'T LIKE THIS! LET'S GET BACK TO WORK... BUT KEEP YOUR EYES OPEN!
WEEEOOOONIIIIIIII WEEEEEEOOOO
AS FOR YOU, VARMINT—DON'T THINK YOU'RE GETTING AWAY WITH THIS! WE'LL FIND OUT WHERE YOU'VE TAKEN OUR MONEY AND WE'LL GET IT ALL BACK, DOWN TO THE LAST CENT!
AHA...
THOSE AREN'T LUMBERJACKS! AND, WHAT'S MORE...
WEEEOOOONIIIIIIII WEEEEEEOOOO

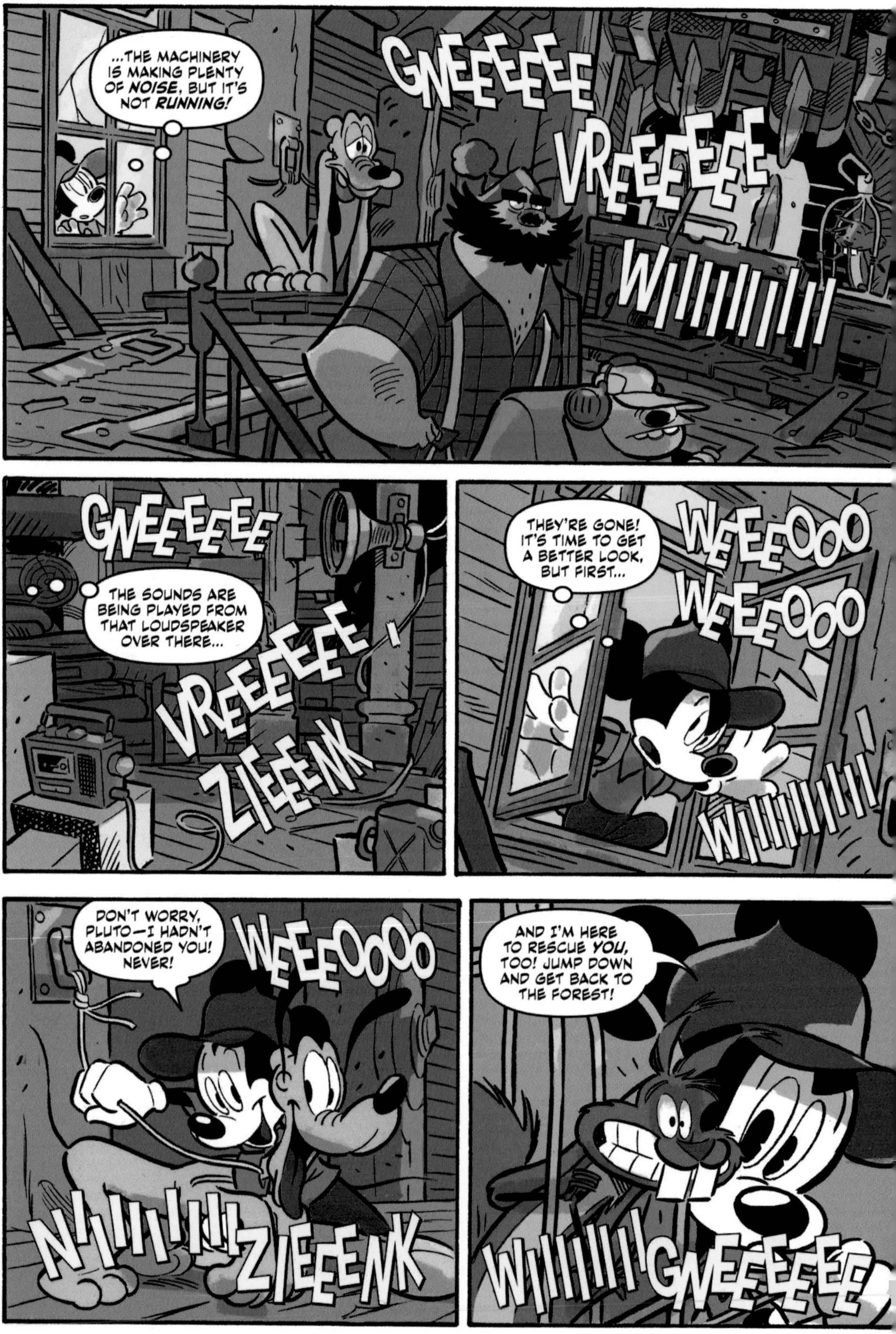
...THE MACHINERY IS MAKING PLENTY OF NOISE, BUT IT'S NOT RUNNING!
GNEEEEEE
VREEEEEE
WIIIIIIIII
GNEEEEEE
THE SOUNDS ARE BEING PLAYED FROM THAT LOUDSPEAKER OVER THERE...
VREEEEEE
ZIEEENK
THEY'RE GONE! IT'S TIME TO GET A BETTER LOOK, BUT FIRST...
WEEEOOO
WEEEOOO
WIIIIIIIII
DON'T WORRY, PLUTO—I HADN'T ABANDONED YOU! NEVER!
WEEEOOOO
NIIIIIIIII
ZIEEENK
AND I'M HERE TO RESCUE YOU, TOO! JUMP DOWN AND GET BACK TO THE FOREST!
WIIIIIIIII
GNEEEEEE

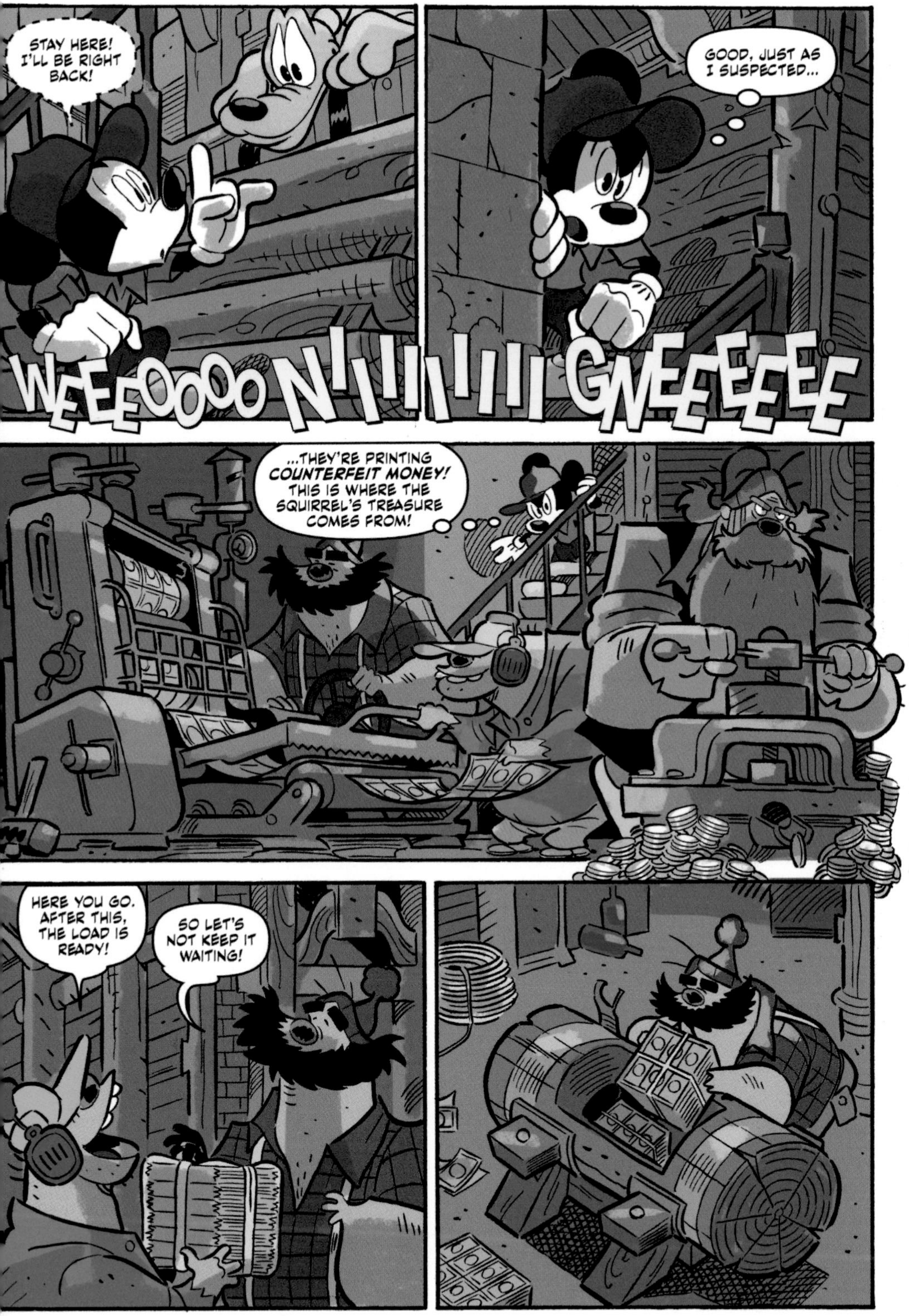
STAY HERE! I'LL BE RIGHT BACK!
GOOD, JUST AS I SUSPECTED...
WEEEOOOO NIIIIIIIII GNEEEEEE
...THEY'RE PRINTING COUNTERFEIT MONEY! THIS IS WHERE THE SQUIRREL'S TREASURE COMES FROM!
HERE YOU GO. AFTER THIS, THE LOAD IS READY!
SO LET'S NOT KEEP IT WAITING!

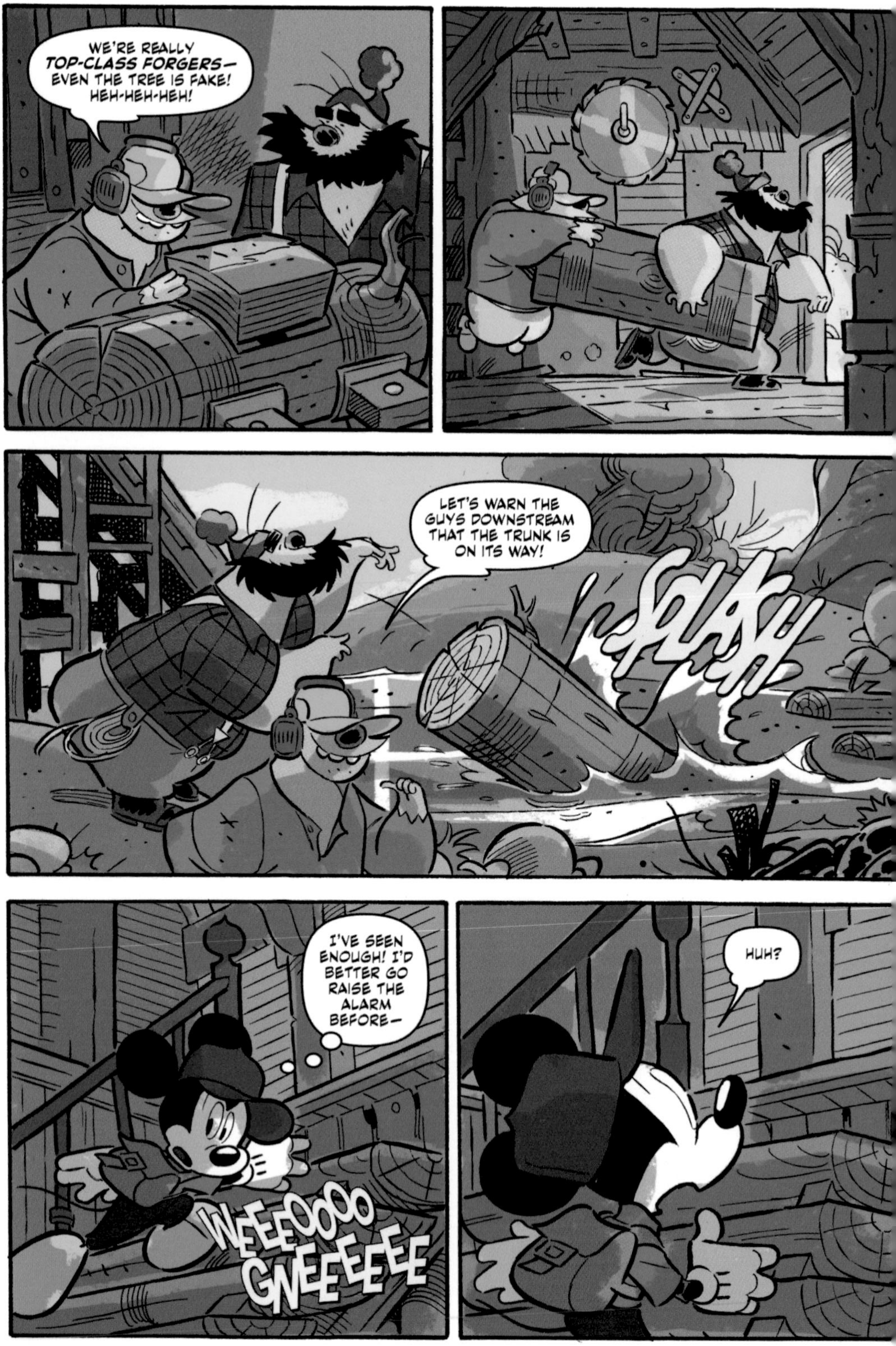
WE'RE REALLY TOP-CLASS FORGERS— EVEN THE TREE IS FAKE! HEH-HEH-HEH!
LET'S WARN THE GUYS DOWNSTREAM THAT THE TRUNK IS ON ITS WAY!
SPLASH
I'VE SEEN ENOUGH! I'D BETTER GO RAISE THE ALARM BEFORE—
WEEEOOOO GWEEEEEE
HUH?

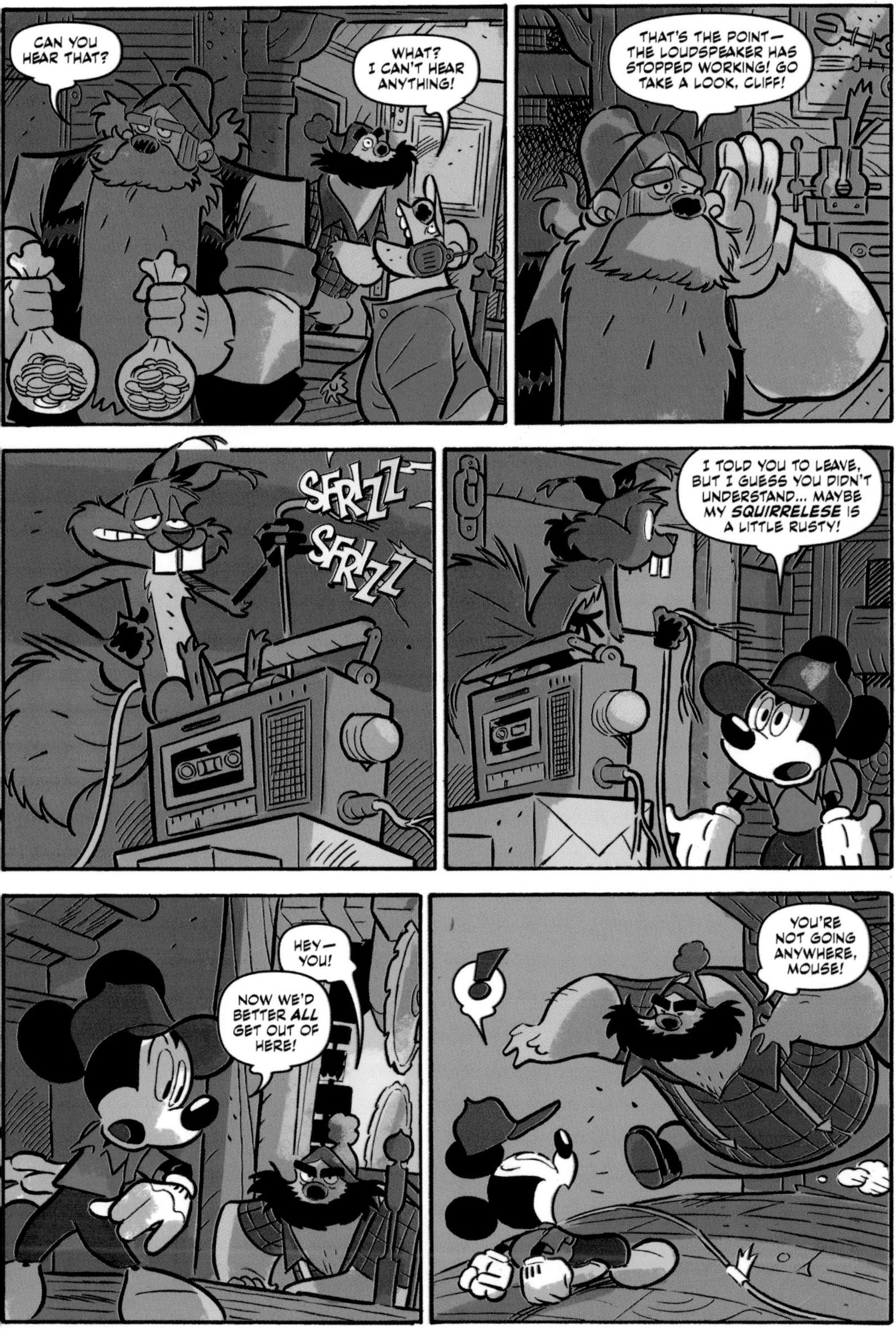
CAN YOU HEAR THAT?
WHAT? I CAN'T HEAR ANYTHING!
THAT'S THE POINT— THE LOUDSPEAKER HAS STOPPED WORKING! GO TAKE A LOOK, CLIFF!
SFRIZZZ
SFRIZZZ
I TOLD YOU TO LEAVE, BUT I GUESS YOU DIDN'T UNDERSTAND... MAYBE MY ***SQUIRRELESE*** IS A LITTLE RUSTY!
HEY— YOU!
NOW WE'D BETTER ***ALL*** GET OUT OF HERE!
!
YOU'RE NOT GOING ANYWHERE, MOUSE!

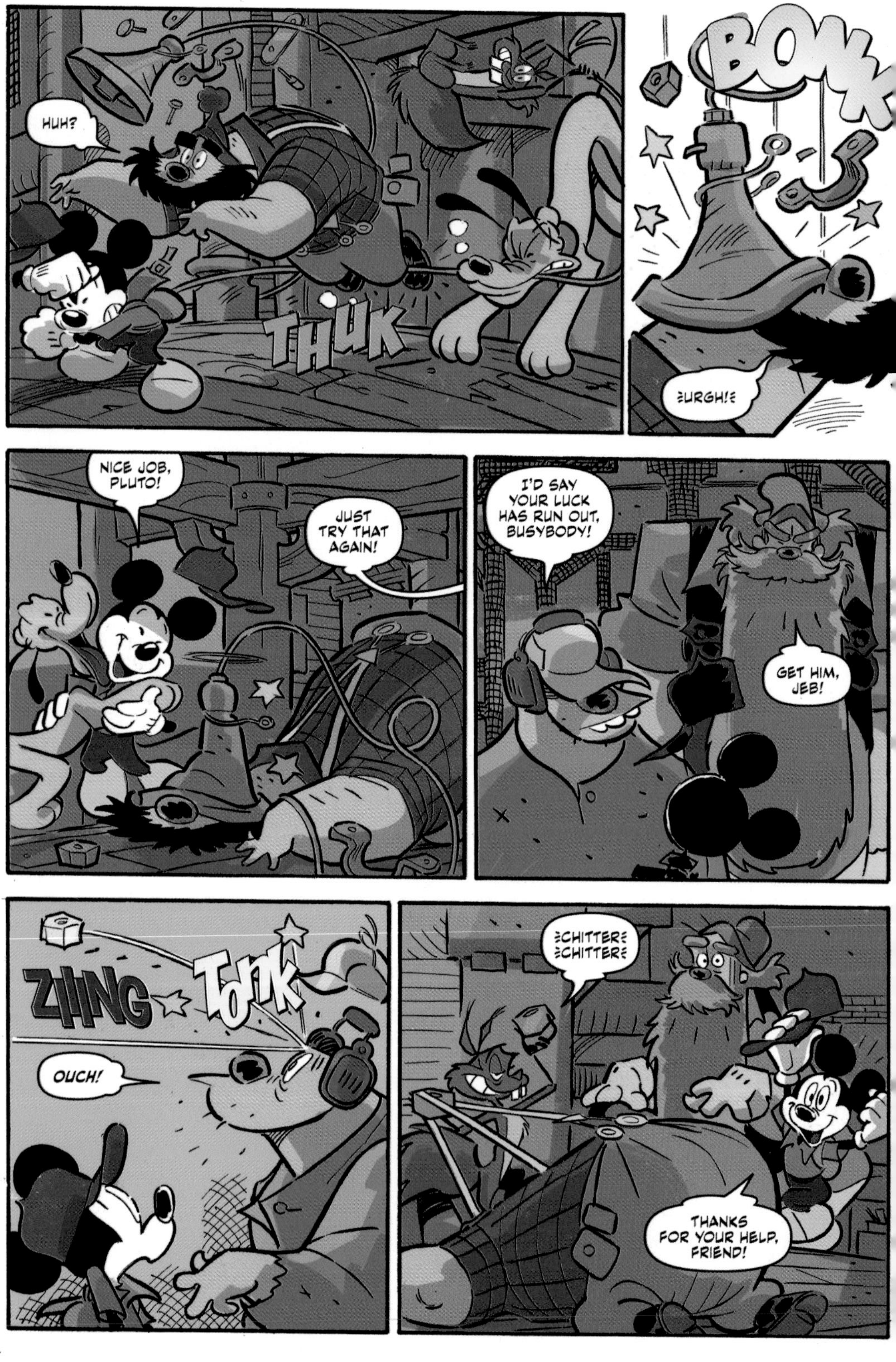
HUH?
THUK
BONK
URGH!
NICE JOB, PLUTO!
JUST TRY THAT AGAIN!
I'D SAY YOUR LUCK HAS RUN OUT, BUSYBODY!
GET HIM, JEB!
ZING
TONK
OUCH!
CHITTER CHITTER
THANKS FOR YOUR HELP, FRIEND!

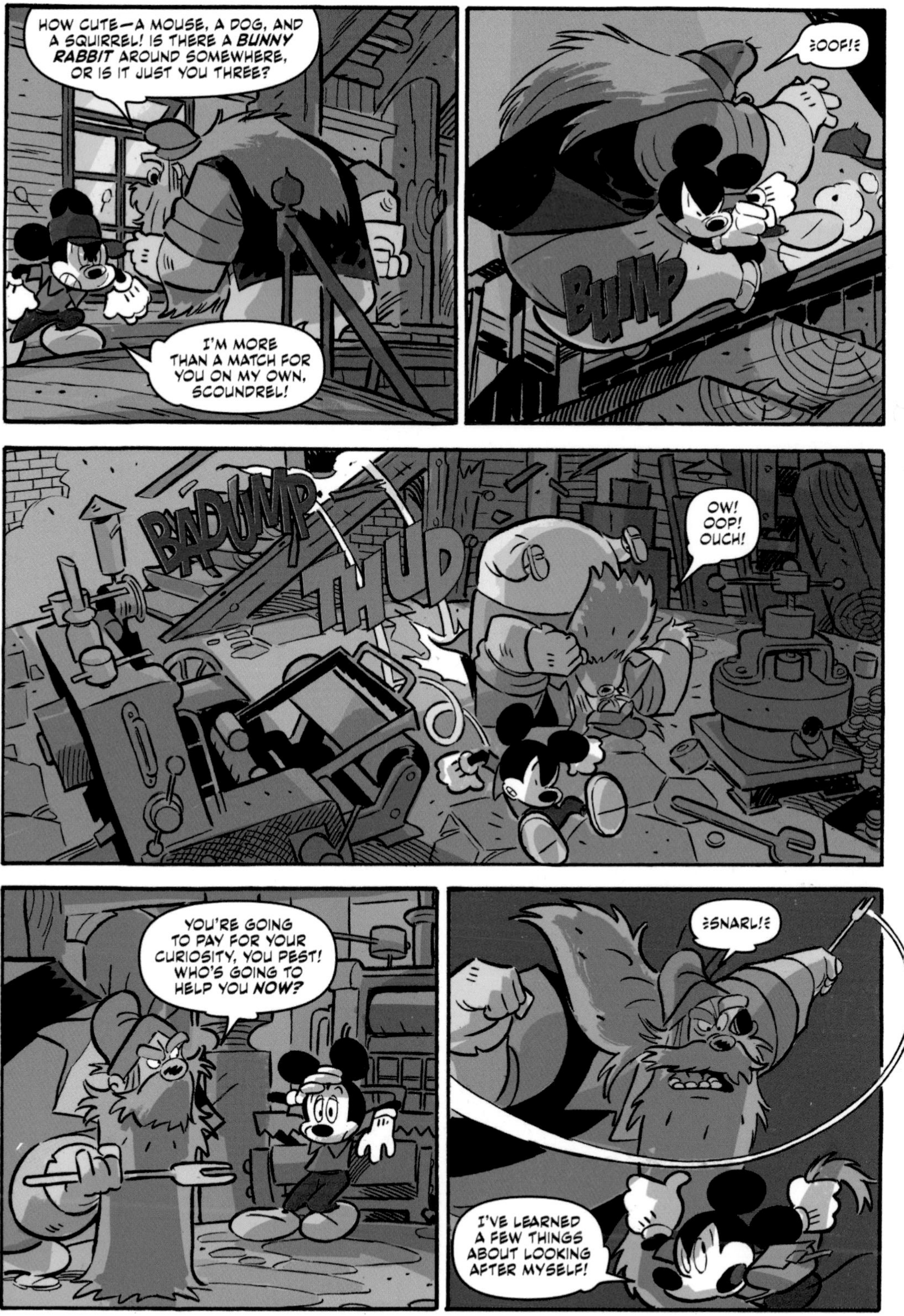
HOW CUTE—A MOUSE, A DOG, AND A SQUIRREL! IS THERE A *BUNNY RABBIT* AROUND SOMEWHERE, OR IS IT JUST YOU THREE?
I'M MORE THAN A MATCH FOR YOU ON MY OWN, SCOUNDREL!
OOF!
BUMP
BADUMP
THUD
OW! OOP! OUCH!
YOU'RE GOING TO PAY FOR YOUR CURIOSITY, YOU PEST! WHO'S GOING TO HELP YOU *NOW?*
SNARL!
I'VE LEARNED A FEW THINGS ABOUT LOOKING AFTER MYSELF!

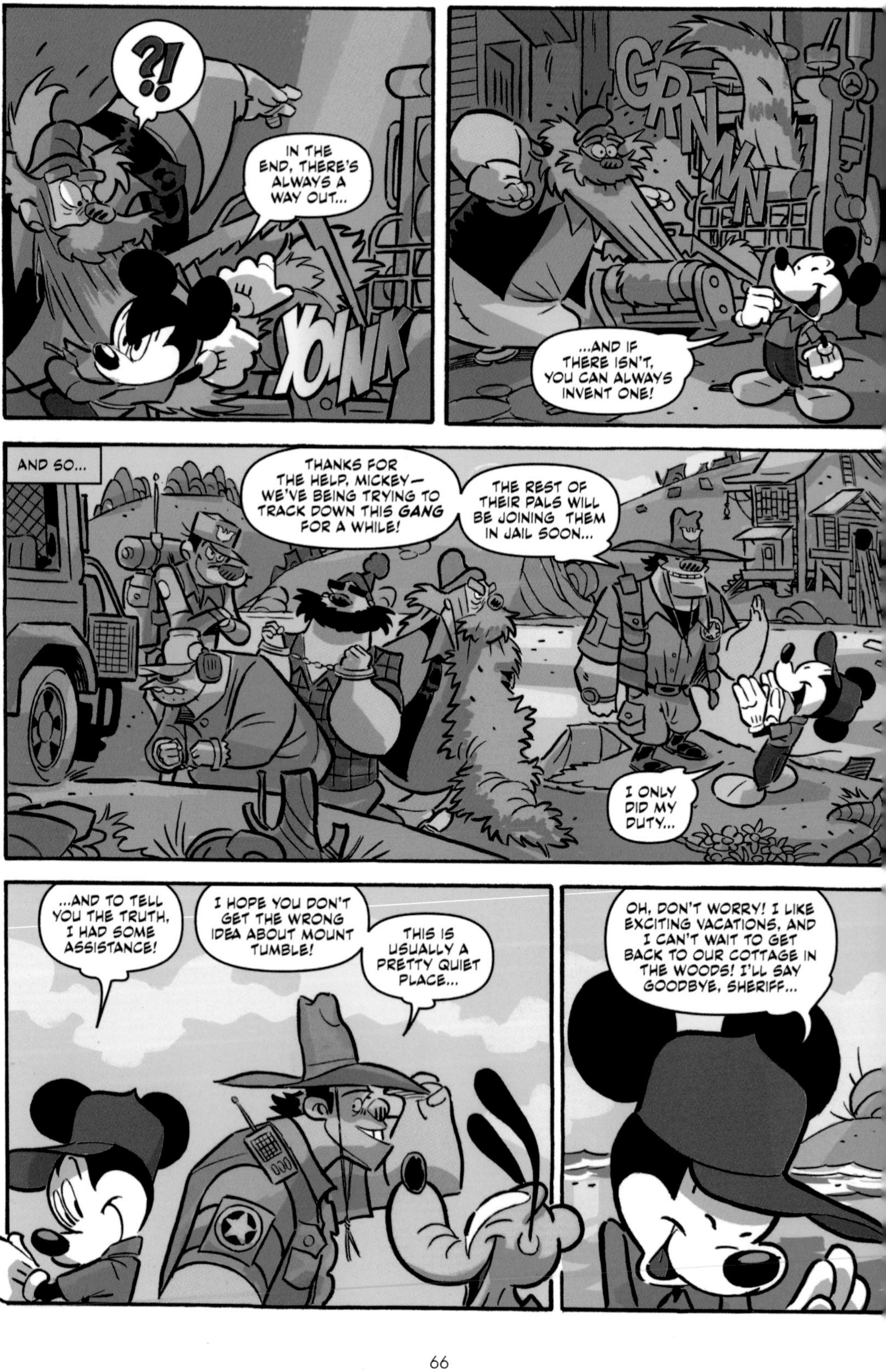
?!
IN THE END, THERE'S ALWAYS A WAY OUT...
YOINK
GRNYYN
...AND IF THERE ISN'T, YOU CAN ALWAYS INVENT ONE!
AND SO...
THANKS FOR THE HELP, MICKEY—WE'VE BEING TRYING TO TRACK DOWN THIS GANG FOR A WHILE!
THE REST OF THEIR PALS WILL BE JOINING THEM IN JAIL SOON...
I ONLY DID MY DUTY...
...AND TO TELL YOU THE TRUTH, I HAD SOME ASSISTANCE!
I HOPE YOU DON'T GET THE WRONG IDEA ABOUT MOUNT TUMBLE!
THIS IS USUALLY A PRETTY QUIET PLACE...
OH, DON'T WORRY! I LIKE EXCITING VACATIONS, AND I CAN'T WAIT TO GET BACK TO OUR COTTAGE IN THE WOODS! I'LL SAY GOODBYE, SHERIFF...

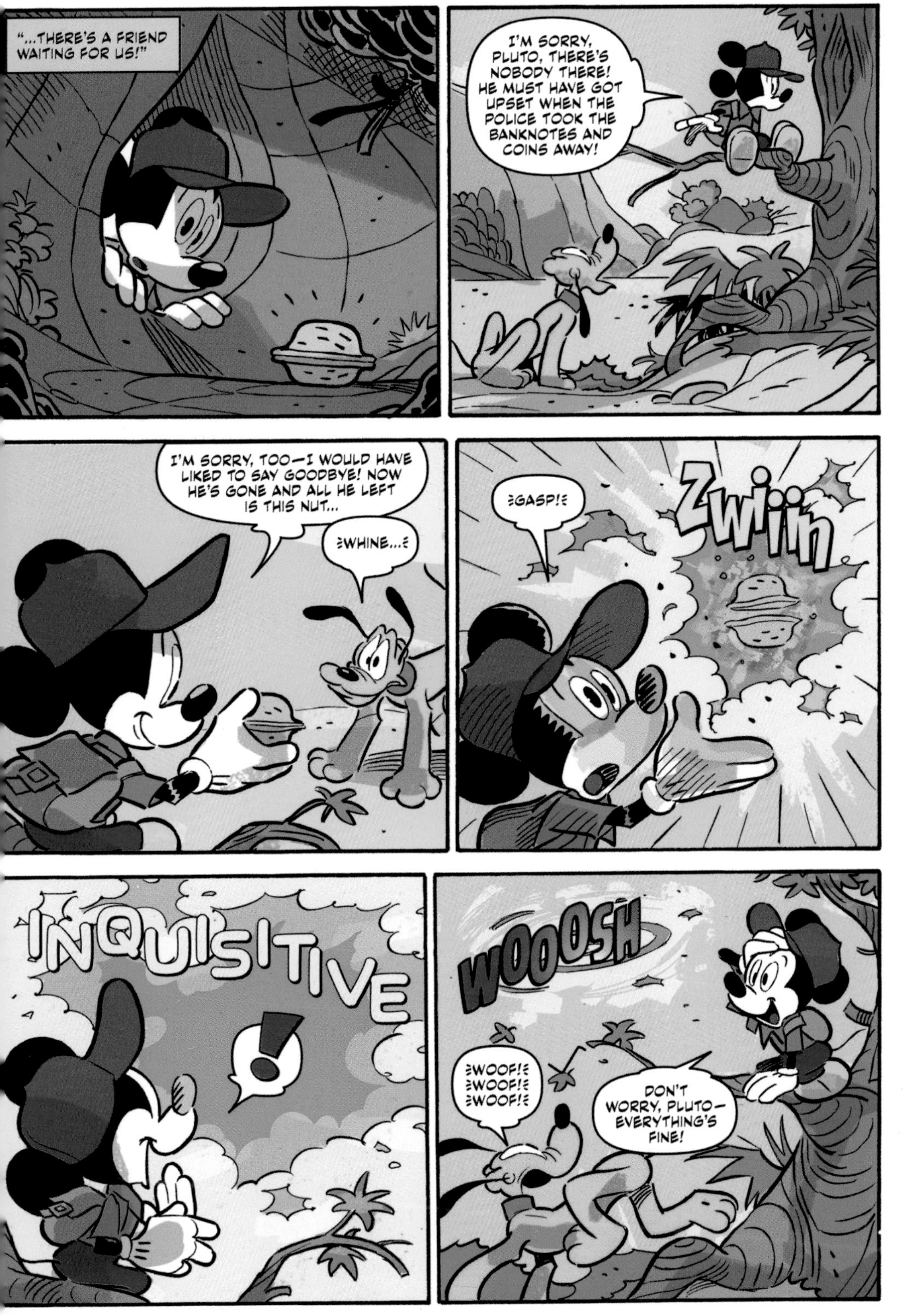
"...THERE'S A FRIEND WAITING FOR US!"
I'M SORRY, PLUTO, THERE'S NOBODY THERE! HE MUST HAVE GOT UPSET WHEN THE POLICE TOOK THE BANKNOTES AND COINS AWAY!
I'M SORRY, TOO—I WOULD HAVE LIKED TO SAY GOODBYE! NOW HE'S GONE AND ALL HE LEFT IS THIS NUT...
WHINE...
GASP!
ZWIIIN
INQUISITIVE
!
WOOOSH
WOOF! WOOF! WOOF!
DON'T WORRY, PLUTO—EVERYTHING'S FINE!

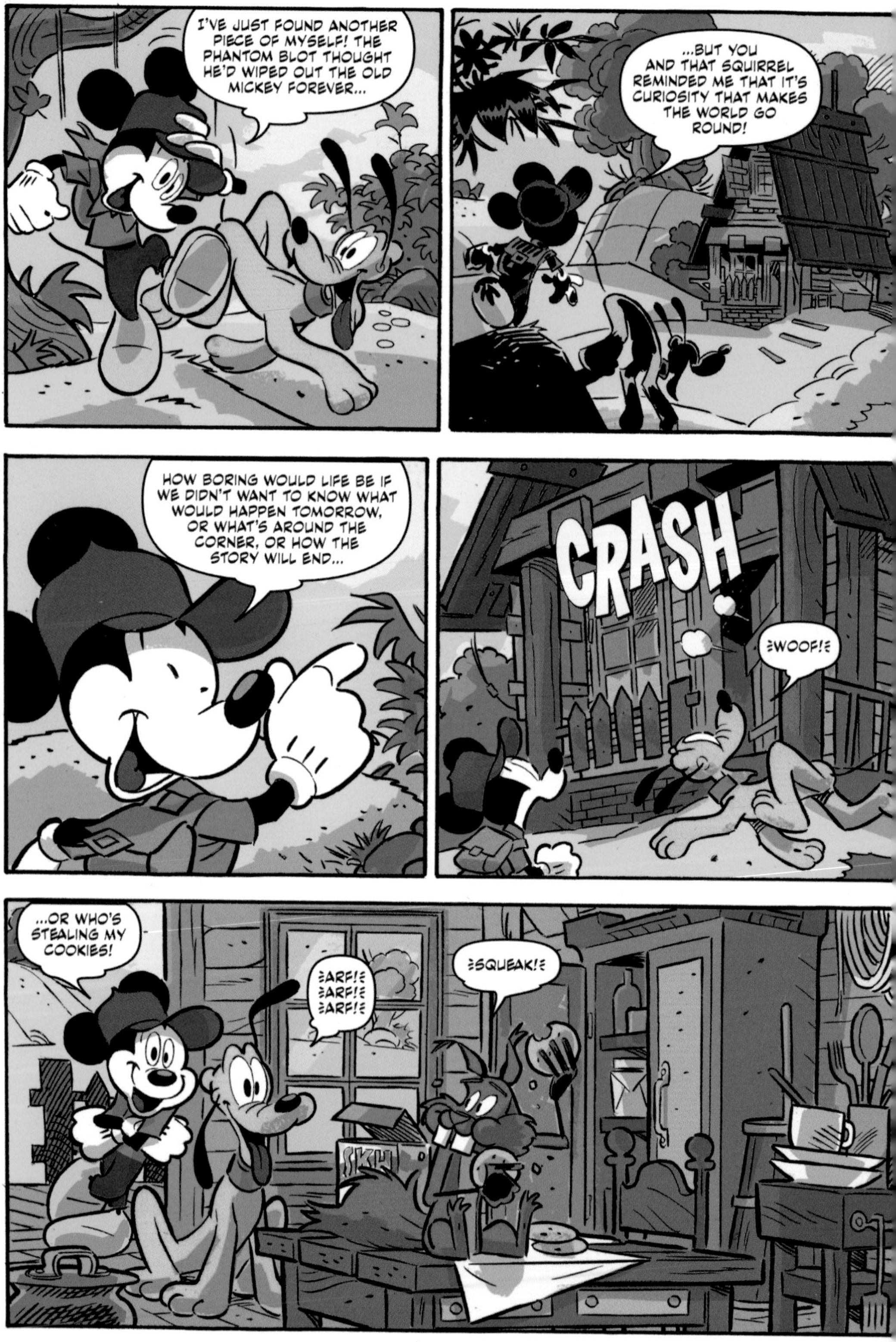
I'VE JUST FOUND ANOTHER PIECE OF MYSELF! THE PHANTOM BLOT THOUGHT HE'D WIPED OUT THE OLD MICKEY FOREVER...
...BUT YOU AND THAT SQUIRREL REMINDED ME THAT IT'S CURIOSITY THAT MAKES THE WORLD GO ROUND!
HOW BORING WOULD LIFE BE IF WE DIDN'T WANT TO KNOW WHAT WOULD HAPPEN TOMORROW, OR WHAT'S AROUND THE CORNER, OR HOW THE STORY WILL END...
CRASH
WOOF!
...OR WHO'S STEALING MY COOKIES!
ARF! ARF! ARF!
SQUEAK!

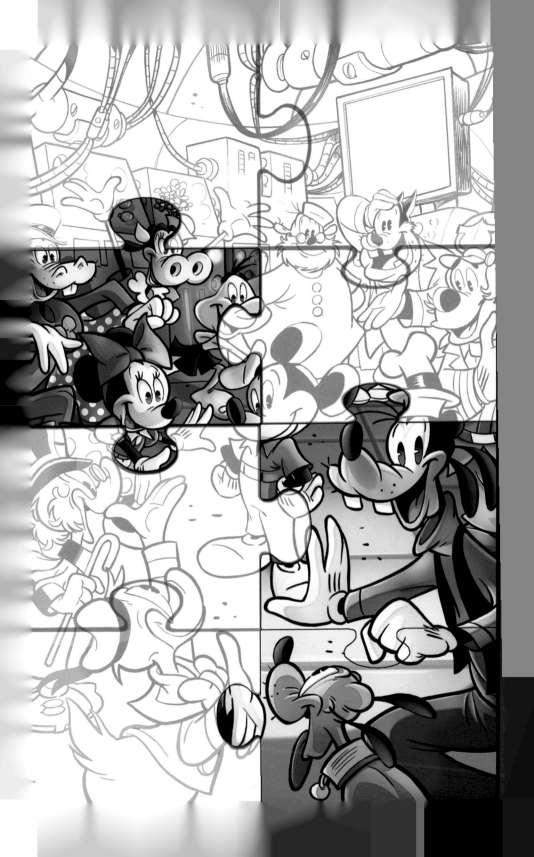

Art by MARCO MAZZARELLO
Colors by EDIZIONI BD

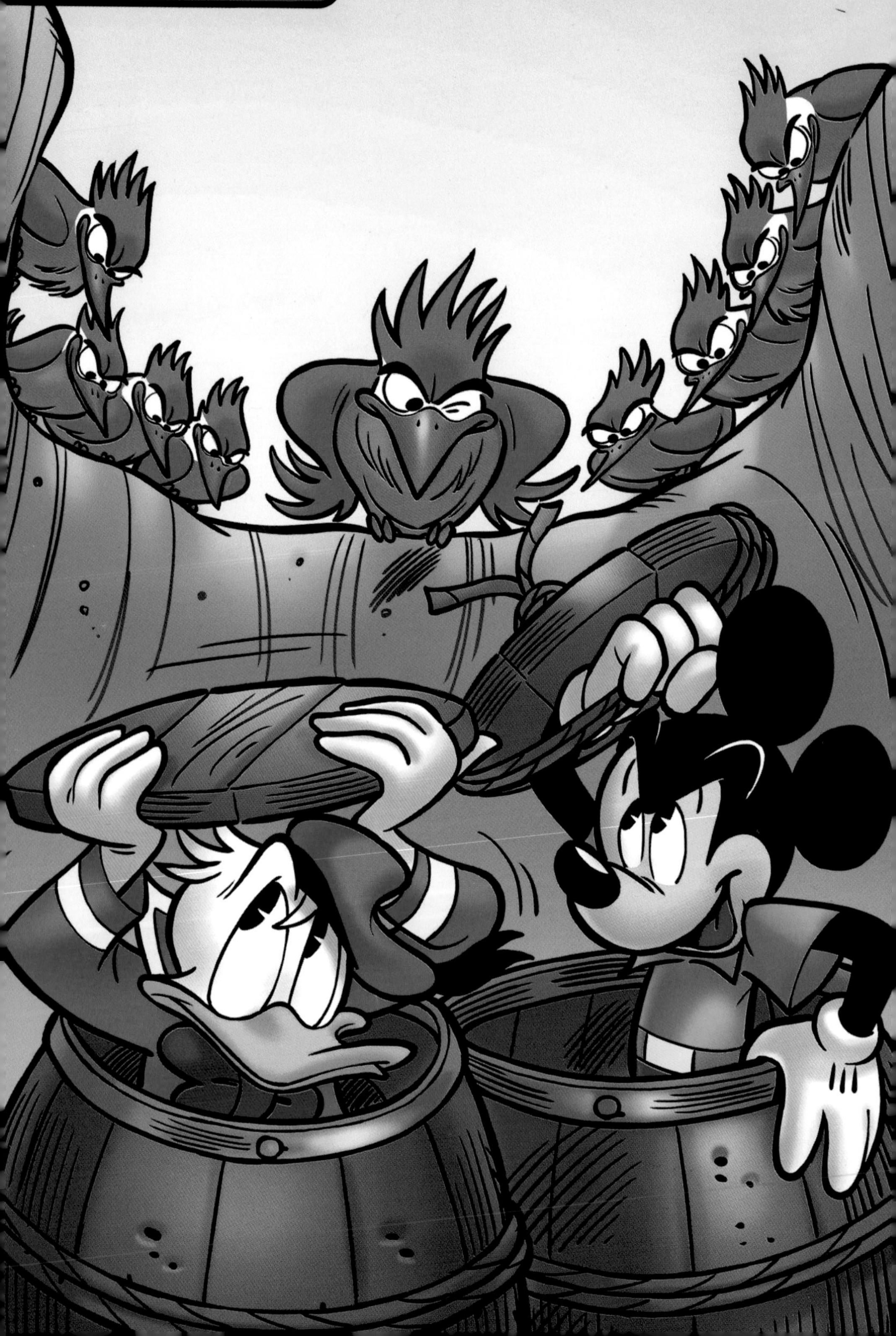

CHAPTER 4: THE HEROES OF MOUNT RATTMORE

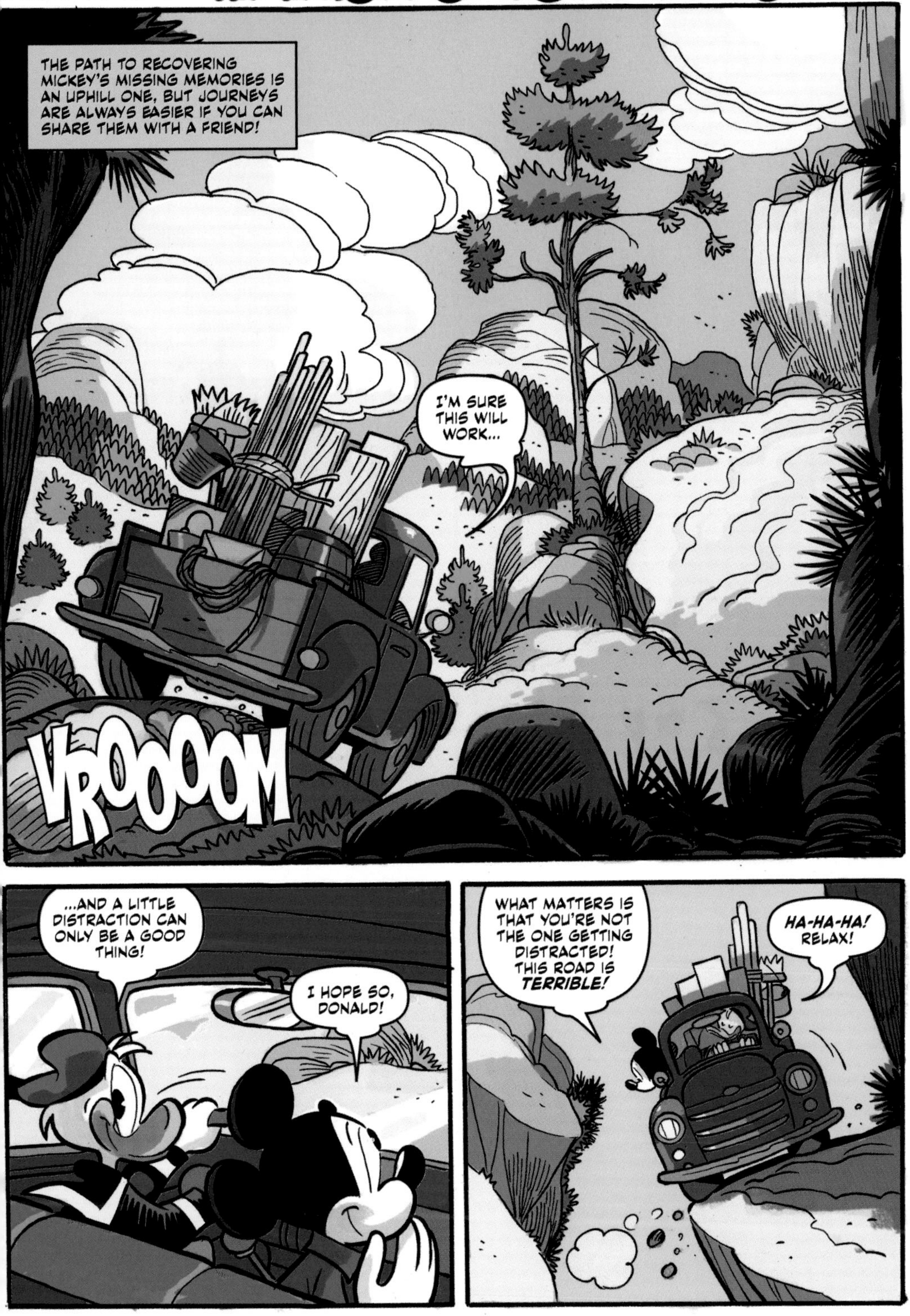

THE PATH TO RECOVERING MICKEY'S MISSING MEMORIES IS AN UPHILL ONE, BUT JOURNEYS ARE ALWAYS EASIER IF YOU CAN SHARE THEM WITH A FRIEND!
I'M SURE THIS WILL WORK...
VROOOOM
...AND A LITTLE DISTRACTION CAN ONLY BE A GOOD THING!
I HOPE SO, DONALD!
WHAT MATTERS IS THAT YOU'RE NOT THE ONE GETTING DISTRACTED! THIS ROAD IS *TERRIBLE!*
HA-HA-HA! RELAX!

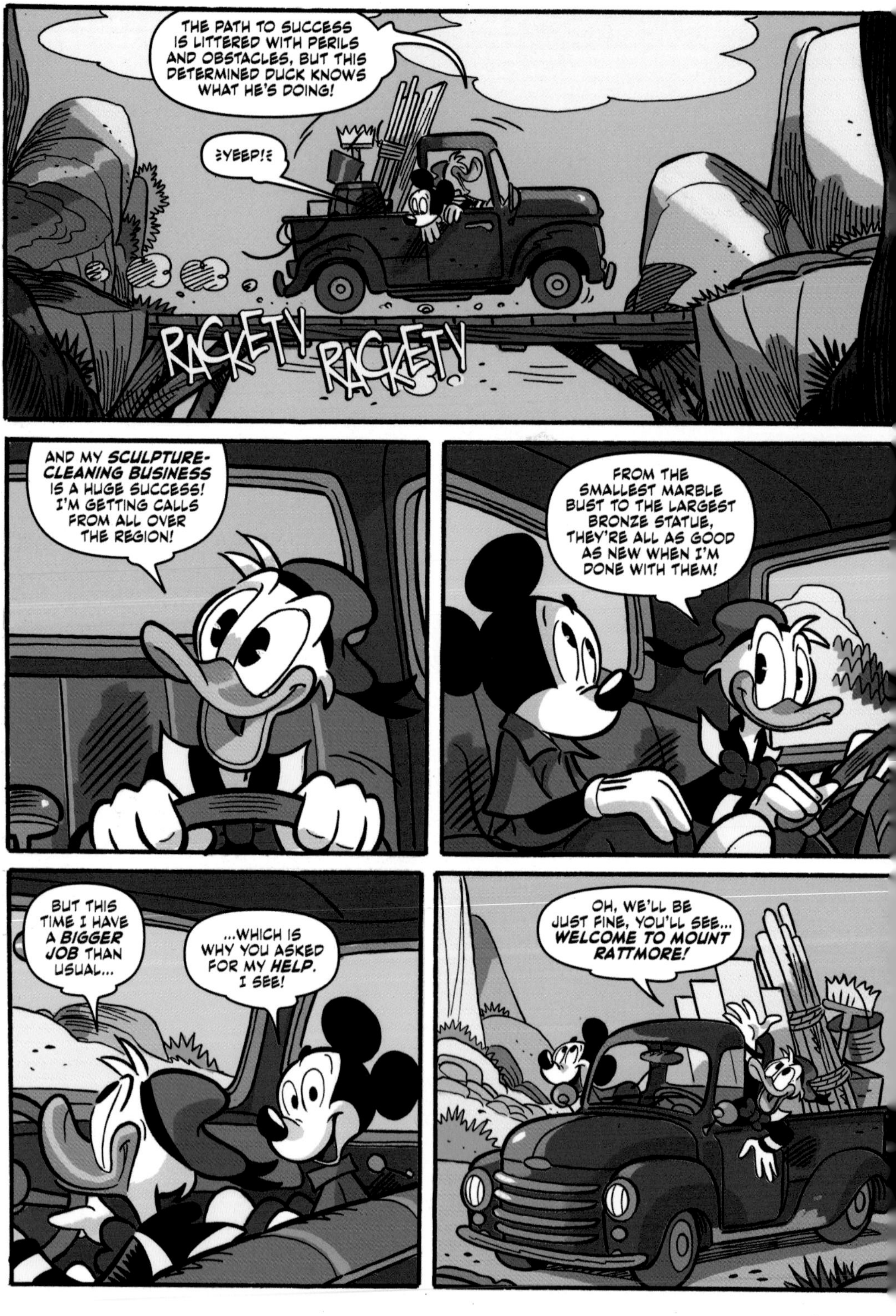
THE PATH TO SUCCESS IS LITTERED WITH PERILS AND OBSTACLES, BUT THIS DETERMINED DUCK KNOWS WHAT HE'S DOING!
YEEP!
RACKETY RACKETY
AND MY *SCULPTURE-CLEANING BUSINESS* IS A HUGE SUCCESS! I'M GETTING CALLS FROM ALL OVER THE REGION!
FROM THE SMALLEST MARBLE BUST TO THE LARGEST BRONZE STATUE, THEY'RE ALL AS GOOD AS NEW WHEN I'M DONE WITH THEM!
BUT THIS TIME I HAVE A *BIGGER JOB* THAN USUAL...
...WHICH IS WHY YOU ASKED FOR MY *HELP*. I SEE!
OH, WE'LL BE JUST FINE, YOU'LL SEE... *WELCOME TO MOUNT RATTMORE!*

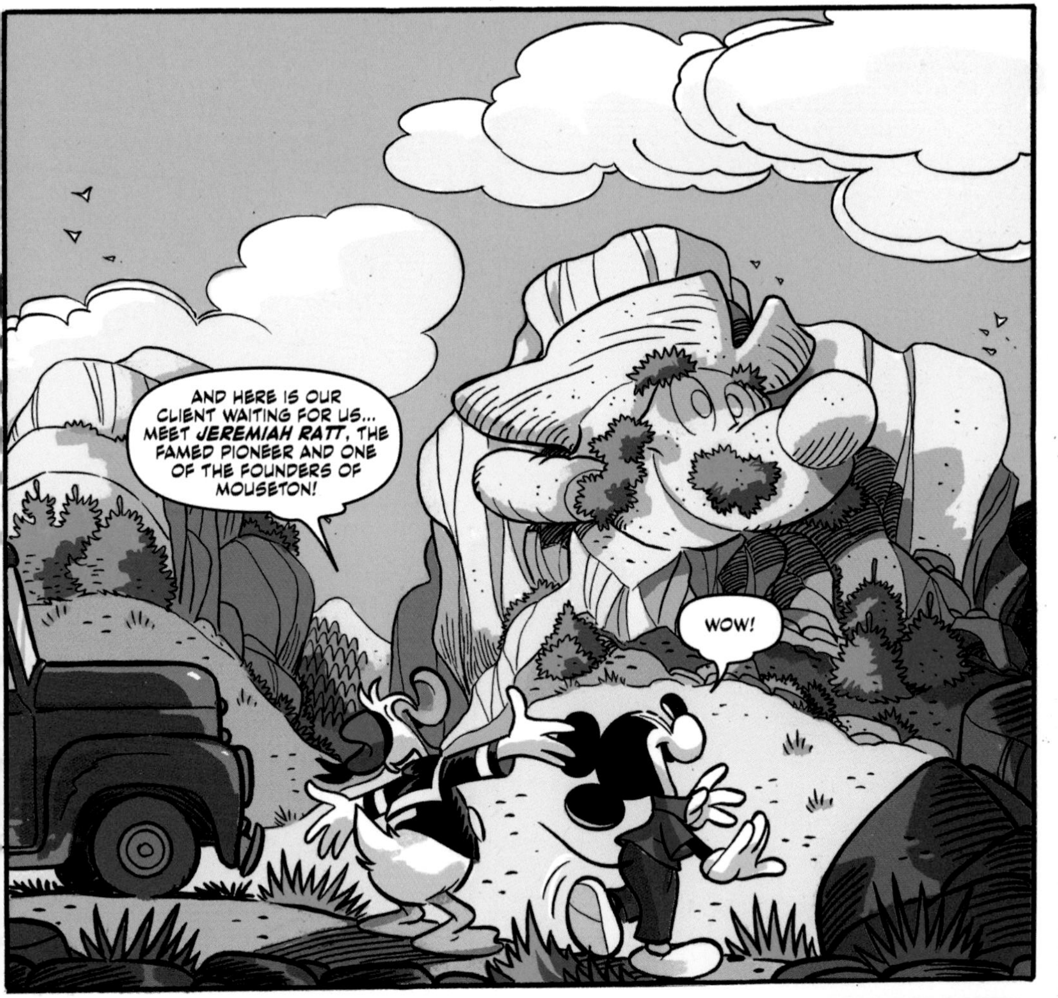
AND HERE IS OUR CLIENT WAITING FOR US... MEET JEREMIAH RATT, THE FAMED PIONEER AND ONE OF THE FOUNDERS OF MOUSETON!
WOW!

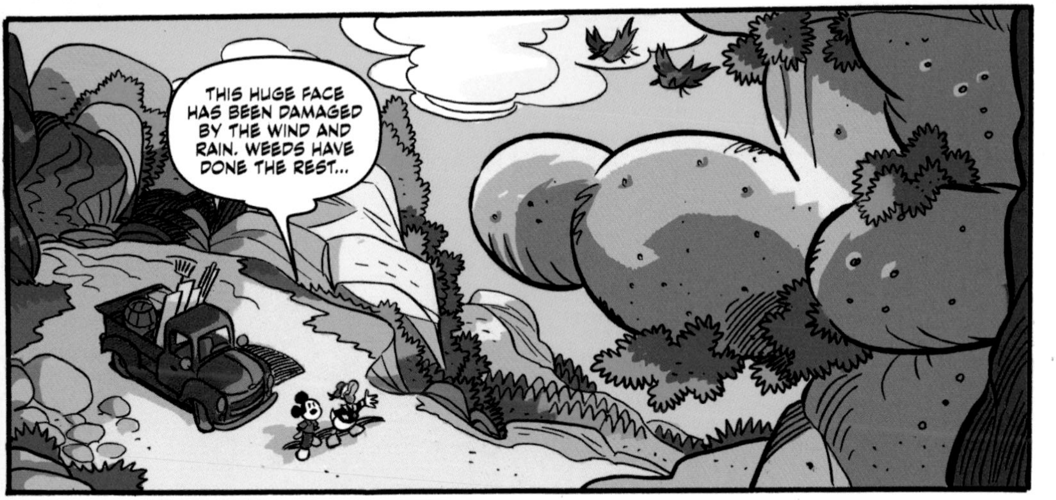
THIS HUGE FACE HAS BEEN DAMAGED BY THE WIND AND RAIN. WEEDS HAVE DONE THE REST...

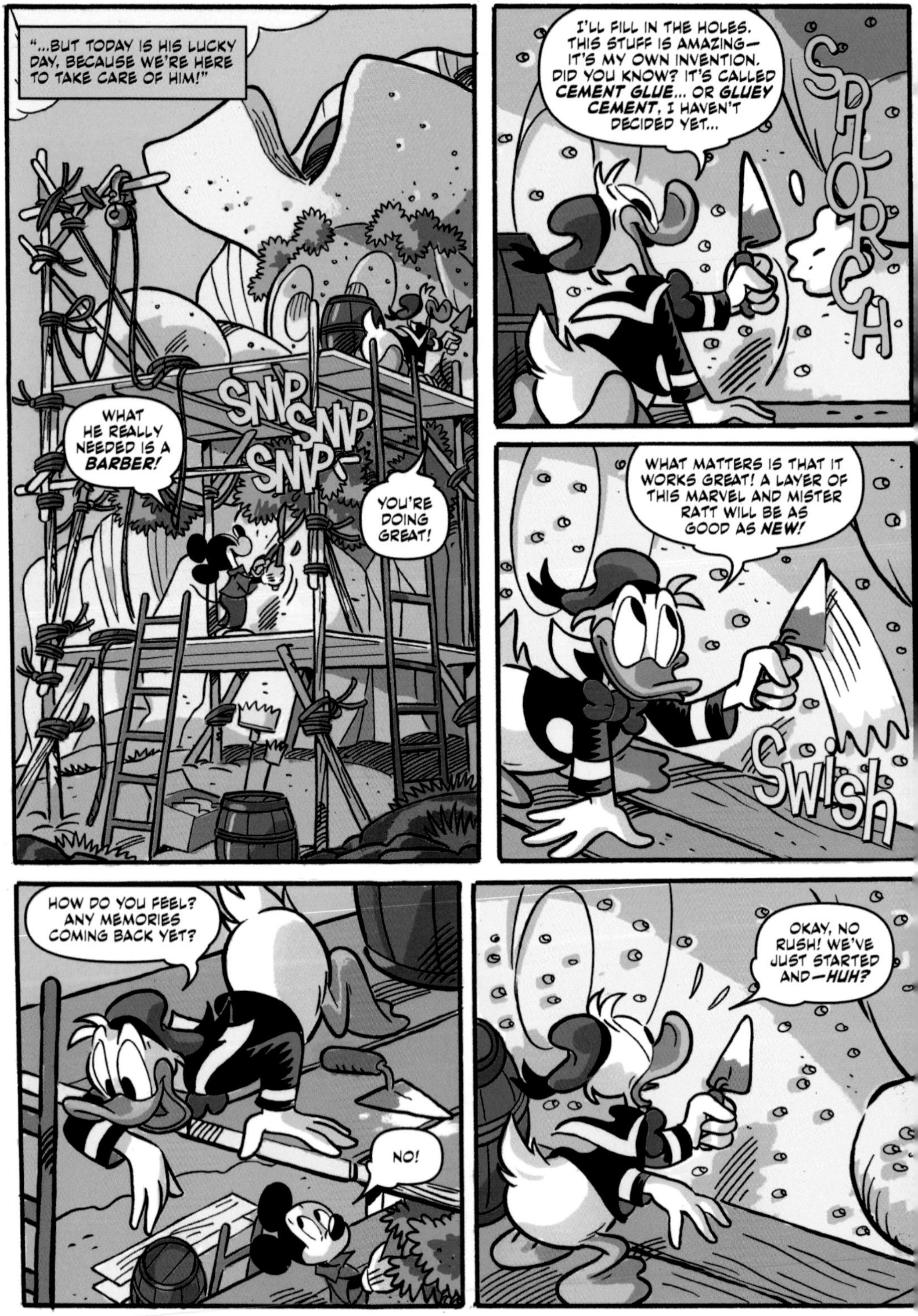
"...BUT TODAY IS HIS LUCKY DAY, BECAUSE WE'RE HERE TO TAKE CARE OF HIM!"
SNIP SNIP SNIP
WHAT HE REALLY NEEDED IS A *BARBER!*
YOU'RE DOING GREAT!
I'LL FILL IN THE HOLES. THIS STUFF IS AMAZING— IT'S MY OWN INVENTION. DID YOU KNOW? IT'S CALLED *CEMENT GLUE*... OR *GLUEY CEMENT*, I HAVEN'T DECIDED YET...
SPLORCH
WHAT MATTERS IS THAT IT WORKS GREAT! A LAYER OF THIS MARVEL AND MISTER RATT WILL BE AS GOOD AS *NEW!*
SWISH
HOW DO YOU FEEL? ANY MEMORIES COMING BACK YET?
NO!
OKAY, NO RUSH! WE'VE JUST STARTED AND—*HUH?*

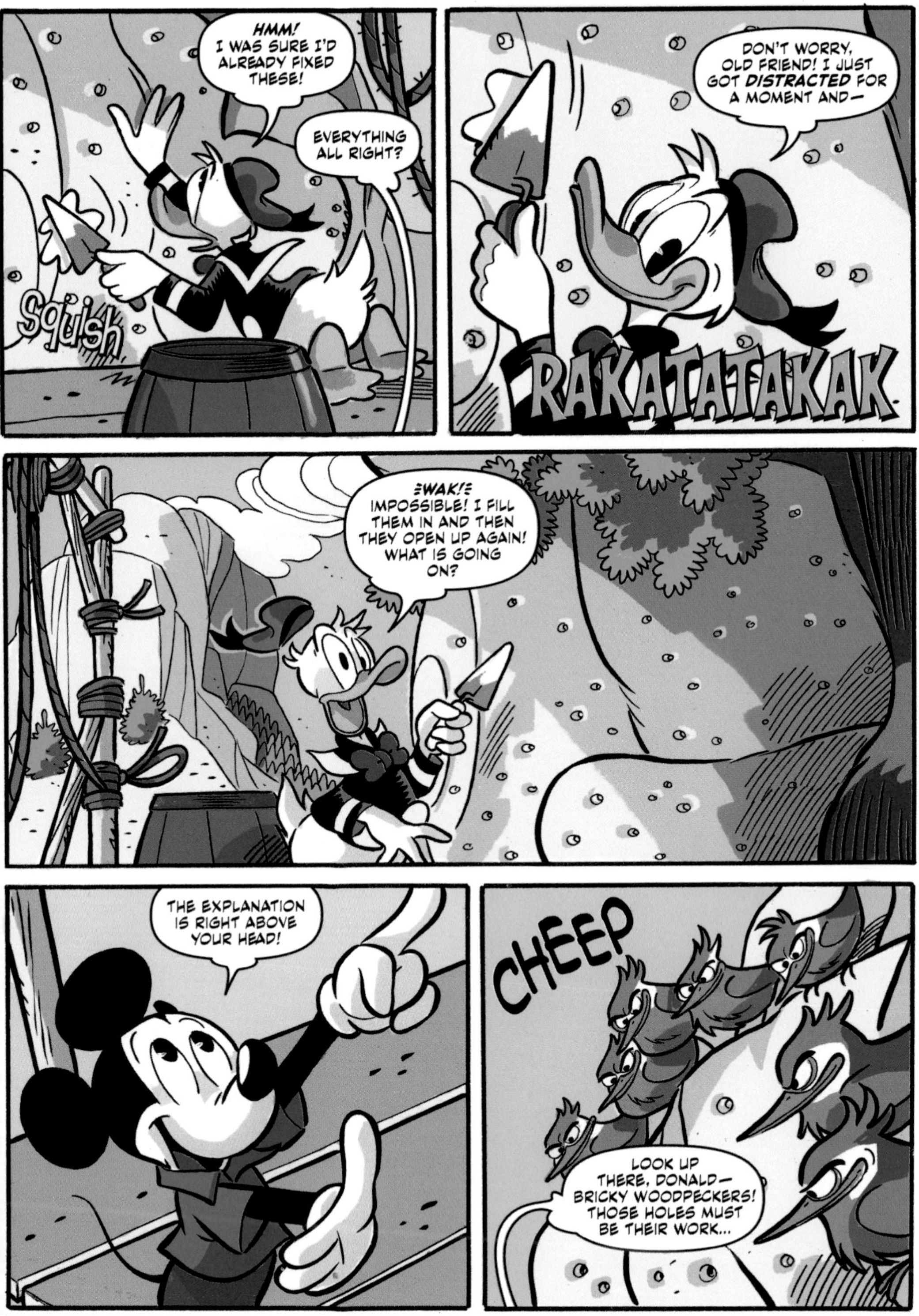
HMM! I WAS SURE I'D ALREADY FIXED THESE!
EVERYTHING ALL RIGHT?
SQUISH
DON'T WORRY, OLD FRIEND! I JUST GOT DISTRACTED FOR A MOMENT AND—
RAKATATAKAK
WAK! IMPOSSIBLE! I FILL THEM IN AND THEN THEY OPEN UP AGAIN! WHAT IS GOING ON?
THE EXPLANATION IS RIGHT ABOVE YOUR HEAD!
CHEEP
LOOK UP THERE, DONALD— BRICKY WOODPECKERS! THOSE HOLES MUST BE THEIR WORK...

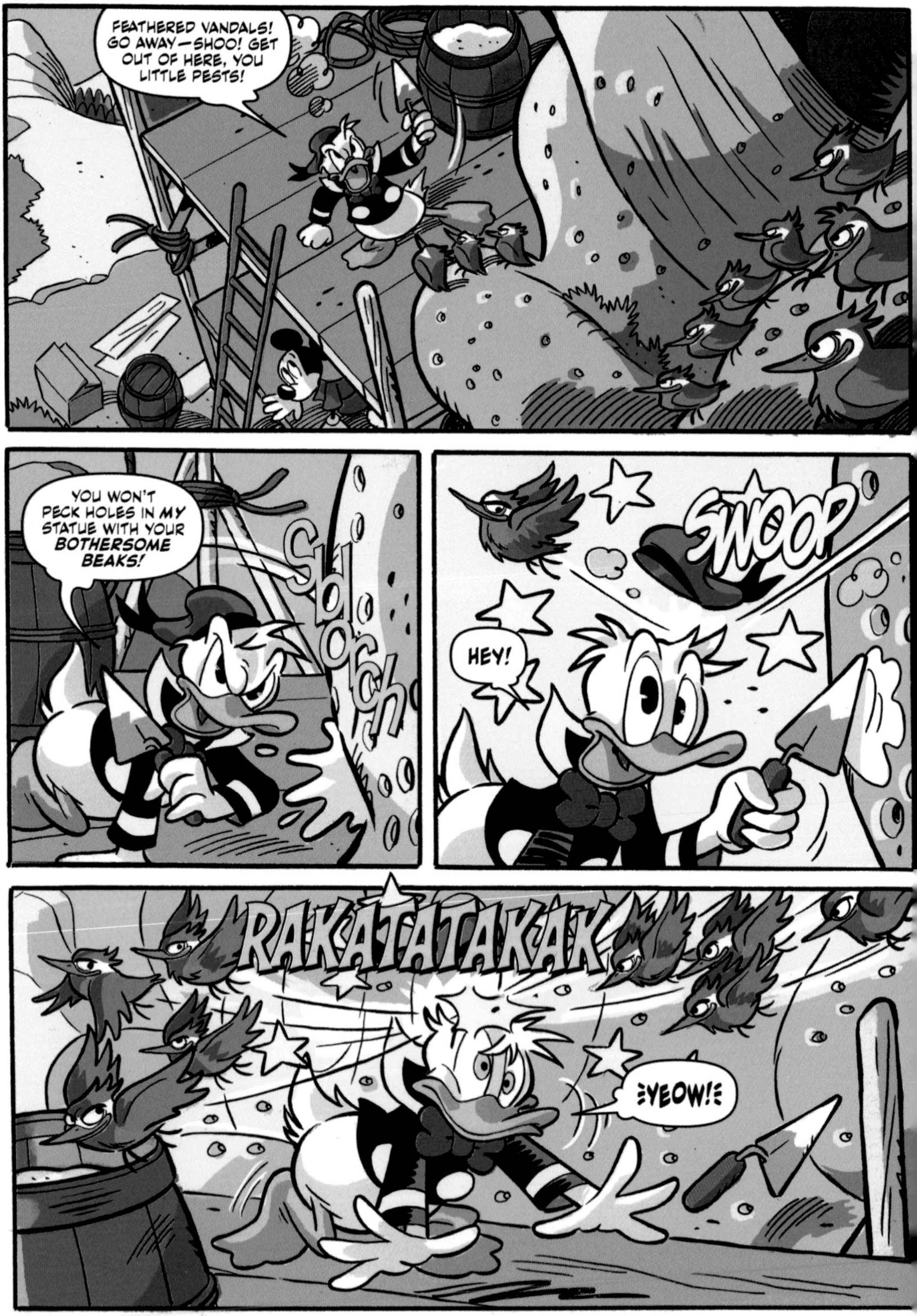

FEATHERED VANDALS! GO AWAY—SHOO! GET OUT OF HERE, YOU LITTLE PESTS!
YOU WON'T PECK HOLES IN MY STATUE WITH YOUR BOTHERSOME BEAKS!
SBLORCH
SWOOP
HEY!
RAKATATAKAK
YEOW!

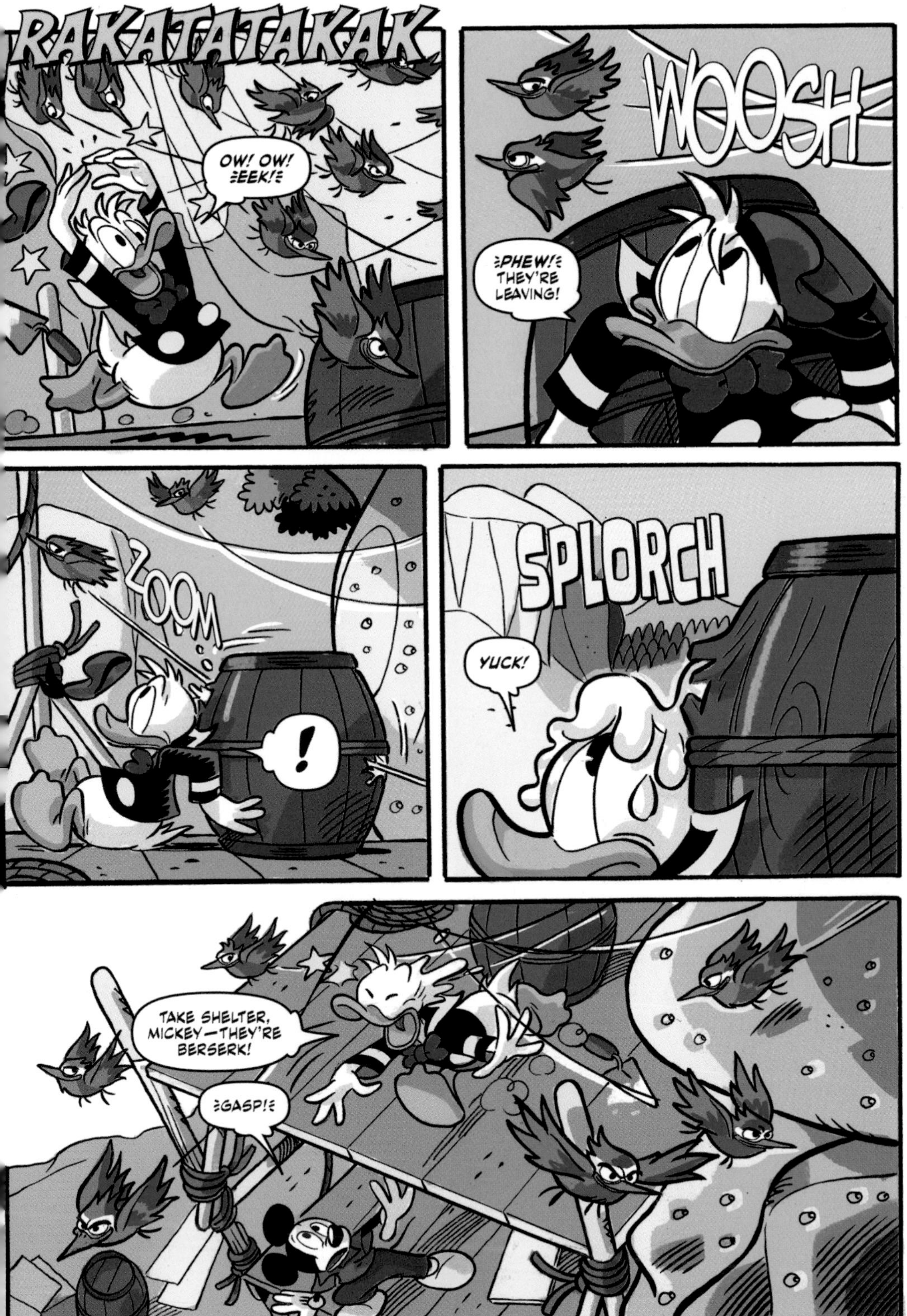
RAKATATAKAK
OW! OW! EEK!
WOOSH
PHEW! THEY'RE LEAVING!
ZOOM
!
SPLORCH
YUCK!
TAKE SHELTER, MICKEY—THEY'RE BERSERK!
GASP!

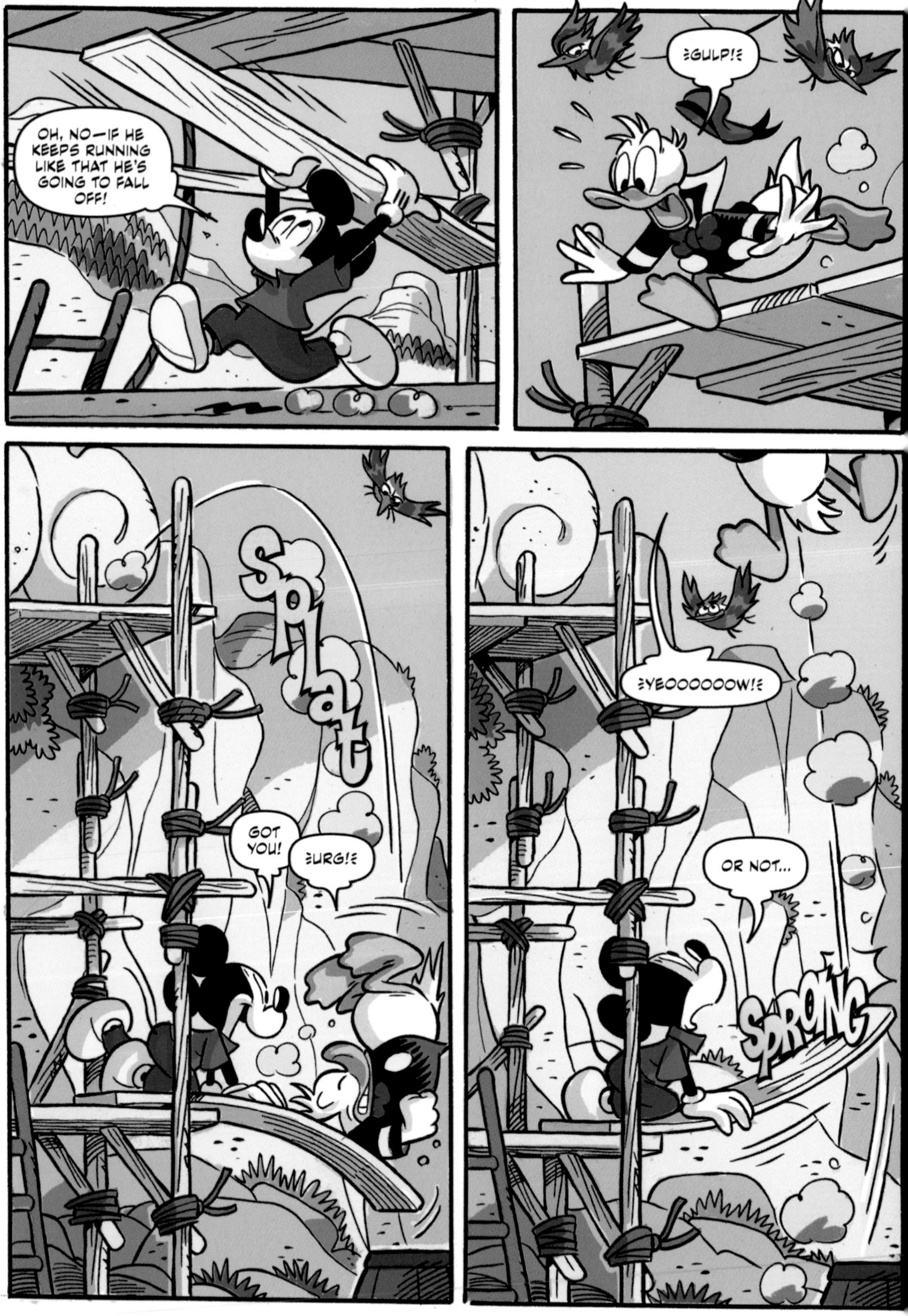
OH, NO—IF HE KEEPS RUNNING LIKE THAT HE'S GOING TO FALL OFF!
GULP!
SPLAT
GOT YOU!
URG!
YEOOOOOOW!
OR NOT...
SPRONG

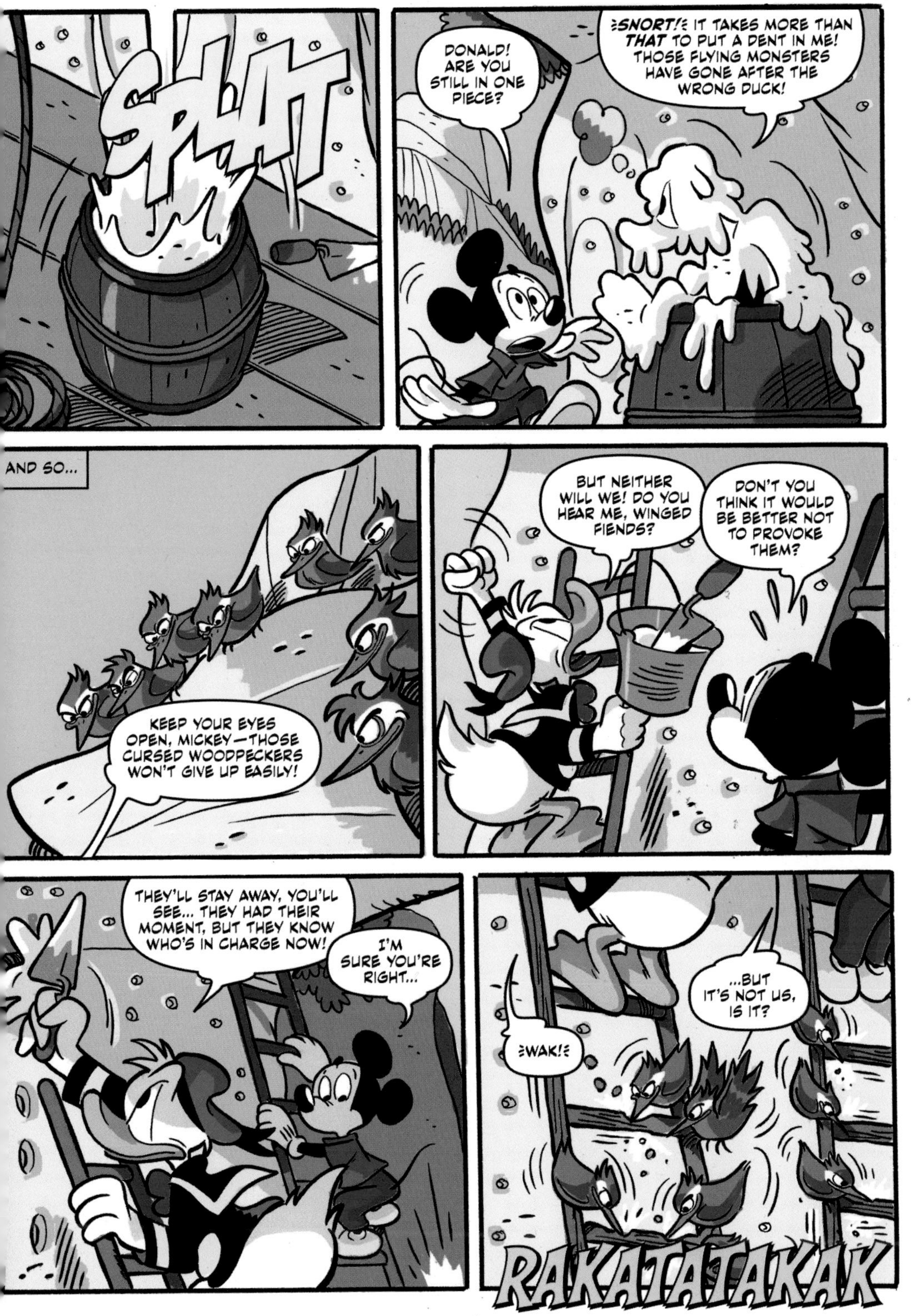
SPLAT
DONALD! ARE YOU STILL IN ONE PIECE?
SNORT! IT TAKES MORE THAN THAT TO PUT A DENT IN ME! THOSE FLYING MONSTERS HAVE GONE AFTER THE WRONG DUCK!
AND SO...
KEEP YOUR EYES OPEN, MICKEY—THOSE CURSED WOODPECKERS WON'T GIVE UP EASILY!
BUT NEITHER WILL WE! DO YOU HEAR ME, WINGED FIENDS?
DON'T YOU THINK IT WOULD BE BETTER NOT TO PROVOKE THEM?
THEY'LL STAY AWAY, YOU'LL SEE... THEY HAD THEIR MOMENT, BUT THEY KNOW WHO'S IN CHARGE NOW!
I'M SURE YOU'RE RIGHT...
...BUT IT'S NOT US, IS IT?
WAK!
RAKATATAKAK

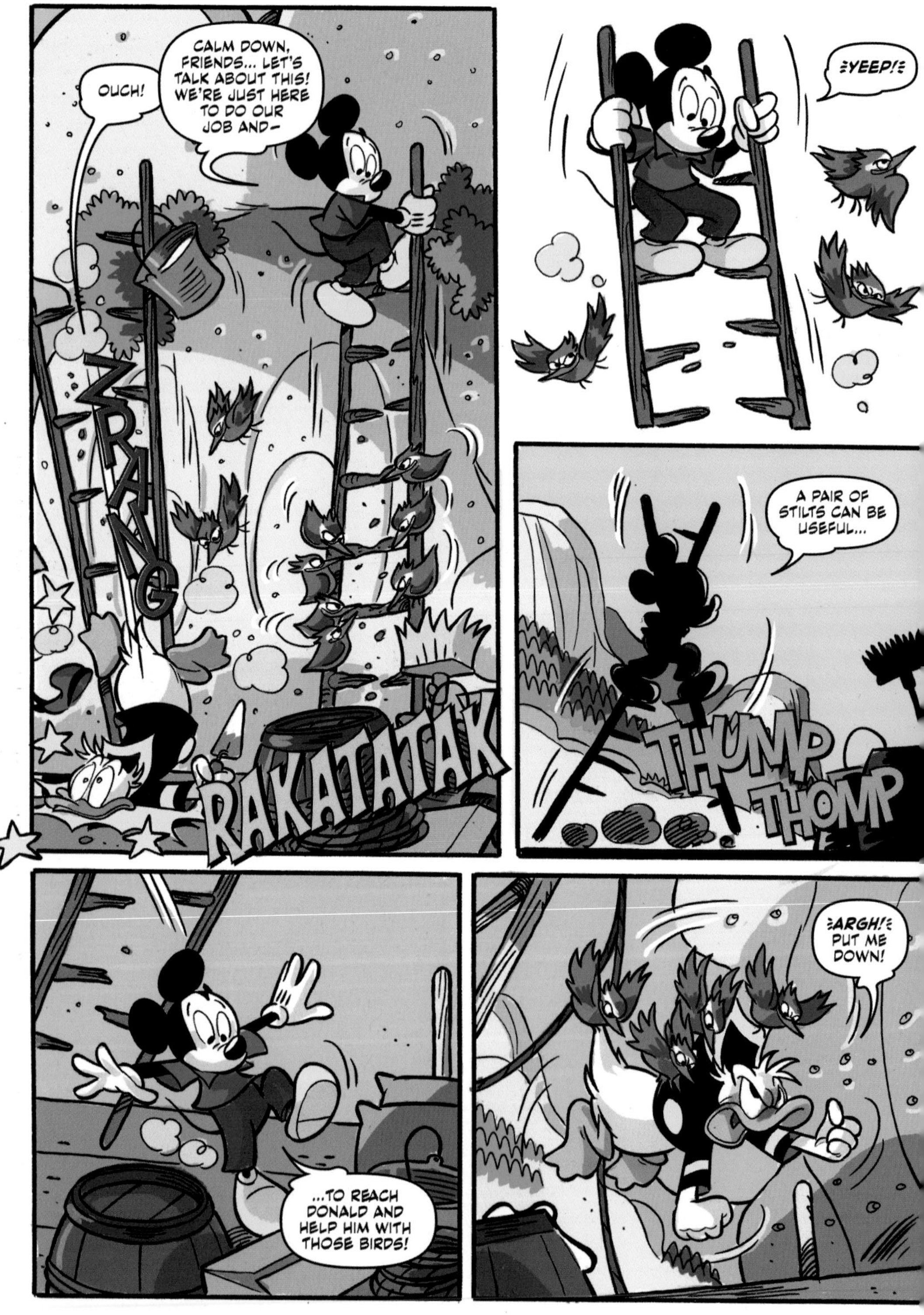
OUCH!
CALM DOWN, FRIENDS... LET'S TALK ABOUT THIS! WE'RE JUST HERE TO DO OUR JOB AND—
ZZRANG
RAKATATAK
YEEP!
A PAIR OF STILTS CAN BE USEFUL...
THUMP THOMP
...TO REACH DONALD AND HELP HIM WITH THOSE BIRDS!
ARGH! PUT ME DOWN!

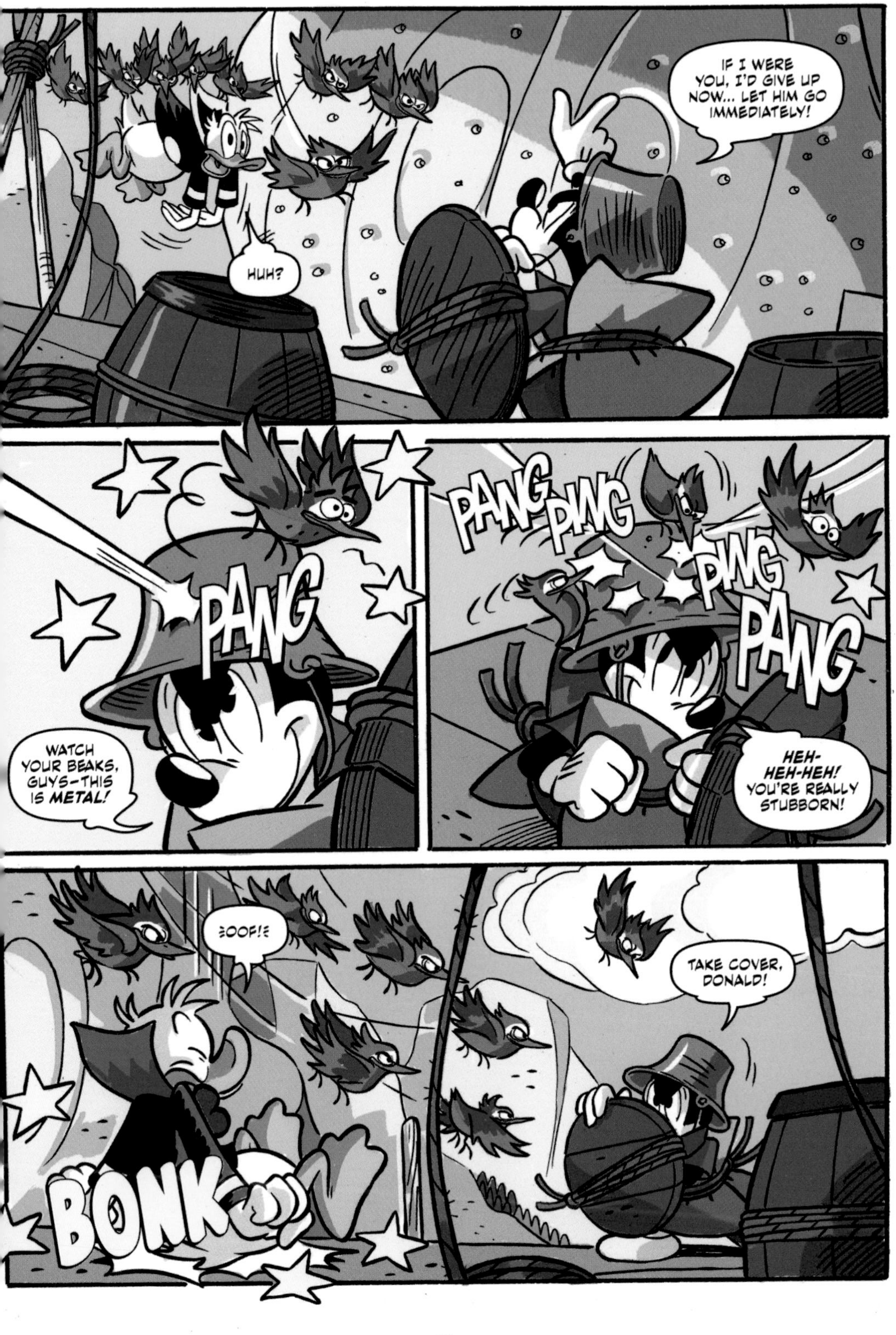
IF I WERE YOU, I'D GIVE UP NOW... LET HIM GO IMMEDIATELY!
HUH?
PANG
WATCH YOUR BEAKS, GUYS–THIS IS METAL!
PANG PING
PING
PANG
HEH-HEH-HEH! YOU'RE REALLY STUBBORN!
OOF!
BONK
TAKE COVER, DONALD!

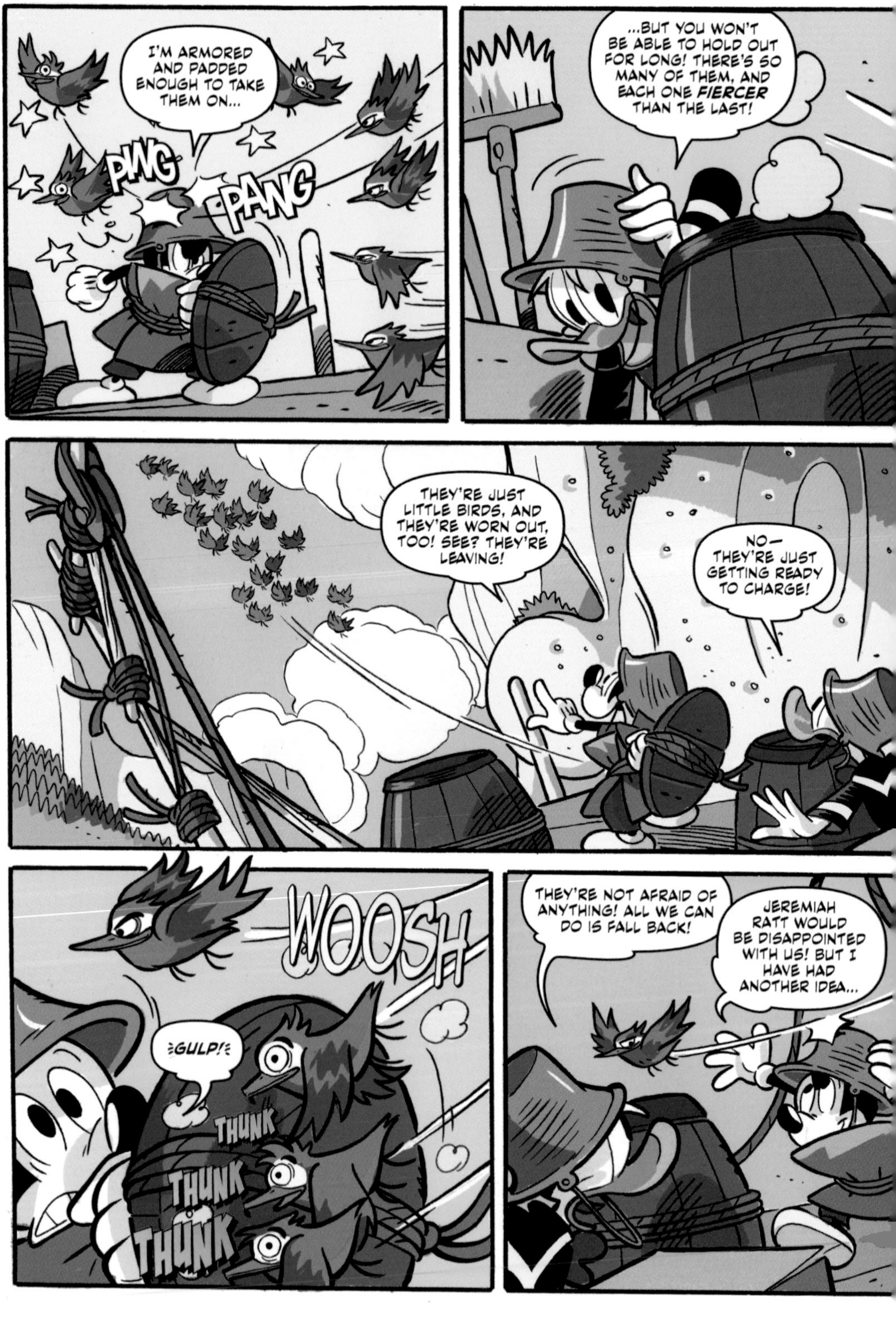
I'M ARMORED AND PADDED ENOUGH TO TAKE THEM ON...
PING
PANG
...BUT YOU WON'T BE ABLE TO HOLD OUT FOR LONG! THERE'S SO MANY OF THEM, AND EACH ONE FIERCER THAN THE LAST!
THEY'RE JUST LITTLE BIRDS, AND THEY'RE WORN OUT, TOO! SEE? THEY'RE LEAVING!
NO— THEY'RE JUST GETTING READY TO CHARGE!
WOOSH
GULP!
THUNK
THUNK
THUNK
THEY'RE NOT AFRAID OF ANYTHING! ALL WE CAN DO IS FALL BACK!
JEREMIAH RATT WOULD BE DISAPPOINTED WITH US! BUT I HAVE HAD ANOTHER IDEA...

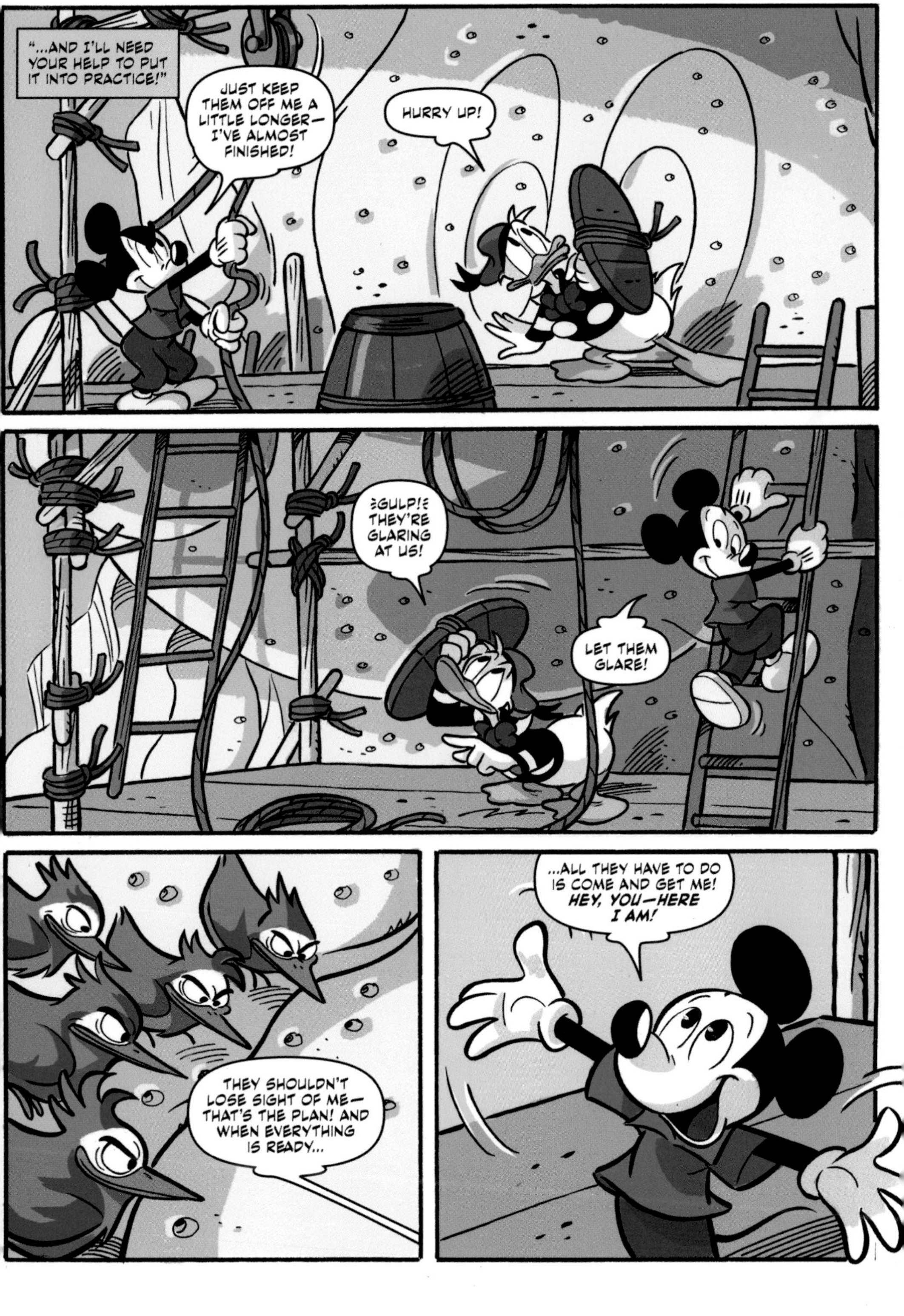
"...AND I'LL NEED YOUR HELP TO PUT IT INTO PRACTICE!"
JUST KEEP THEM OFF ME A LITTLE LONGER— I'VE ALMOST FINISHED!
HURRY UP!
GULP! THEY'RE GLARING AT US!
LET THEM GLARE!
THEY SHOULDN'T LOSE SIGHT OF ME— THAT'S THE PLAN! AND WHEN EVERYTHING IS READY...
...ALL THEY HAVE TO DO IS COME AND GET ME! *HEY, YOU—HERE I AM!*

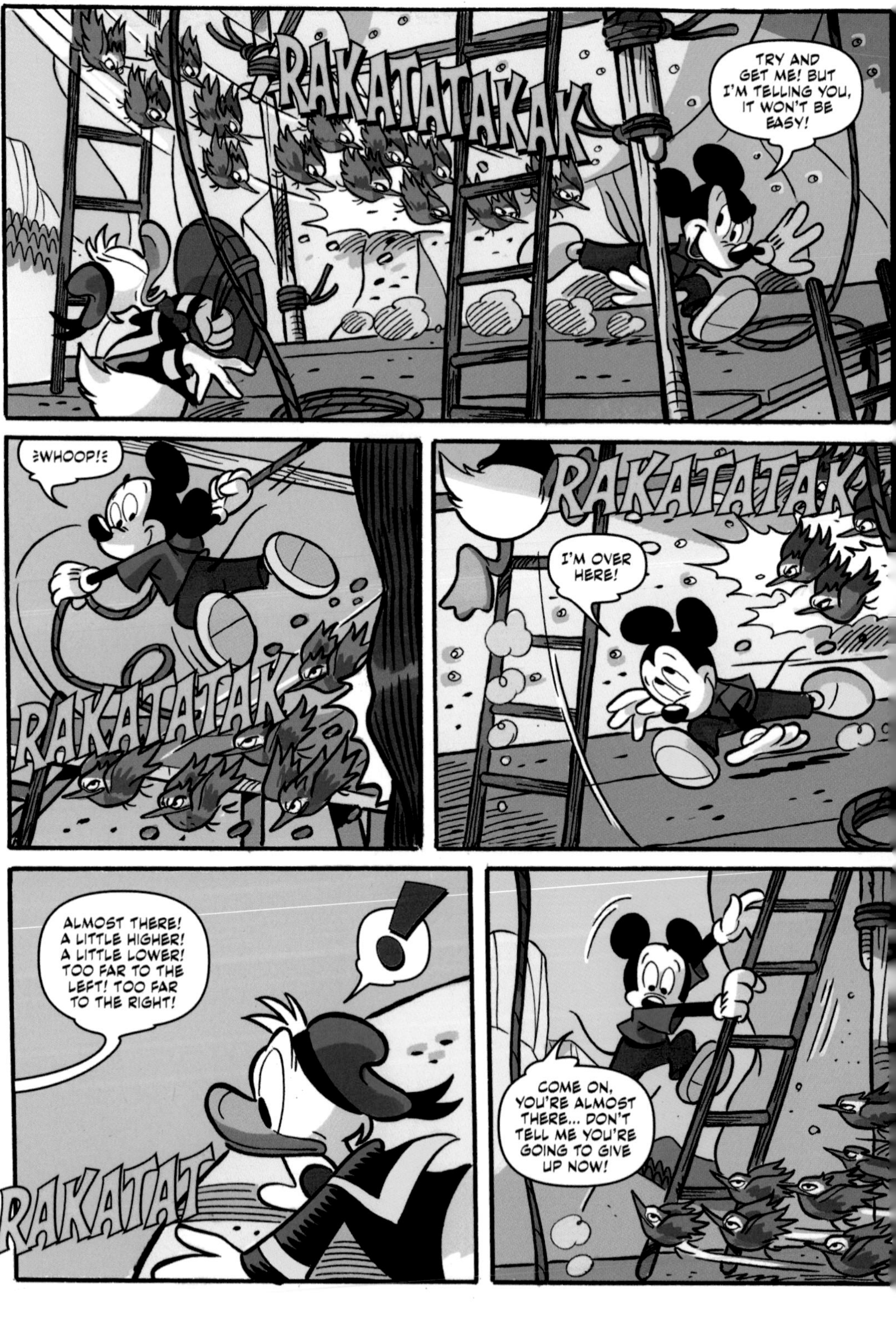
RAKATATAKAK
TRY AND GET ME! BUT I'M TELLING YOU, IT WON'T BE EASY!
WHOOP!
RAKATATAK
RAKATATAK
I'M OVER HERE!
ALMOST THERE! A LITTLE HIGHER! A LITTLE LOWER! TOO FAR TO THE LEFT! TOO FAR TO THE RIGHT!
!
RAKATAT
COME ON, YOU'RE ALMOST THERE... DON'T TELL ME YOU'RE GOING TO GIVE UP NOW!

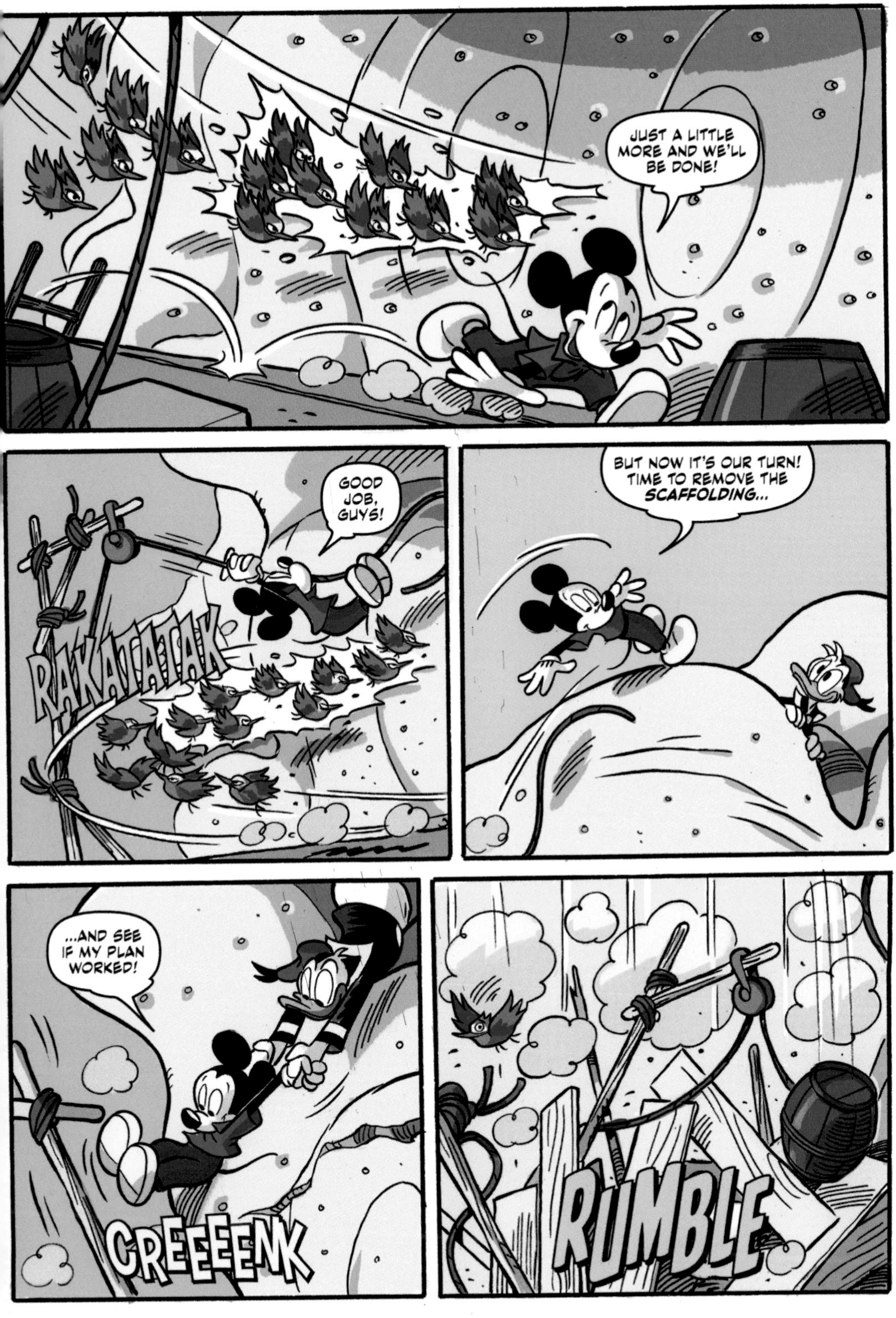
JUST A LITTLE MORE AND WE'LL BE DONE!
GOOD JOB, GUYS!
RAKATATAK
BUT NOW IT'S OUR TURN! TIME TO REMOVE THE SCAFFOLDING...
...AND SEE IF MY PLAN WORKED!
CREEEEENK
RUMBLE

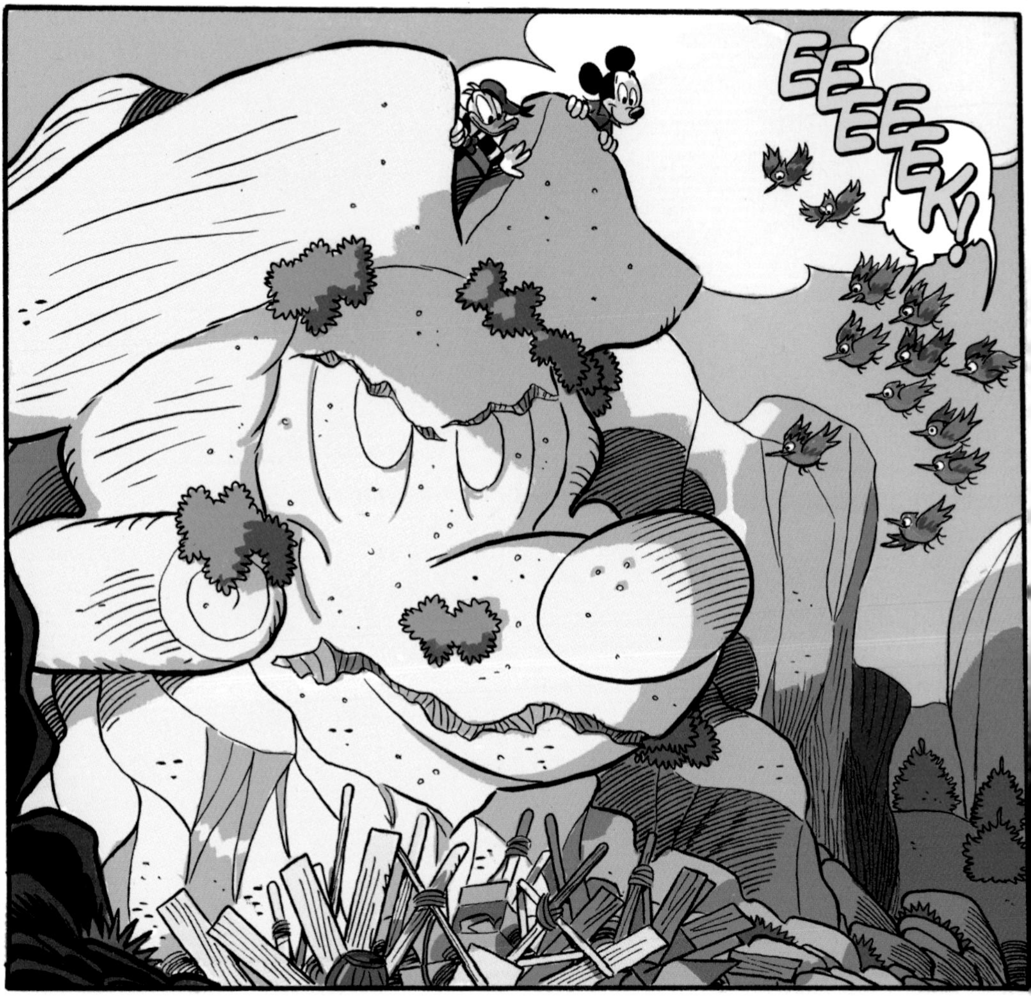
EEEEEK!

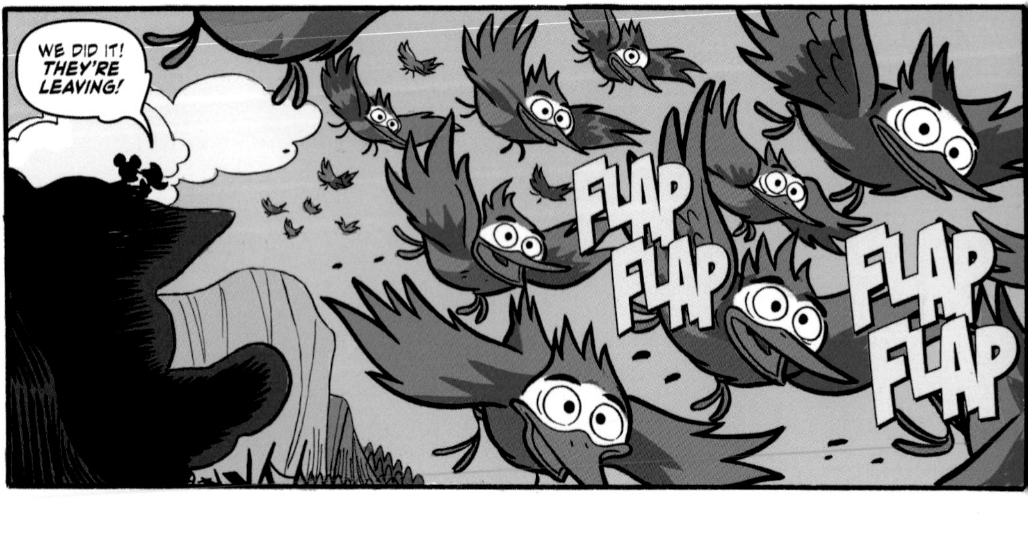
WE DID IT! THEY'RE LEAVING!
FLAP
FLAP
FLAP
FLAP

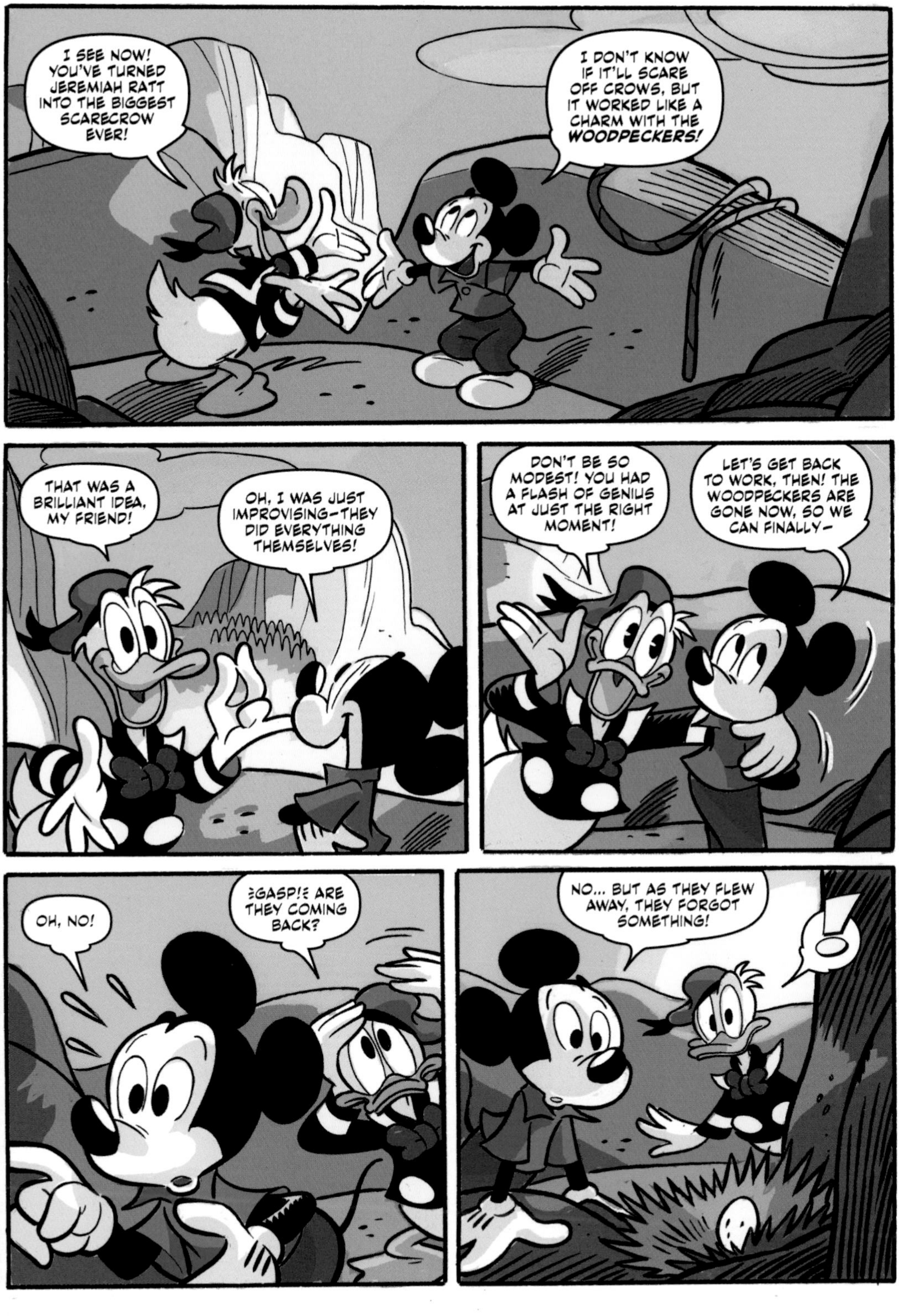
I SEE NOW! YOU'VE TURNED JEREMIAH RATT INTO THE BIGGEST SCARECROW EVER!
I DON'T KNOW IF IT'LL SCARE OFF CROWS, BUT IT WORKED LIKE A CHARM WITH THE *WOODPECKERS!*
THAT WAS A BRILLIANT IDEA, MY FRIEND!
OH, I WAS JUST IMPROVISING—THEY DID EVERYTHING THEMSELVES!
DON'T BE SO MODEST! YOU HAD A FLASH OF GENIUS AT JUST THE RIGHT MOMENT!
LET'S GET BACK TO WORK, THEN! THE WOODPECKERS ARE GONE NOW, SO WE CAN FINALLY—
OH, NO!
⦚GASP!⦚ ARE THEY COMING BACK?
NO... BUT AS THEY FLEW AWAY, THEY FORGOT SOMETHING!
!

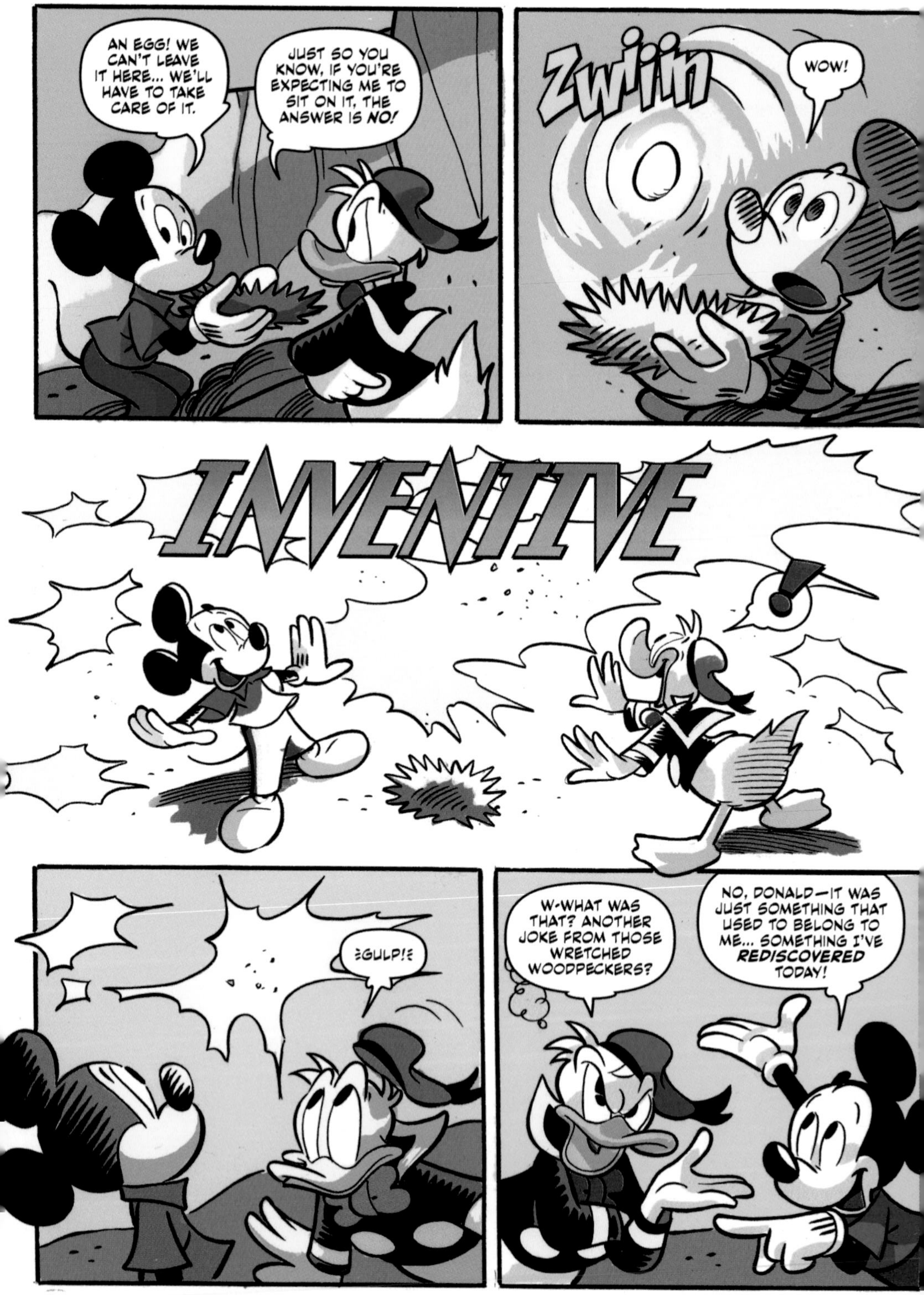
AN EGG! WE CAN'T LEAVE IT HERE... WE'LL HAVE TO TAKE CARE OF IT.
JUST SO YOU KNOW, IF YOU'RE EXPECTING ME TO SIT ON IT, THE ANSWER IS NO!
ZWIIN
WOW!
INVENTIVE
!
GULP!
W-WHAT WAS THAT? ANOTHER JOKE FROM THOSE WRETCHED WOODPECKERS?
NO, DONALD—IT WAS JUST SOMETHING THAT USED TO BELONG TO ME... SOMETHING I'VE REDISCOVERED TODAY!

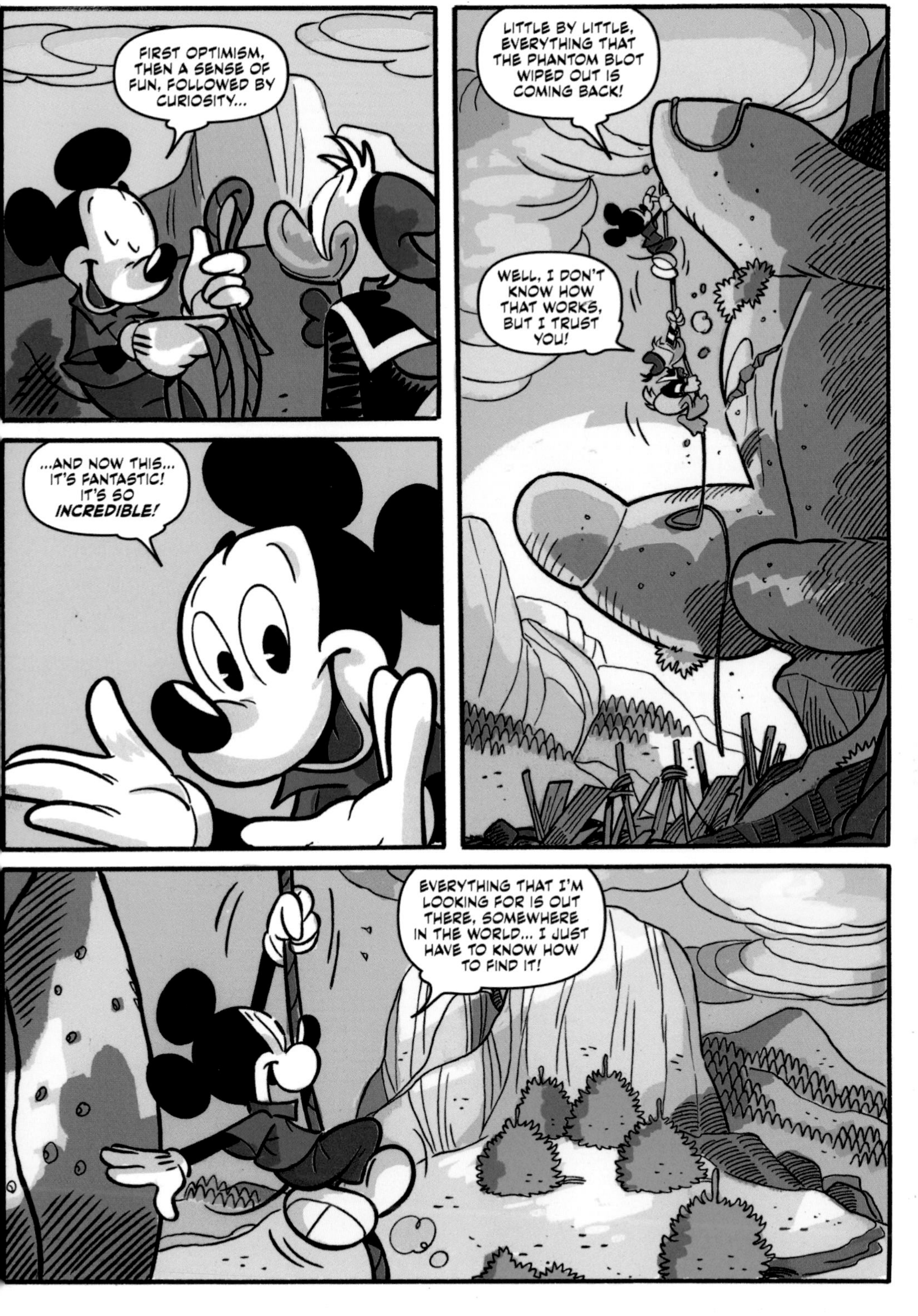
FIRST OPTIMISM, THEN A SENSE OF FUN, FOLLOWED BY CURIOSITY...
...AND NOW THIS... IT'S FANTASTIC! IT'S SO *INCREDIBLE!*
LITTLE BY LITTLE, EVERYTHING THAT THE PHANTOM BLOT WIPED OUT IS COMING BACK!
WELL, I DON'T KNOW HOW THAT WORKS, BUT I TRUST YOU!
EVERYTHING THAT I'M LOOKING FOR IS OUT THERE, SOMEWHERE IN THE WORLD... I JUST HAVE TO KNOW HOW TO FIND IT!

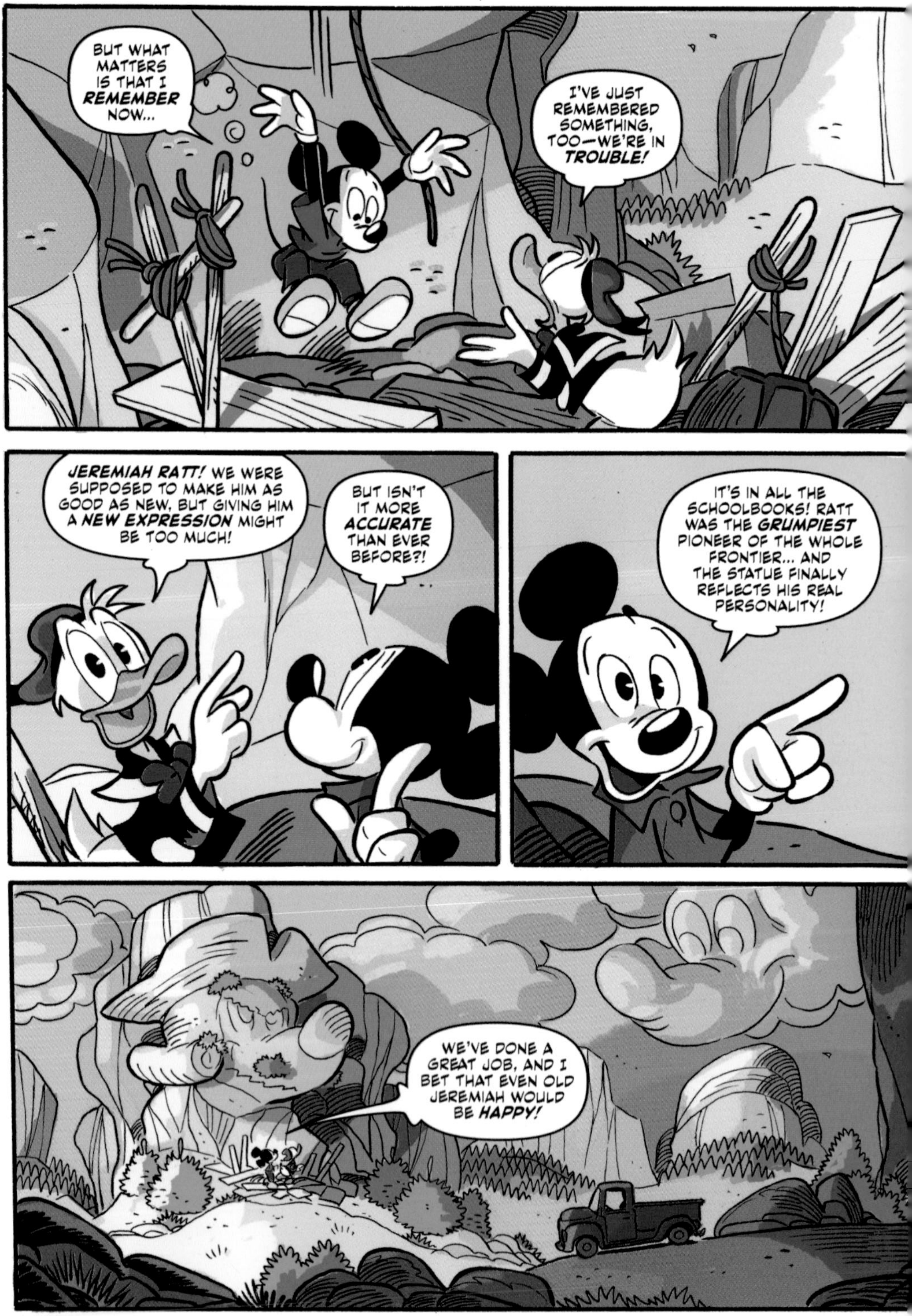
BUT WHAT MATTERS IS THAT I REMEMBER NOW...
I'VE JUST REMEMBERED SOMETHING, TOO—WE'RE IN TROUBLE!
JEREMIAH RATT! WE WERE SUPPOSED TO MAKE HIM AS GOOD AS NEW, BUT GIVING HIM A NEW EXPRESSION MIGHT BE TOO MUCH!
BUT ISN'T IT MORE ACCURATE THAN EVER BEFORE?!
IT'S IN ALL THE SCHOOLBOOKS! RATT WAS THE GRUMPIEST PIONEER OF THE WHOLE FRONTIER... AND THE STATUE FINALLY REFLECTS HIS REAL PERSONALITY!
WE'VE DONE A GREAT JOB, AND I BET THAT EVEN OLD JEREMIAH WOULD BE HAPPY!

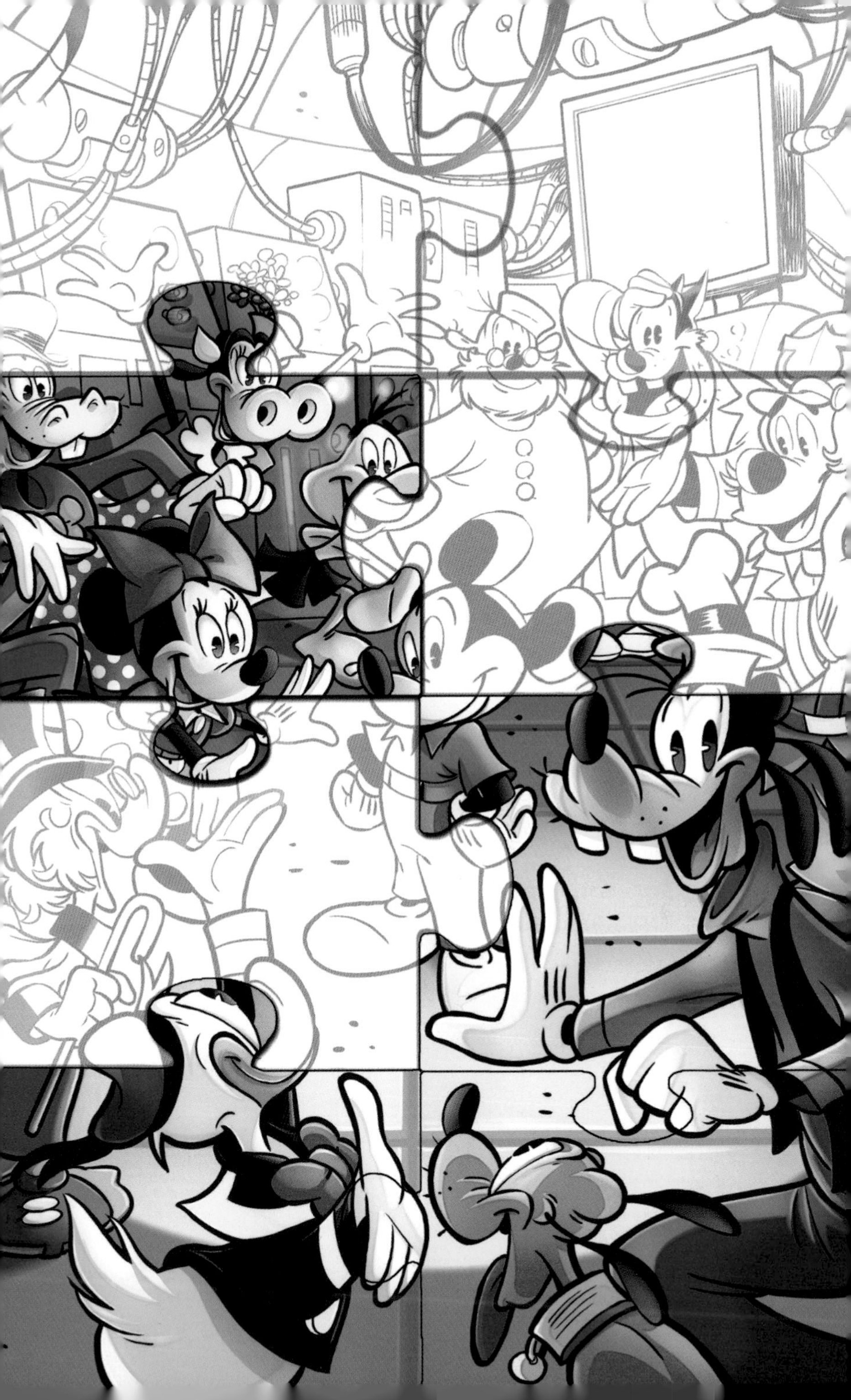

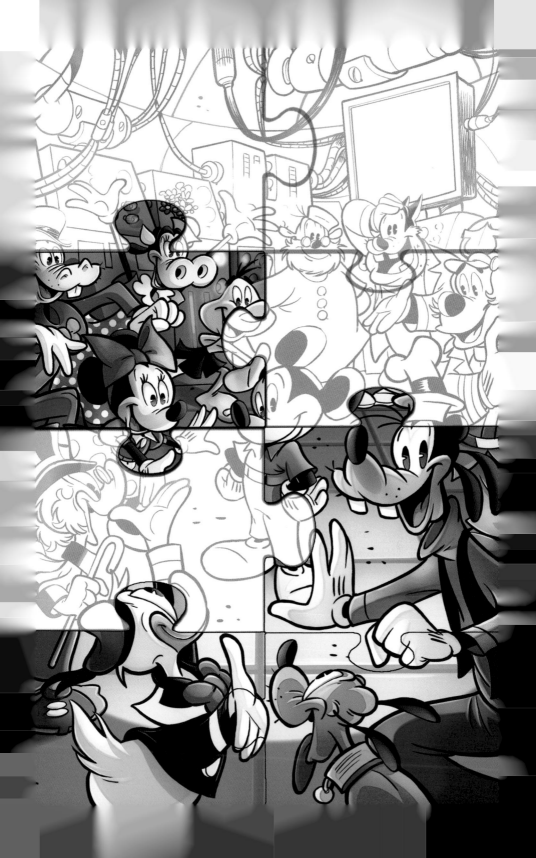

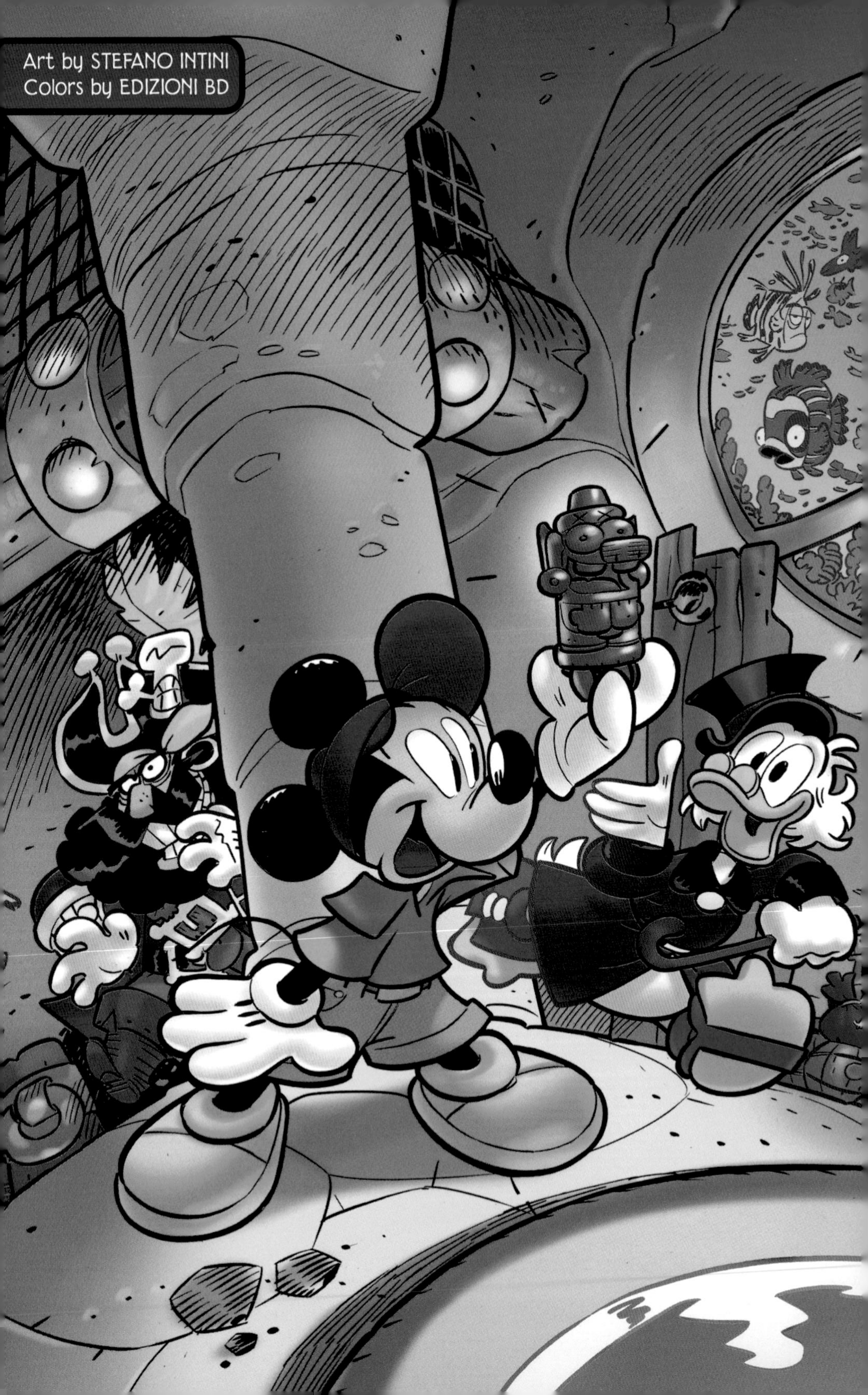
Art by STEFANO INTINI
Colors by EDIZIONI BD

CHAPTER 5: THE SPRING OF TIME

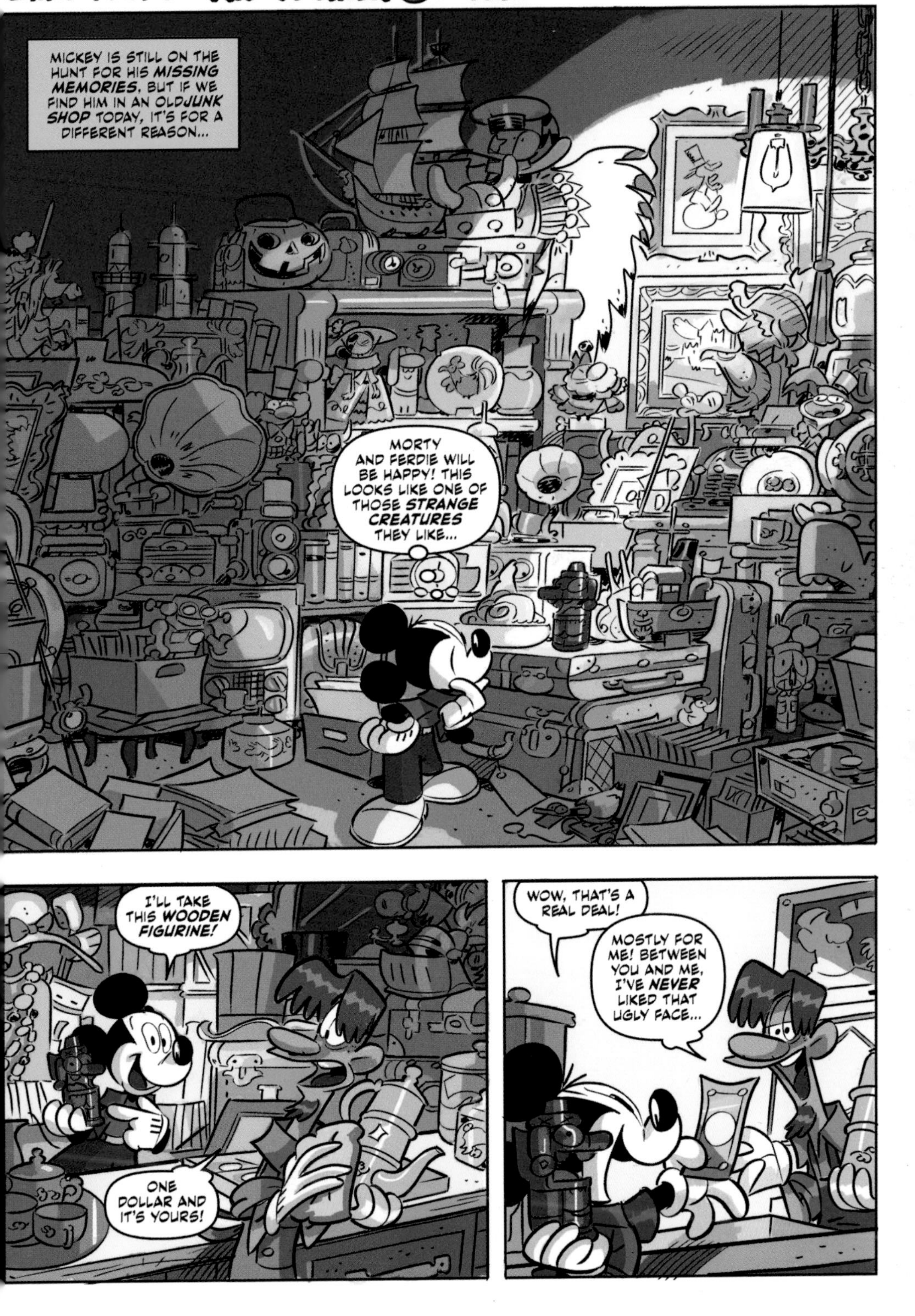
MICKEY IS STILL ON THE HUNT FOR HIS MISSING MEMORIES, BUT IF WE FIND HIM IN AN OLD JUNK SHOP TODAY, IT'S FOR A DIFFERENT REASON...
MORTY AND FERDIE WILL BE HAPPY! THIS LOOKS LIKE ONE OF THOSE STRANGE CREATURES THEY LIKE...
I'LL TAKE THIS WOODEN FIGURINE!
ONE DOLLAR AND IT'S YOURS!
WOW, THAT'S A REAL DEAL!
MOSTLY FOR ME! BETWEEN YOU AND ME, I'VE NEVER LIKED THAT UGLY FACE...

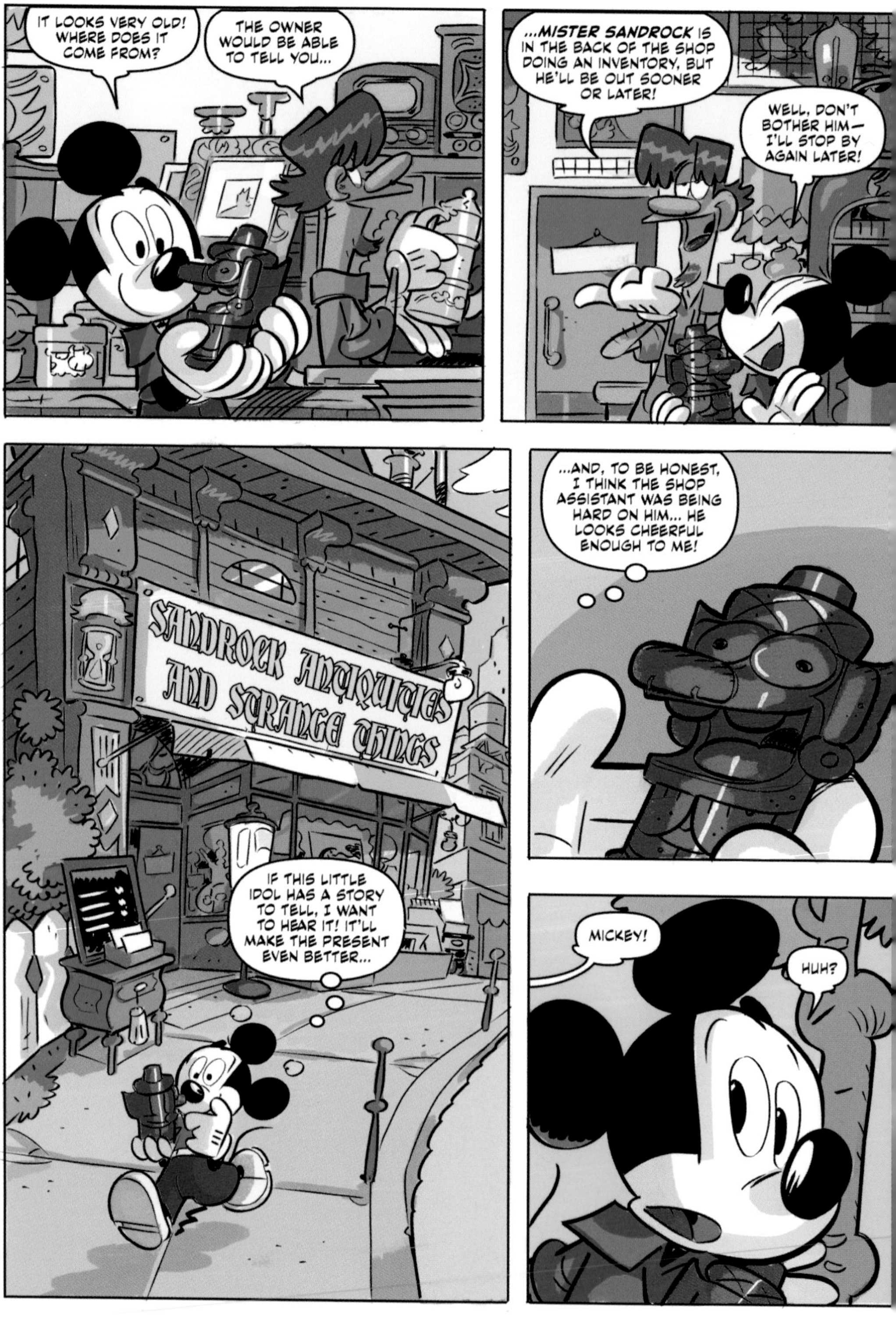
IT LOOKS VERY OLD! WHERE DOES IT COME FROM?
THE OWNER WOULD BE ABLE TO TELL YOU...
...MISTER SANDROCK IS IN THE BACK OF THE SHOP DOING AN INVENTORY, BUT HE'LL BE OUT SOONER OR LATER!
WELL, DON'T BOTHER HIM— I'LL STOP BY AGAIN LATER!
SANDROCK ANTIQUITIES AND STRANGE THINGS
IF THIS LITTLE IDOL HAS A STORY TO TELL, I WANT TO HEAR IT! IT'LL MAKE THE PRESENT EVEN BETTER...
...AND, TO BE HONEST, I THINK THE SHOP ASSISTANT WAS BEING HARD ON HIM... HE LOOKS CHEERFUL ENOUGH TO ME!
MICKEY!
HUH?

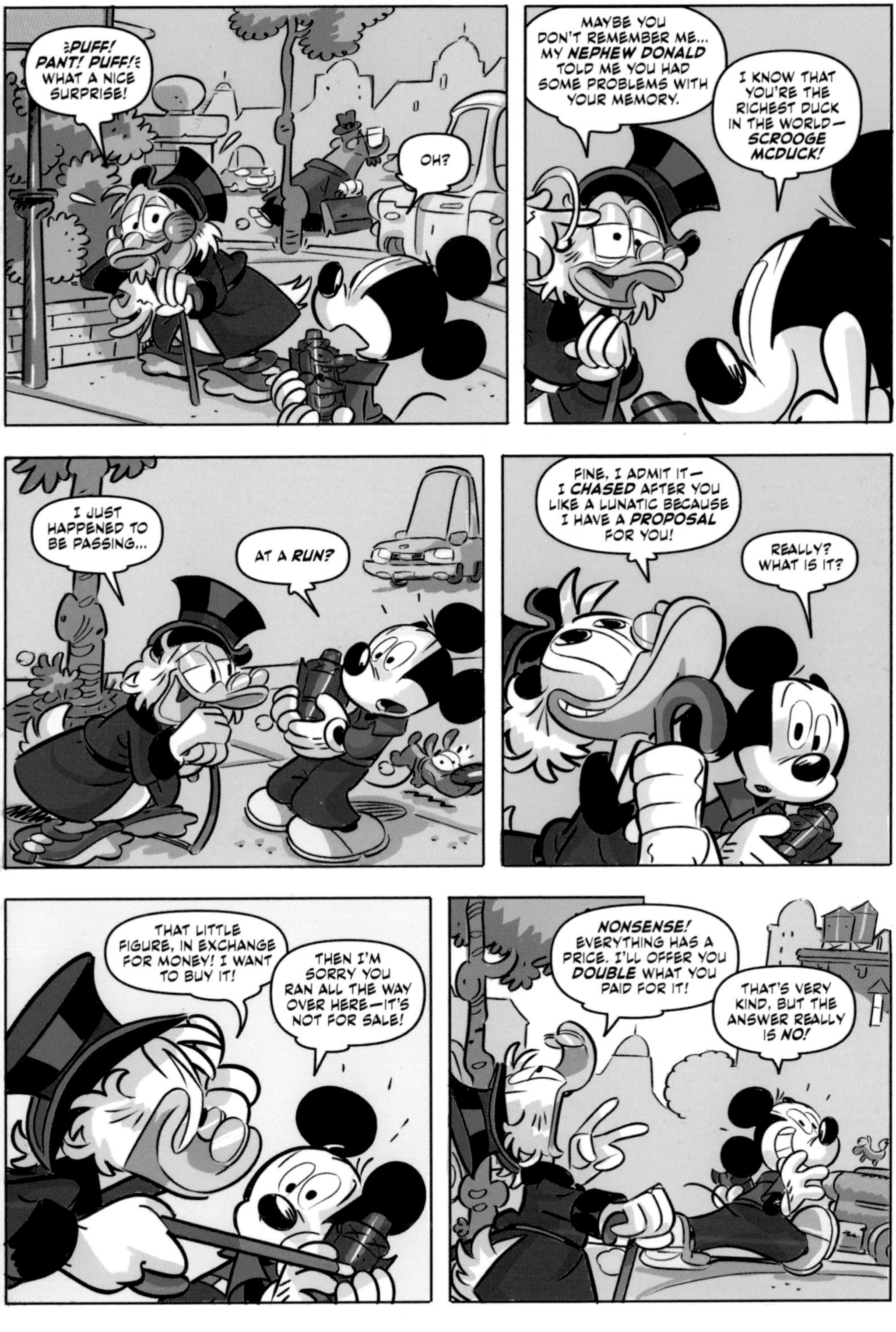
PUFF! PANT! PUFF! WHAT A NICE SURPRISE!
OH?
MAYBE YOU DON'T REMEMBER ME... MY NEPHEW DONALD TOLD ME YOU HAD SOME PROBLEMS WITH YOUR MEMORY.
I KNOW THAT YOU'RE THE RICHEST DUCK IN THE WORLD—SCROOGE MCDUCK!
I JUST HAPPENED TO BE PASSING...
AT A RUN?
FINE, I ADMIT IT—I CHASED AFTER YOU LIKE A LUNATIC BECAUSE I HAVE A PROPOSAL FOR YOU!
REALLY? WHAT IS IT?
THAT LITTLE FIGURE, IN EXCHANGE FOR MONEY! I WANT TO BUY IT!
THEN I'M SORRY YOU RAN ALL THE WAY OVER HERE—IT'S NOT FOR SALE!
NONSENSE! EVERYTHING HAS A PRICE. I'LL OFFER YOU DOUBLE WHAT YOU PAID FOR IT!
THAT'S VERY KIND, BUT THE ANSWER REALLY IS NO!

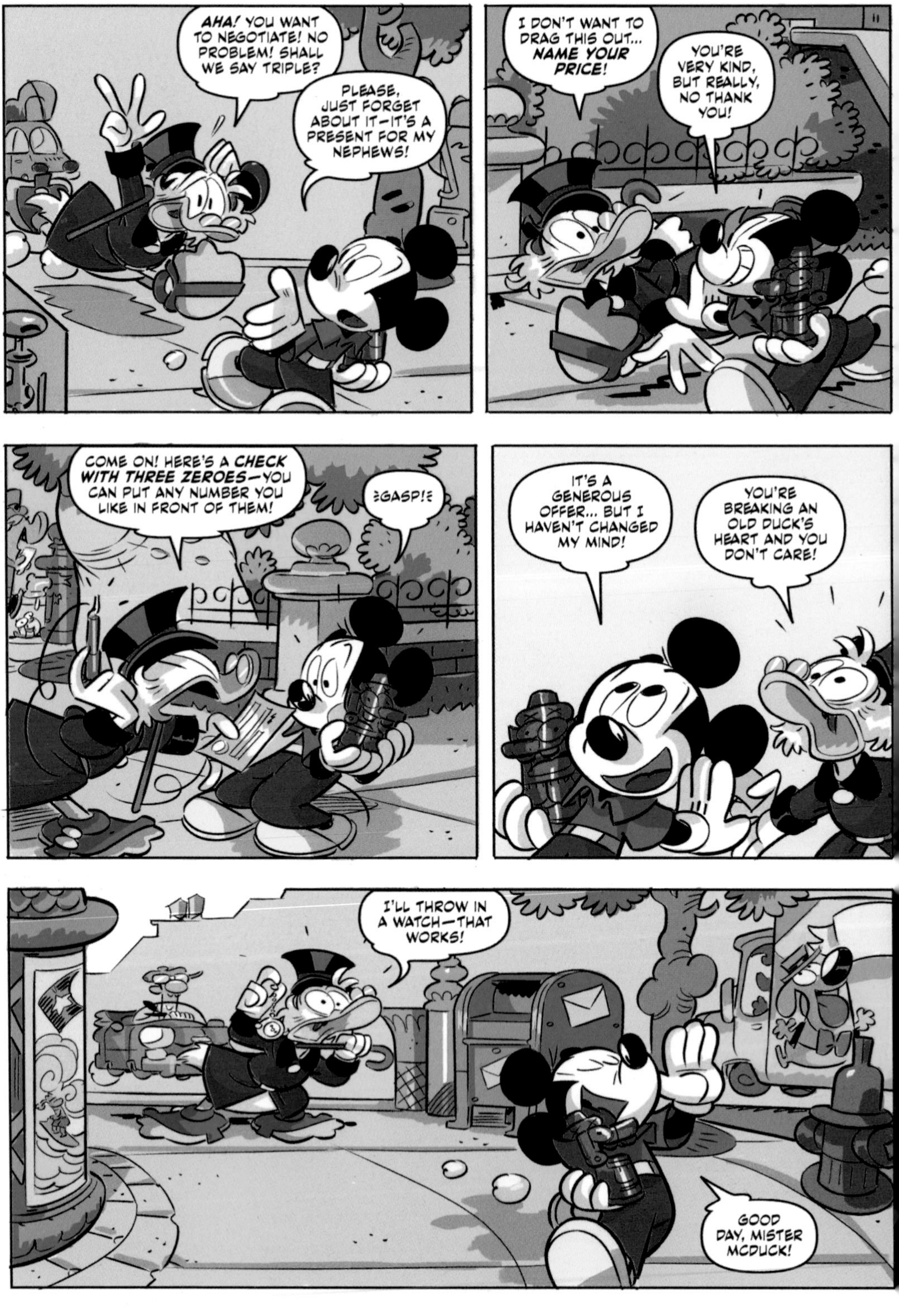
AHA! YOU WANT TO NEGOTIATE! NO PROBLEM! SHALL WE SAY TRIPLE?
PLEASE, JUST FORGET ABOUT IT—IT'S A PRESENT FOR MY NEPHEWS!
I DON'T WANT TO DRAG THIS OUT... NAME YOUR PRICE!
YOU'RE VERY KIND, BUT REALLY, NO THANK YOU!
COME ON! HERE'S A CHECK WITH THREE ZEROES—YOU CAN PUT ANY NUMBER YOU LIKE IN FRONT OF THEM!
GASP!
IT'S A GENEROUS OFFER... BUT I HAVEN'T CHANGED MY MIND!
YOU'RE BREAKING AN OLD DUCK'S HEART AND YOU DON'T CARE!
I'LL THROW IN A WATCH—THAT WORKS!
GOOD DAY, MISTER MCDUCK!

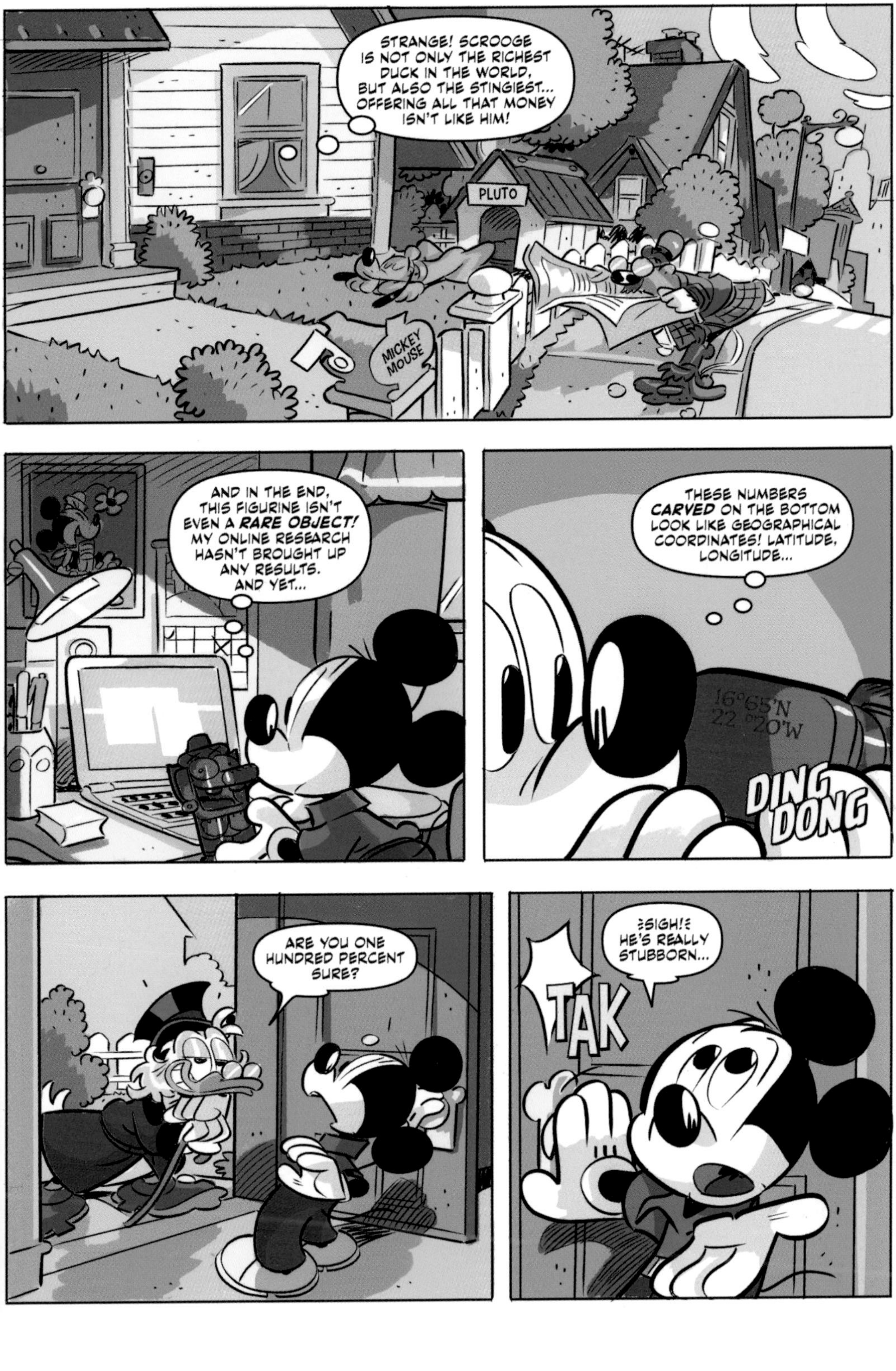
STRANGE! SCROOGE IS NOT ONLY THE RICHEST DUCK IN THE WORLD, BUT ALSO THE STINGIEST... OFFERING ALL THAT MONEY ISN'T LIKE HIM!
PLUTO
MICKEY MOUSE
AND IN THE END, THIS FIGURINE ISN'T EVEN A ***RARE OBJECT!*** MY ONLINE RESEARCH HASN'T BROUGHT UP ANY RESULTS. AND YET...
THESE NUMBERS ***CARVED*** ON THE BOTTOM LOOK LIKE GEOGRAPHICAL COORDINATES! LATITUDE, LONGITUDE...
16°65'N
22°20'W
DING DONG
ARE YOU ONE HUNDRED PERCENT SURE?
TAK
SIGH! HE'S REALLY STUBBORN...

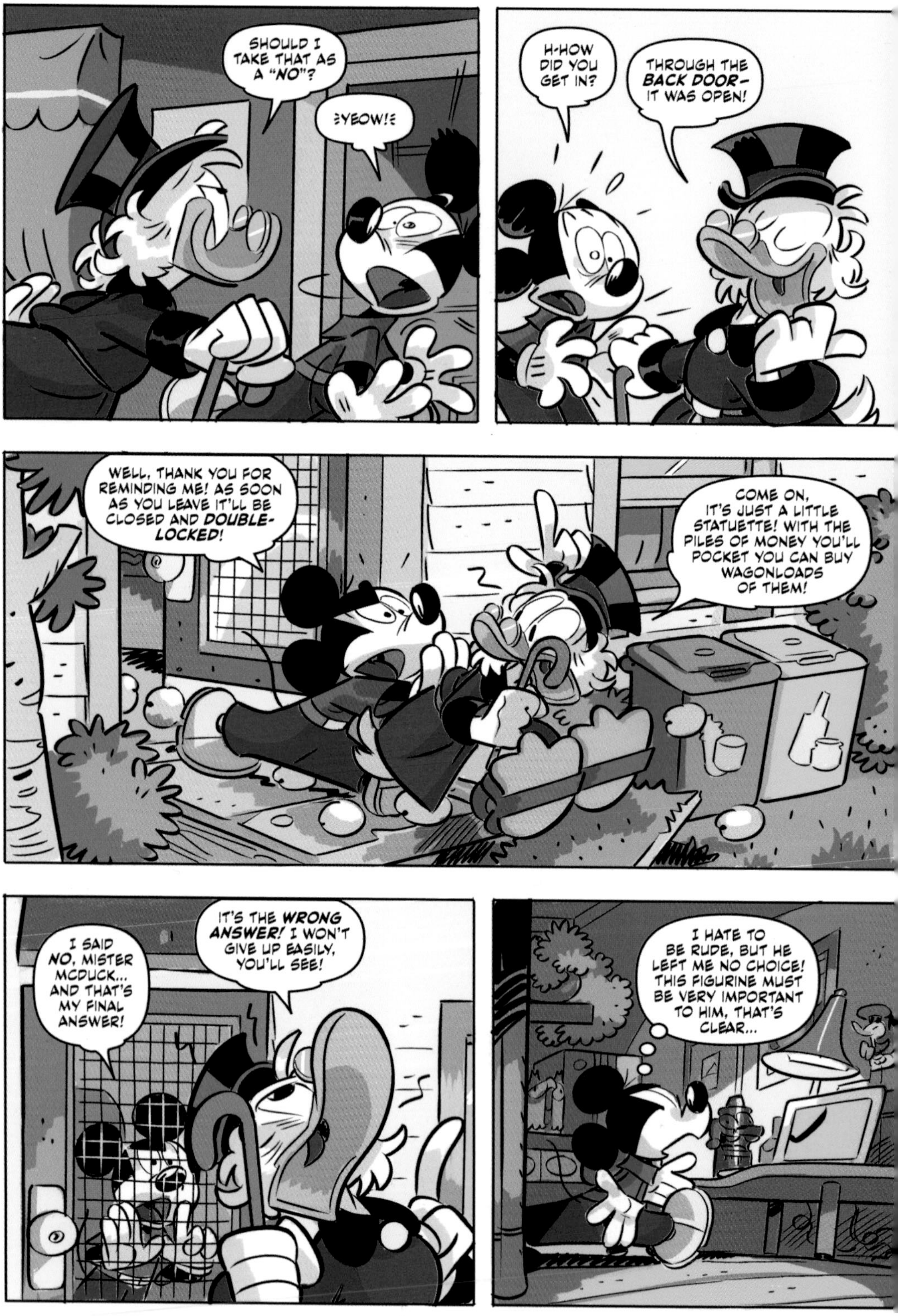
SHOULD I TAKE THAT AS A "NO"?
≷YEOW!≶
H-HOW DID YOU GET IN?
THROUGH THE BACK DOOR– IT WAS OPEN!
WELL, THANK YOU FOR REMINDING ME! AS SOON AS YOU LEAVE IT'LL BE CLOSED AND DOUBLE-LOCKED!
COME ON, IT'S JUST A LITTLE STATUETTE! WITH THE PILES OF MONEY YOU'LL POCKET YOU CAN BUY WAGONLOADS OF THEM!
I SAID NO, MISTER MCDUCK... AND THAT'S MY FINAL ANSWER!
IT'S THE WRONG ANSWER! I WON'T GIVE UP EASILY, YOU'LL SEE!
I HATE TO BE RUDE, BUT HE LEFT ME NO CHOICE! THIS FIGURINE MUST BE VERY IMPORTANT TO HIM, THAT'S CLEAR...

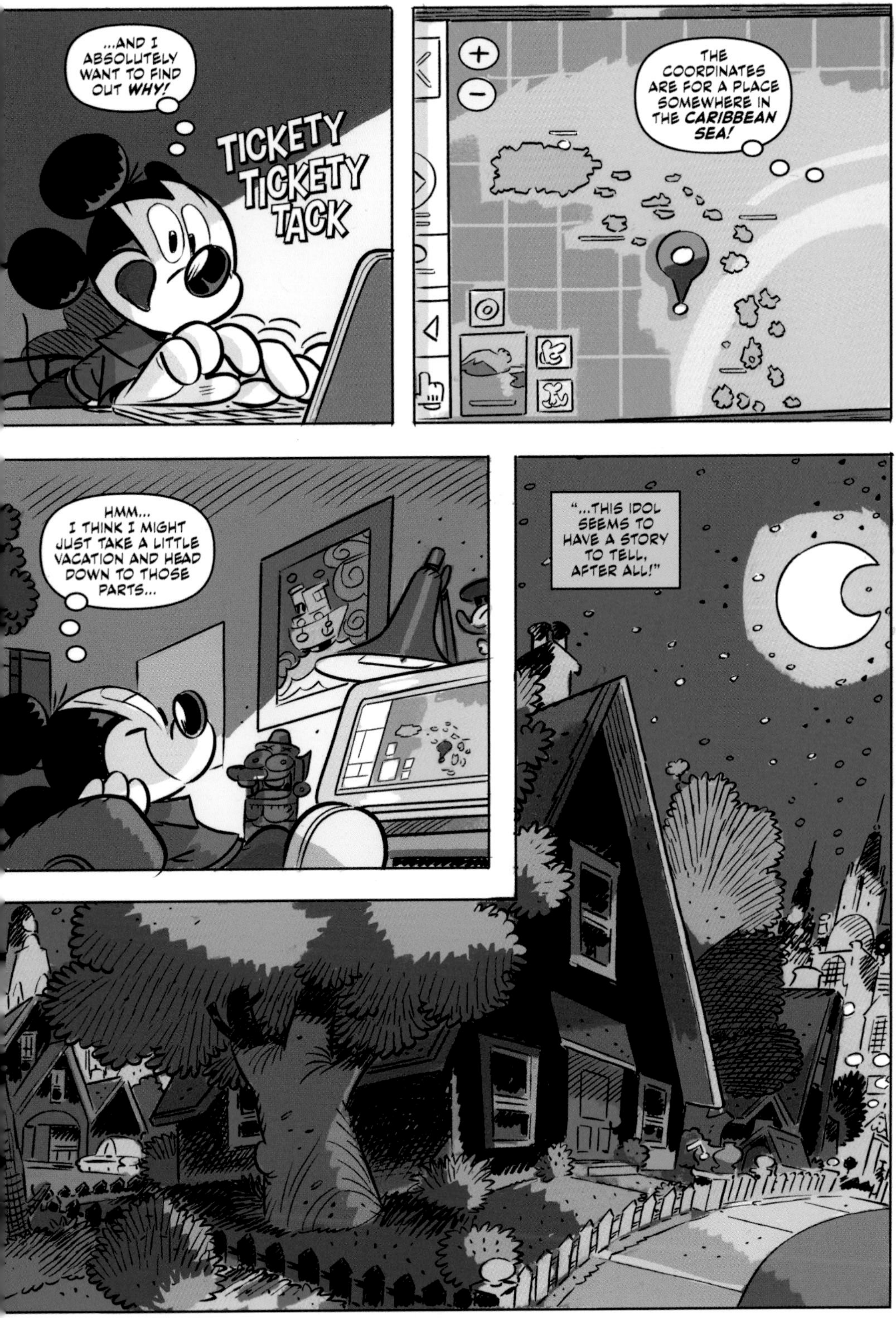
...AND I ABSOLUTELY WANT TO FIND OUT *WHY!*
TICKETY TICKETY TACK
THE COORDINATES ARE FOR A PLACE SOMEWHERE IN THE *CARIBBEAN SEA!*
HMM... I THINK I MIGHT JUST TAKE A LITTLE VACATION AND HEAD DOWN TO THOSE PARTS...
"...THIS IDOL SEEMS TO HAVE A STORY TO TELL, AFTER ALL!"

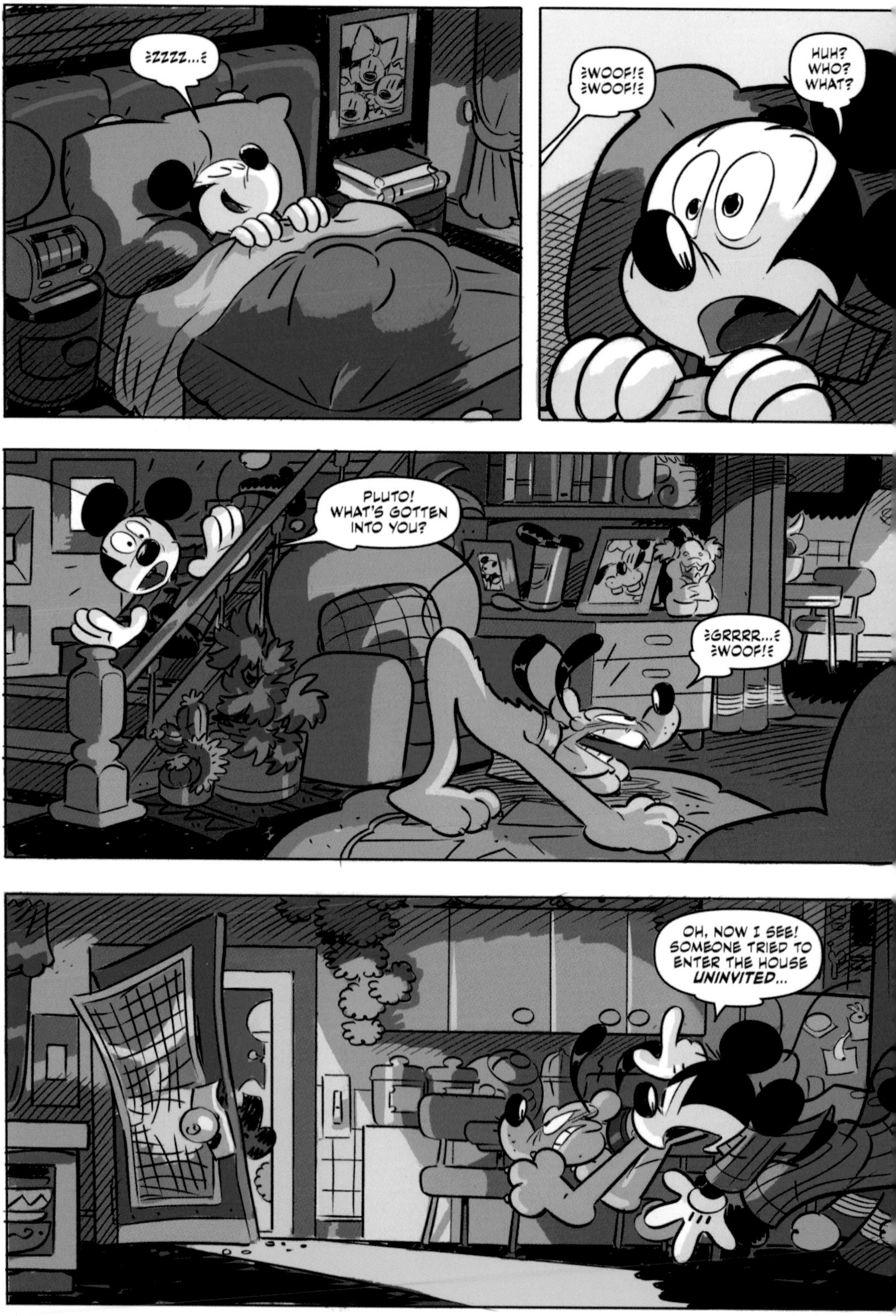
ZZZZ...
WOOF! WOOF!
HUH? WHO? WHAT?
PLUTO! WHAT'S GOTTEN INTO YOU?
GRRRR... WOOF!
OH, NOW I SEE! SOMEONE TRIED TO ENTER THE HOUSE *UNINVITED*...

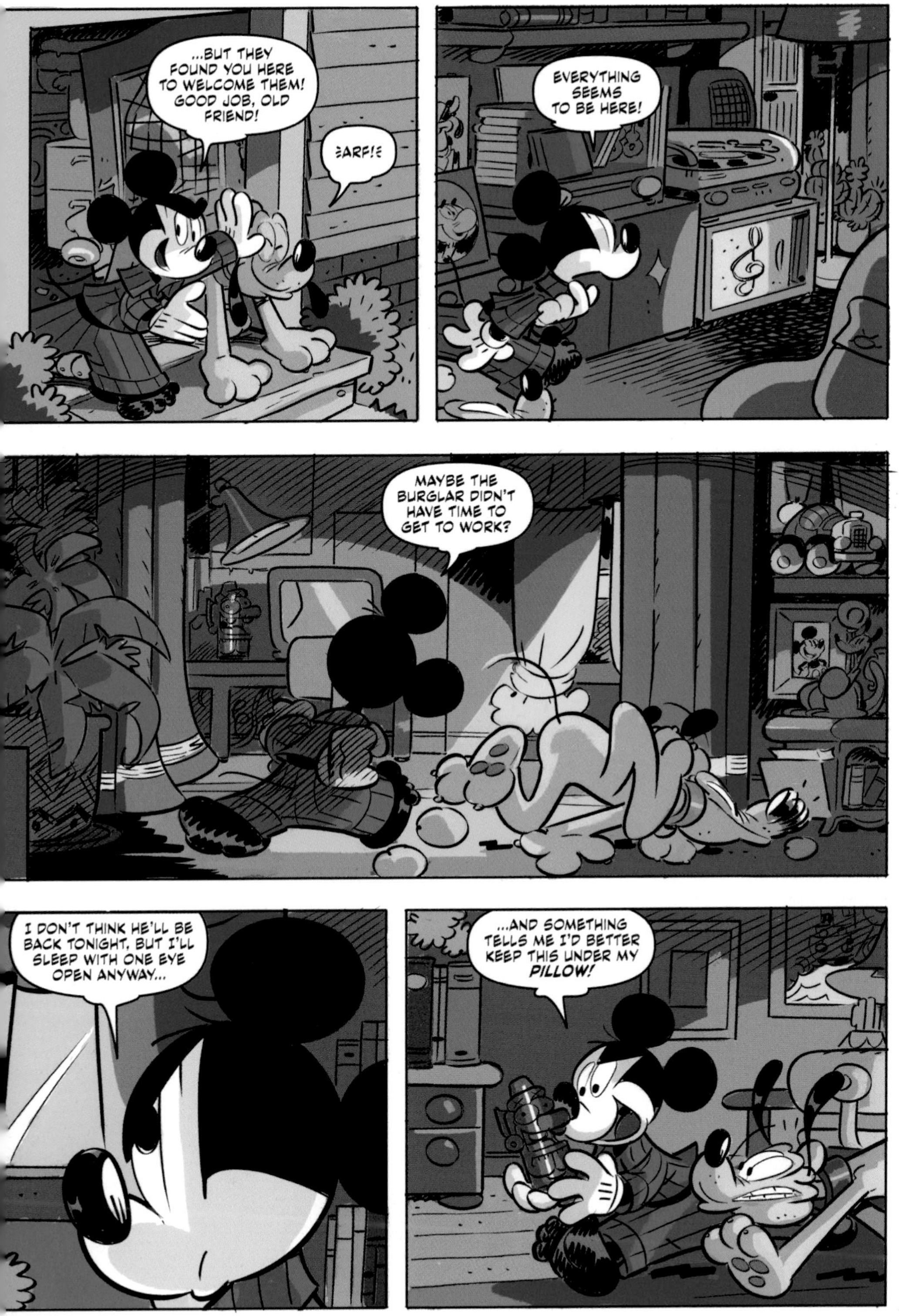
...BUT THEY FOUND YOU HERE TO WELCOME THEM! GOOD JOB, OLD FRIEND!
ARF!
EVERYTHING SEEMS TO BE HERE!
MAYBE THE BURGLAR DIDN'T HAVE TIME TO GET TO WORK?
I DON'T THINK HE'LL BE BACK TONIGHT, BUT I'LL SLEEP WITH ONE EYE OPEN ANYWAY...
...AND SOMETHING TELLS ME I'D BETTER KEEP THIS UNDER MY PILLOW!

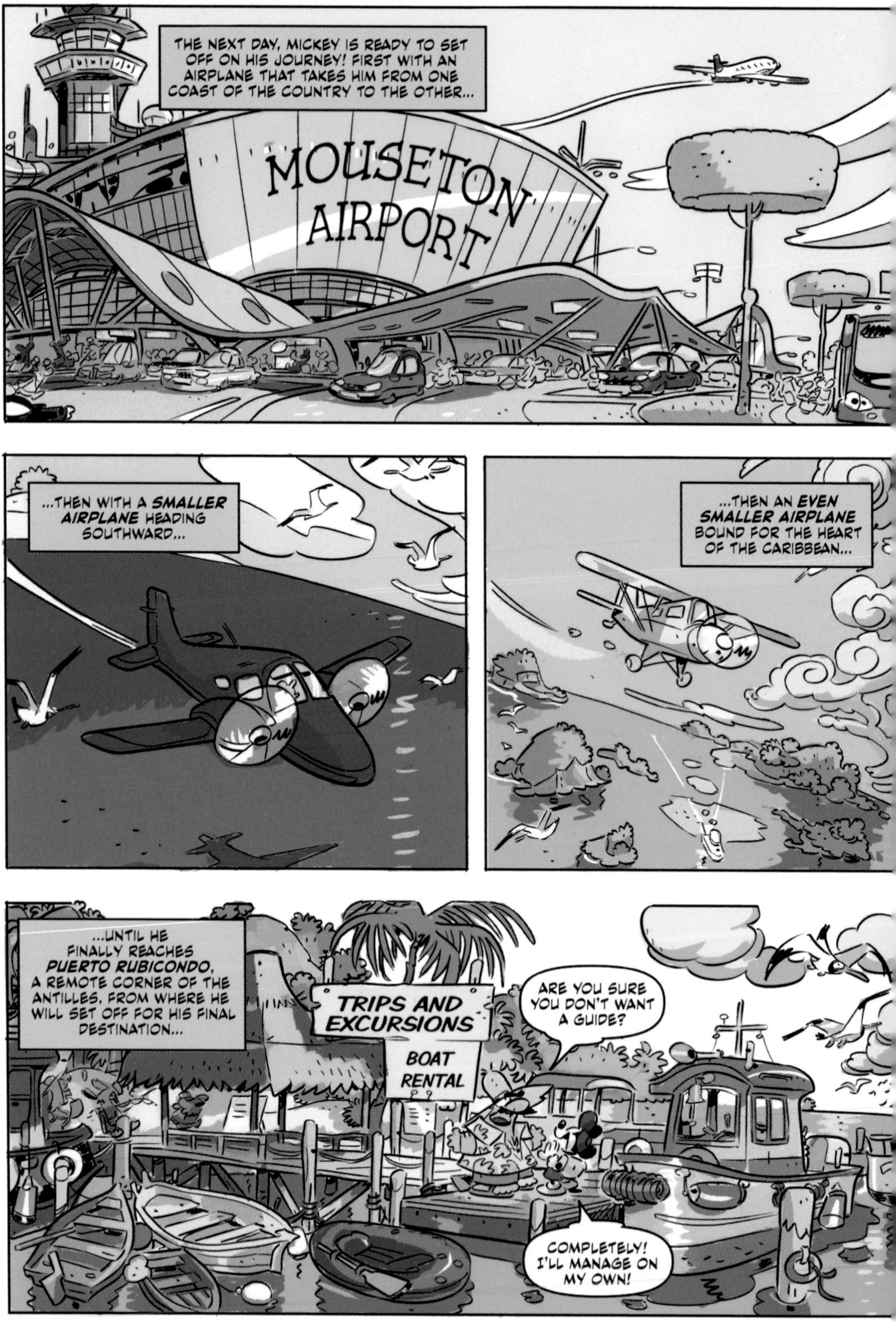
THE NEXT DAY, MICKEY IS READY TO SET OFF ON HIS JOURNEY! FIRST WITH AN AIRPLANE THAT TAKES HIM FROM ONE COAST OF THE COUNTRY TO THE OTHER...
MOUSETON AIRPORT
...THEN WITH A *SMALLER AIRPLANE* HEADING SOUTHWARD...
...THEN AN *EVEN SMALLER AIRPLANE* BOUND FOR THE HEART OF THE CARIBBEAN...
...UNTIL HE FINALLY REACHES *PUERTO RUBICONDO*, A REMOTE CORNER OF THE ANTILLES, FROM WHERE HE WILL SET OFF FOR HIS FINAL DESTINATION...
TRIPS AND EXCURSIONS
BOAT RENTAL
ARE YOU SURE YOU DON'T WANT A GUIDE?
COMPLETELY! I'LL MANAGE ON MY OWN!

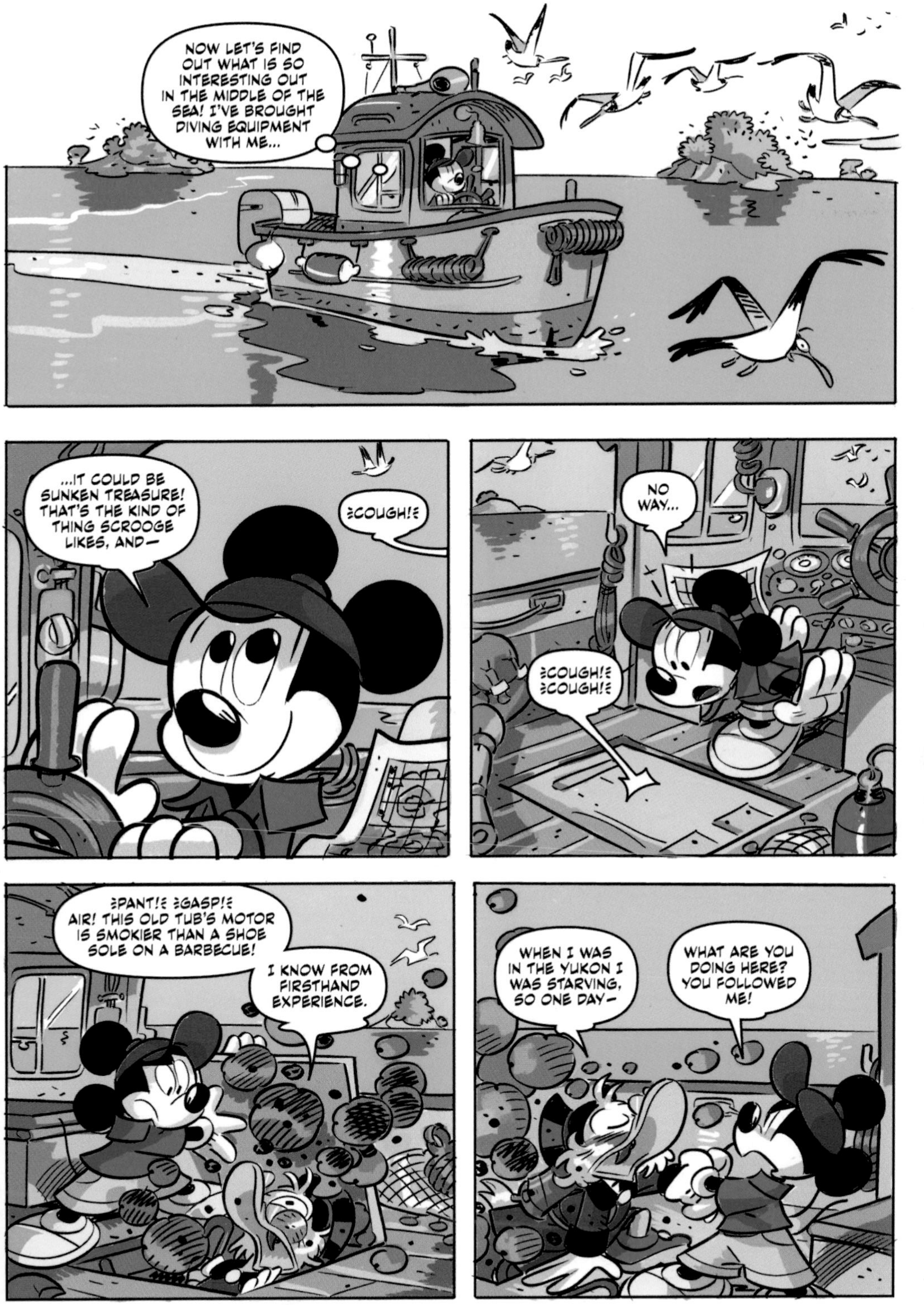
NOW LET'S FIND OUT WHAT IS SO INTERESTING OUT IN THE MIDDLE OF THE SEA! I'VE BROUGHT DIVING EQUIPMENT WITH ME...
...IT COULD BE SUNKEN TREASURE! THAT'S THE KIND OF THING SCROOGE LIKES, AND—
COUGH!
NO WAY...
COUGH! COUGH!
PANT! GASP! AIR! THIS OLD TUB'S MOTOR IS SMOKIER THAN A SHOE SOLE ON A BARBECUE!
I KNOW FROM FIRSTHAND EXPERIENCE.
WHAT ARE YOU DOING HERE? YOU FOLLOWED ME!
WHEN I WAS IN THE YUKON I WAS STARVING, SO ONE DAY—

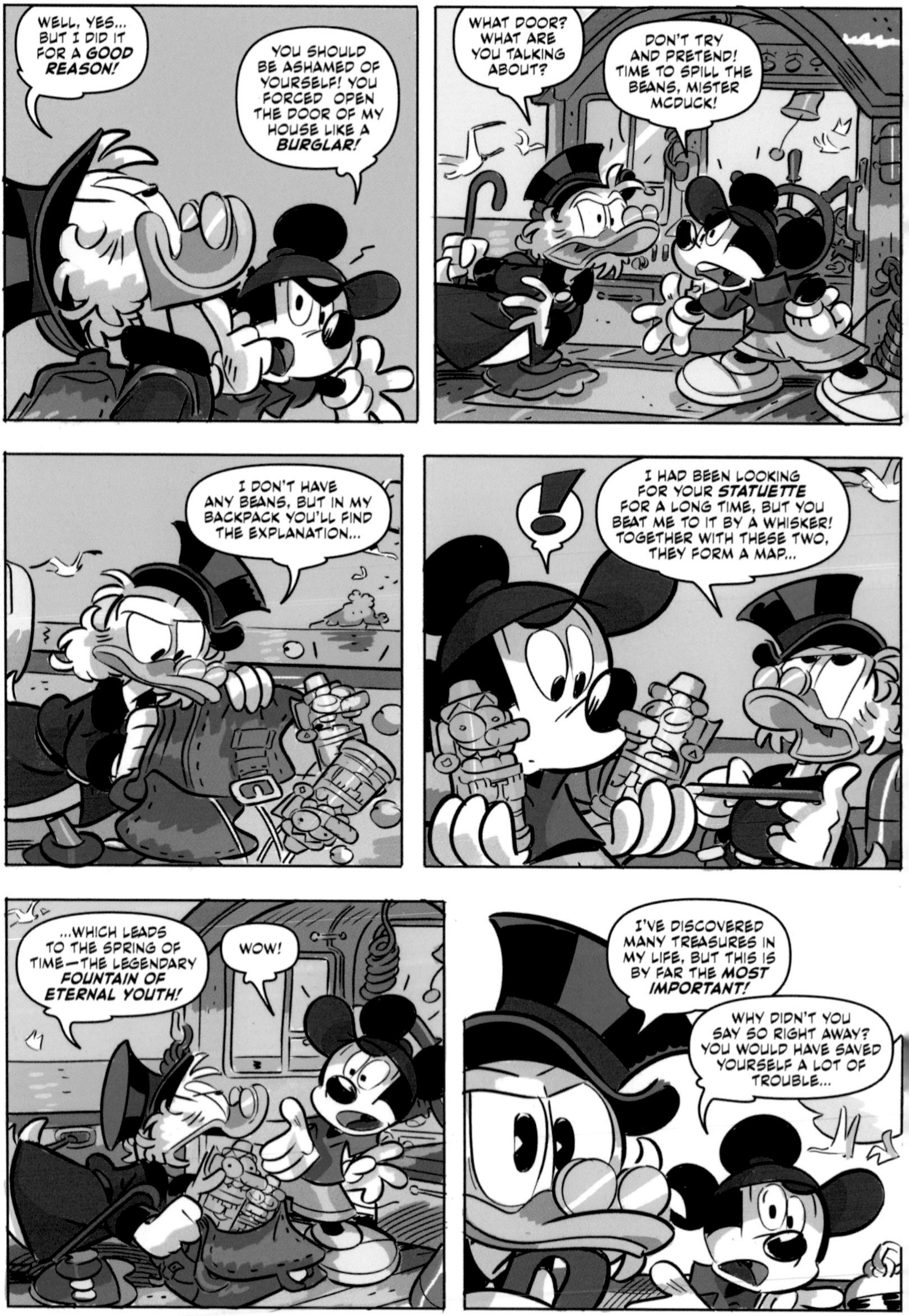
WELL, YES... BUT I DID IT FOR A **GOOD REASON!**
YOU SHOULD BE ASHAMED OF YOURSELF! YOU FORCED OPEN THE DOOR OF MY HOUSE LIKE A **BURGLAR!**
WHAT DOOR? WHAT ARE YOU TALKING ABOUT?
DON'T TRY AND PRETEND! TIME TO SPILL THE BEANS, MISTER MCDUCK!
I DON'T HAVE ANY BEANS, BUT IN MY BACKPACK YOU'LL FIND THE EXPLANATION...
!
I HAD BEEN LOOKING FOR YOUR **STATUETTE** FOR A LONG TIME, BUT YOU BEAT ME TO IT BY A WHISKER! TOGETHER WITH THESE TWO, THEY FORM A MAP...
...WHICH LEADS TO THE SPRING OF TIME—THE LEGENDARY **FOUNTAIN OF ETERNAL YOUTH!**
WOW!
I'VE DISCOVERED MANY TREASURES IN MY LIFE, BUT THIS IS BY FAR THE **MOST IMPORTANT!**
WHY DIDN'T YOU SAY SO RIGHT AWAY? YOU WOULD HAVE SAVED YOURSELF A LOT OF TROUBLE...

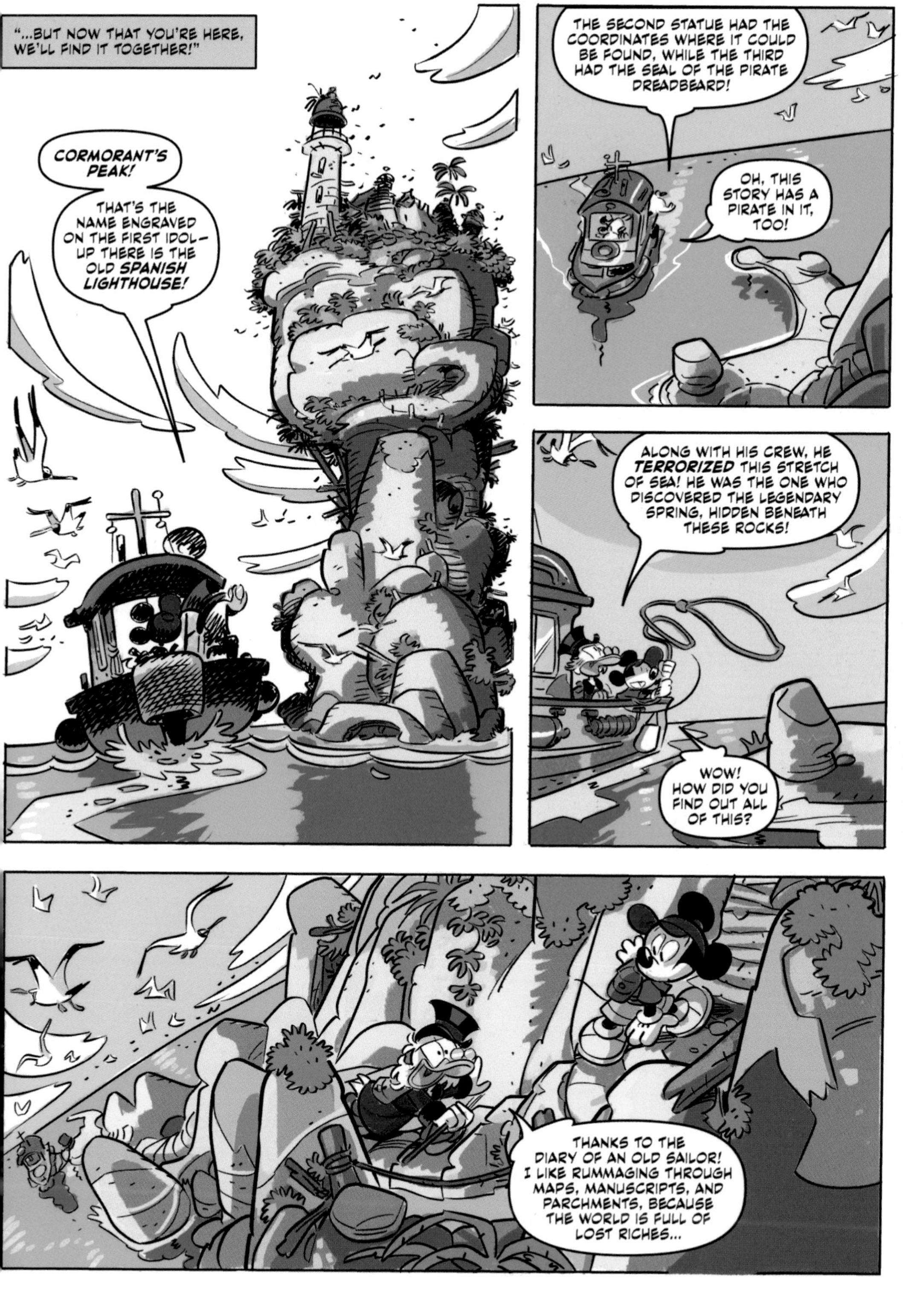
"...BUT NOW THAT YOU'RE HERE, WE'LL FIND IT TOGETHER!"
CORMORANT'S PEAK!
THAT'S THE NAME ENGRAVED ON THE FIRST IDOL— UP THERE IS THE OLD SPANISH LIGHTHOUSE!
THE SECOND STATUE HAD THE COORDINATES WHERE IT COULD BE FOUND, WHILE THE THIRD HAD THE SEAL OF THE PIRATE DREADBEARD!
OH, THIS STORY HAS A PIRATE IN IT, TOO!
ALONG WITH HIS CREW, HE TERRORIZED THIS STRETCH OF SEA! HE WAS THE ONE WHO DISCOVERED THE LEGENDARY SPRING, HIDDEN BENEATH THESE ROCKS!
WOW! HOW DID YOU FIND OUT ALL OF THIS?
THANKS TO THE DIARY OF AN OLD SAILOR! I LIKE RUMMAGING THROUGH MAPS, MANUSCRIPTS, AND PARCHMENTS, BECAUSE THE WORLD IS FULL OF LOST RICHES...

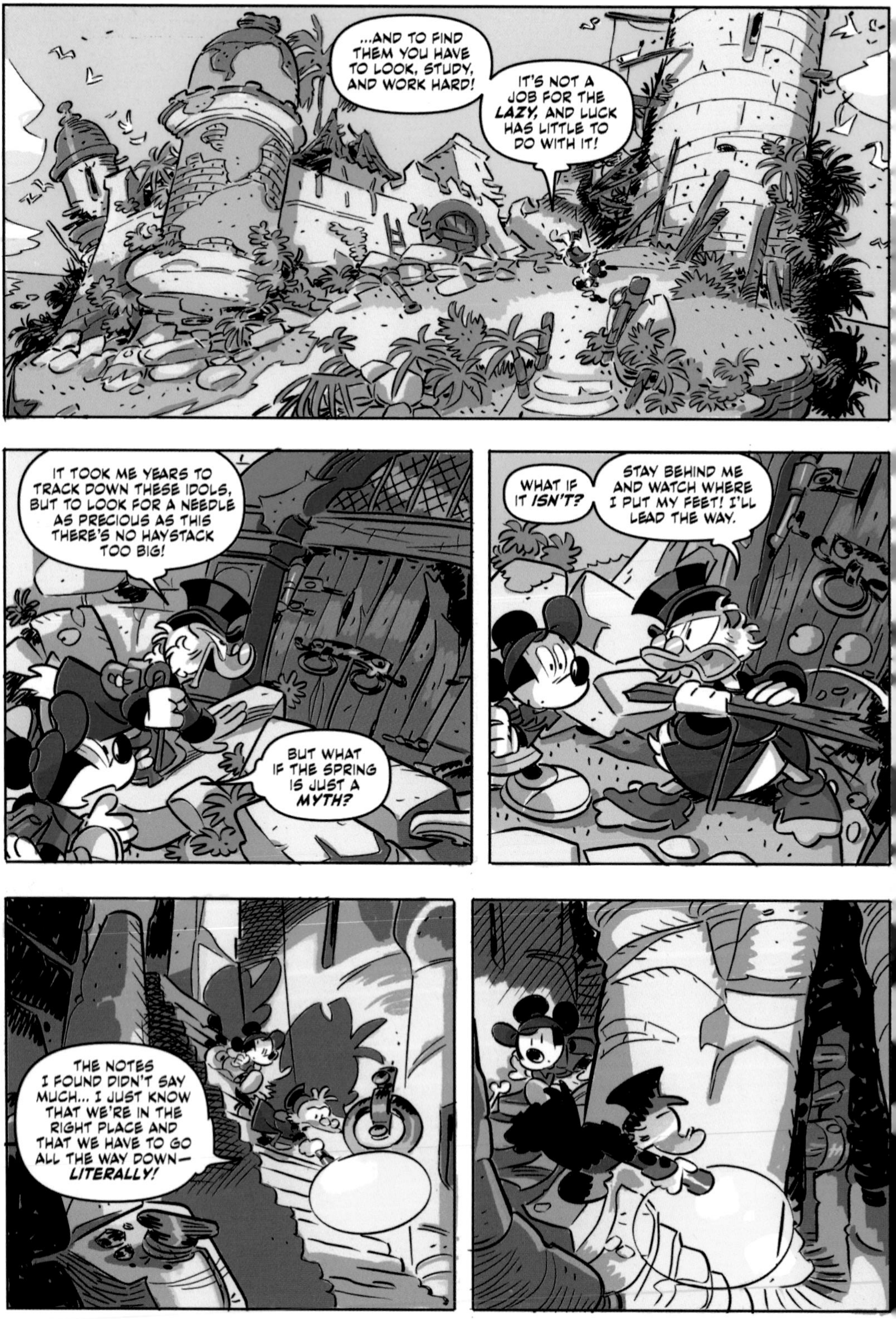
...AND TO FIND THEM YOU HAVE TO LOOK, STUDY, AND WORK HARD!
IT'S NOT A JOB FOR THE *LAZY*, AND LUCK HAS LITTLE TO DO WITH IT!
IT TOOK ME YEARS TO TRACK DOWN THESE IDOLS, BUT TO LOOK FOR A NEEDLE AS PRECIOUS AS THIS THERE'S NO HAYSTACK TOO BIG!
BUT WHAT IF THE SPRING IS JUST A *MYTH?*
WHAT IF IT *ISN'T?*
STAY BEHIND ME AND WATCH WHERE I PUT MY FEET! I'LL LEAD THE WAY.
THE NOTES I FOUND DIDN'T SAY MUCH... I JUST KNOW THAT WE'RE IN THE RIGHT PLACE AND THAT WE HAVE TO GO ALL THE WAY DOWN— *LITERALLY!*

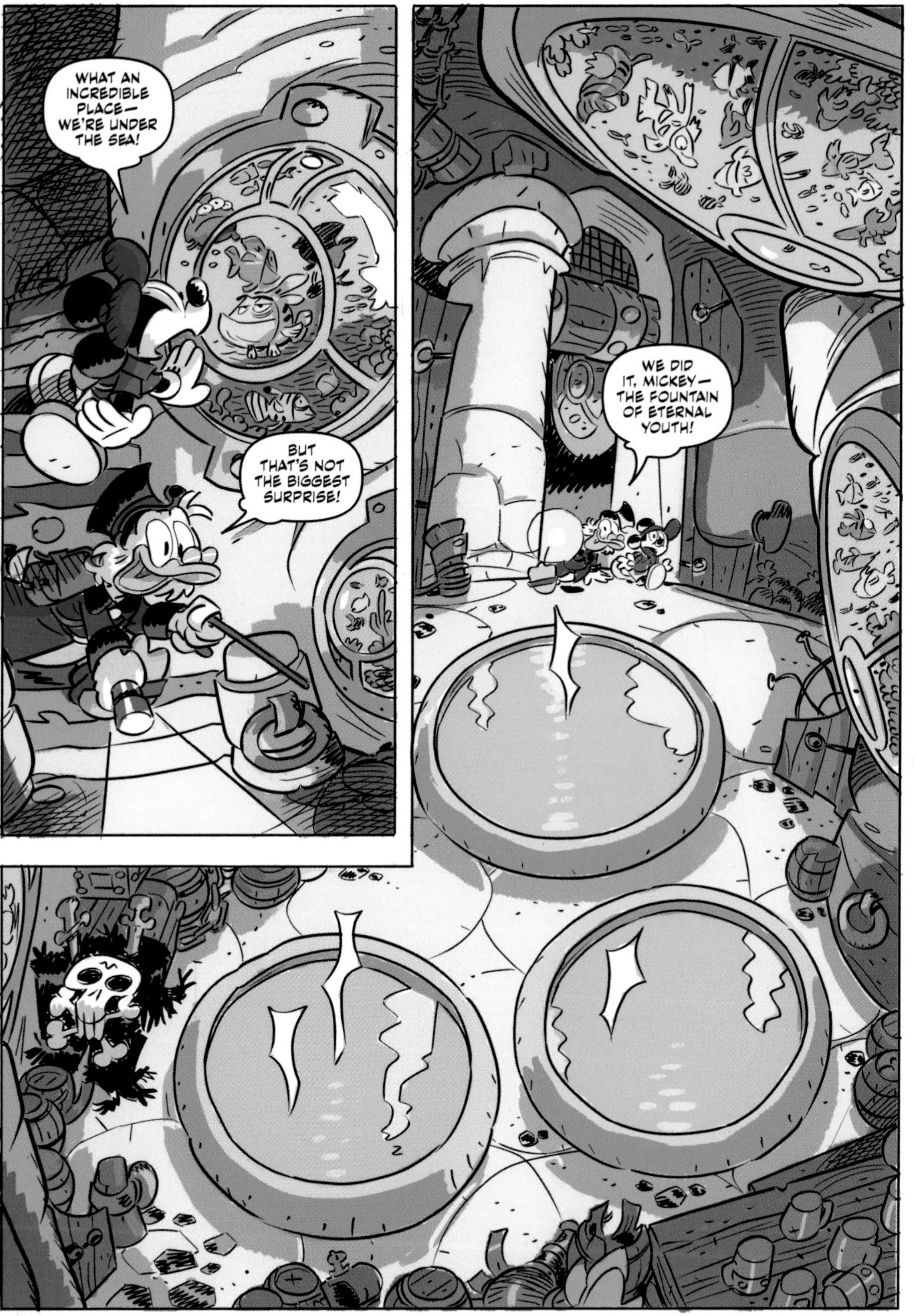
WHAT AN INCREDIBLE PLACE— WE'RE UNDER THE SEA!
BUT THAT'S NOT THE BIGGEST SURPRISE!
WE DID IT, MICKEY— THE FOUNTAIN OF ETERNAL YOUTH!

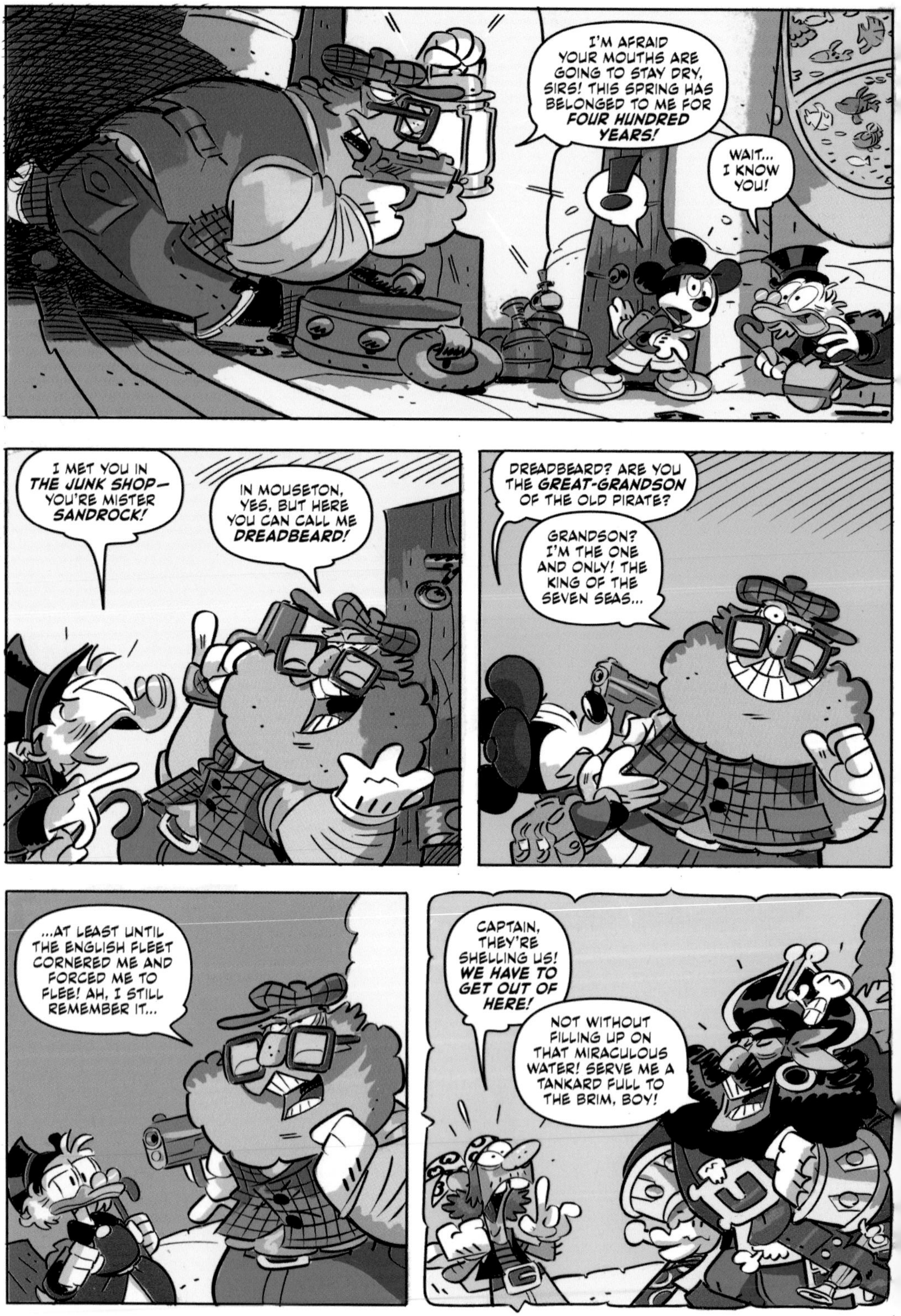
I'M AFRAID YOUR MOUTHS ARE GOING TO STAY DRY, SIRS! THIS SPRING HAS BELONGED TO ME FOR FOUR HUNDRED YEARS!
!
WAIT... I KNOW YOU!
I MET YOU IN THE JUNK SHOP— YOU'RE MISTER SANDROCK!
IN MOUSETON, YES, BUT HERE YOU CAN CALL ME DREADBEARD!
DREADBEARD? ARE YOU THE GREAT-GRANDSON OF THE OLD PIRATE?
GRANDSON? I'M THE ONE AND ONLY! THE KING OF THE SEVEN SEAS...
...AT LEAST UNTIL THE ENGLISH FLEET CORNERED ME AND FORCED ME TO FLEE! AH, I STILL REMEMBER IT...
CAPTAIN, THEY'RE SHELLING US! WE HAVE TO GET OUT OF HERE!
NOT WITHOUT FILLING UP ON THAT MIRACULOUS WATER! SERVE ME A TANKARD FULL TO THE BRIM, BOY!

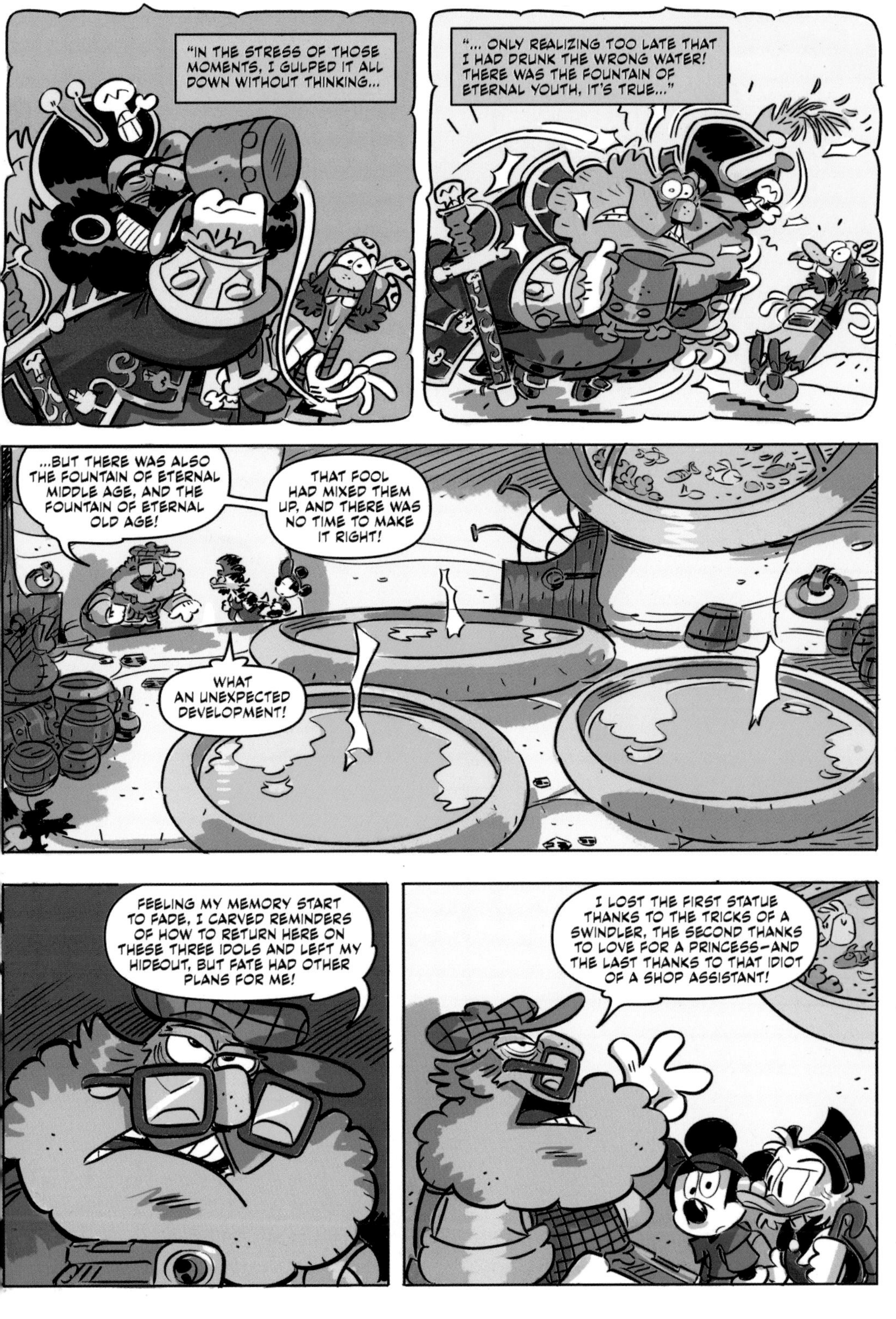
"IN THE STRESS OF THOSE MOMENTS, I GULPED IT ALL DOWN WITHOUT THINKING...
"... ONLY REALIZING TOO LATE THAT I HAD DRUNK THE WRONG WATER! THERE WAS THE FOUNTAIN OF ETERNAL YOUTH, IT'S TRUE..."
...BUT THERE WAS ALSO THE FOUNTAIN OF ETERNAL MIDDLE AGE, AND THE FOUNTAIN OF ETERNAL OLD AGE!
THAT FOOL HAD MIXED THEM UP, AND THERE WAS NO TIME TO MAKE IT RIGHT!
WHAT AN UNEXPECTED DEVELOPMENT!
FEELING MY MEMORY START TO FADE, I CARVED REMINDERS OF HOW TO RETURN HERE ON THESE THREE IDOLS AND LEFT MY HIDEOUT, BUT FATE HAD OTHER PLANS FOR ME!
I LOST THE FIRST STATUE THANKS TO THE TRICKS OF A SWINDLER, THE SECOND THANKS TO LOVE FOR A PRINCESS—AND THE LAST THANKS TO THAT IDIOT OF A SHOP ASSISTANT!

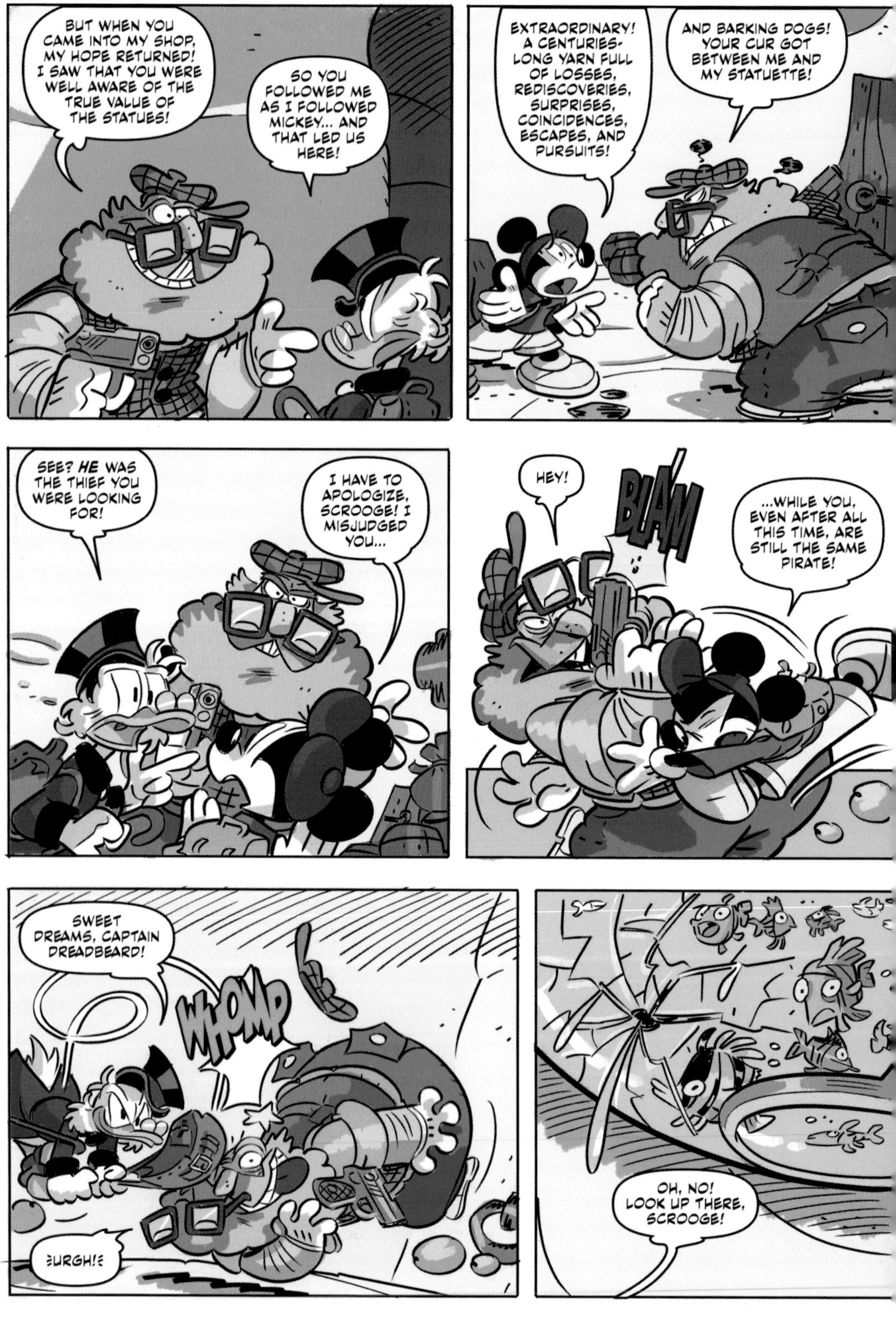
BUT WHEN YOU CAME INTO MY SHOP, MY HOPE RETURNED! I SAW THAT YOU WERE WELL AWARE OF THE TRUE VALUE OF THE STATUES!
SO YOU FOLLOWED ME AS I FOLLOWED MICKEY... AND THAT LED US HERE!
EXTRAORDINARY! A CENTURIES-LONG YARN FULL OF LOSSES, REDISCOVERIES, SURPRISES, COINCIDENCES, ESCAPES, AND PURSUITS!
AND BARKING DOGS! YOUR CUR GOT BETWEEN ME AND MY STATUETTE!
SEE? HE WAS THE THIEF YOU WERE LOOKING FOR!
I HAVE TO APOLOGIZE, SCROOGE! I MISJUDGED YOU...
HEY!
BLAM
...WHILE YOU, EVEN AFTER ALL THIS TIME, ARE STILL THE SAME PIRATE!
SWEET DREAMS, CAPTAIN DREADBEARD!
WHOMP
URGH!
OH, NO! LOOK UP THERE, SCROOGE!

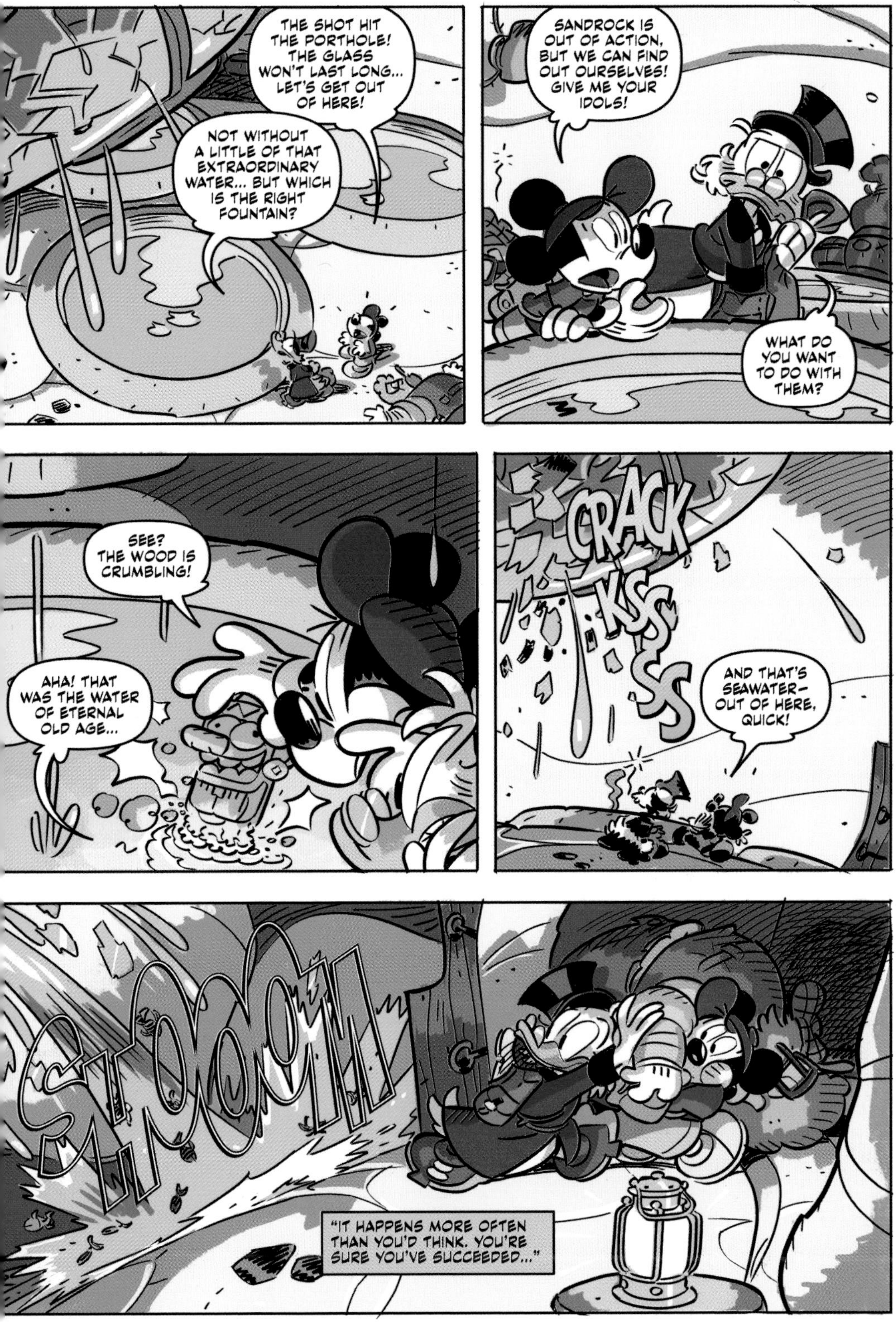

THE SHOT HIT THE PORTHOLE! THE GLASS WON'T LAST LONG... LET'S GET OUT OF HERE!
NOT WITHOUT A LITTLE OF THAT EXTRAORDINARY WATER... BUT WHICH IS THE RIGHT FOUNTAIN?
SANDROCK IS OUT OF ACTION, BUT WE CAN FIND OUT OURSELVES! GIVE ME YOUR IDOLS!
WHAT DO YOU WANT TO DO WITH THEM?
SEE? THE WOOD IS CRUMBLING!
AHA! THAT WAS THE WATER OF ETERNAL OLD AGE...
CRACK
KSSSS
AND THAT'S SEAWATER— OUT OF HERE, QUICK!
SPLOOOOM
"IT HAPPENS MORE OFTEN THAN YOU'D THINK. YOU'RE SURE YOU'VE SUCCEEDED..."

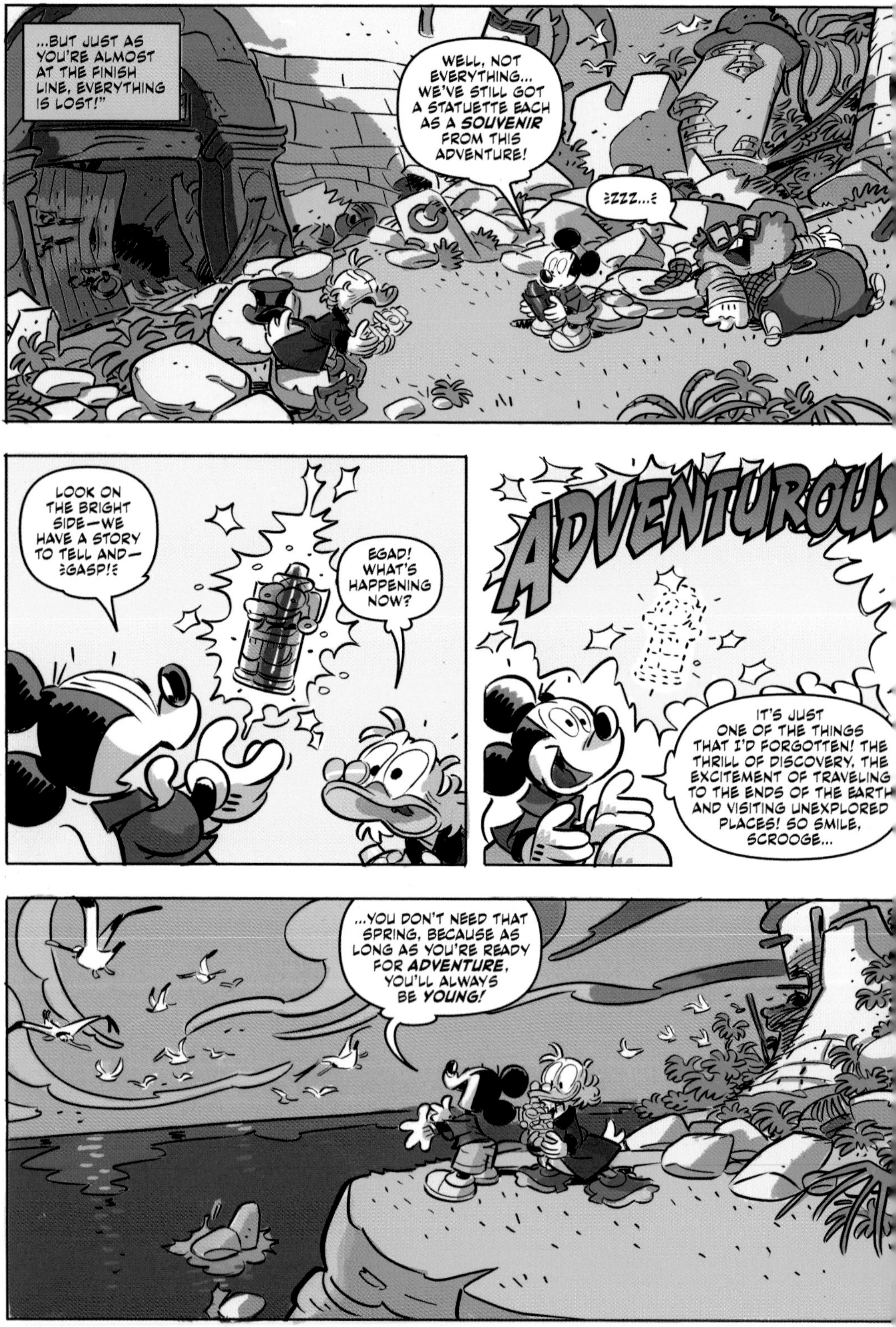
...BUT JUST AS YOU'RE ALMOST AT THE FINISH LINE, EVERYTHING IS LOST!"
WELL, NOT EVERYTHING... WE'VE STILL GOT A STATUETTE EACH AS A SOUVENIR FROM THIS ADVENTURE!
ZZZ...
LOOK ON THE BRIGHT SIDE—WE HAVE A STORY TO TELL AND— GASP!
EGAD! WHAT'S HAPPENING NOW?
ADVENTUROUS
IT'S JUST ONE OF THE THINGS THAT I'D FORGOTTEN! THE THRILL OF DISCOVERY. THE EXCITEMENT OF TRAVELING TO THE ENDS OF THE EARTH AND VISITING UNEXPLORED PLACES! SO SMILE, SCROOGE...
...YOU DON'T NEED THAT SPRING, BECAUSE AS LONG AS YOU'RE READY FOR ADVENTURE, YOU'LL ALWAYS BE YOUNG!

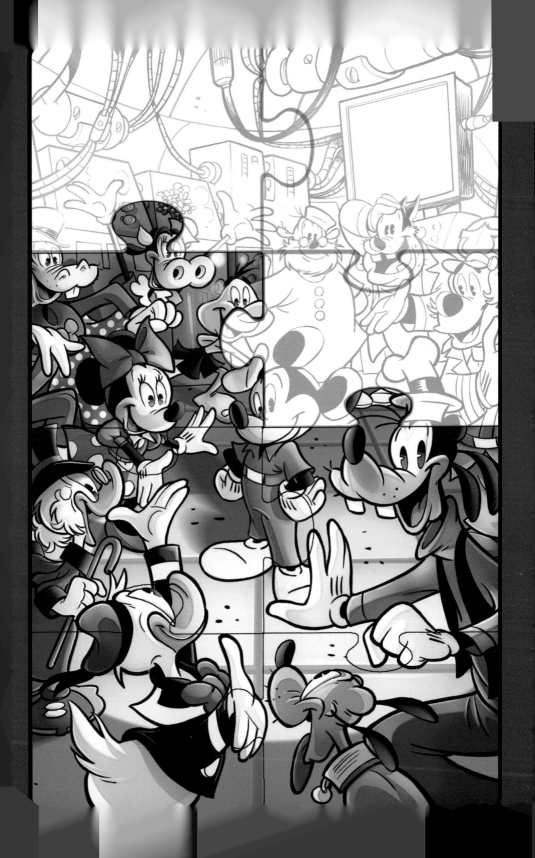

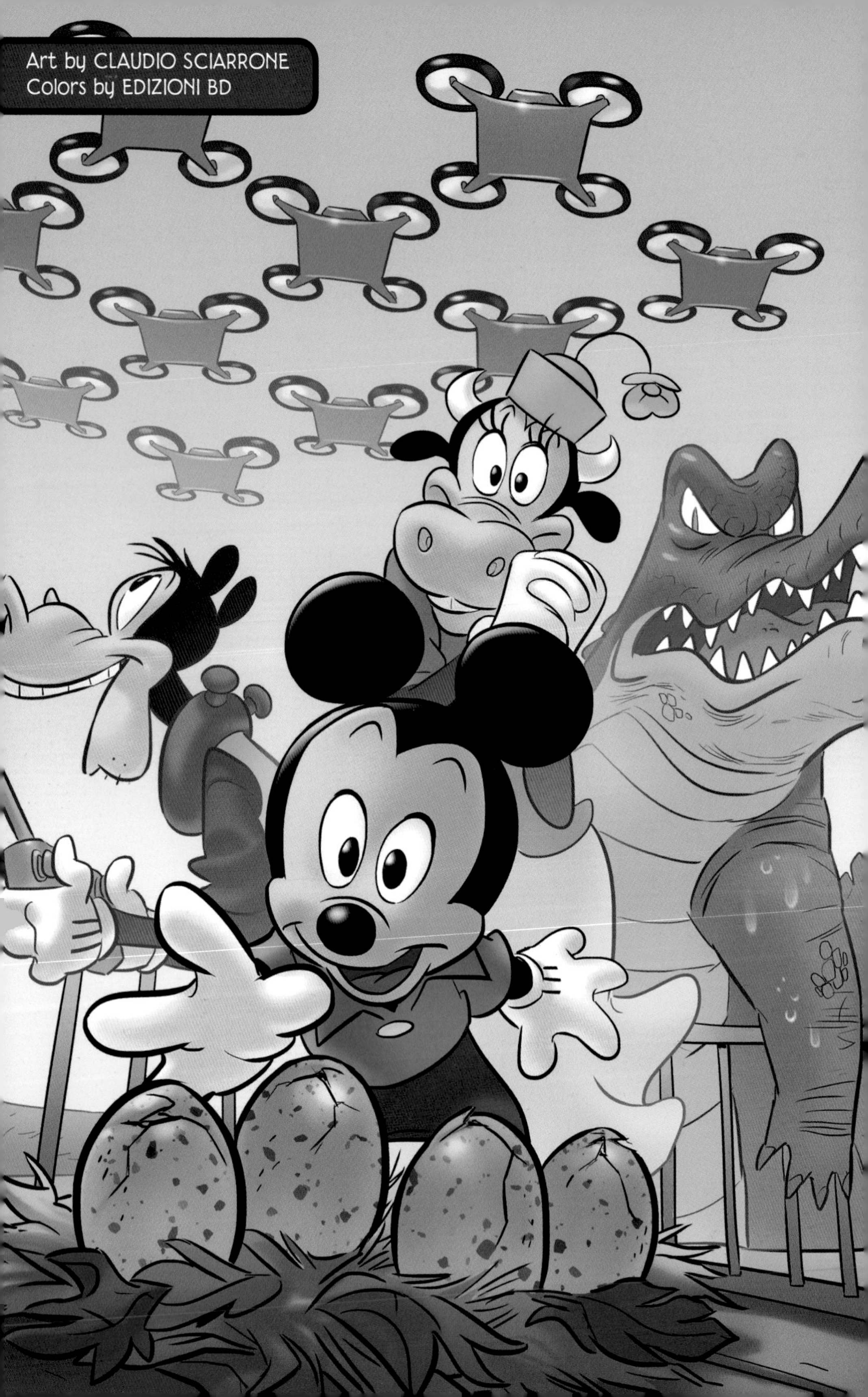
Art by CLAUDIO SCIARRONE
Colors by EDIZIONI BD

CHAPTER 6: THE QUEEN OF THE RIVER

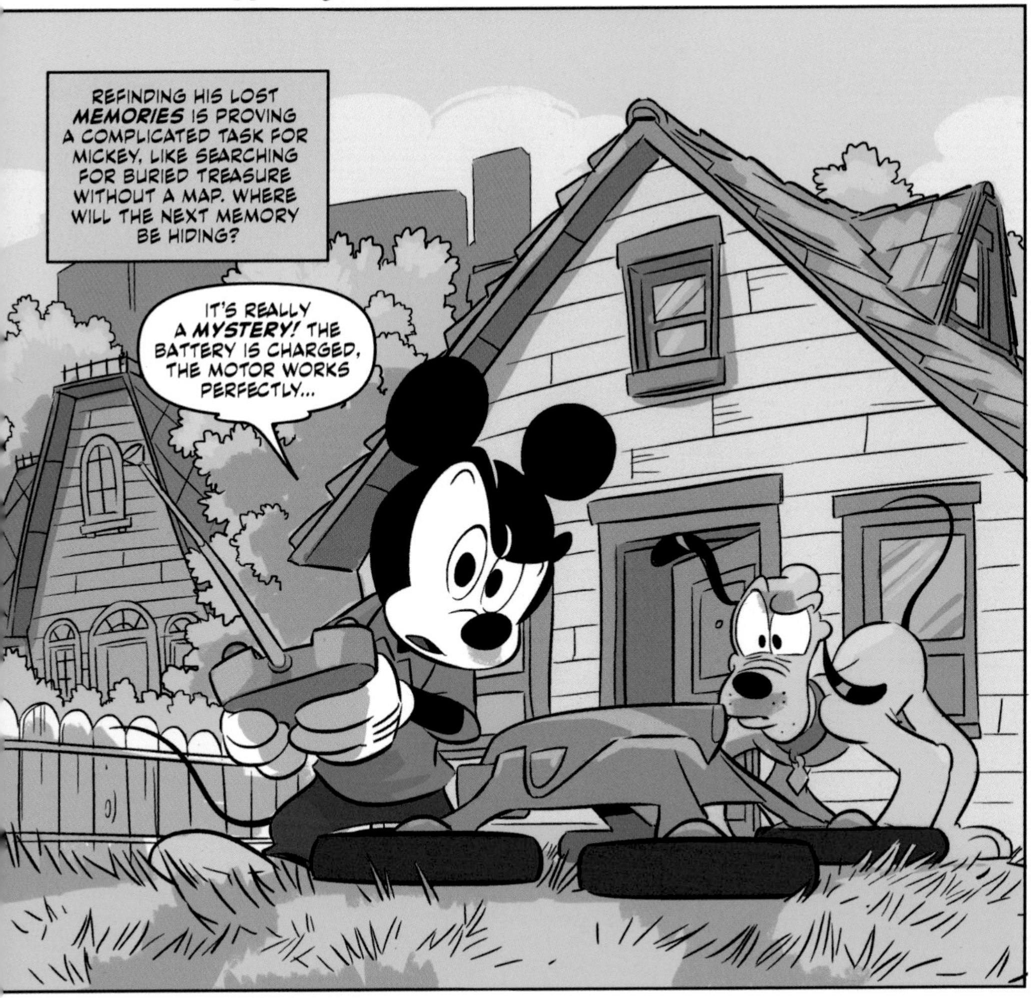
REFINDING HIS LOST MEMORIES IS PROVING A COMPLICATED TASK FOR MICKEY, LIKE SEARCHING FOR BURIED TREASURE WITHOUT A MAP. WHERE WILL THE NEXT MEMORY BE HIDING?
IT'S REALLY A MYSTERY! THE BATTERY IS CHARGED, THE MOTOR WORKS PERFECTLY...

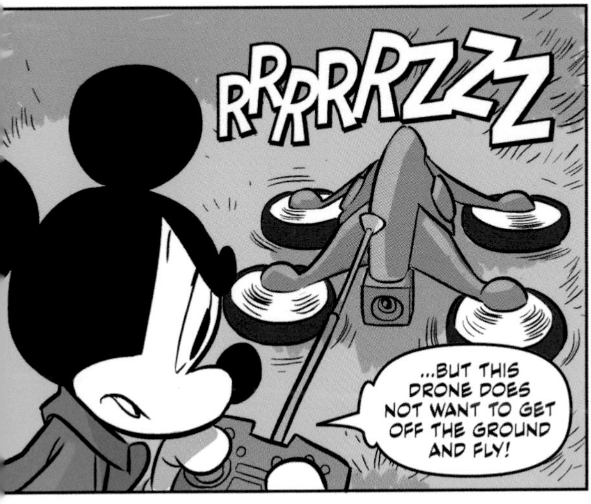
RRRRRZZZ
...BUT THIS DRONE DOES NOT WANT TO GET OFF THE GROUND AND FLY!

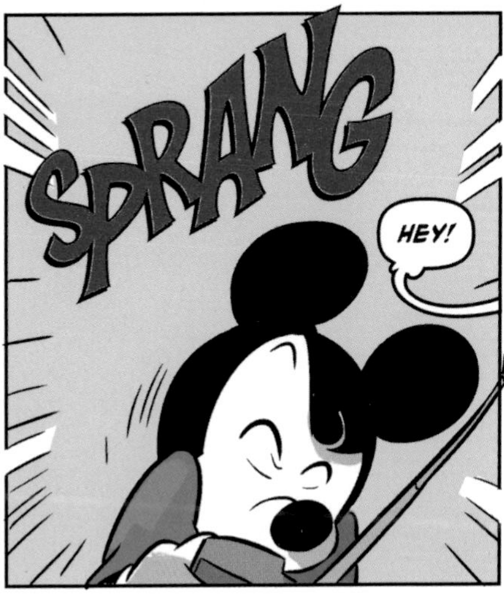
SPRANG
HEY!

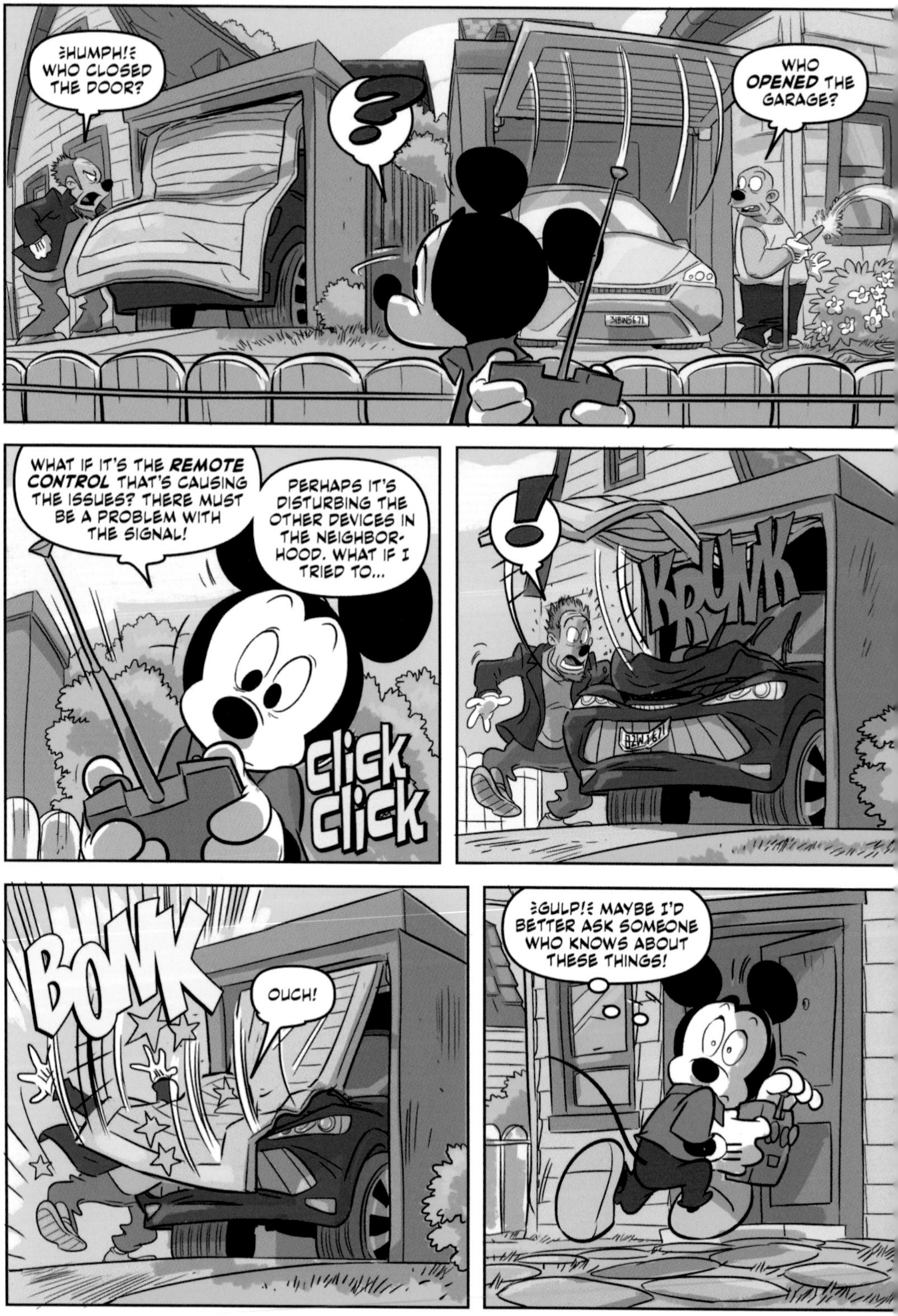

HUMPH! WHO CLOSED THE DOOR?
?
WHO OPENED THE GARAGE?
WHAT IF IT'S THE REMOTE CONTROL THAT'S CAUSING THE ISSUES? THERE MUST BE A PROBLEM WITH THE SIGNAL!
PERHAPS IT'S DISTURBING THE OTHER DEVICES IN THE NEIGHBOR-HOOD. WHAT IF I TRIED TO...
CLICK CLICK
!
KRUNK
BONK
OUCH!
GULP! MAYBE I'D BETTER ASK SOMEONE WHO KNOWS ABOUT THESE THINGS!

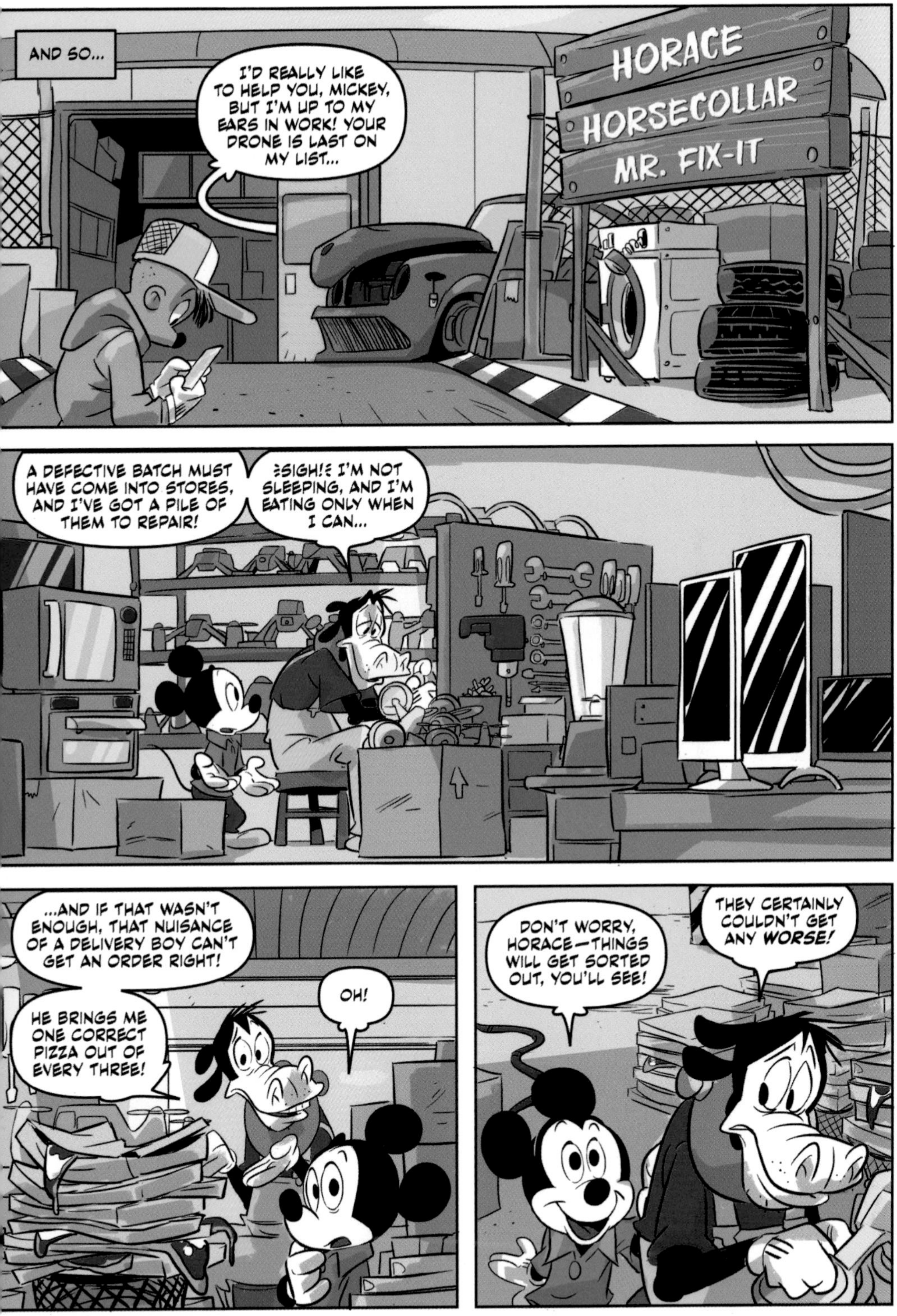
AND SO...
I'D REALLY LIKE TO HELP YOU, MICKEY, BUT I'M UP TO MY EARS IN WORK! YOUR DRONE IS LAST ON MY LIST...
HORACE HORSECOLLAR MR. FIX-IT
A DEFECTIVE BATCH MUST HAVE COME INTO STORES, AND I'VE GOT A PILE OF THEM TO REPAIR!
⪖SIGH!⪕ I'M NOT SLEEPING, AND I'M EATING ONLY WHEN I CAN...
...AND IF THAT WASN'T ENOUGH, THAT NUISANCE OF A DELIVERY BOY CAN'T GET AN ORDER RIGHT!
HE BRINGS ME ONE CORRECT PIZZA OUT OF EVERY THREE!
OH!
DON'T WORRY, HORACE—THINGS WILL GET SORTED OUT, YOU'LL SEE!
THEY CERTAINLY COULDN'T GET ANY *WORSE!*

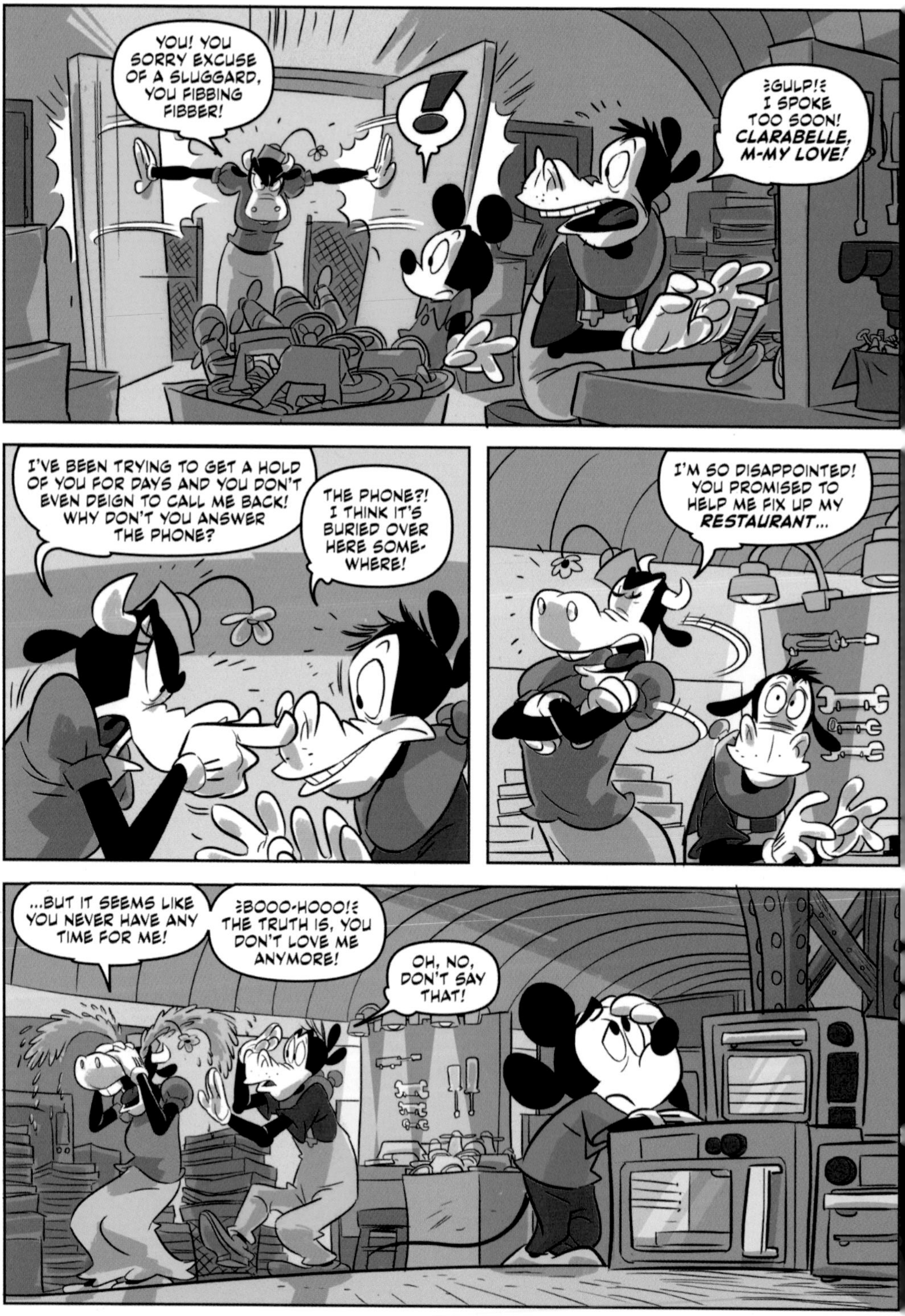
YOU! YOU SORRY EXCUSE OF A SLUGGARD, YOU FIBBING FIBBER!
!
GULP! I SPOKE TOO SOON! CLARABELLE, M-MY LOVE!
I'VE BEEN TRYING TO GET A HOLD OF YOU FOR DAYS AND YOU DON'T EVEN DEIGN TO CALL ME BACK! WHY DON'T YOU ANSWER THE PHONE?
THE PHONE?! I THINK IT'S BURIED OVER HERE SOME-WHERE!
I'M SO DISAPPOINTED! YOU PROMISED TO HELP ME FIX UP MY RESTAURANT...
...BUT IT SEEMS LIKE YOU NEVER HAVE ANY TIME FOR ME!
BOOO-HOOO! THE TRUTH IS, YOU DON'T LOVE ME ANYMORE!
OH, NO, DON'T SAY THAT!

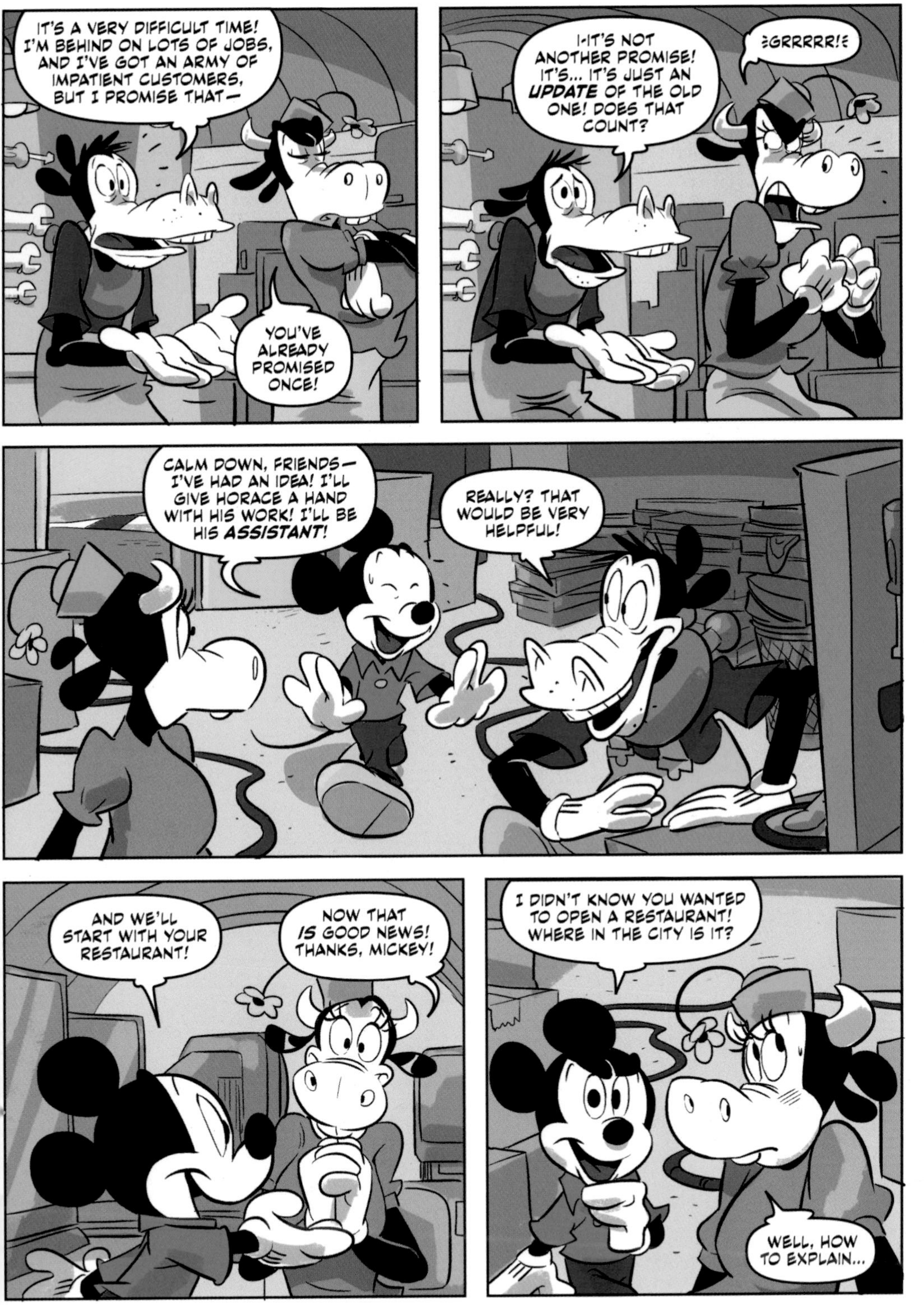
IT'S A VERY DIFFICULT TIME! I'M BEHIND ON LOTS OF JOBS, AND I'VE GOT AN ARMY OF IMPATIENT CUSTOMERS, BUT I PROMISE THAT—
YOU'VE ALREADY PROMISED ONCE!
I-IT'S NOT ANOTHER PROMISE! IT'S... IT'S JUST AN UPDATE OF THE OLD ONE! DOES THAT COUNT?
GRRRRR!
CALM DOWN, FRIENDS— I'VE HAD AN IDEA! I'LL GIVE HORACE A HAND WITH HIS WORK! I'LL BE HIS ASSISTANT!
REALLY? THAT WOULD BE VERY HELPFUL!
AND WE'LL START WITH YOUR RESTAURANT!
NOW THAT IS GOOD NEWS! THANKS, MICKEY!
I DIDN'T KNOW YOU WANTED TO OPEN A RESTAURANT! WHERE IN THE CITY IS IT?
WELL, HOW TO EXPLAIN...

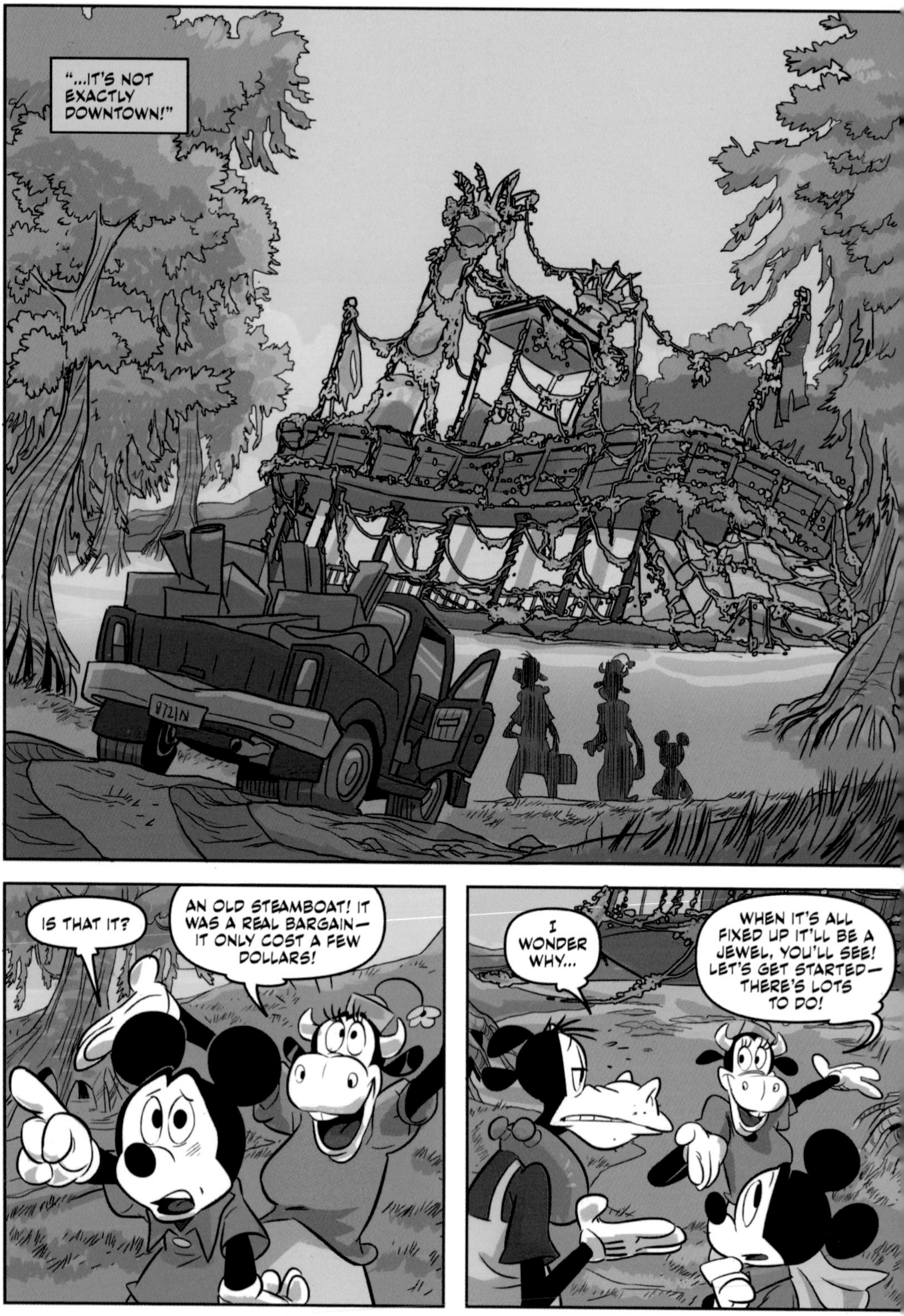
"...IT'S NOT EXACTLY DOWNTOWN!"
IS THAT IT?
AN OLD STEAMBOAT! IT WAS A REAL BARGAIN— IT ONLY COST A FEW DOLLARS!
I WONDER WHY...
WHEN IT'S ALL FIXED UP IT'LL BE A JEWEL, YOU'LL SEE! LET'S GET STARTED— THERE'S LOTS TO DO!

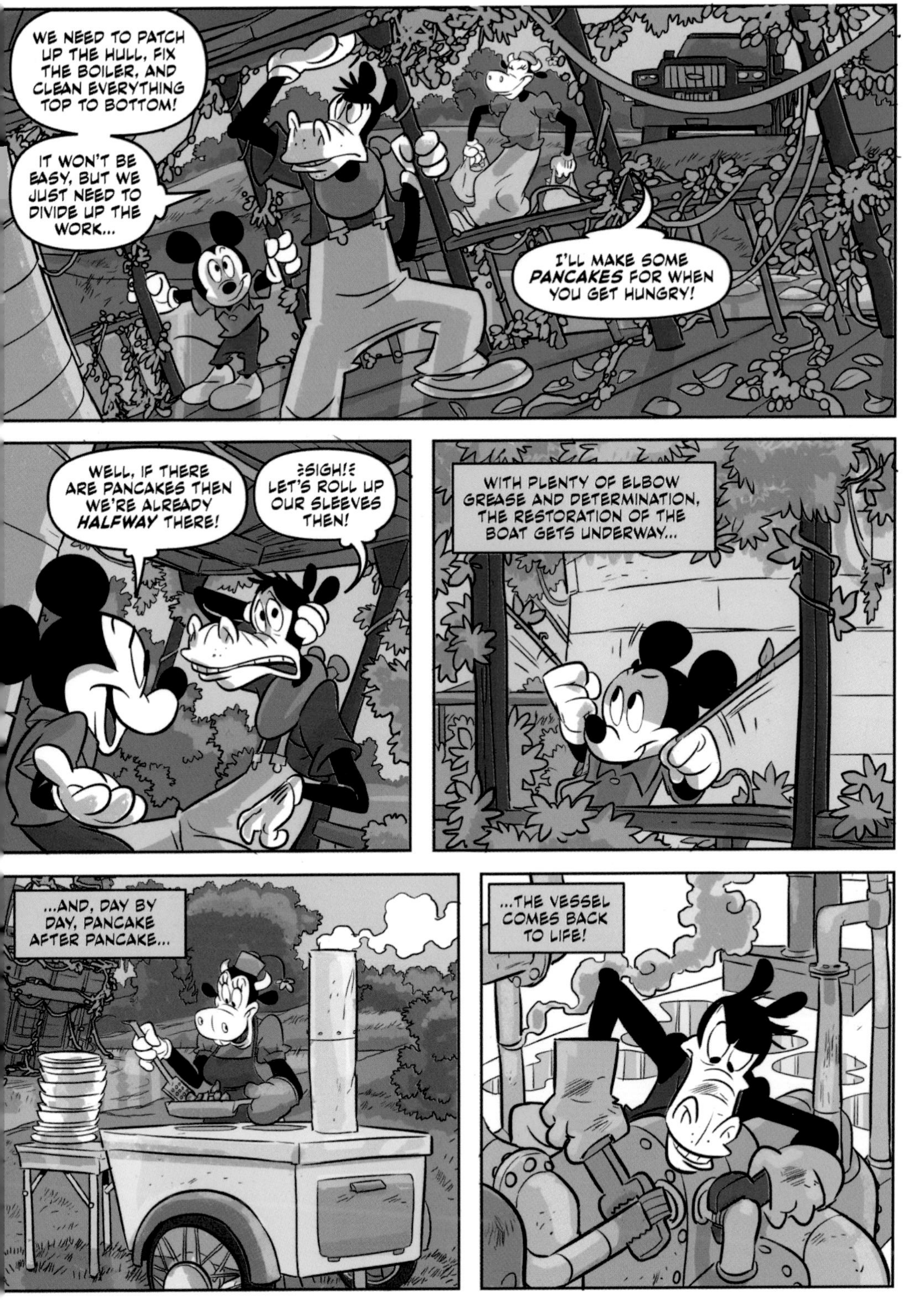
WE NEED TO PATCH UP THE HULL, FIX THE BOILER, AND CLEAN EVERYTHING TOP TO BOTTOM!
IT WON'T BE EASY, BUT WE JUST NEED TO DIVIDE UP THE WORK...
I'LL MAKE SOME *PANCAKES* FOR WHEN YOU GET HUNGRY!
WELL, IF THERE ARE PANCAKES THEN WE'RE ALREADY *HALFWAY* THERE!
SIGH! LET'S ROLL UP OUR SLEEVES THEN!
WITH PLENTY OF ELBOW GREASE AND DETERMINATION, THE RESTORATION OF THE BOAT GETS UNDERWAY...
...AND, DAY BY DAY, PANCAKE AFTER PANCAKE...
...THE VESSEL COMES BACK TO LIFE!

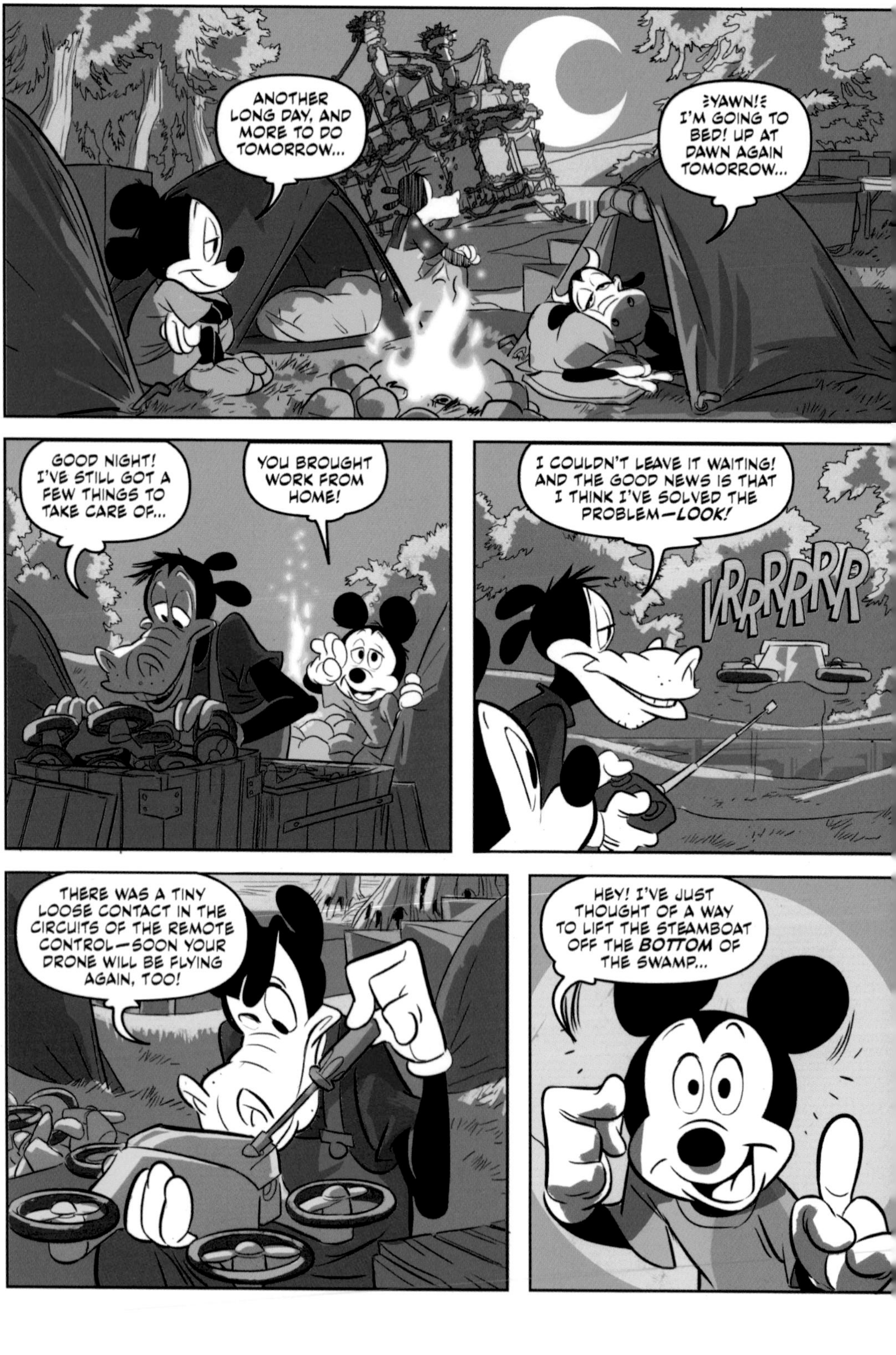
ANOTHER LONG DAY, AND MORE TO DO TOMORROW...
≥YAWN!≤ I'M GOING TO BED! UP AT DAWN AGAIN TOMORROW...
GOOD NIGHT! I'VE STILL GOT A FEW THINGS TO TAKE CARE OF...
YOU BROUGHT WORK FROM HOME!
I COULDN'T LEAVE IT WAITING! AND THE GOOD NEWS IS THAT I THINK I'VE SOLVED THE PROBLEM—*LOOK!*
VRRRRRR
THERE WAS A TINY LOOSE CONTACT IN THE CIRCUITS OF THE REMOTE CONTROL—SOON YOUR DRONE WILL BE FLYING AGAIN, TOO!
HEY! I'VE JUST THOUGHT OF A WAY TO LIFT THE STEAMBOAT OFF THE *BOTTOM* OF THE SWAMP...

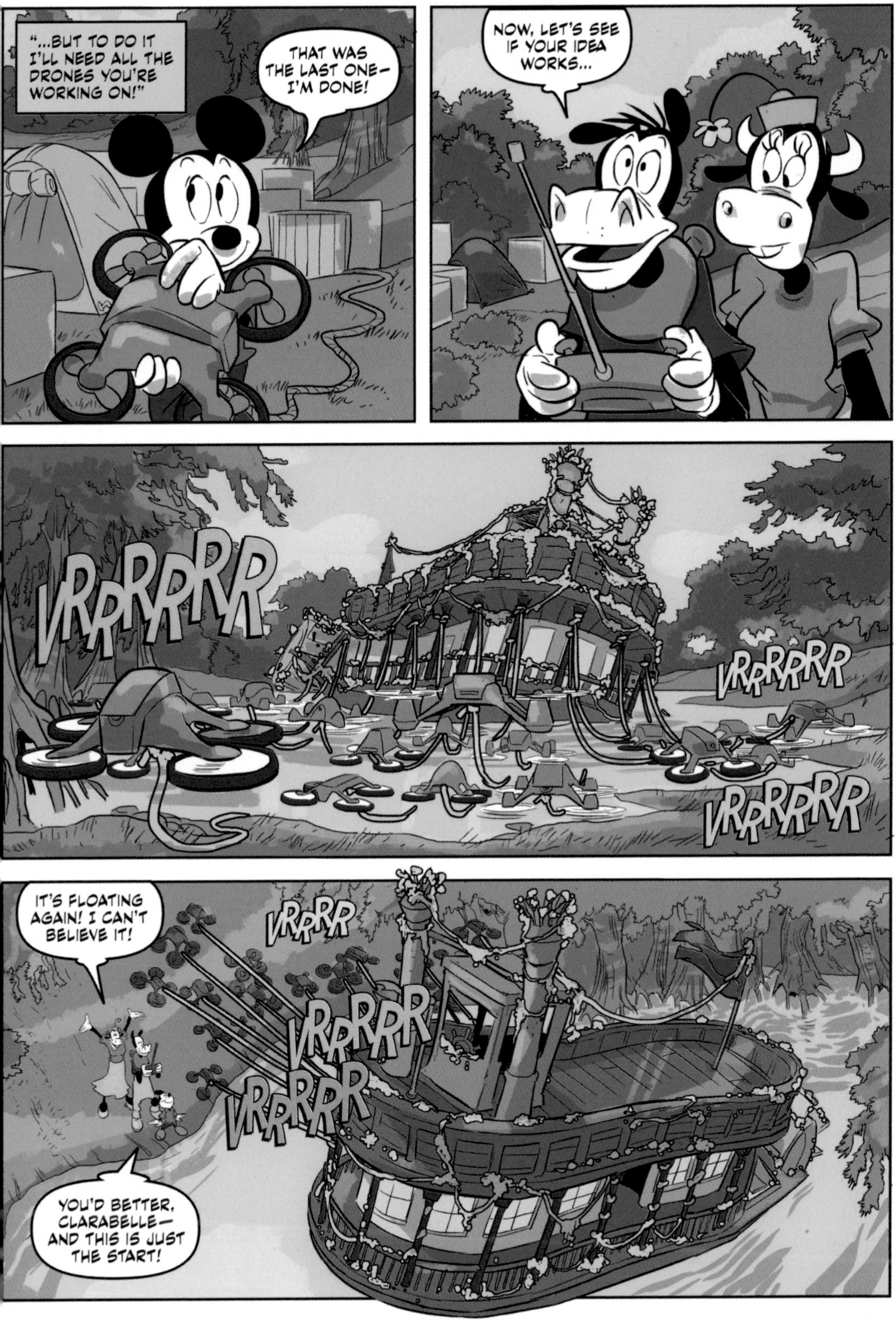
"...BUT TO DO IT I'LL NEED ALL THE DRONES YOU'RE WORKING ON!"
THAT WAS THE LAST ONE— I'M DONE!
NOW, LET'S SEE IF YOUR IDEA WORKS...
VRRRRRRR
VRRRRRRR
VRRRRRRR
IT'S FLOATING AGAIN! I CAN'T BELIEVE IT!
VRRRR
VRRRRRR
VRRRRR
YOU'D BETTER, CLARABELLE— AND THIS IS JUST THE START!

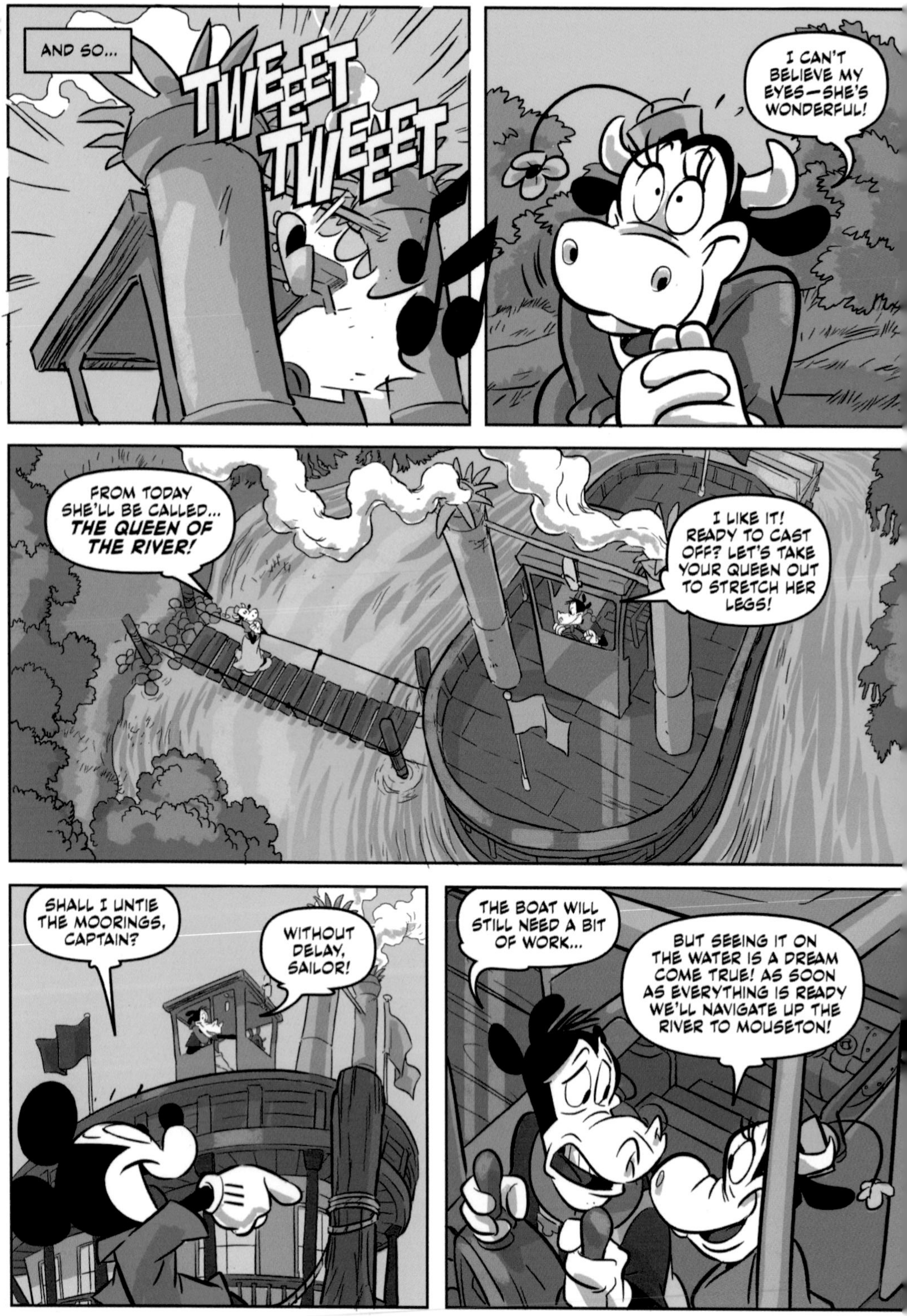
AND SO...
TWEEEET TWEEEET
I CAN'T BELIEVE MY EYES—SHE'S WONDERFUL!
FROM TODAY SHE'LL BE CALLED... THE QUEEN OF THE RIVER!
I LIKE IT! READY TO CAST OFF? LET'S TAKE YOUR QUEEN OUT TO STRETCH HER LEGS!
SHALL I UNTIE THE MOORINGS, CAPTAIN?
WITHOUT DELAY, SAILOR!
THE BOAT WILL STILL NEED A BIT OF WORK...
BUT SEEING IT ON THE WATER IS A DREAM COME TRUE! AS SOON AS EVERYTHING IS READY WE'LL NAVIGATE UP THE RIVER TO MOUSETON!

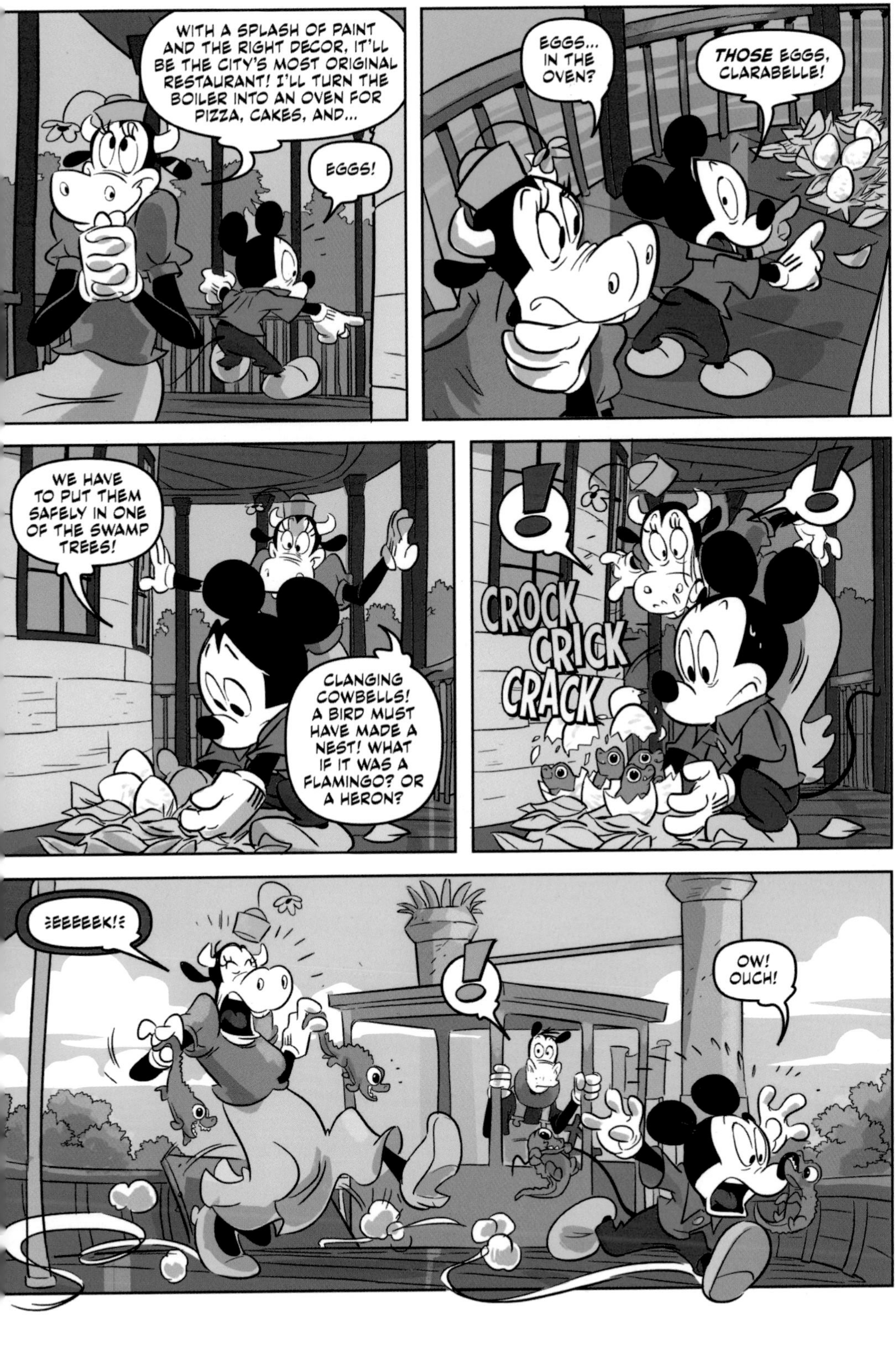
WITH A SPLASH OF PAINT AND THE RIGHT DECOR, IT'LL BE THE CITY'S MOST ORIGINAL RESTAURANT! I'LL TURN THE BOILER INTO AN OVEN FOR PIZZA, CAKES, AND...
EGGS!
EGGS... IN THE OVEN?
THOSE EGGS, CLARABELLE!
WE HAVE TO PUT THEM SAFELY IN ONE OF THE SWAMP TREES!
CLANGING COWBELLS! A BIRD MUST HAVE MADE A NEST! WHAT IF IT WAS A FLAMINGO? OR A HERON?
!
!
CROCK
CRICK
CRACK
EEEEEEK!
!
OW! OUCH!

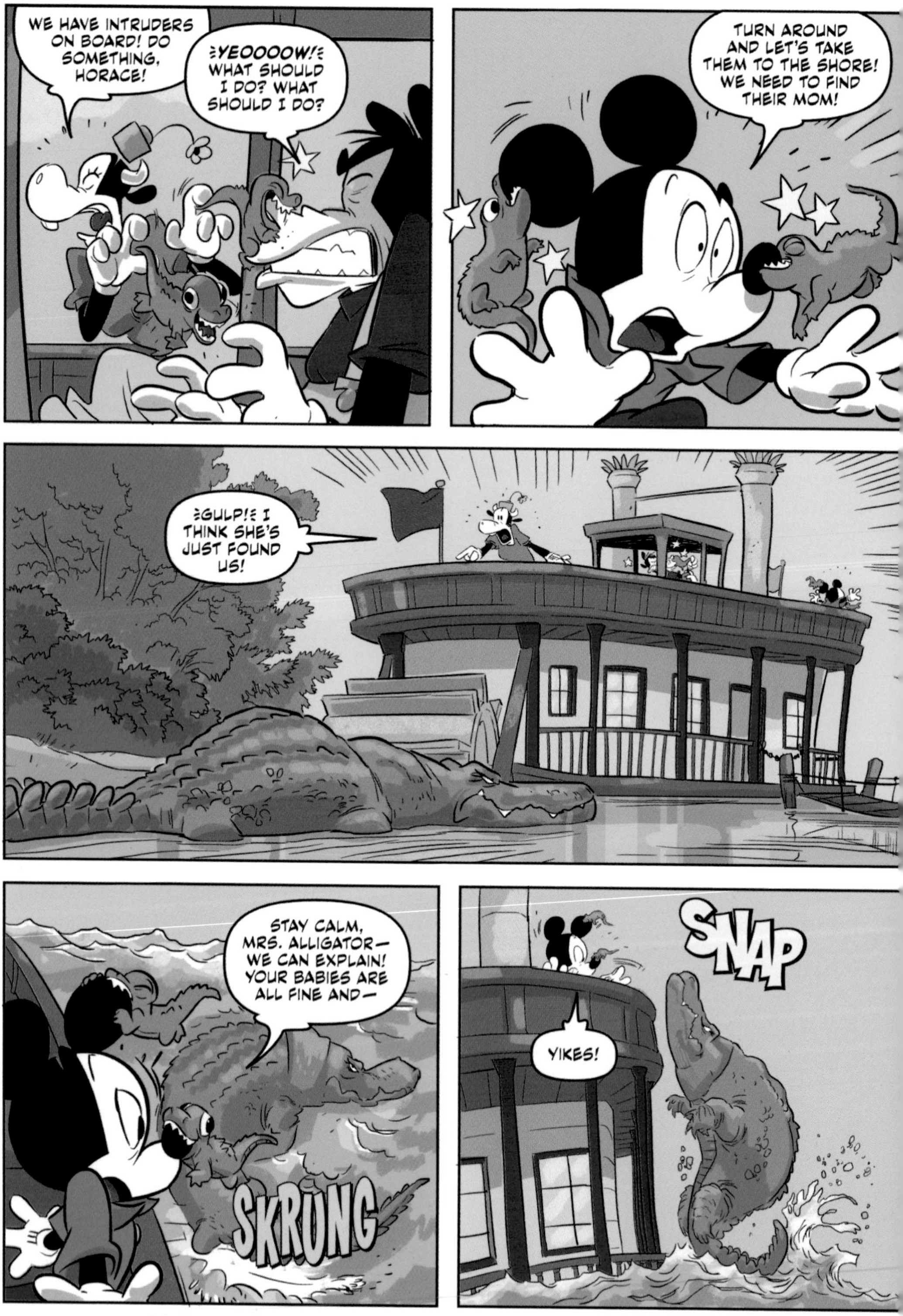
WE HAVE INTRUDERS ON BOARD! DO SOMETHING, HORACE!
YEOOOOW! WHAT SHOULD I DO? WHAT SHOULD I DO?
TURN AROUND AND LET'S TAKE THEM TO THE SHORE! WE NEED TO FIND THEIR MOM!
GULP! I THINK SHE'S JUST FOUND US!
STAY CALM, MRS. ALLIGATOR— WE CAN EXPLAIN! YOUR BABIES ARE ALL FINE AND—
SKRUNG
SNAP
YIKES!

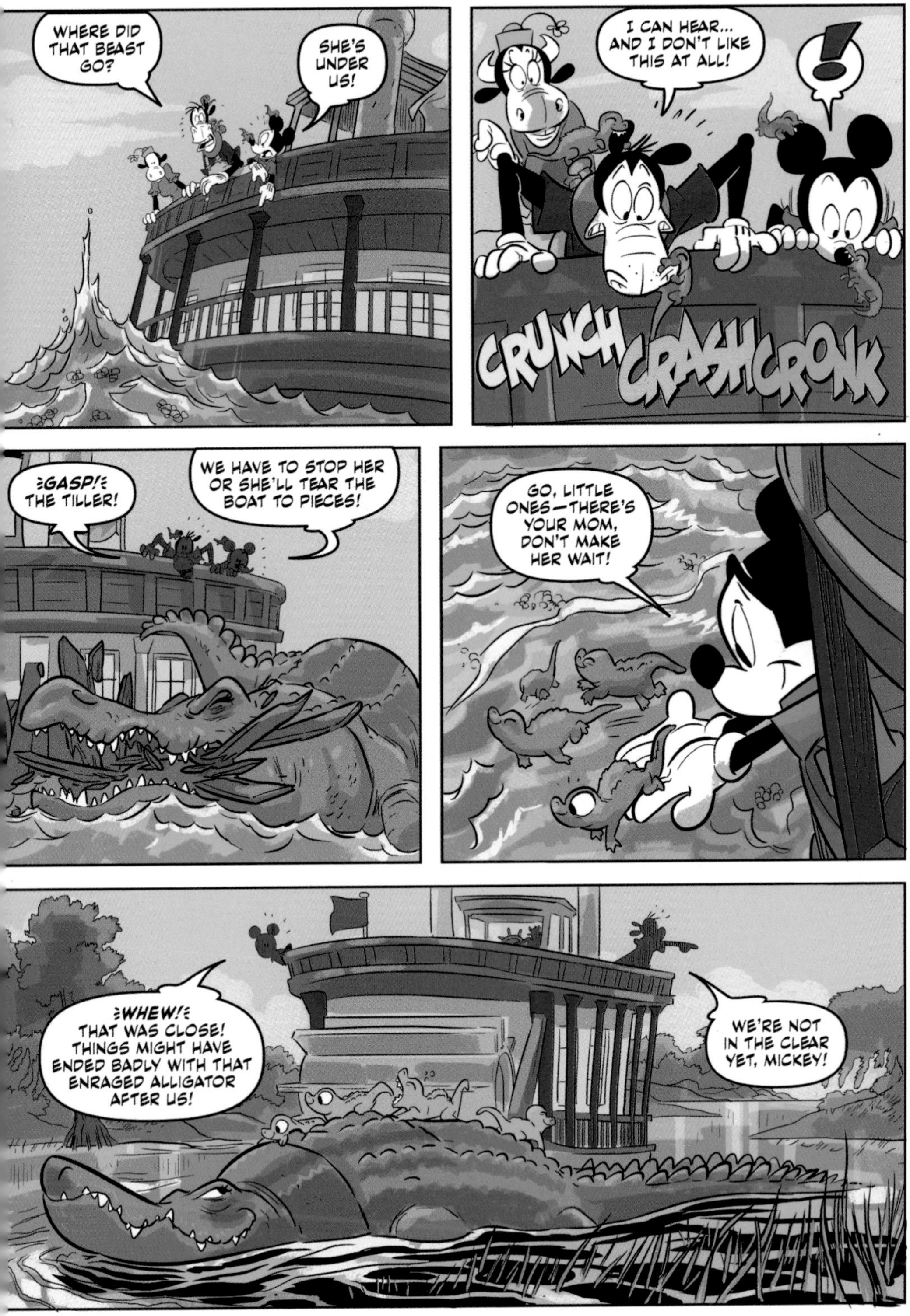
WHERE DID THAT BEAST GO?
SHE'S UNDER US!
I CAN HEAR... AND I DON'T LIKE THIS AT ALL!
!
CRUNCH CRASH CRONK
GASP! THE TILLER!
WE HAVE TO STOP HER OR SHE'LL TEAR THE BOAT TO PIECES!
GO, LITTLE ONES—THERE'S YOUR MOM, DON'T MAKE HER WAIT!
WHEW! THAT WAS CLOSE! THINGS MIGHT HAVE ENDED BADLY WITH THAT ENRAGED ALLIGATOR AFTER US!
WE'RE NOT IN THE CLEAR YET, MICKEY!

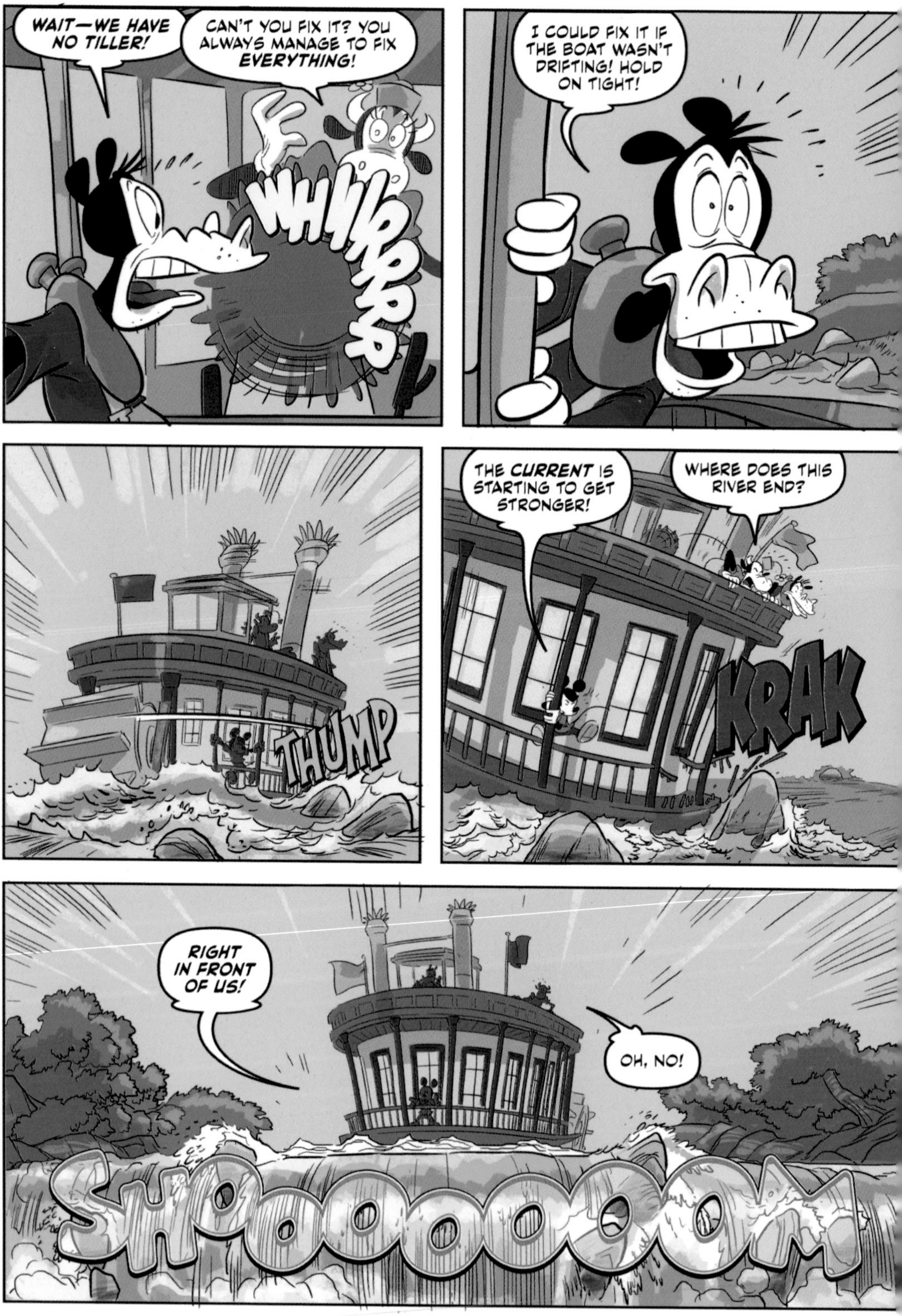
WAIT—WE HAVE NO TILLER!
CAN'T YOU FIX IT? YOU ALWAYS MANAGE TO FIX EVERYTHING!
WHHIRRRRR
I COULD FIX IT IF THE BOAT WASN'T DRIFTING! HOLD ON TIGHT!
THUMP
THE CURRENT IS STARTING TO GET STRONGER!
WHERE DOES THIS RIVER END?
KRAK
RIGHT IN FRONT OF US!
OH, NO!
SHOOOOOOOM

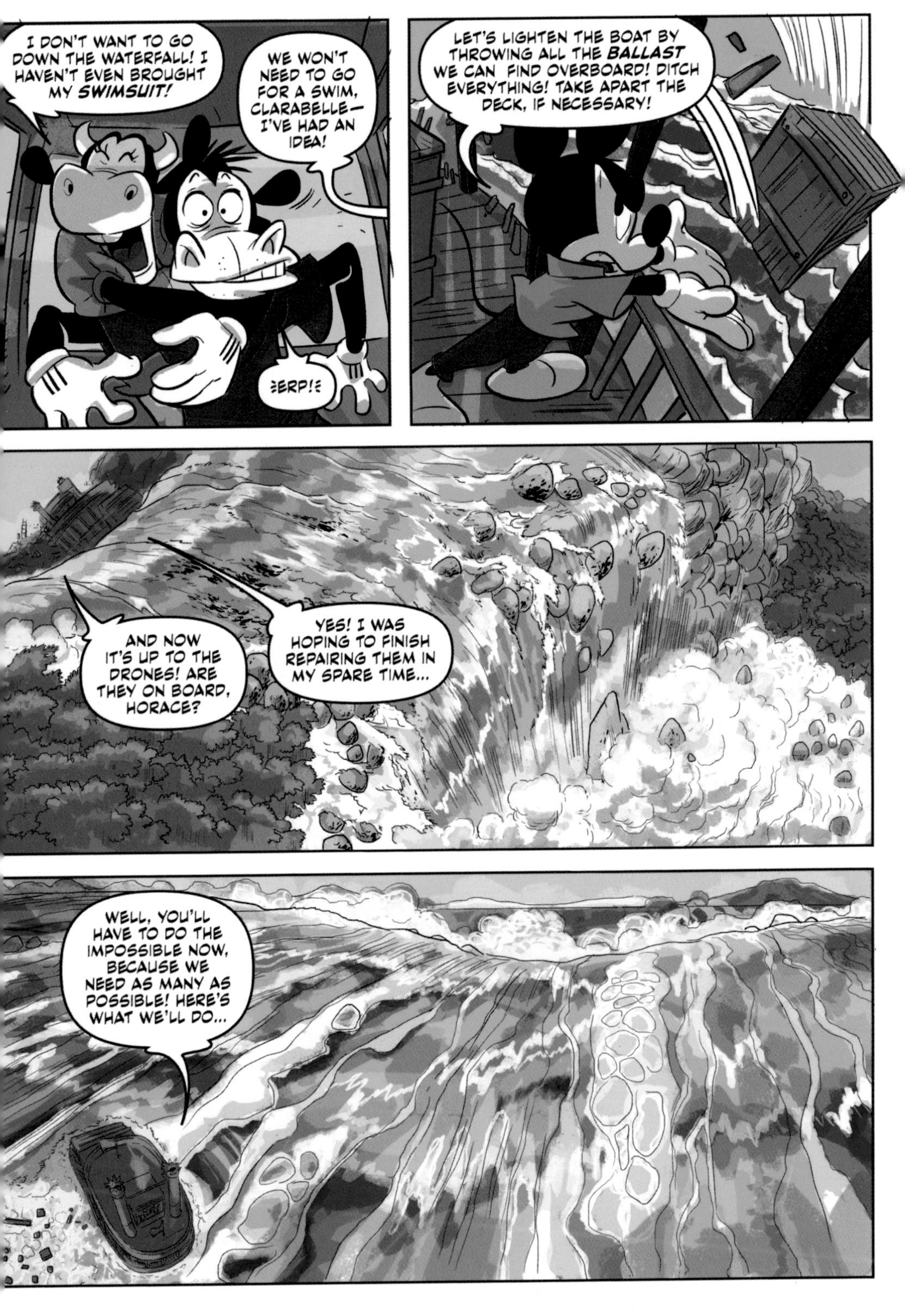
I DON'T WANT TO GO DOWN THE WATERFALL! I HAVEN'T EVEN BROUGHT MY SWIMSUIT!
WE WON'T NEED TO GO FOR A SWIM, CLARABELLE— I'VE HAD AN IDEA!
ERP!
LET'S LIGHTEN THE BOAT BY THROWING ALL THE BALLAST WE CAN FIND OVERBOARD! DITCH EVERYTHING! TAKE APART THE DECK, IF NECESSARY!
AND NOW IT'S UP TO THE DRONES! ARE THEY ON BOARD, HORACE?
YES! I WAS HOPING TO FINISH REPAIRING THEM IN MY SPARE TIME...
WELL, YOU'LL HAVE TO DO THE IMPOSSIBLE NOW, BECAUSE WE NEED AS MANY AS POSSIBLE! HERE'S WHAT WE'LL DO...

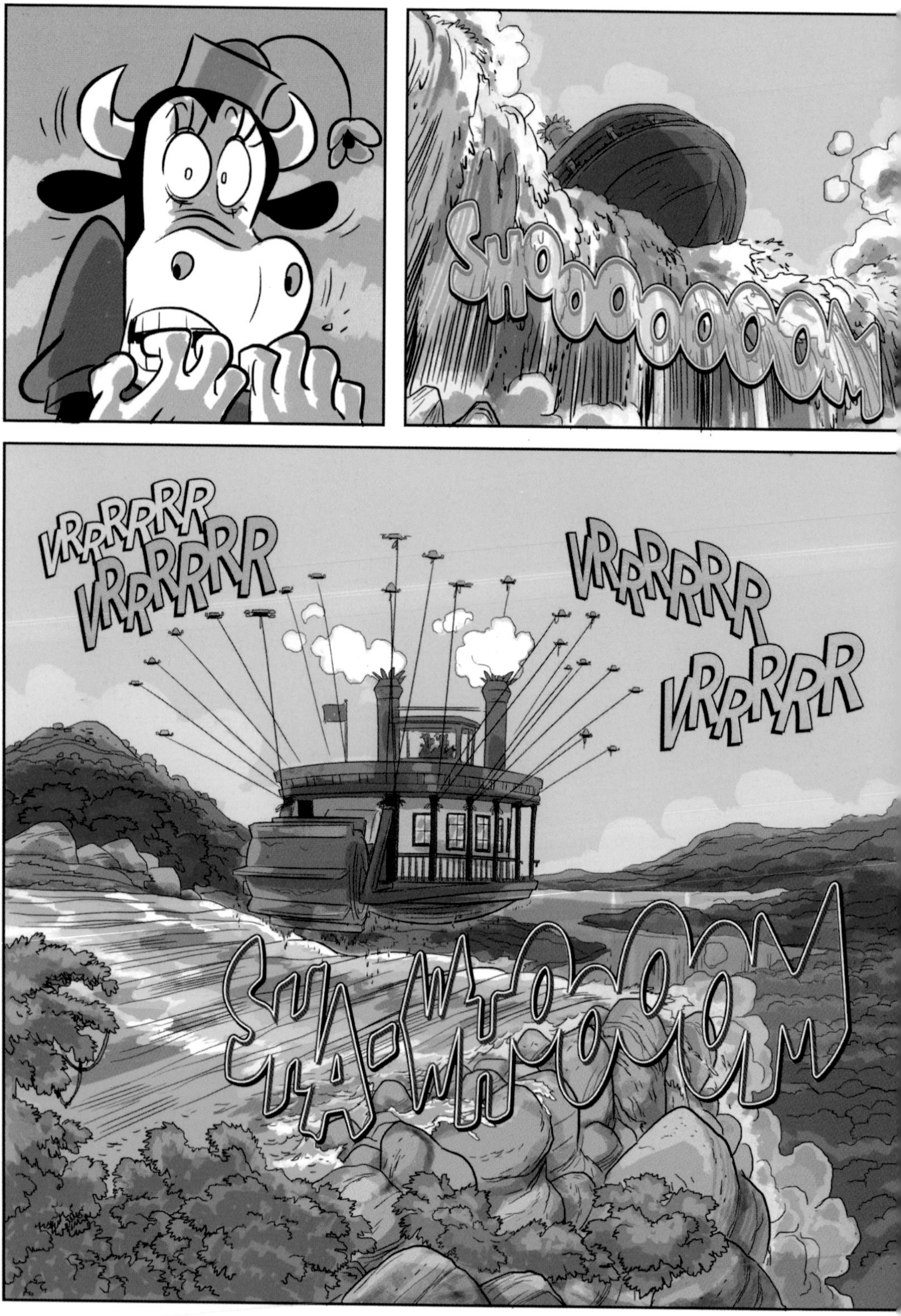
SHOOOOOOOM
VRRRRRR
VRRRRRR
VRRRRRR
VRRRRR
SHA-WHOOOOM

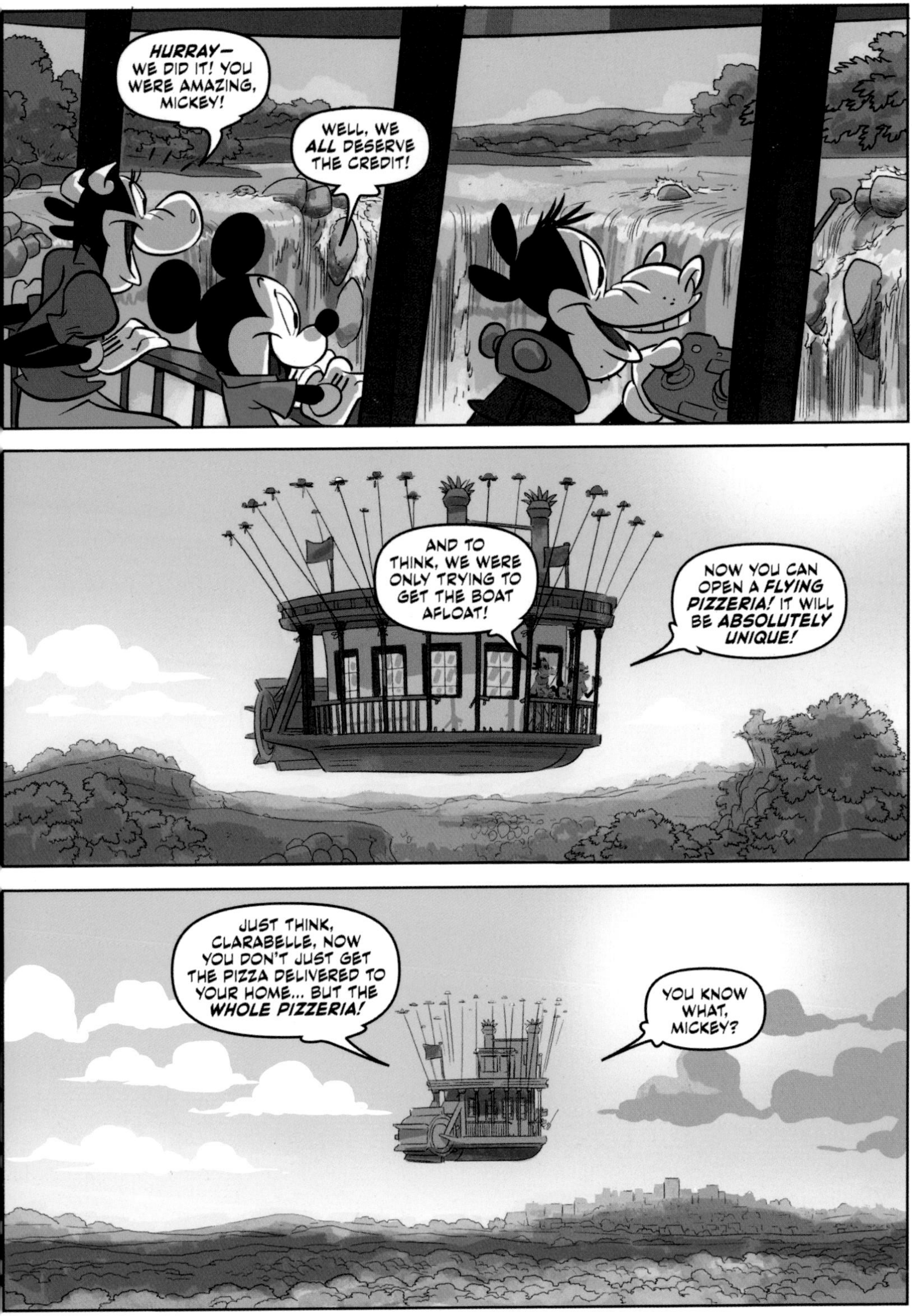
HURRAY— WE DID IT! YOU WERE AMAZING, MICKEY!
WELL, WE ALL DESERVE THE CREDIT!
AND TO THINK, WE WERE ONLY TRYING TO GET THE BOAT AFLOAT!
NOW YOU CAN OPEN A FLYING PIZZERIA! IT WILL BE ABSOLUTELY UNIQUE!
JUST THINK, CLARABELLE, NOW YOU DON'T JUST GET THE PIZZA DELIVERED TO YOUR HOME... BUT THE WHOLE PIZZERIA!
YOU KNOW WHAT, MICKEY?

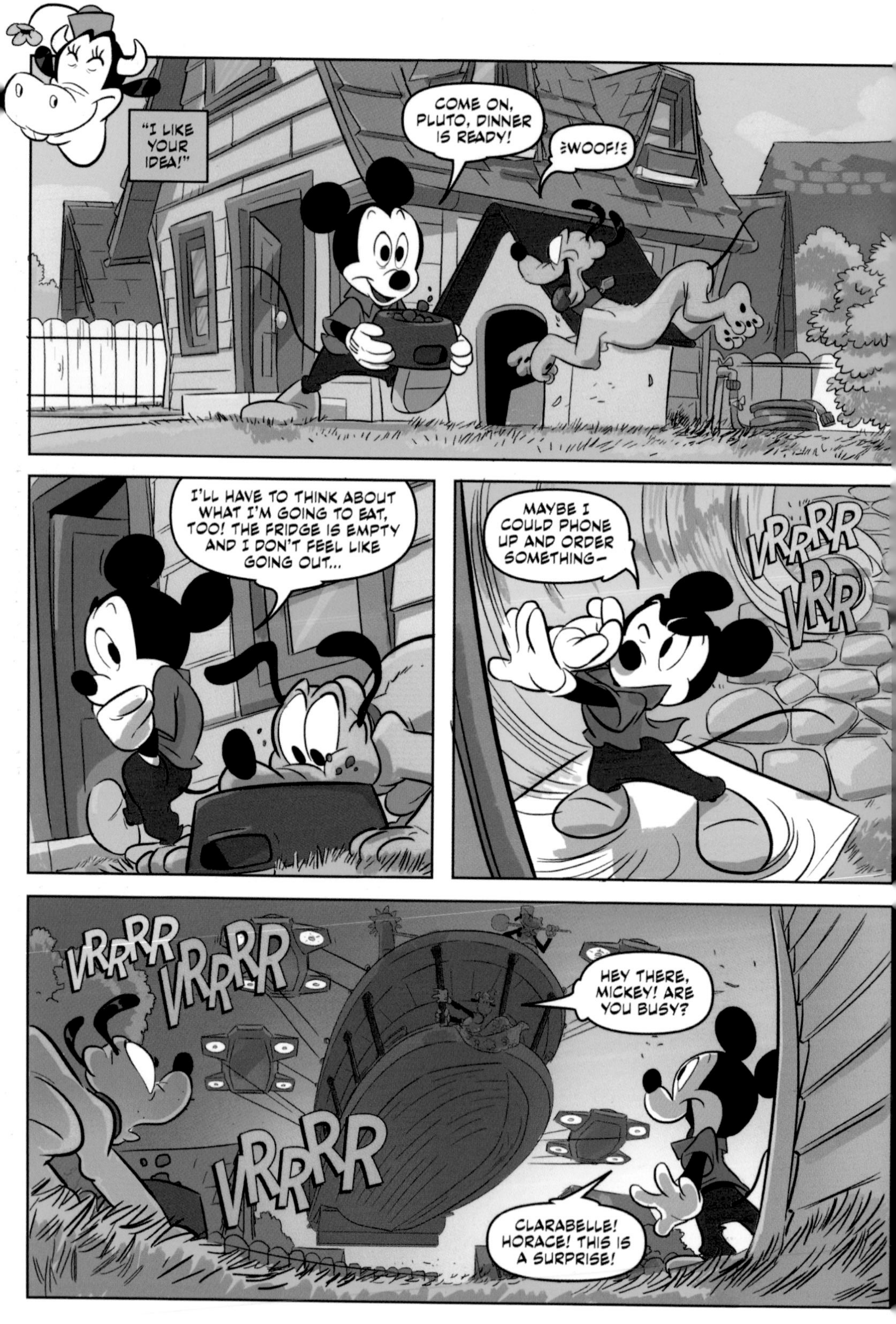
"I LIKE YOUR IDEA!"
COME ON, PLUTO, DINNER IS READY!
WOOF!
I'LL HAVE TO THINK ABOUT WHAT I'M GOING TO EAT, TOO! THE FRIDGE IS EMPTY AND I DON'T FEEL LIKE GOING OUT...
MAYBE I COULD PHONE UP AND ORDER SOMETHING–
VRRRR
VRR
VRRRR
VRRRR
HEY THERE, MICKEY! ARE YOU BUSY?
VRRRR
CLARABELLE! HORACE! THIS IS A SURPRISE!

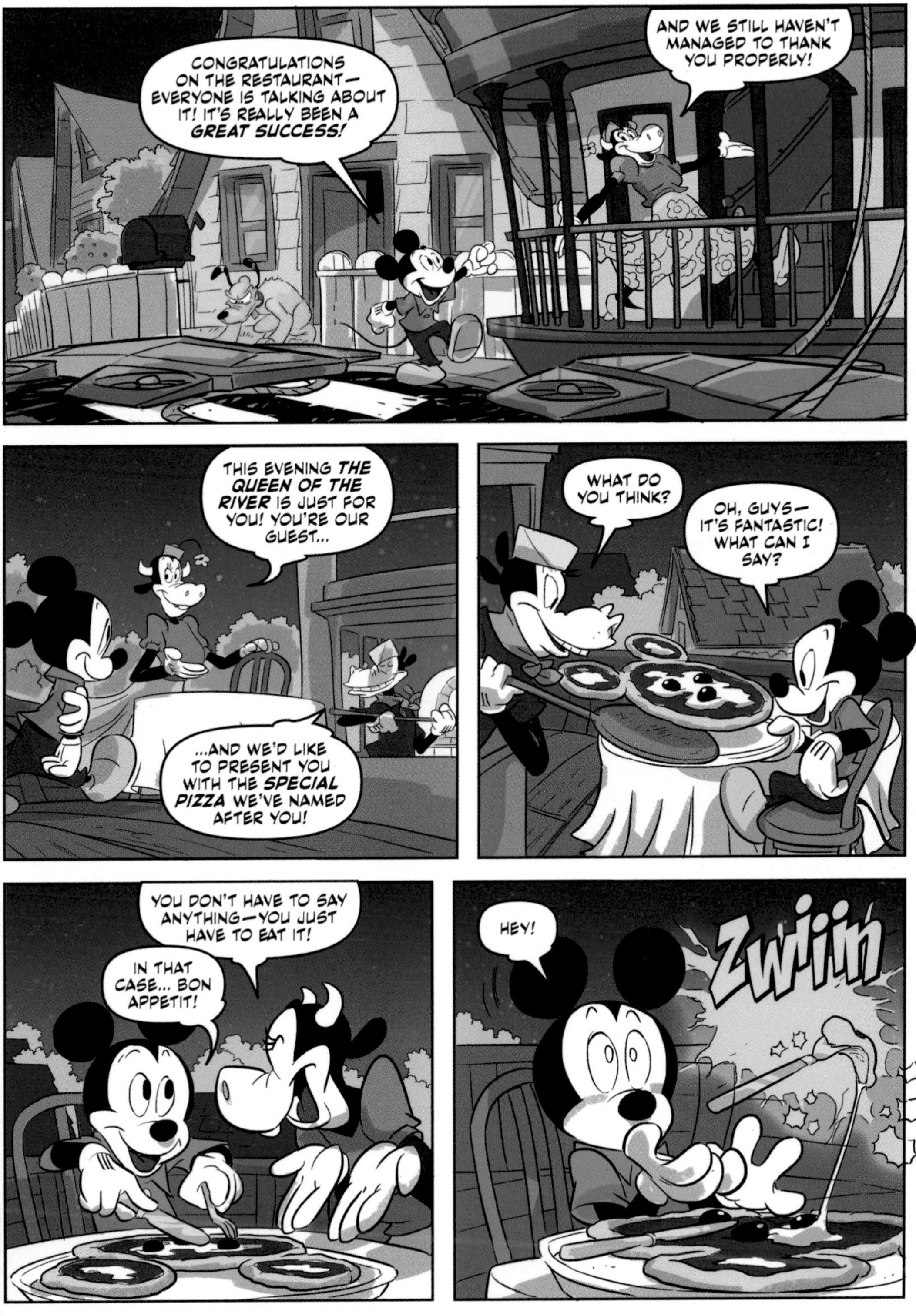
CONGRATULATIONS ON THE RESTAURANT— EVERYONE IS TALKING ABOUT IT! IT'S REALLY BEEN A GREAT SUCCESS!
AND WE STILL HAVEN'T MANAGED TO THANK YOU PROPERLY!
THIS EVENING THE QUEEN OF THE RIVER IS JUST FOR YOU! YOU'RE OUR GUEST...
...AND WE'D LIKE TO PRESENT YOU WITH THE SPECIAL PIZZA WE'VE NAMED AFTER YOU!
WHAT DO YOU THINK?
OH, GUYS— IT'S FANTASTIC! WHAT CAN I SAY?
YOU DON'T HAVE TO SAY ANYTHING—YOU JUST HAVE TO EAT IT!
IN THAT CASE... BON APPETIT!
HEY!
ZWIIM

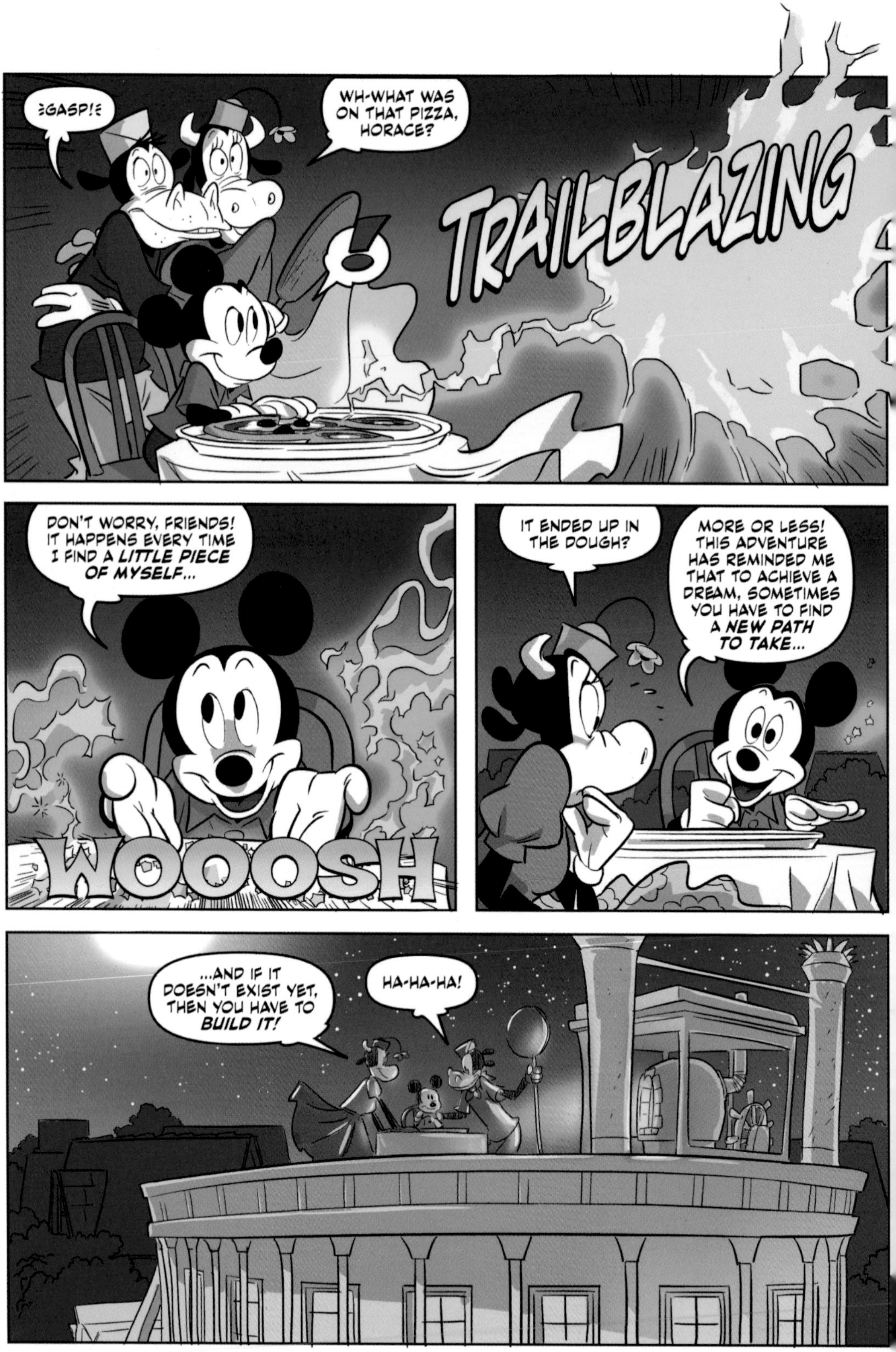
GASP!
WH-WHAT WAS ON THAT PIZZA, HORACE?
!
TRAILBLAZING
DON'T WORRY, FRIENDS! IT HAPPENS EVERY TIME I FIND A LITTLE PIECE OF MYSELF...
WOOOSH
IT ENDED UP IN THE DOUGH?
MORE OR LESS! THIS ADVENTURE HAS REMINDED ME THAT TO ACHIEVE A DREAM, SOMETIMES YOU HAVE TO FIND A NEW PATH TO TAKE...
...AND IF IT DOESN'T EXIST YET, THEN YOU HAVE TO BUILD IT!
HA-HA-HA!

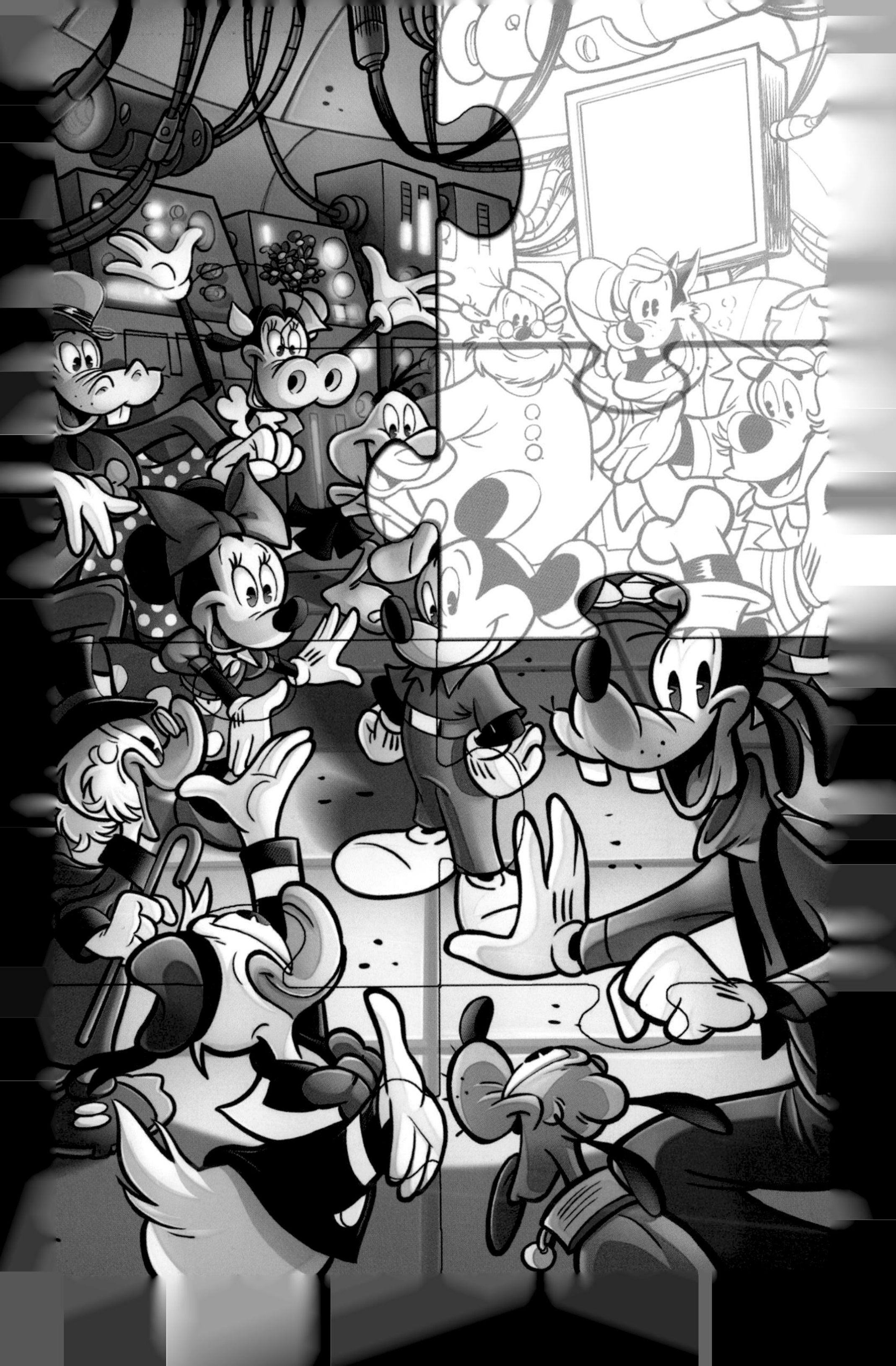

Art by LORENZO PASTROVICCHIO
Colors by EDIZIONI BD

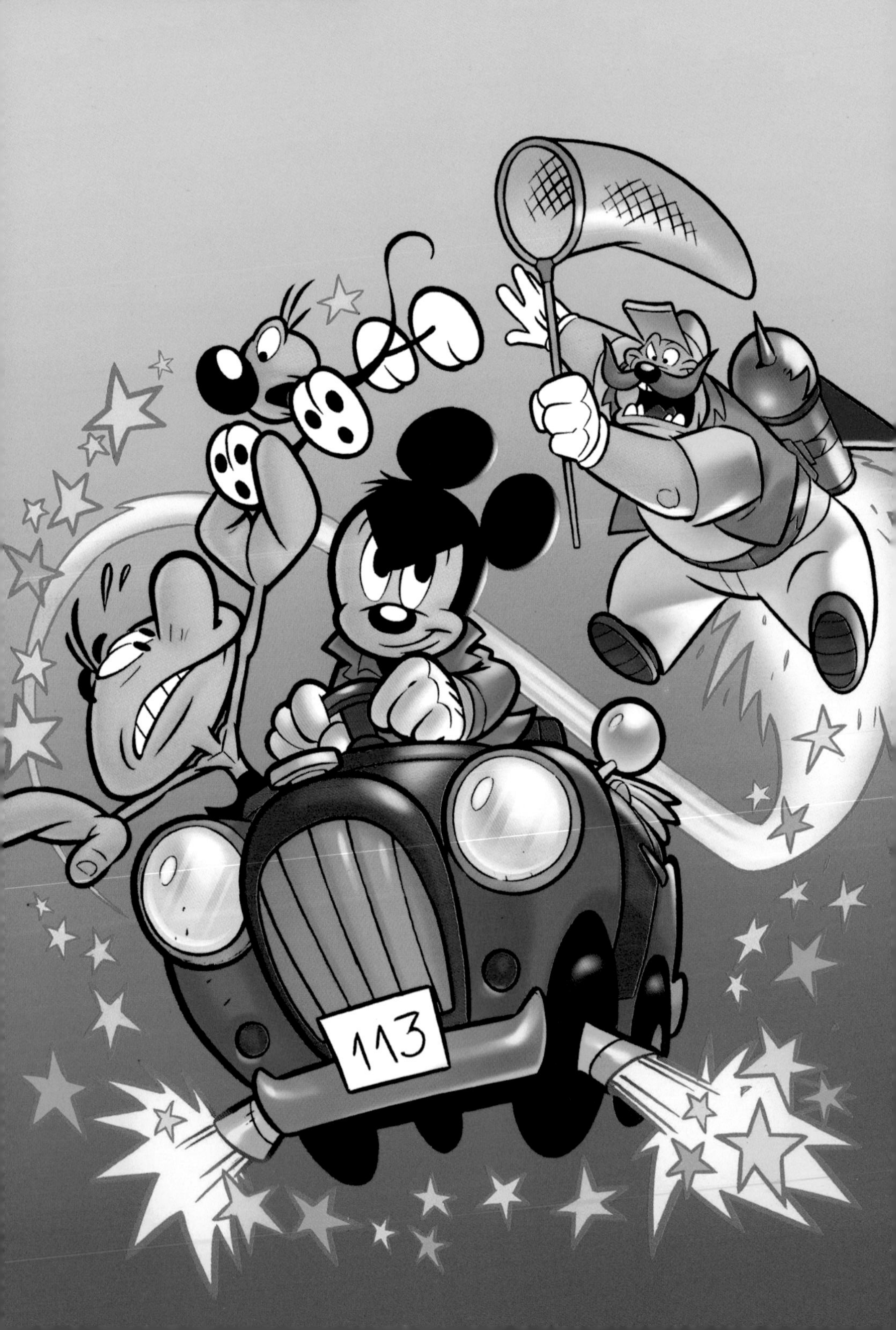
113

CHAPTER 7: THREAT FROM THE FUTURE

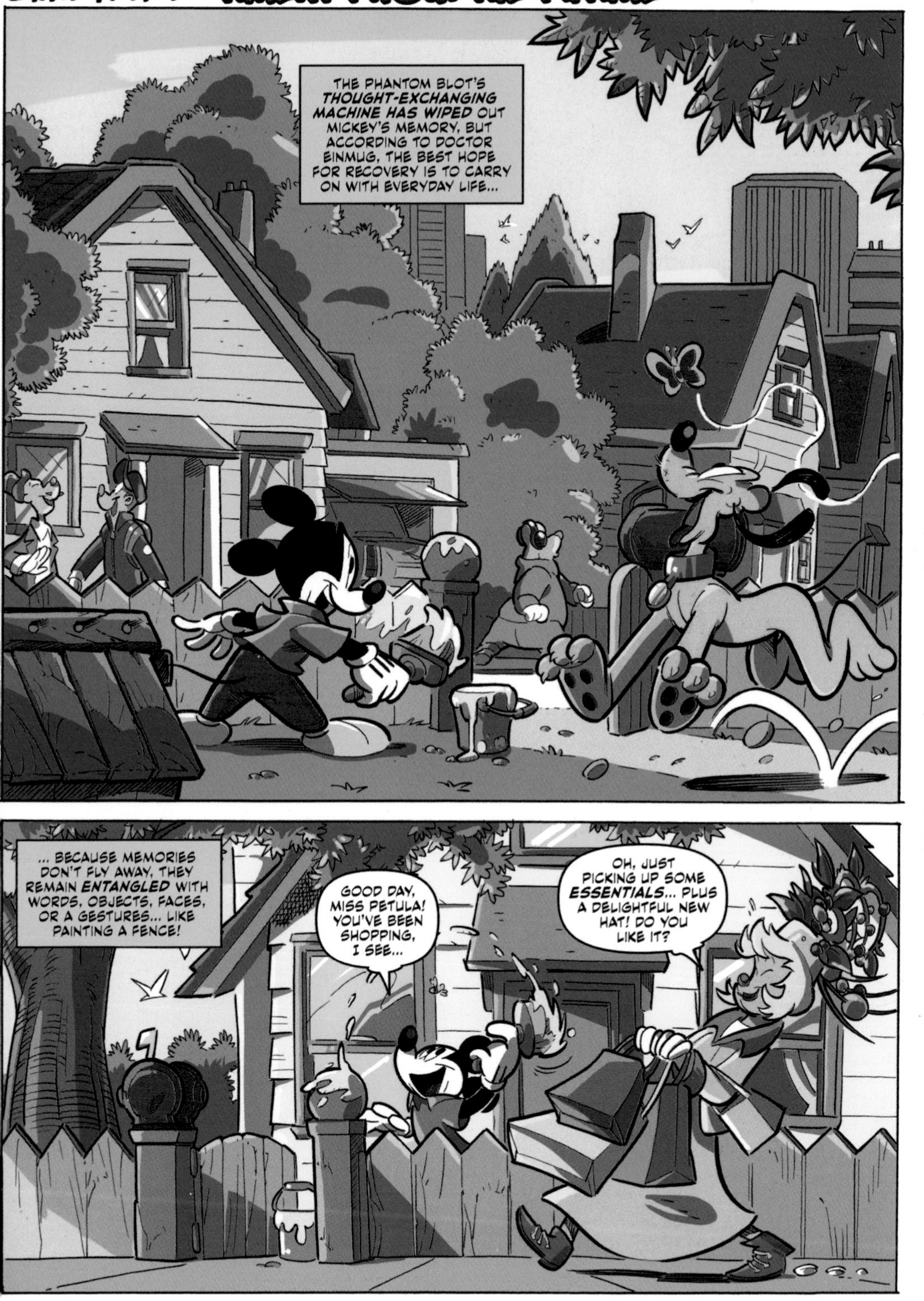
THE PHANTOM BLOT'S ***THOUGHT-EXCHANGING MACHINE HAS WIPED*** OUT MICKEY'S MEMORY, BUT ACCORDING TO DOCTOR EINMUG, THE BEST HOPE FOR RECOVERY IS TO CARRY ON WITH EVERYDAY LIFE...
... BECAUSE MEMORIES DON'T FLY AWAY, THEY REMAIN ***ENTANGLED*** WITH WORDS, OBJECTS, FACES, OR A GESTURES... LIKE PAINTING A FENCE!
GOOD DAY, MISS PETULA! YOU'VE BEEN SHOPPING, I SEE...
OH, JUST PICKING UP SOME ***ESSENTIALS***... PLUS A DELIGHTFUL NEW HAT! DO YOU LIKE IT?

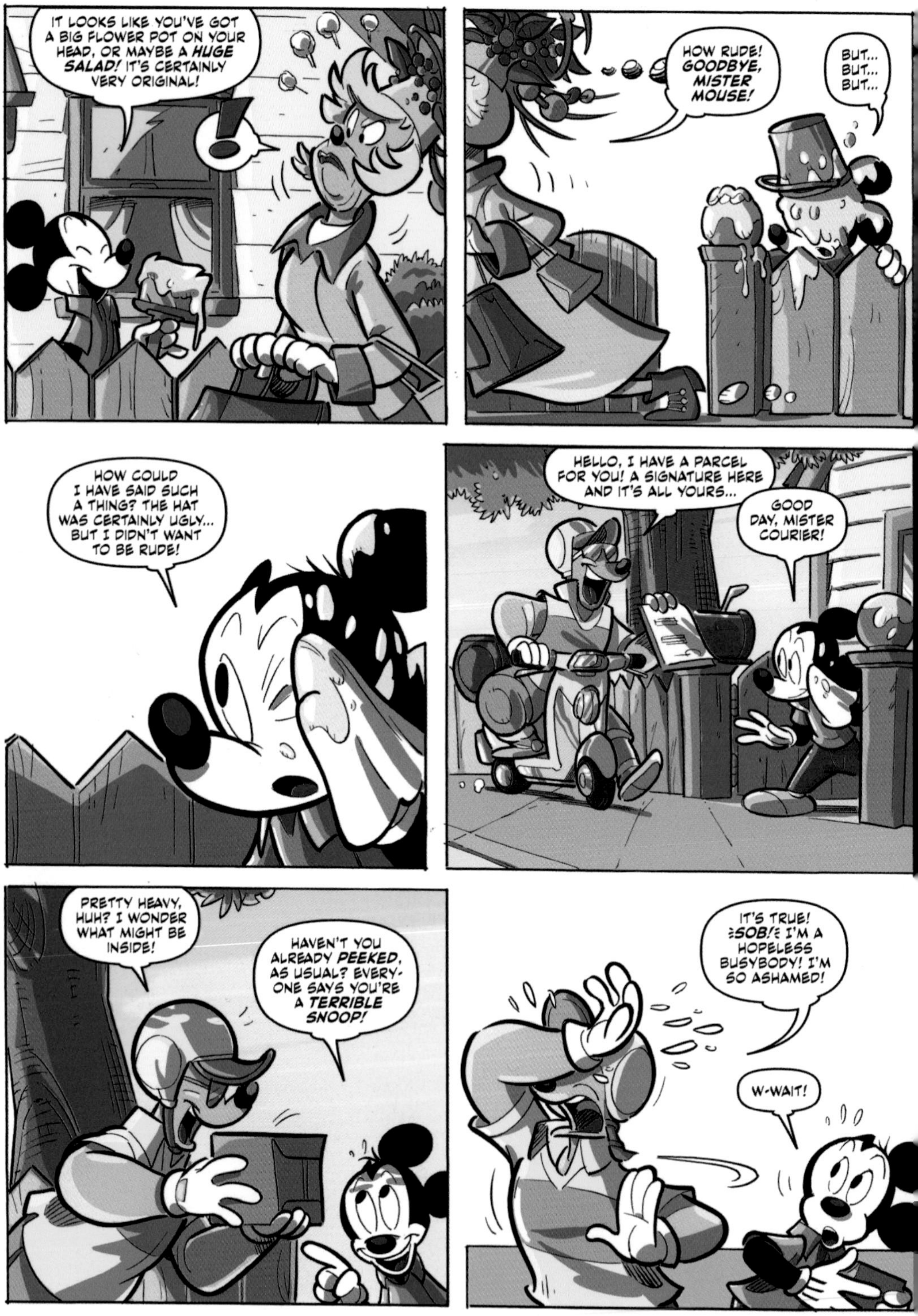
IT LOOKS LIKE YOU'VE GOT A BIG FLOWER POT ON YOUR HEAD, OR MAYBE A *HUGE SALAD!* IT'S CERTAINLY VERY ORIGINAL!
!
HOW RUDE! *GOODBYE, MISTER MOUSE!*
BUT... BUT... BUT...
HOW COULD I HAVE SAID SUCH A THING? THE HAT WAS CERTAINLY UGLY... BUT I DIDN'T WANT TO BE RUDE!
HELLO, I HAVE A PARCEL FOR YOU! A SIGNATURE HERE AND IT'S ALL YOURS...
GOOD DAY, MISTER COURIER!
PRETTY HEAVY, HUH? I WONDER WHAT MIGHT BE INSIDE!
HAVEN'T YOU ALREADY *PEEKED*, AS USUAL? EVERY-ONE SAYS YOU'RE A *TERRIBLE SNOOP!*
IT'S TRUE! *SOB!* I'M A HOPELESS BUSYBODY! I'M SO ASHAMED!
W-WAIT!

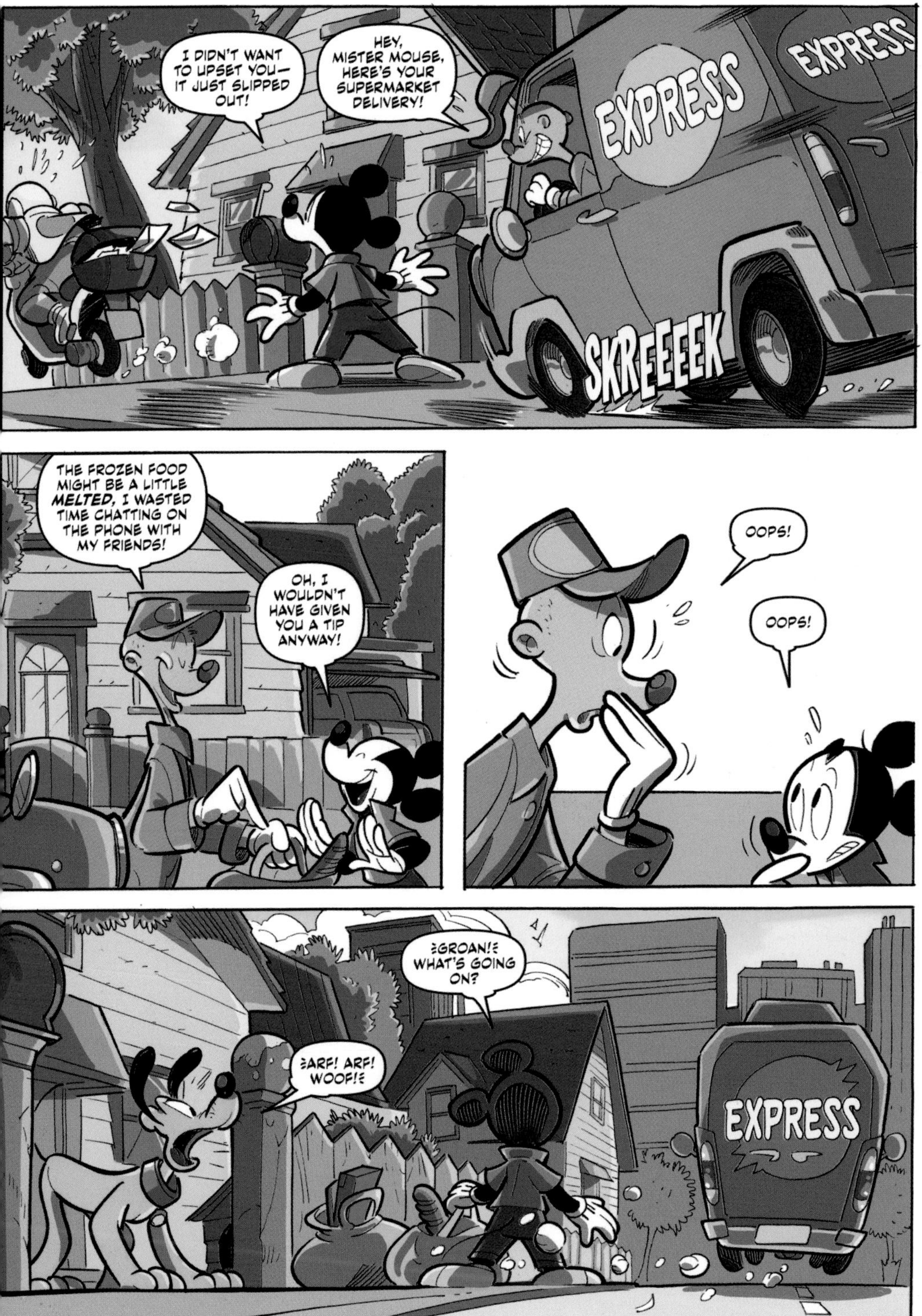
I DIDN'T WANT TO UPSET YOU— IT JUST SLIPPED OUT!
HEY, MISTER MOUSE, HERE'S YOUR SUPERMARKET DELIVERY!
EXPRESS
EXPRESS
SKREEEEK
THE FROZEN FOOD MIGHT BE A LITTLE MELTED, I WASTED TIME CHATTING ON THE PHONE WITH MY FRIENDS!
OH, I WOULDN'T HAVE GIVEN YOU A TIP ANYWAY!
OOPS!
OOPS!
GROAN! WHAT'S GOING ON?
ARF! ARF! WOOF!
EXPRESS

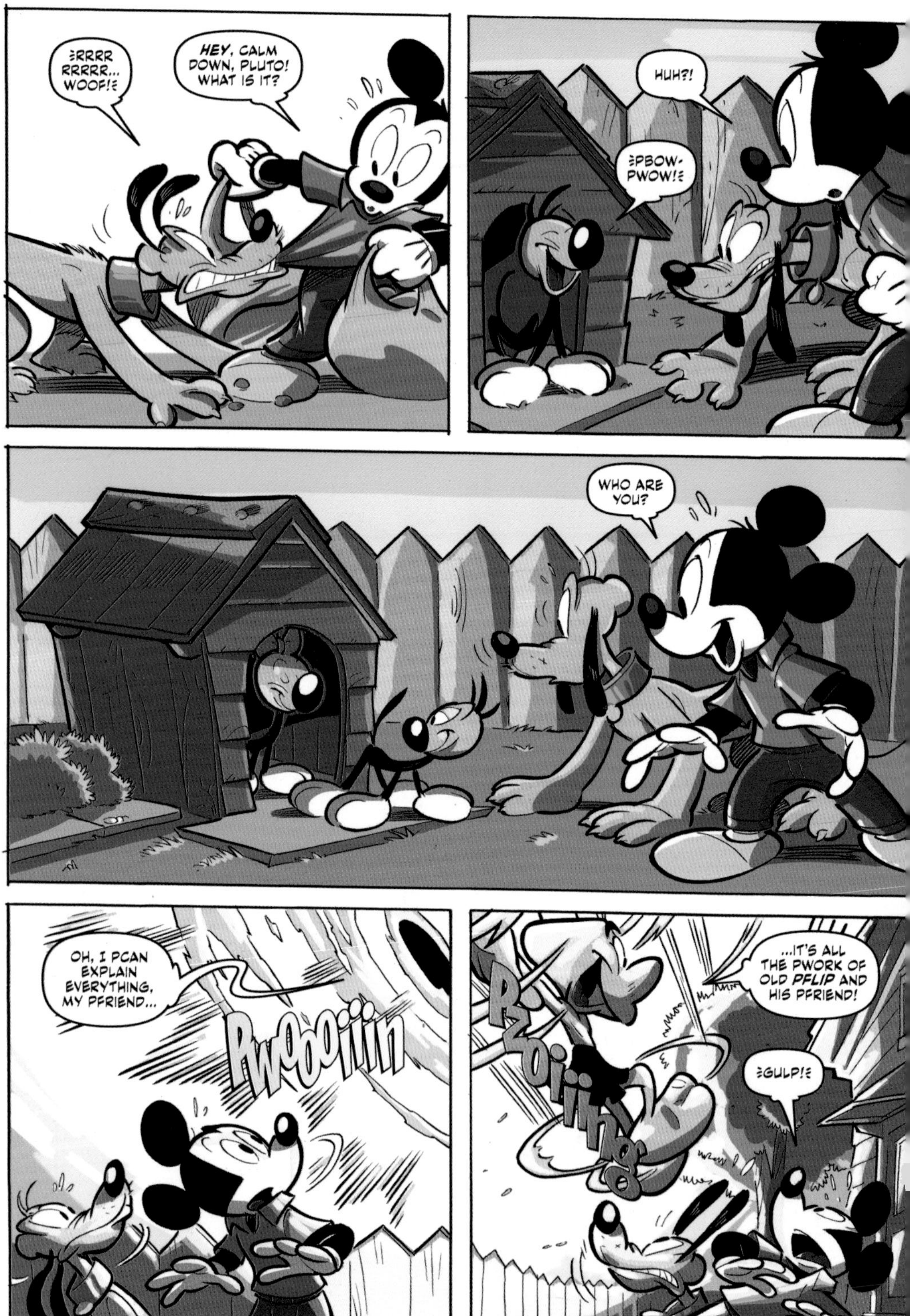
ƎRRRR RRRRR... WOOF!Ǝ
HEY, CALM DOWN, PLUTO! WHAT IS IT?
HUH?!
ƎPBOW-PWOW!Ǝ
WHO ARE YOU?
OH, I PCAN EXPLAIN EVERYTHING, MY PFRIEND...
PWOOOIIIN
...IT'S ALL THE PWORK OF OLD PFLIP AND HIS PFRIEND!
BOIIING
ƎGULP!Ǝ

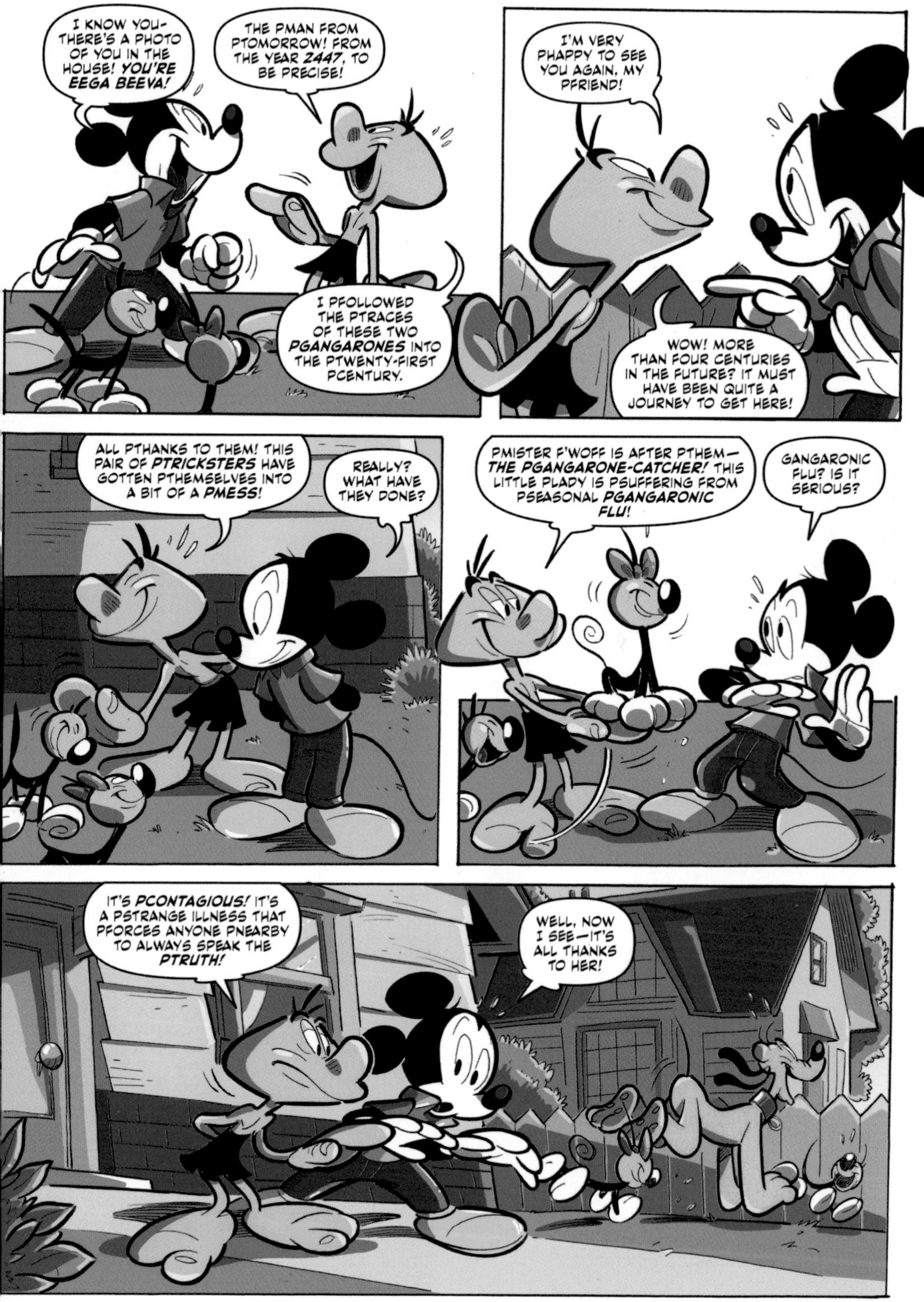
I KNOW YOU- THERE'S A PHOTO OF YOU IN THE HOUSE! YOU'RE EEGA BEEVA!
THE PMAN FROM PTOMORROW! FROM THE YEAR 2447, TO BE PRECISE!
I PFOLLOWED THE PTRACES OF THESE TWO PGANGARONES INTO THE PTWENTY-FIRST PCENTURY.
I'M VERY PHAPPY TO SEE YOU AGAIN, MY PFRIEND!
WOW! MORE THAN FOUR CENTURIES IN THE FUTURE? IT MUST HAVE BEEN QUITE A JOURNEY TO GET HERE!
ALL PTHANKS TO THEM! THIS PAIR OF PTRICKSTERS HAVE GOTTEN PTHEMSELVES INTO A BIT OF A PMESS!
REALLY? WHAT HAVE THEY DONE?
PMISTER F'WOFF IS AFTER PTHEM—THE PGANGARONE-CATCHER! THIS LITTLE PLADY IS PSUFFERING FROM PSEASONAL PGANGARONIC FLU!
GANGARONIC FLU? IS IT SERIOUS?
IT'S PCONTAGIOUS! IT'S A PSTRANGE ILLNESS THAT PFORCES ANYONE PNEARBY TO ALWAYS SPEAK THE PTRUTH!
WELL, NOW I SEE—IT'S ALL THANKS TO HER!

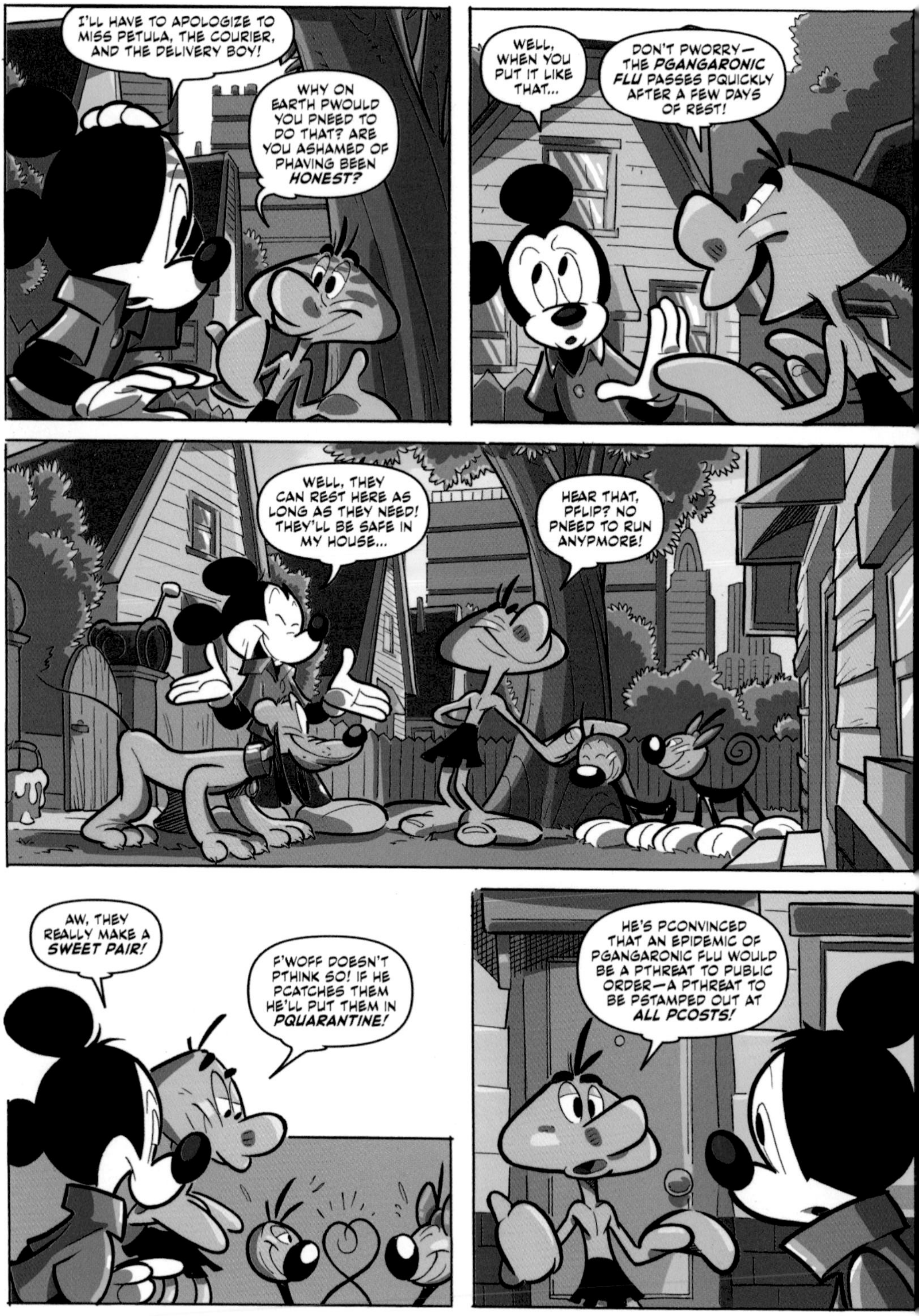
I'LL HAVE TO APOLOGIZE TO MISS PETULA, THE COURIER, AND THE DELIVERY BOY!
WHY ON EARTH PWOULD YOU PNEED TO DO THAT? ARE YOU ASHAMED OF PHAVING BEEN **HONEST?**
WELL, WHEN YOU PUT IT LIKE THAT...
DON'T PWORRY— THE **PGANGARONIC FLU** PASSES PQUICKLY AFTER A FEW DAYS OF REST!
WELL, THEY CAN REST HERE AS LONG AS THEY NEED! THEY'LL BE SAFE IN MY HOUSE...
HEAR THAT, PFLIP? NO PNEED TO RUN ANYMORE!
AW, THEY REALLY MAKE A **SWEET PAIR!**
F'WOFF DOESN'T PTHINK SO! IF HE PCATCHES THEM HE'LL PUT THEM IN **PQUARANTINE!**
HE'S PCONVINCED THAT AN EPIDEMIC OF PGANGARONIC FLU WOULD BE A PTHREAT TO PUBLIC ORDER—A PTHREAT TO BE PSTAMPED OUT AT **ALL PCOSTS!**

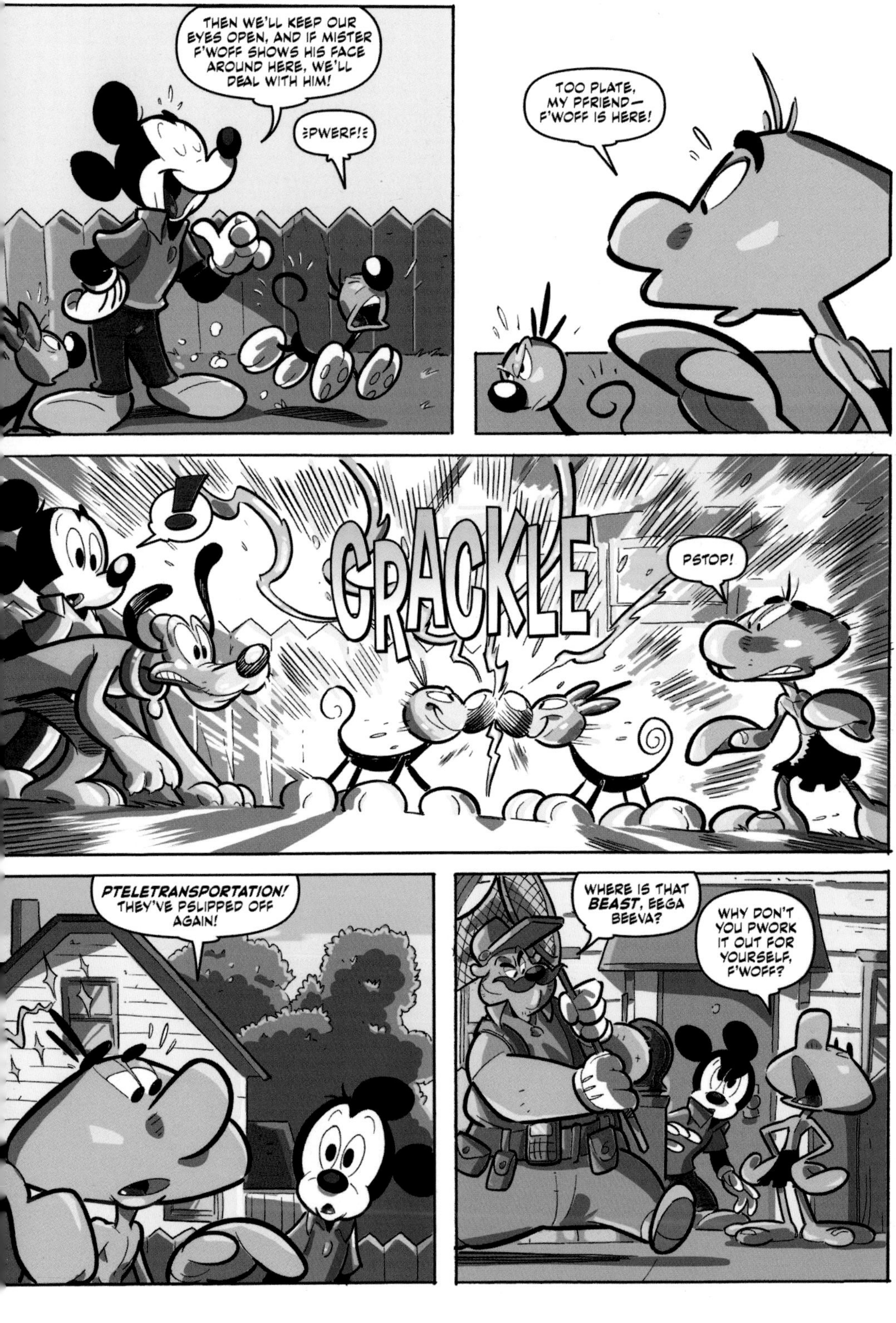

THEN WE'LL KEEP OUR EYES OPEN, AND IF MISTER F'WOFF SHOWS HIS FACE AROUND HERE, WE'LL DEAL WITH HIM!
PWERF!
TOO PLATE, MY PFRIEND— F'WOFF IS HERE!
!
CRACKLE
PSTOP!
PTELETRANSPORTATION! THEY'VE PSLIPPED OFF AGAIN!
WHERE IS THAT BEAST, EEGA BEEVA?
WHY DON'T YOU PWORK IT OUT FOR YOURSELF, F'WOFF?

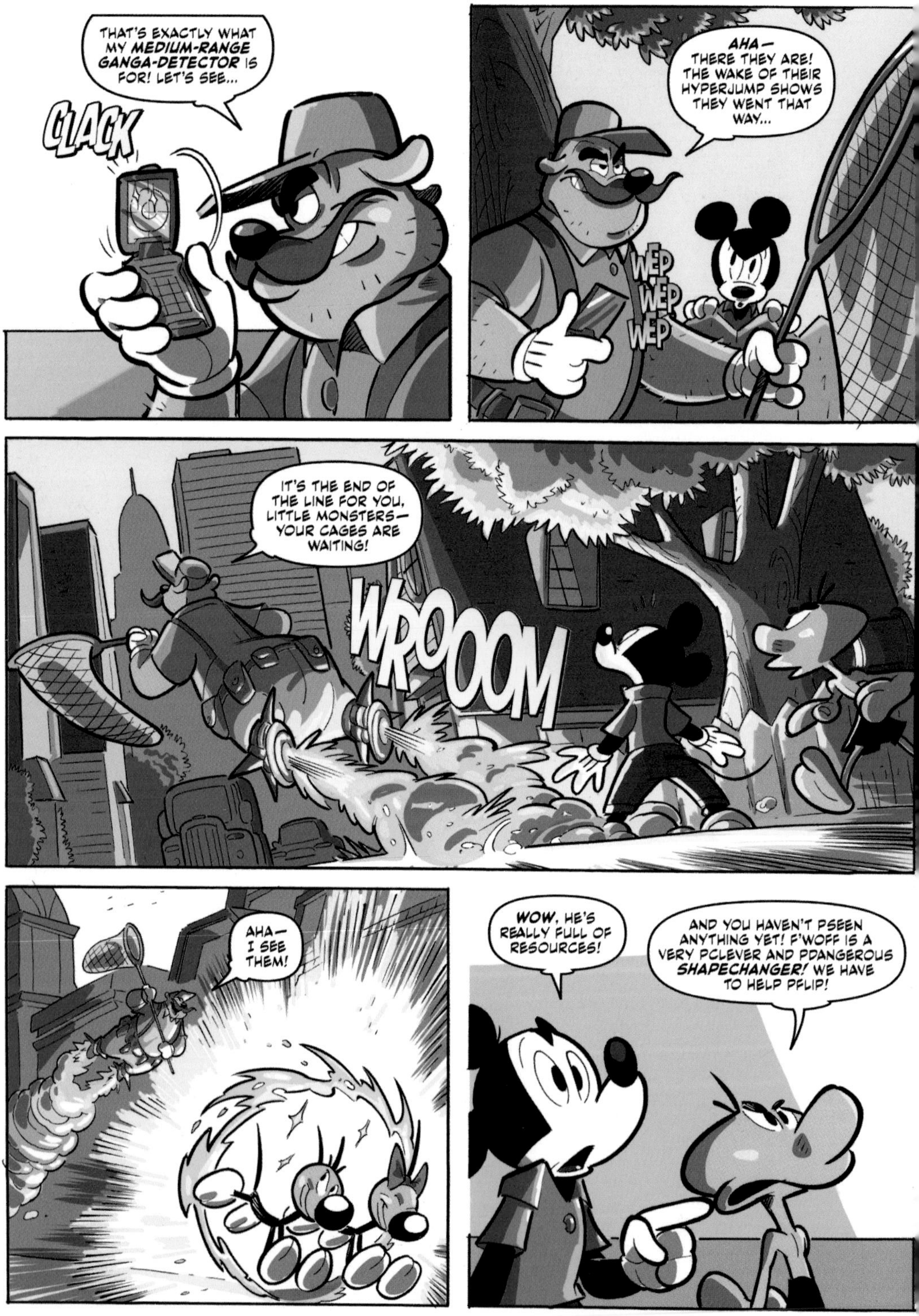
THAT'S EXACTLY WHAT MY MEDIUM-RANGE GANGA-DETECTOR IS FOR! LET'S SEE...
CLACK
AHA— THERE THEY ARE! THE WAKE OF THEIR HYPERJUMP SHOWS THEY WENT THAT WAY...
WEP WEP WEP
IT'S THE END OF THE LINE FOR YOU, LITTLE MONSTERS— YOUR CAGES ARE WAITING!
WROOOM
AHA— I SEE THEM!
WOW, HE'S REALLY FULL OF RESOURCES!
AND YOU HAVEN'T PSEEN ANYTHING YET! F'WOFF IS A VERY PCLEVER AND PDANGEROUS SHAPECHANGER! WE HAVE TO HELP PFLIP!

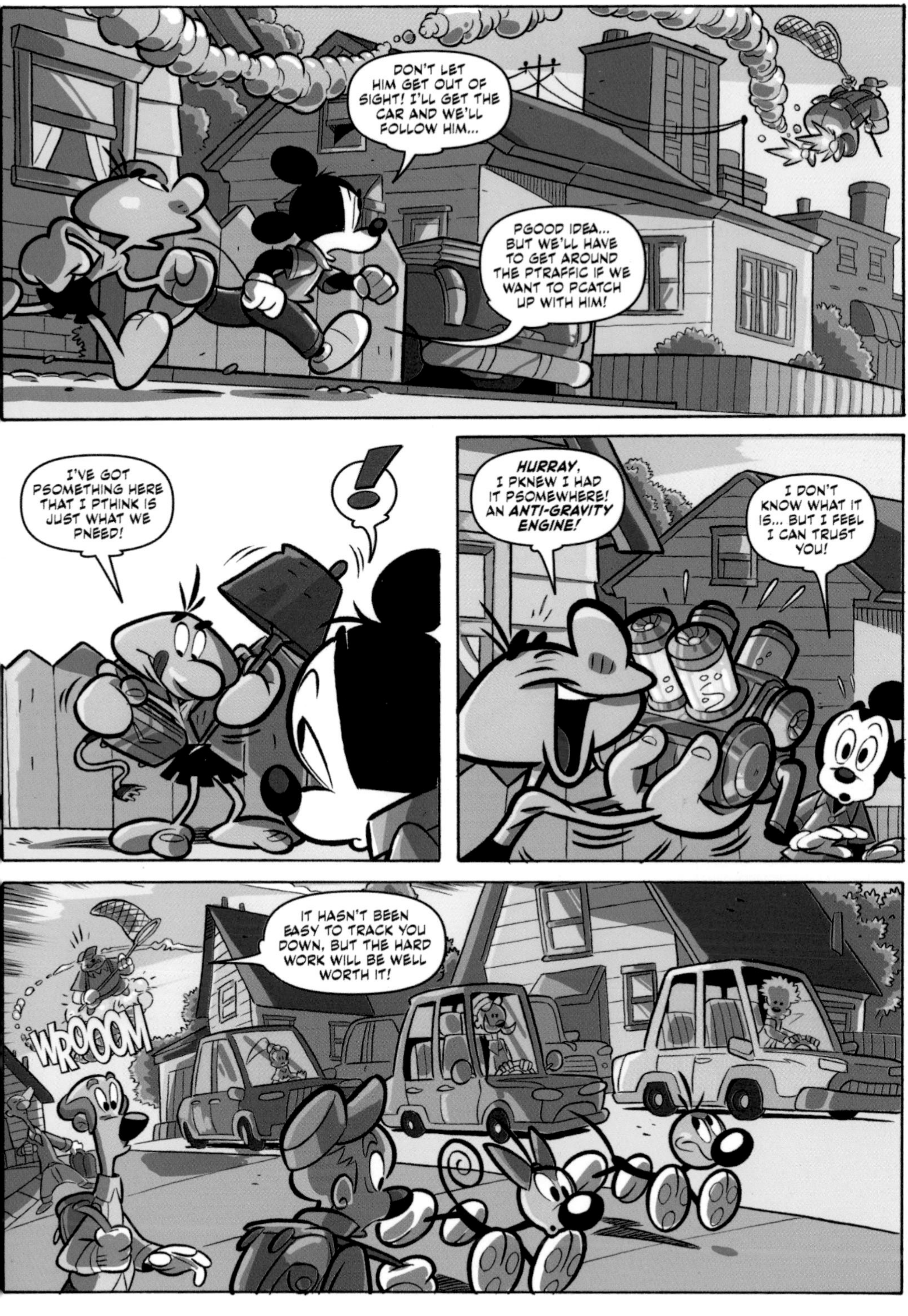
DON'T LET HIM GET OUT OF SIGHT! I'LL GET THE CAR AND WE'LL FOLLOW HIM...
PGOOD IDEA... BUT WE'LL HAVE TO GET AROUND THE PTRAFFIC IF WE WANT TO PCATCH UP WITH HIM!
I'VE GOT PSOMETHING HERE THAT I PTHINK IS JUST WHAT WE PNEED!
!
HURRAY, I PKNEW I HAD IT PSOMEWHERE! AN ANTI-GRAVITY ENGINE!
I DON'T KNOW WHAT IT IS... BUT I FEEL I CAN TRUST YOU!
WROOOM
IT HASN'T BEEN EASY TO TRACK YOU DOWN, BUT THE HARD WORK WILL BE WELL WORTH IT!

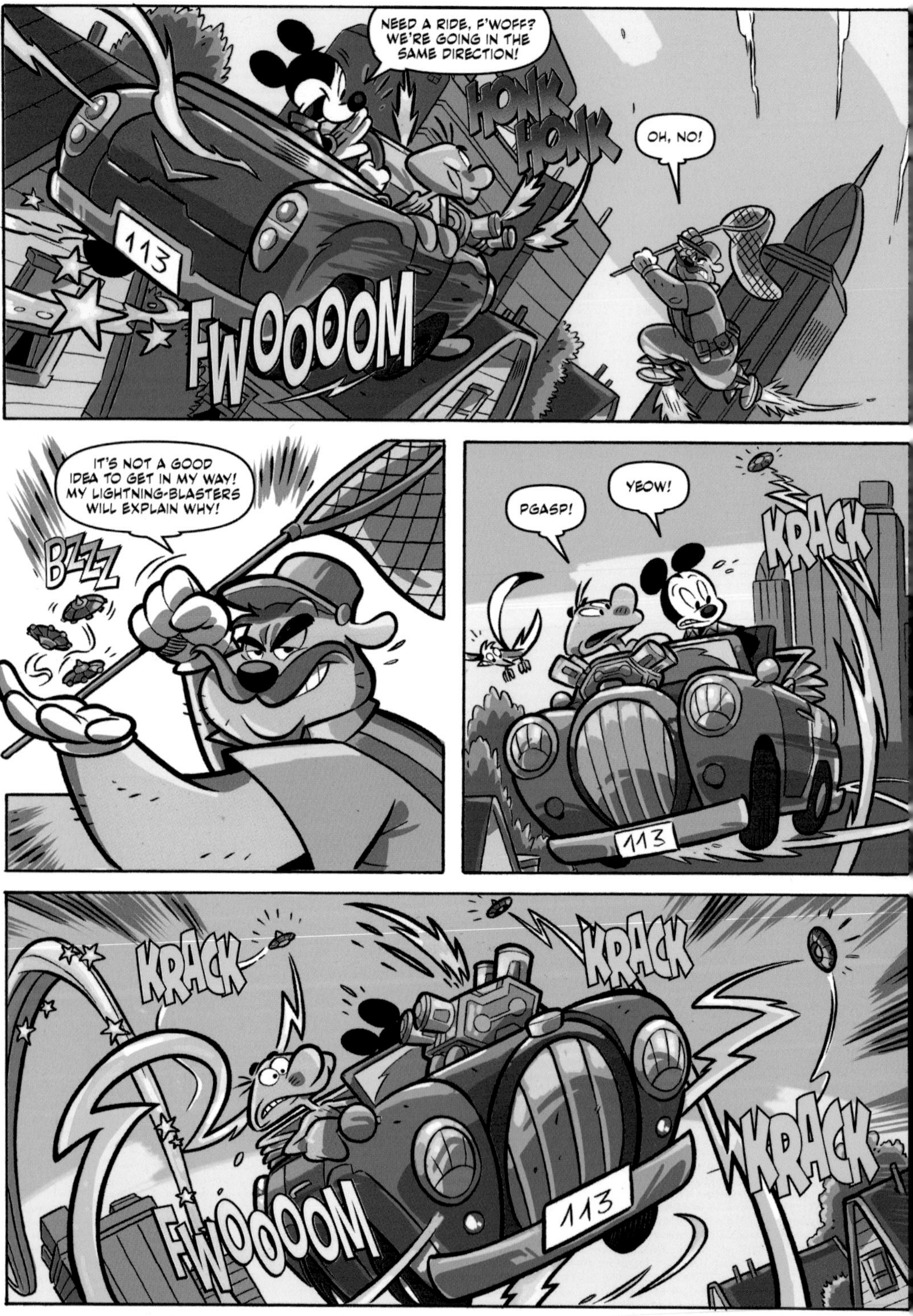
NEED A RIDE, F'WOFF? WE'RE GOING IN THE SAME DIRECTION!
HONK HONK
OH, NO!
113
FWOOOOM
IT'S NOT A GOOD IDEA TO GET IN MY WAY! MY LIGHTNING-BLASTERS WILL EXPLAIN WHY!
BZZZ
PGASP!
YEOW!
KRACK
113
KRACK
KRACK
KRACK
FWOOOOM
113

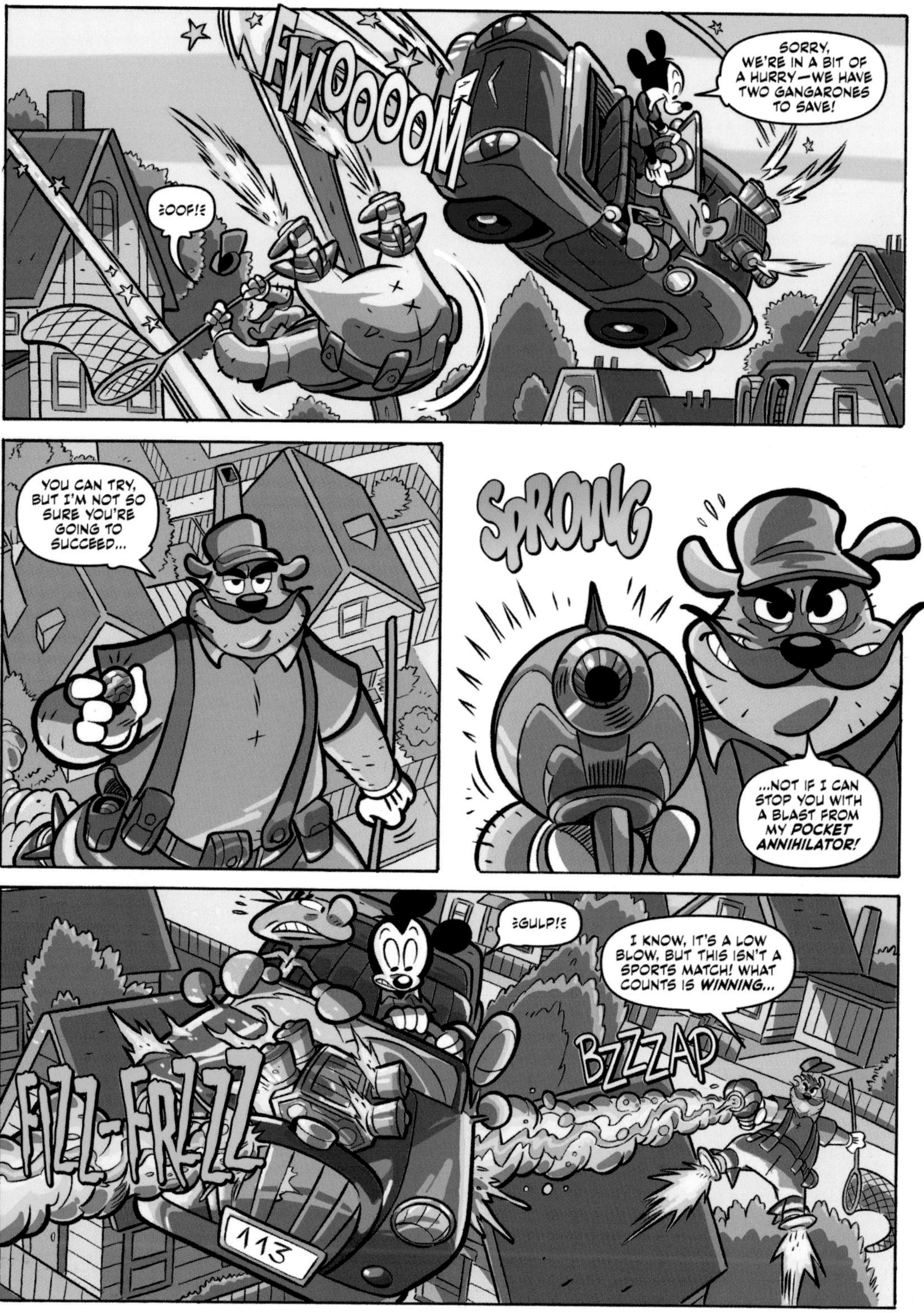
FWOOOOM
SORRY, WE'RE IN A BIT OF A HURRY—WE HAVE TWO GANGARONES TO SAVE!
OOF!
YOU CAN TRY, BUT I'M NOT SO SURE YOU'RE GOING TO SUCCEED...
SPRONG
...NOT IF I CAN STOP YOU WITH A BLAST FROM MY POCKET ANNIHILATOR!
GULP!
I KNOW, IT'S A LOW BLOW, BUT THIS ISN'T A SPORTS MATCH! WHAT COUNTS IS WINNING...
BZZZAP
FIZZ-FRZZZ
113

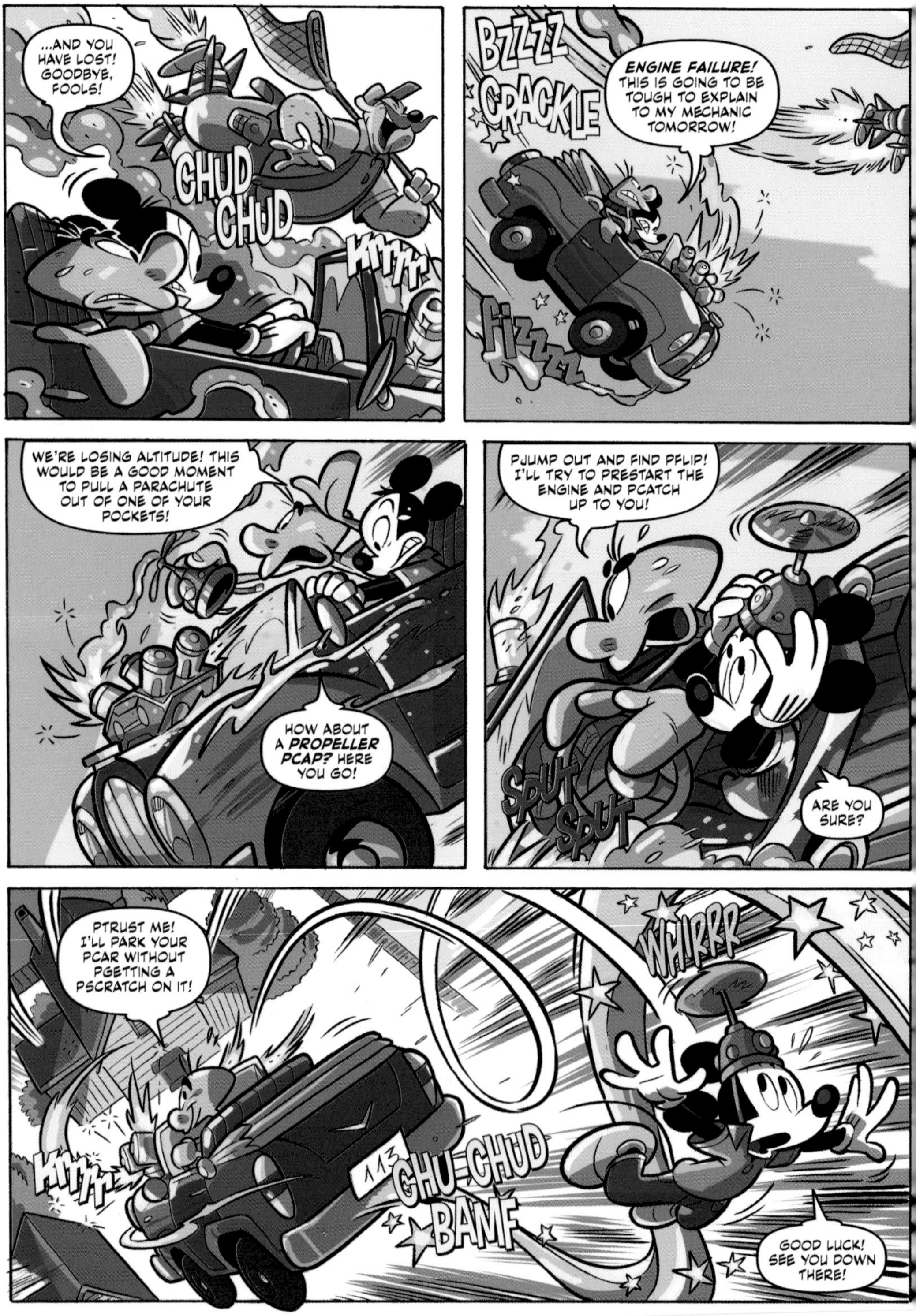
...AND YOU HAVE LOST! GOODBYE, FOOLS!
CHUD CHUD
KRRRR
BZZZZ
CRACKLE
ENGINE FAILURE! THIS IS GOING TO BE TOUGH TO EXPLAIN TO MY MECHANIC TOMORROW!
FIZZZZ
WE'RE LOSING ALTITUDE! THIS WOULD BE A GOOD MOMENT TO PULL A PARACHUTE OUT OF ONE OF YOUR POCKETS!
HOW ABOUT A PROPELLER PCAP? HERE YOU GO!
PJUMP OUT AND FIND PFLIP! I'LL TRY TO PRESTART THE ENGINE AND PCATCH UP TO YOU!
SPUT SPUT
ARE YOU SURE?
PTRUST ME! I'LL PARK YOUR PCAR WITHOUT PGETTING A PSCRATCH ON IT!
WHIRRR
KRRRRR
113
CHU CHUD
BAMF
GOOD LUCK! SEE YOU DOWN THERE!

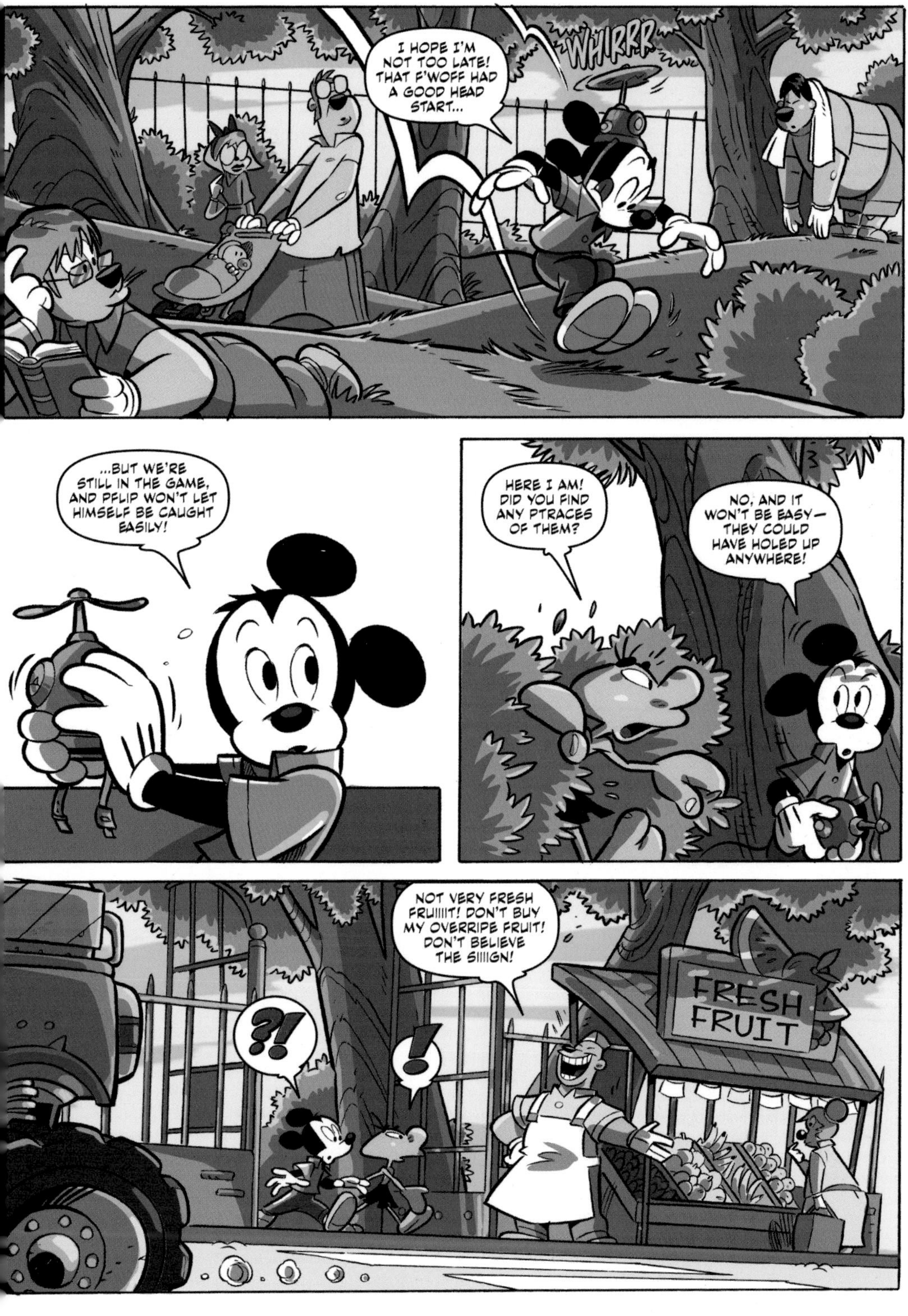
WHIRRR
I HOPE I'M NOT TOO LATE! THAT F'WOFF HAD A GOOD HEAD START...
...BUT WE'RE STILL IN THE GAME, AND PFLIP WON'T LET HIMSELF BE CAUGHT EASILY!
HERE I AM! DID YOU FIND ANY PTRACES OF THEM?
NO, AND IT WON'T BE EASY— THEY COULD HAVE HOLED UP ANYWHERE!
NOT VERY FRESH FRUIIIIIT! DON'T BUY MY OVERRIPE FRUIT! DON'T BELIEVE THE SIIIIGN!
?!
!
FRESH FRUIT

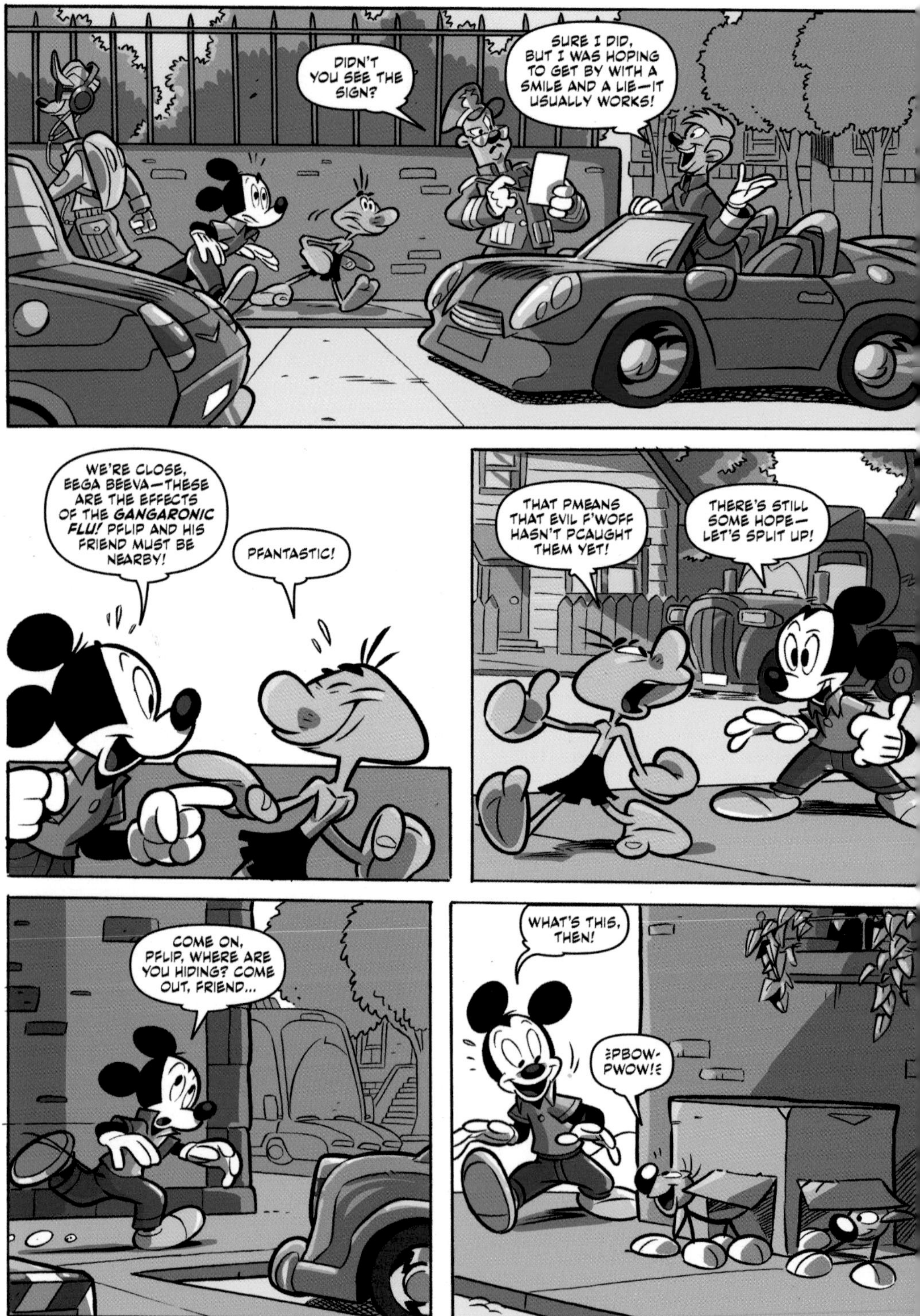
DIDN'T YOU SEE THE SIGN?
SURE I DID, BUT I WAS HOPING TO GET BY WITH A SMILE AND A LIE—IT USUALLY WORKS!
WE'RE CLOSE, EEGA BEEVA—THESE ARE THE EFFECTS OF THE *GANGARONIC FLU!* PFLIP AND HIS FRIEND MUST BE NEARBY!
PFANTASTIC!
THAT PMEANS THAT EVIL F'WOFF HASN'T PCAUGHT THEM YET!
THERE'S STILL SOME HOPE—LET'S SPLIT UP!
COME ON, PFLIP, WHERE ARE YOU HIDING? COME OUT, FRIEND...
WHAT'S THIS, THEN!
PBOW-PWOW!

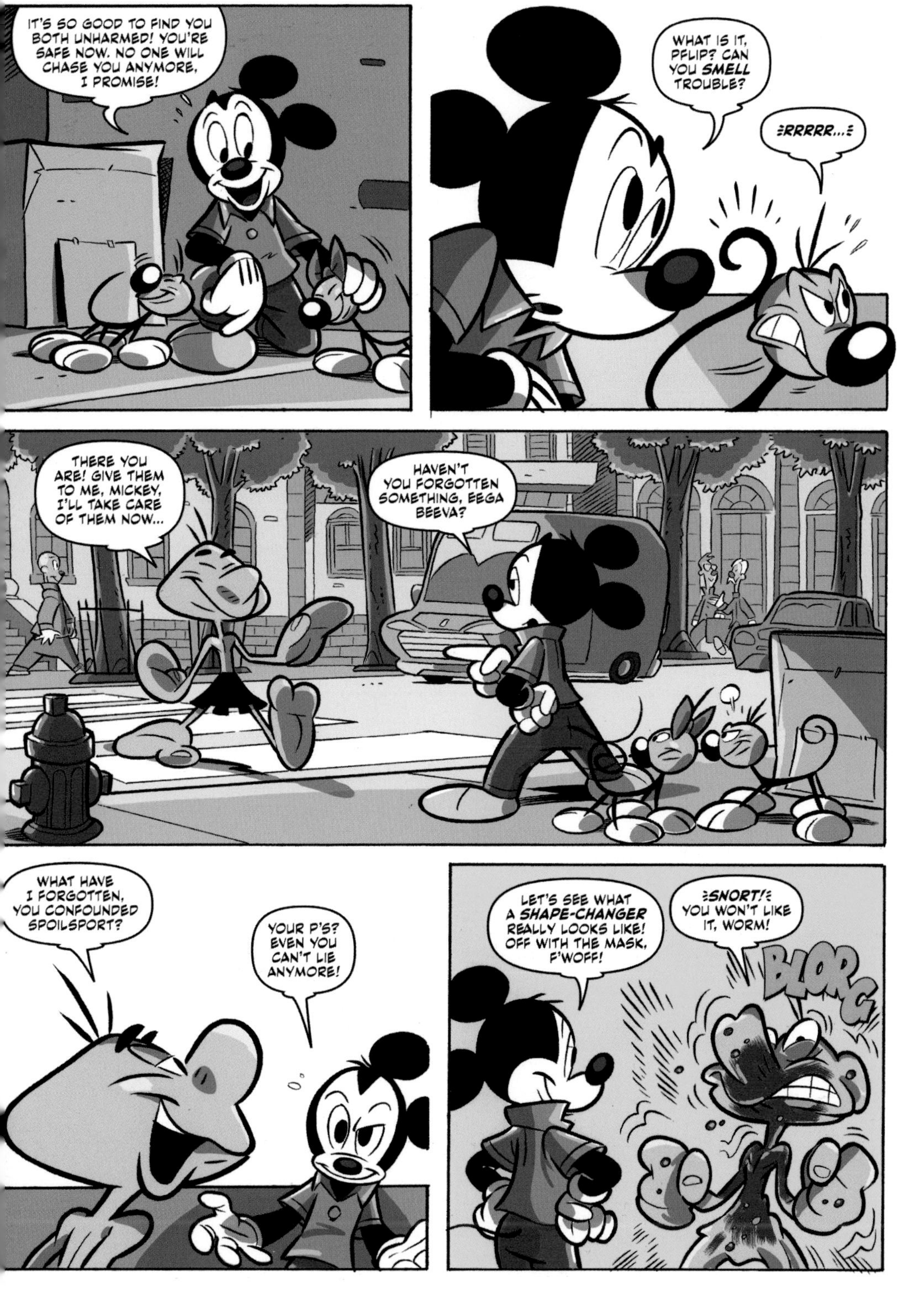

IT'S SO GOOD TO FIND YOU BOTH UNHARMED! YOU'RE SAFE NOW. NO ONE WILL CHASE YOU ANYMORE, I PROMISE!
WHAT IS IT, PFLIP? CAN YOU SMELL TROUBLE?
RRRRR...
THERE YOU ARE! GIVE THEM TO ME, MICKEY. I'LL TAKE CARE OF THEM NOW...
HAVEN'T YOU FORGOTTEN SOMETHING, EEGA BEEVA?
WHAT HAVE I FORGOTTEN, YOU CONFOUNDED SPOILSPORT?
YOUR P'S? EVEN YOU CAN'T LIE ANYMORE!
LET'S SEE WHAT A SHAPE-CHANGER REALLY LOOKS LIKE! OFF WITH THE MASK, F'WOFF!
SNORT! YOU WON'T LIKE IT, WORM!
BLORG

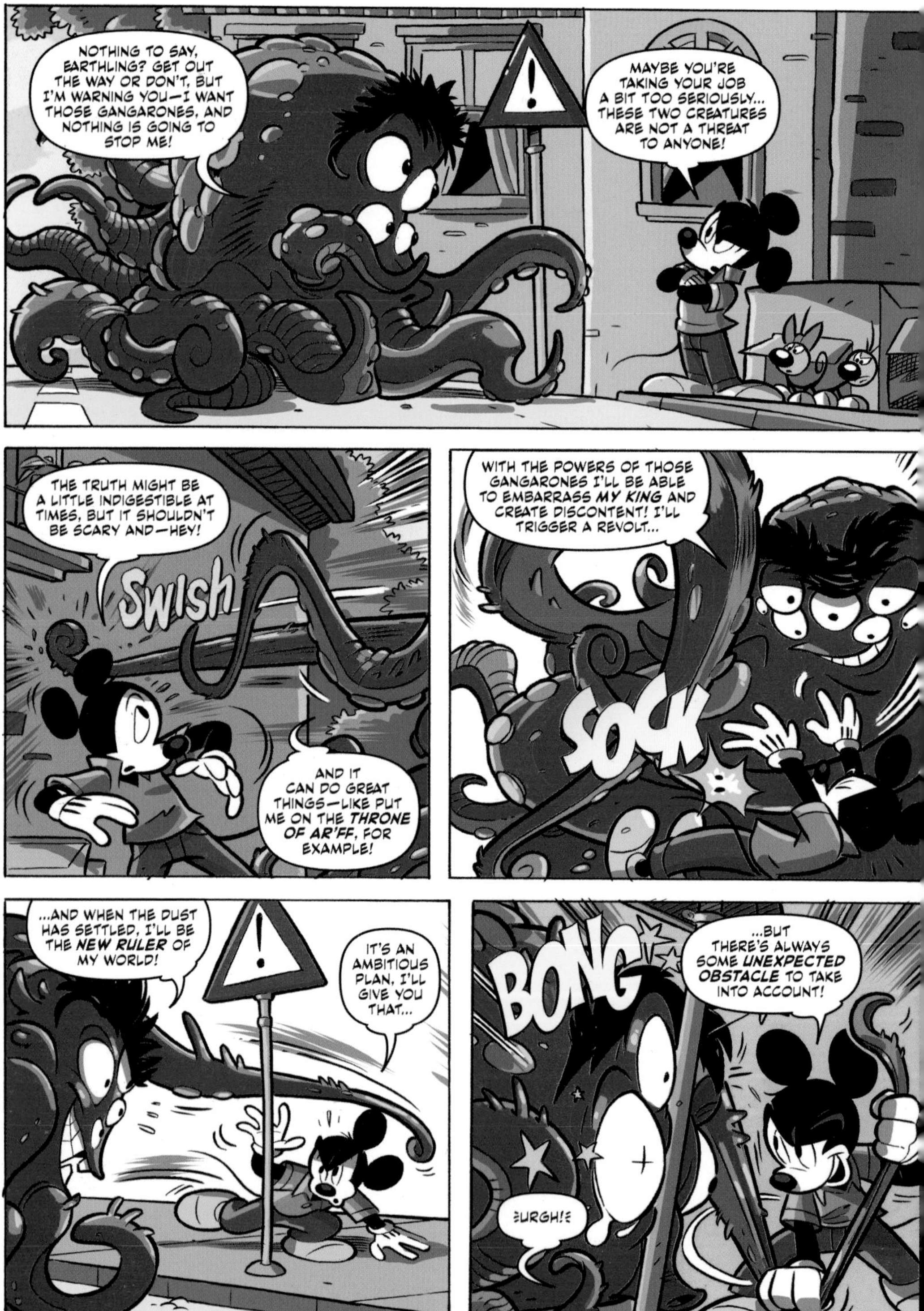

NOTHING TO SAY, EARTHLING? GET OUT THE WAY OR DON'T, BUT I'M WARNING YOU—I WANT THOSE GANGARONES, AND NOTHING IS GOING TO STOP ME!
MAYBE YOU'RE TAKING YOUR JOB A BIT TOO SERIOUSLY... THESE TWO CREATURES ARE NOT A THREAT TO ANYONE!
THE TRUTH MIGHT BE A LITTLE INDIGESTIBLE AT TIMES, BUT IT SHOULDN'T BE SCARY AND—HEY!
SWISH
AND IT CAN DO GREAT THINGS—LIKE PUT ME ON THE THRONE OF AR'FF, FOR EXAMPLE!
WITH THE POWERS OF THOSE GANGARONES I'LL BE ABLE TO EMBARRASS MY KING AND CREATE DISCONTENT! I'LL TRIGGER A REVOLT...
SOCK
...AND WHEN THE DUST HAS SETTLED, I'LL BE THE NEW RULER OF MY WORLD!
IT'S AN AMBITIOUS PLAN, I'LL GIVE YOU THAT...
BONG
...BUT THERE'S ALWAYS SOME UNEXPECTED OBSTACLE TO TAKE INTO ACCOUNT!
URGH!

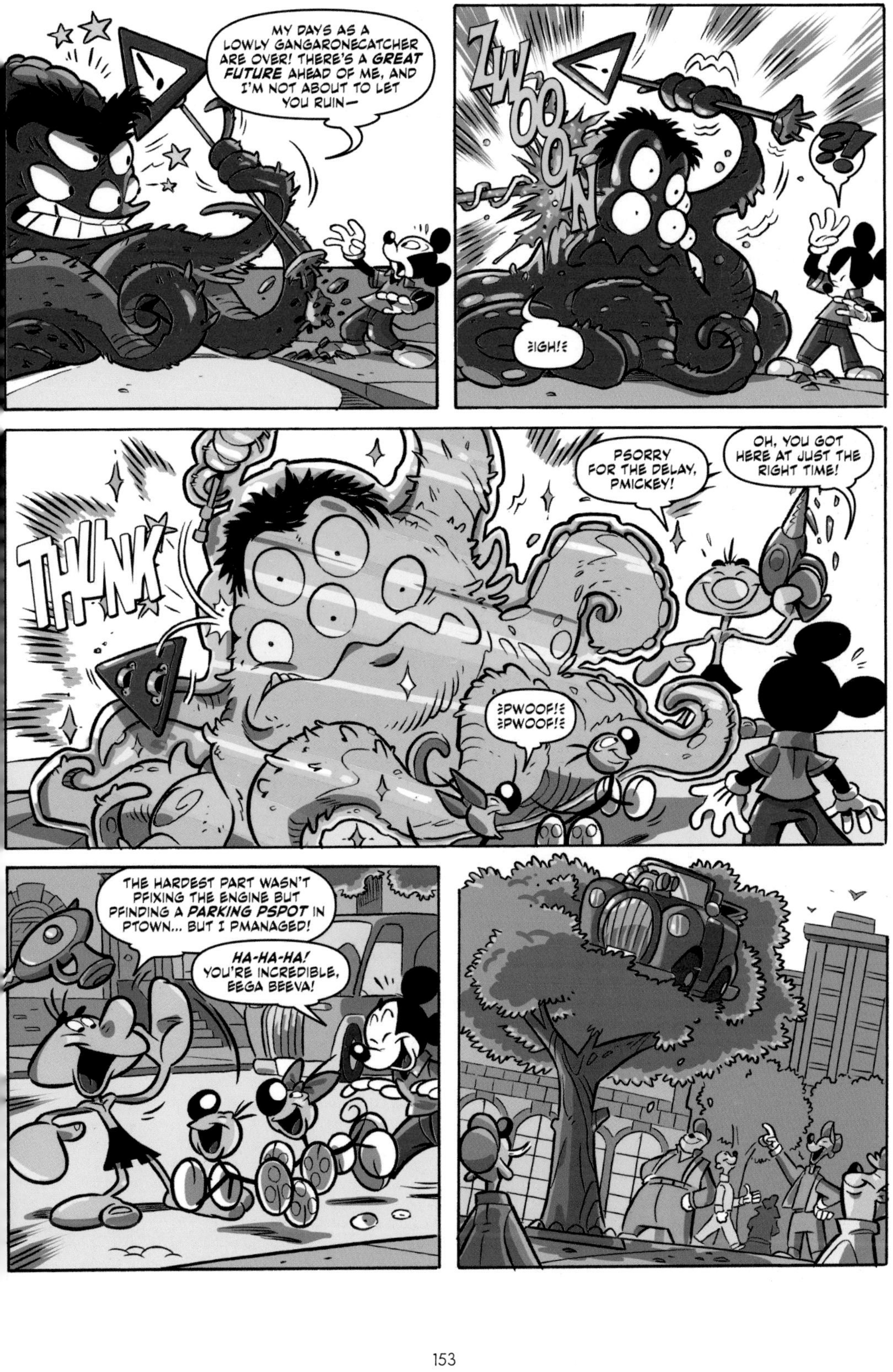
MY DAYS AS A LOWLY GANGARONECATCHER ARE OVER! THERE'S A **GREAT FUTURE** AHEAD OF ME, AND I'M NOT ABOUT TO LET YOU RUIN—
ZWOOOON
?!
EIGH!
THUNK
PSORRY FOR THE DELAY, PMICKEY!
OH, YOU GOT HERE AT JUST THE RIGHT TIME!
PWOOF! PWOOF!
THE HARDEST PART WASN'T PFIXING THE ENGINE BUT PFINDING A **PARKING PSPOT** IN PTOWN... BUT I PMANAGED!
HA-HA-HA! YOU'RE INCREDIBLE, EEGA BEEVA!

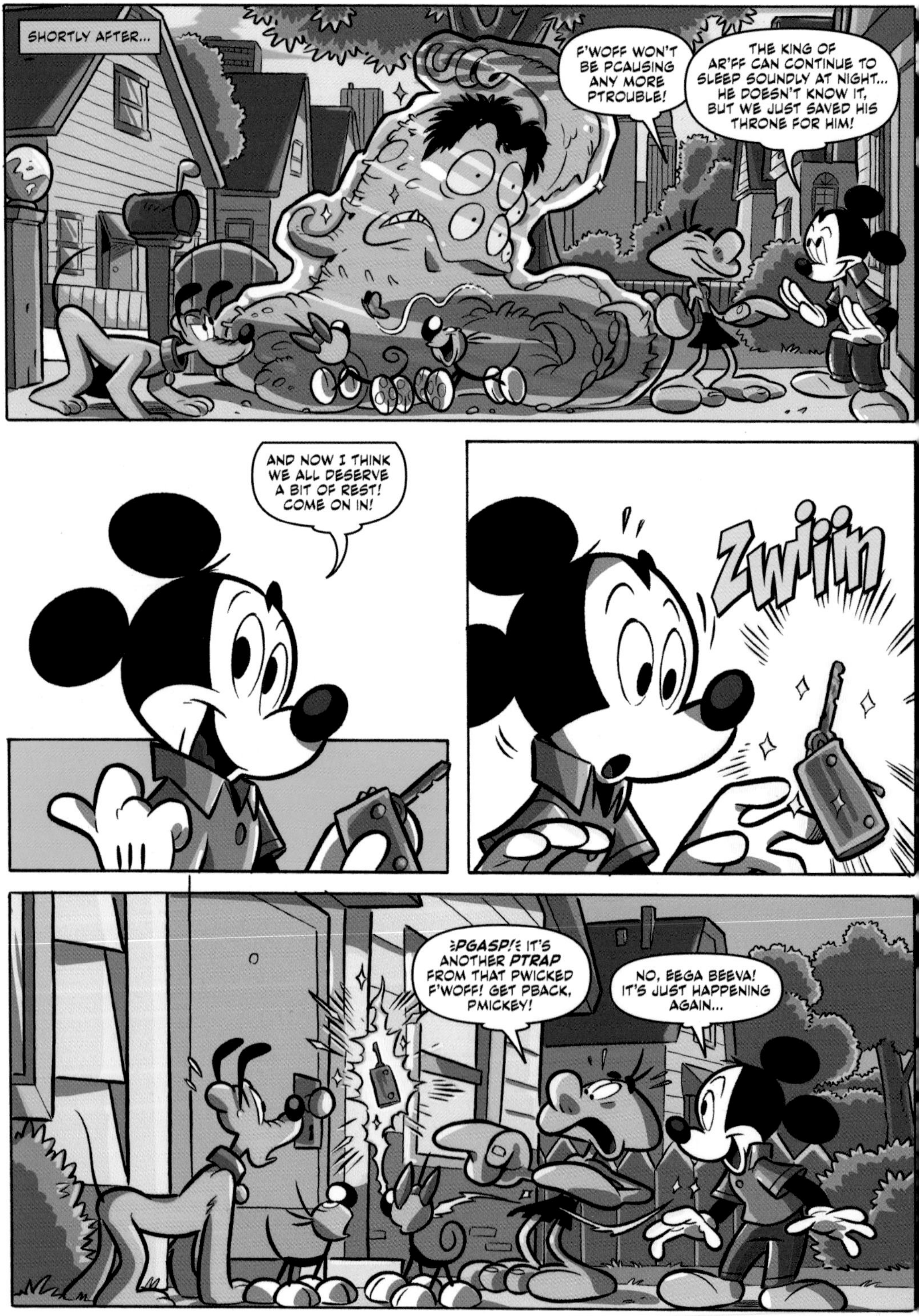
SHORTLY AFTER...
F'WOFF WON'T BE PCAUSING ANY MORE PTROUBLE!
THE KING OF AR'FF CAN CONTINUE TO SLEEP SOUNDLY AT NIGHT... HE DOESN'T KNOW IT, BUT WE JUST SAVED HIS THRONE FOR HIM!
AND NOW I THINK WE ALL DESERVE A BIT OF REST! COME ON IN!
ZWIIN
PGASP! IT'S ANOTHER *PTRAP* FROM THAT PWICKED F'WOFF! GET PBACK, PMICKEY!
NO, EEGA BEEVA! IT'S JUST HAPPENING AGAIN...

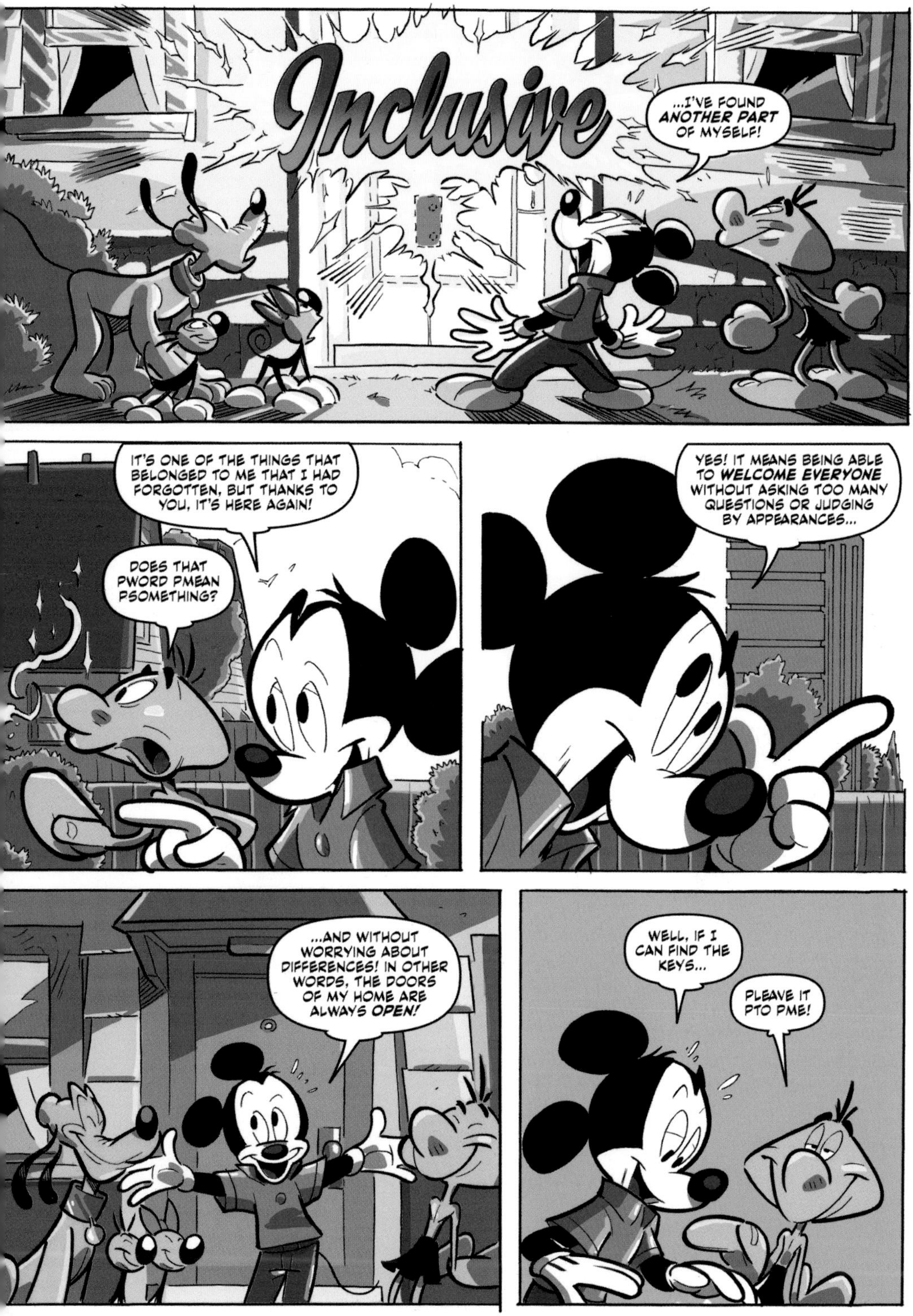
Inclusive
...I'VE FOUND ANOTHER PART OF MYSELF!
IT'S ONE OF THE THINGS THAT BELONGED TO ME THAT I HAD FORGOTTEN, BUT THANKS TO YOU, IT'S HERE AGAIN!
DOES THAT PWORD PMEAN PSOMETHING?
YES! IT MEANS BEING ABLE TO WELCOME EVERYONE WITHOUT ASKING TOO MANY QUESTIONS OR JUDGING BY APPEARANCES...
...AND WITHOUT WORRYING ABOUT DIFFERENCES! IN OTHER WORDS, THE DOORS OF MY HOME ARE ALWAYS OPEN!
WELL, IF I CAN FIND THE KEYS...
PLEAVE IT PTO PME!

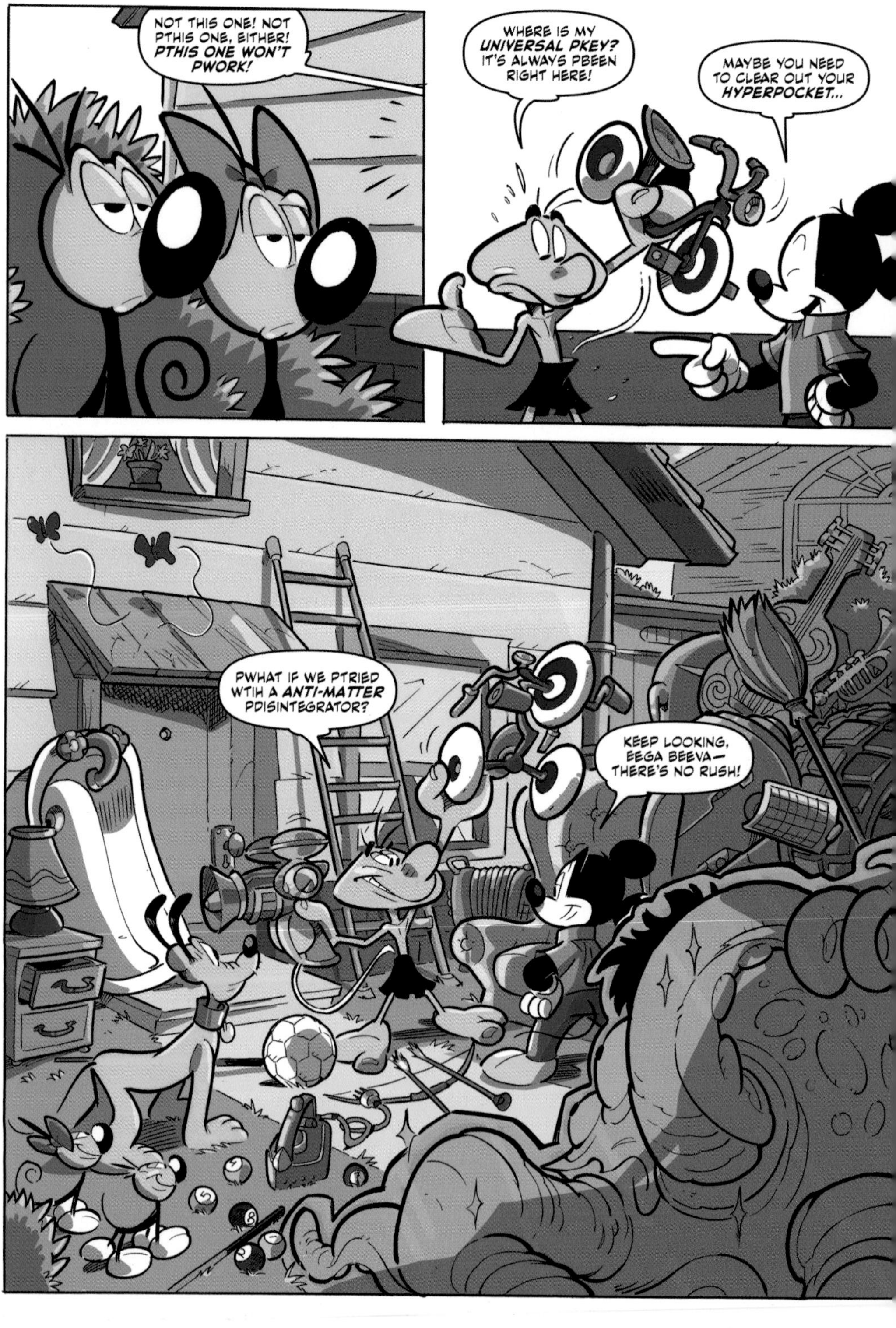
NOT THIS ONE! NOT PTHIS ONE, EITHER! PTHIS ONE WON'T PWORK!
WHERE IS MY UNIVERSAL PKEY? IT'S ALWAYS PBEEN RIGHT HERE!
MAYBE YOU NEED TO CLEAR OUT YOUR HYPERPOCKET...
PWHAT IF WE PTRIED WTIH A ANTI-MATTER PDISINTEGRATOR?
KEEP LOOKING, EEGA BEEVA— THERE'S NO RUSH!

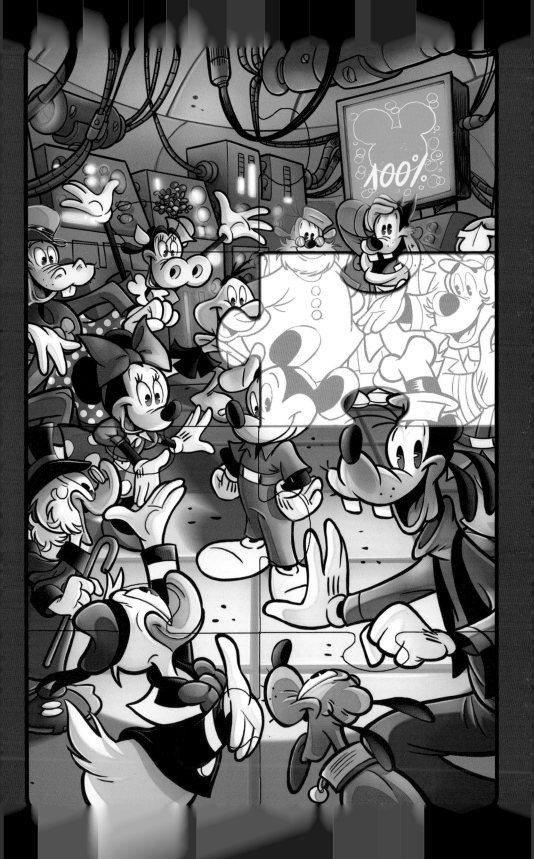

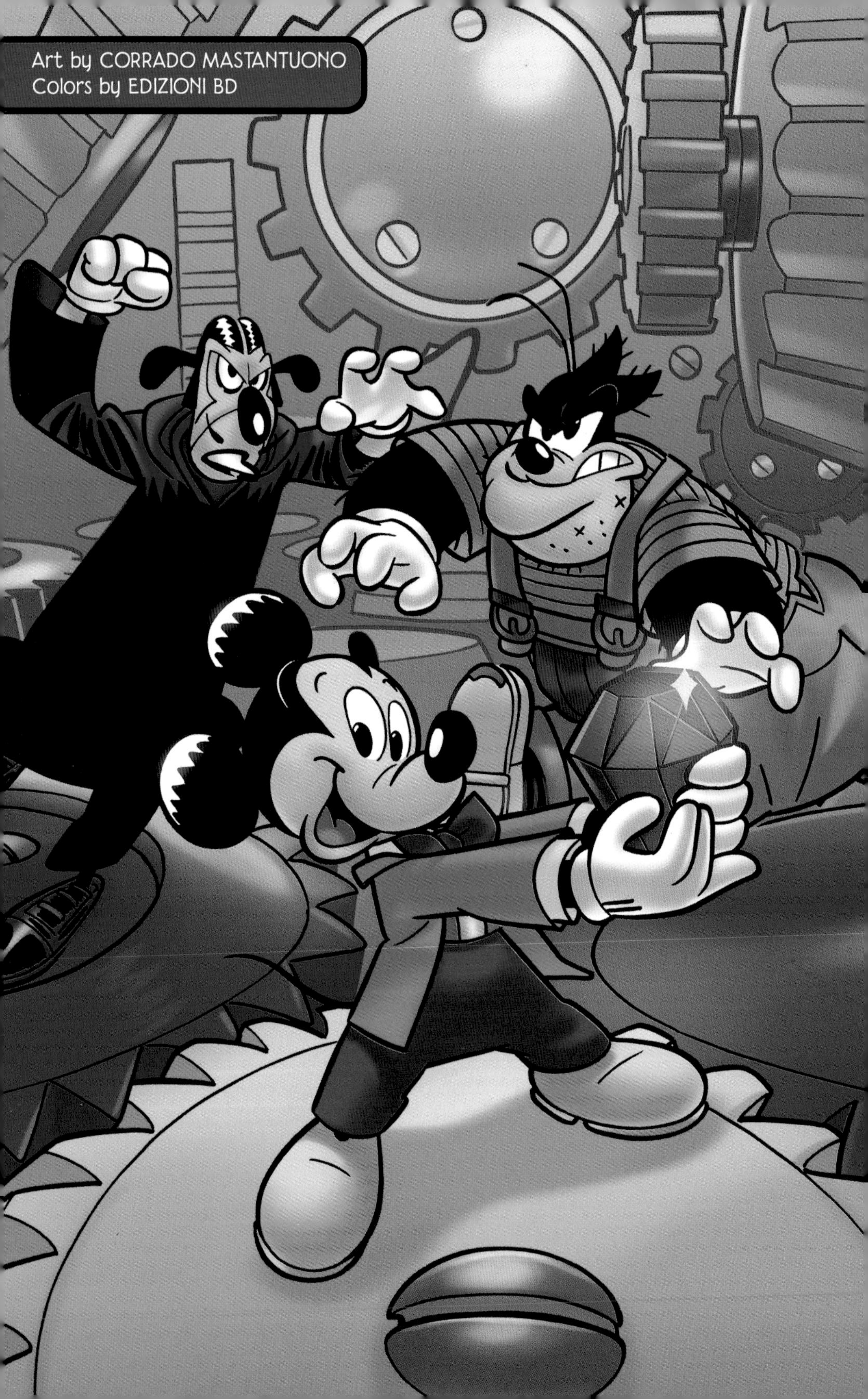
Art by CORRADO MASTANTUONO
Colors by EDIZIONI BD

CHAPTER 8: THE MEMORY MACHINE

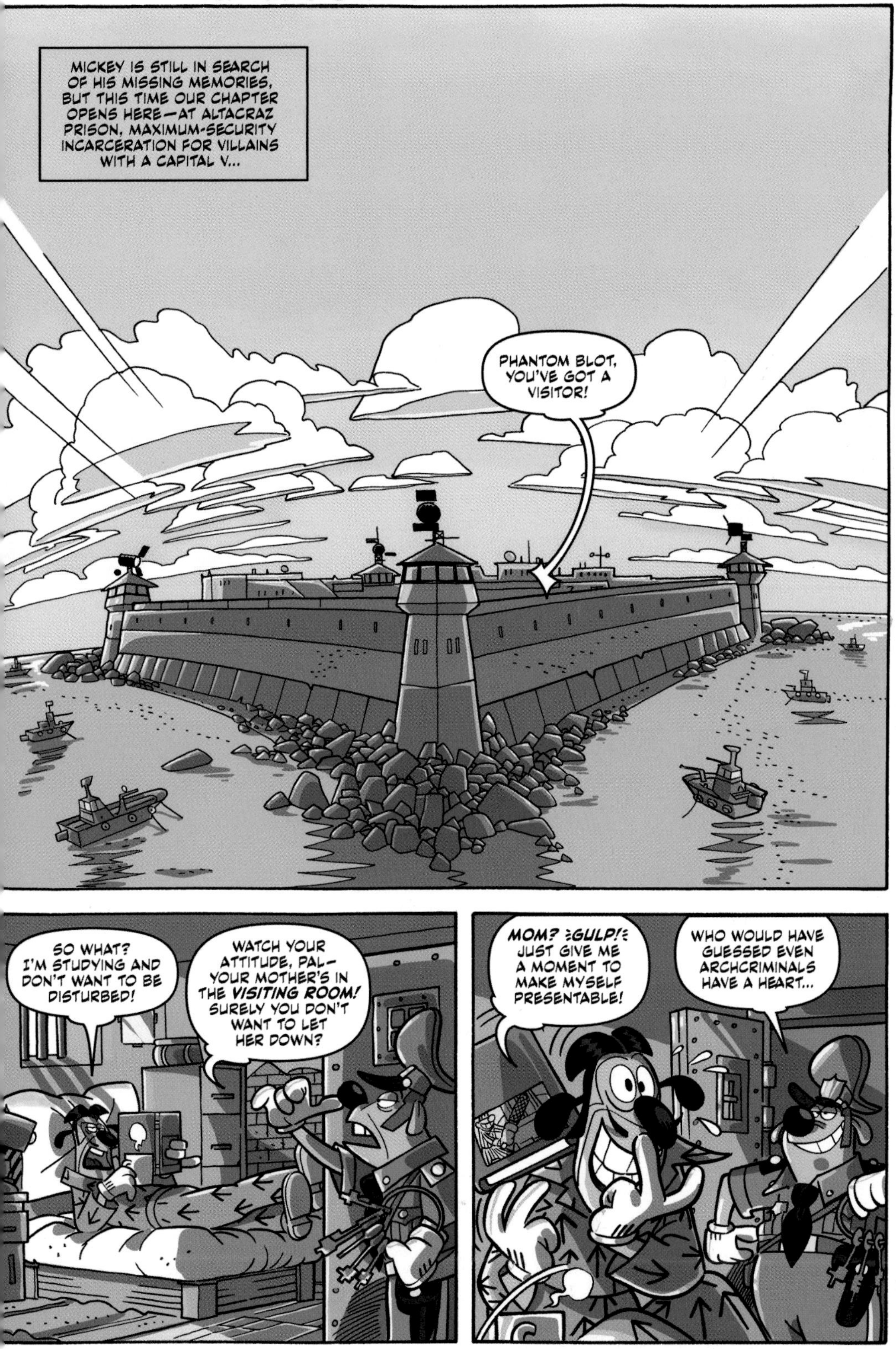
MICKEY IS STILL IN SEARCH OF HIS MISSING MEMORIES, BUT THIS TIME OUR CHAPTER OPENS HERE—AT ALTACRAZ PRISON, MAXIMUM-SECURITY INCARCERATION FOR VILLAINS WITH A CAPITAL V...
PHANTOM BLOT, YOU'VE GOT A VISITOR!
SO WHAT? I'M STUDYING AND DON'T WANT TO BE DISTURBED!
WATCH YOUR ATTITUDE, PAL—YOUR MOTHER'S IN THE *VISITING ROOM!* SURELY YOU DON'T WANT TO LET HER DOWN?
MOM? *GULP!* JUST GIVE ME A MOMENT TO MAKE MYSELF PRESENTABLE!
WHO WOULD HAVE GUESSED EVEN ARCHCRIMINALS HAVE A HEART...

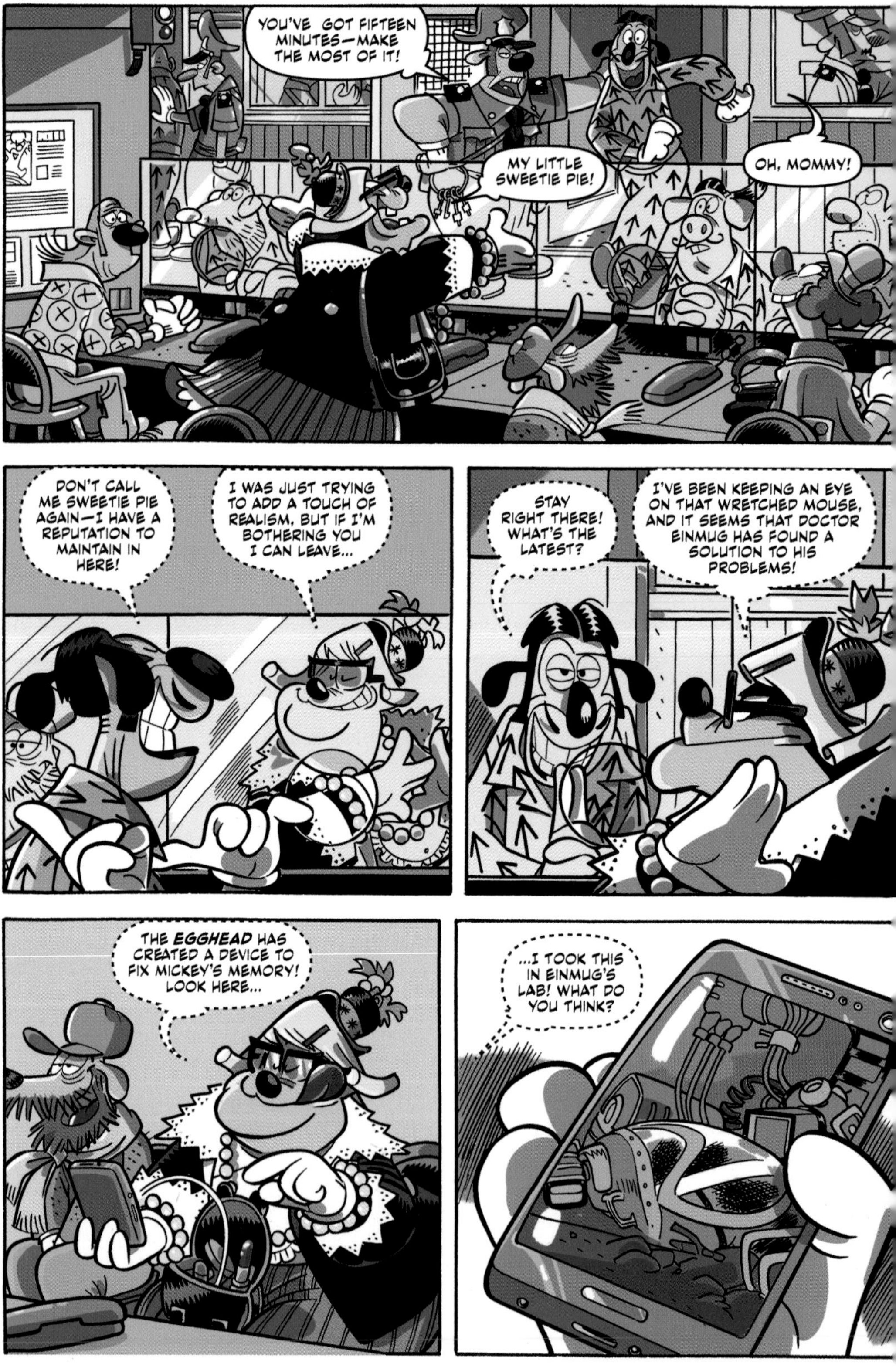

YOU'VE GOT FIFTEEN MINUTES—MAKE THE MOST OF IT!
MY LITTLE SWEETIE PIE!
OH, MOMMY!
DON'T CALL ME SWEETIE PIE AGAIN—I HAVE A REPUTATION TO MAINTAIN IN HERE!
I WAS JUST TRYING TO ADD A TOUCH OF REALISM, BUT IF I'M BOTHERING YOU I CAN LEAVE...
STAY RIGHT THERE! WHAT'S THE LATEST?
I'VE BEEN KEEPING AN EYE ON THAT WRETCHED MOUSE, AND IT SEEMS THAT DOCTOR EINMUG HAS FOUND A SOLUTION TO HIS PROBLEMS!
THE *EGGHEAD* HAS CREATED A DEVICE TO FIX MICKEY'S MEMORY! LOOK HERE...
...I TOOK THIS IN EINMUG'S LAB! WHAT DO YOU THINK?

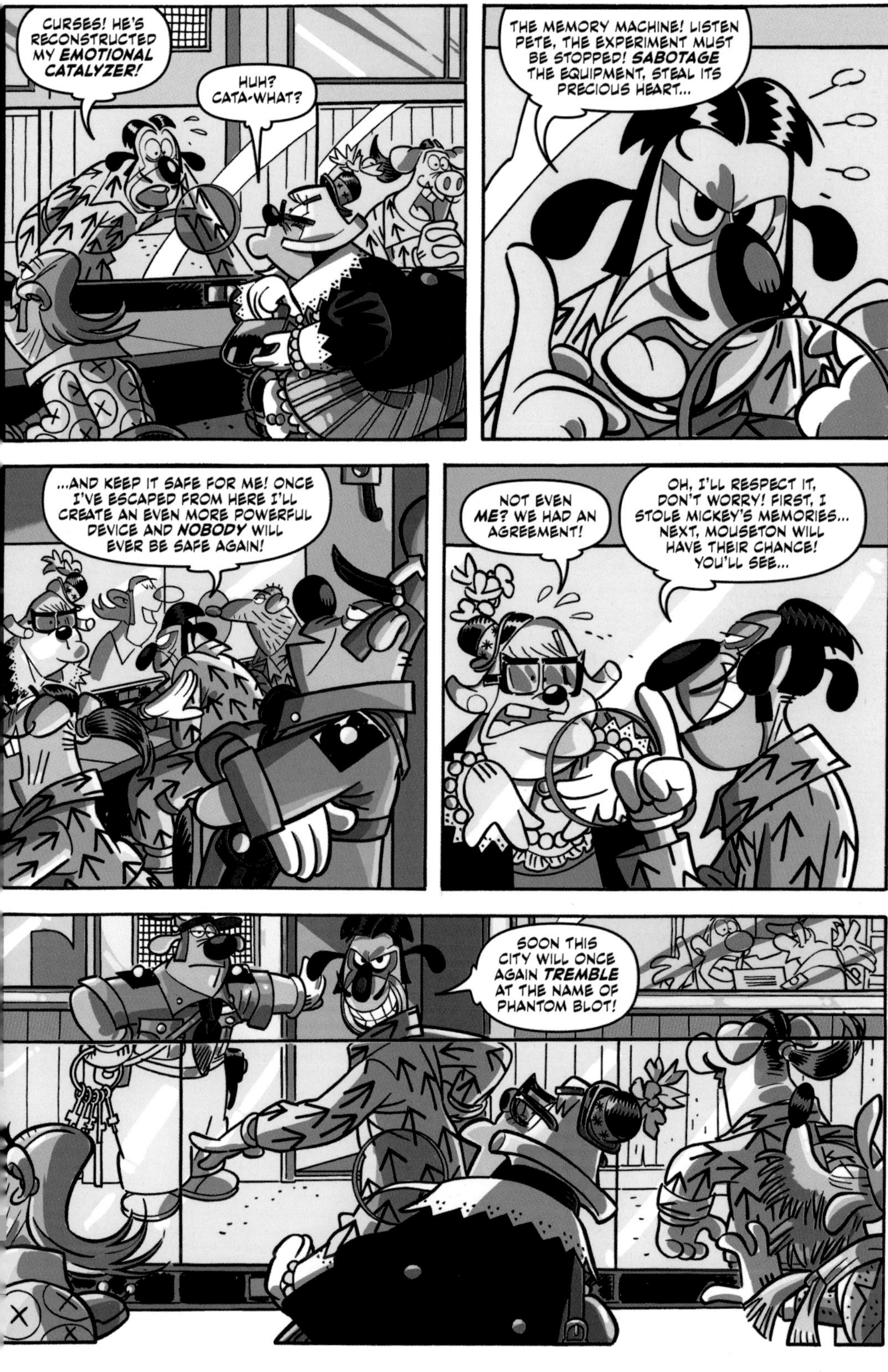
CURSES! HE'S RECONSTRUCTED MY EMOTIONAL CATALYZER!
HUH? CATA-WHAT?
THE MEMORY MACHINE! LISTEN PETE, THE EXPERIMENT MUST BE STOPPED! SABOTAGE THE EQUIPMENT, STEAL ITS PRECIOUS HEART...
...AND KEEP IT SAFE FOR ME! ONCE I'VE ESCAPED FROM HERE I'LL CREATE AN EVEN MORE POWERFUL DEVICE AND NOBODY WILL EVER BE SAFE AGAIN!
NOT EVEN ME? WE HAD AN AGREEMENT!
OH, I'LL RESPECT IT, DON'T WORRY! FIRST, I STOLE MICKEY'S MEMORIES... NEXT, MOUSETON WILL HAVE THEIR CHANCE! YOU'LL SEE...
SOON THIS CITY WILL ONCE AGAIN TREMBLE AT THE NAME OF PHANTOM BLOT!

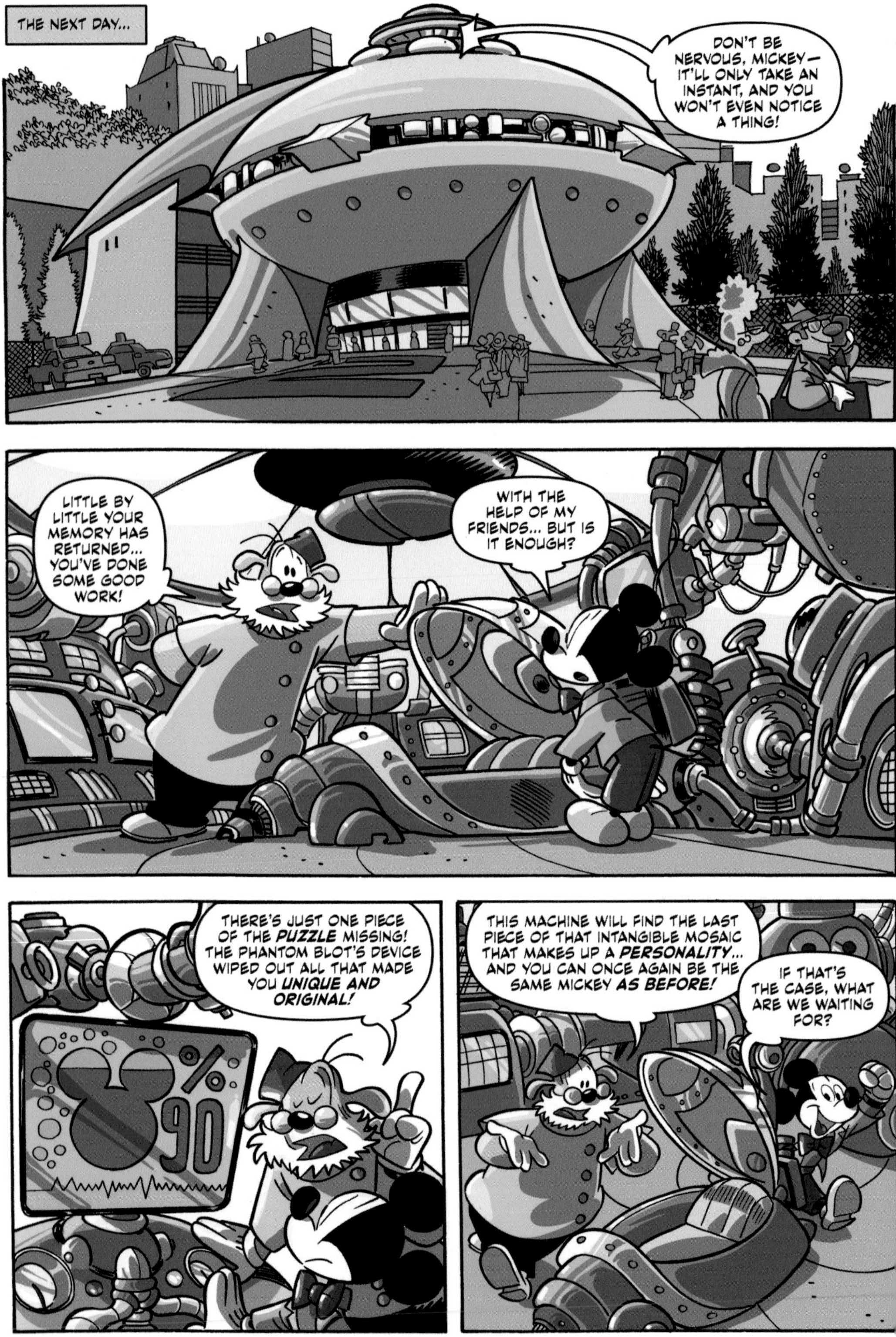
THE NEXT DAY...
DON'T BE NERVOUS, MICKEY— IT'LL ONLY TAKE AN INSTANT, AND YOU WON'T EVEN NOTICE A THING!
LITTLE BY LITTLE YOUR MEMORY HAS RETURNED... YOU'VE DONE SOME GOOD WORK!
WITH THE HELP OF MY FRIENDS... BUT IS IT ENOUGH?
THERE'S JUST ONE PIECE OF THE PUZZLE MISSING! THE PHANTOM BLOT'S DEVICE WIPED OUT ALL THAT MADE YOU UNIQUE AND ORIGINAL!
% 90
THIS MACHINE WILL FIND THE LAST PIECE OF THAT INTANGIBLE MOSAIC THAT MAKES UP A PERSONALITY... AND YOU CAN ONCE AGAIN BE THE SAME MICKEY AS BEFORE!
IF THAT'S THE CASE, WHAT ARE WE WAITING FOR?

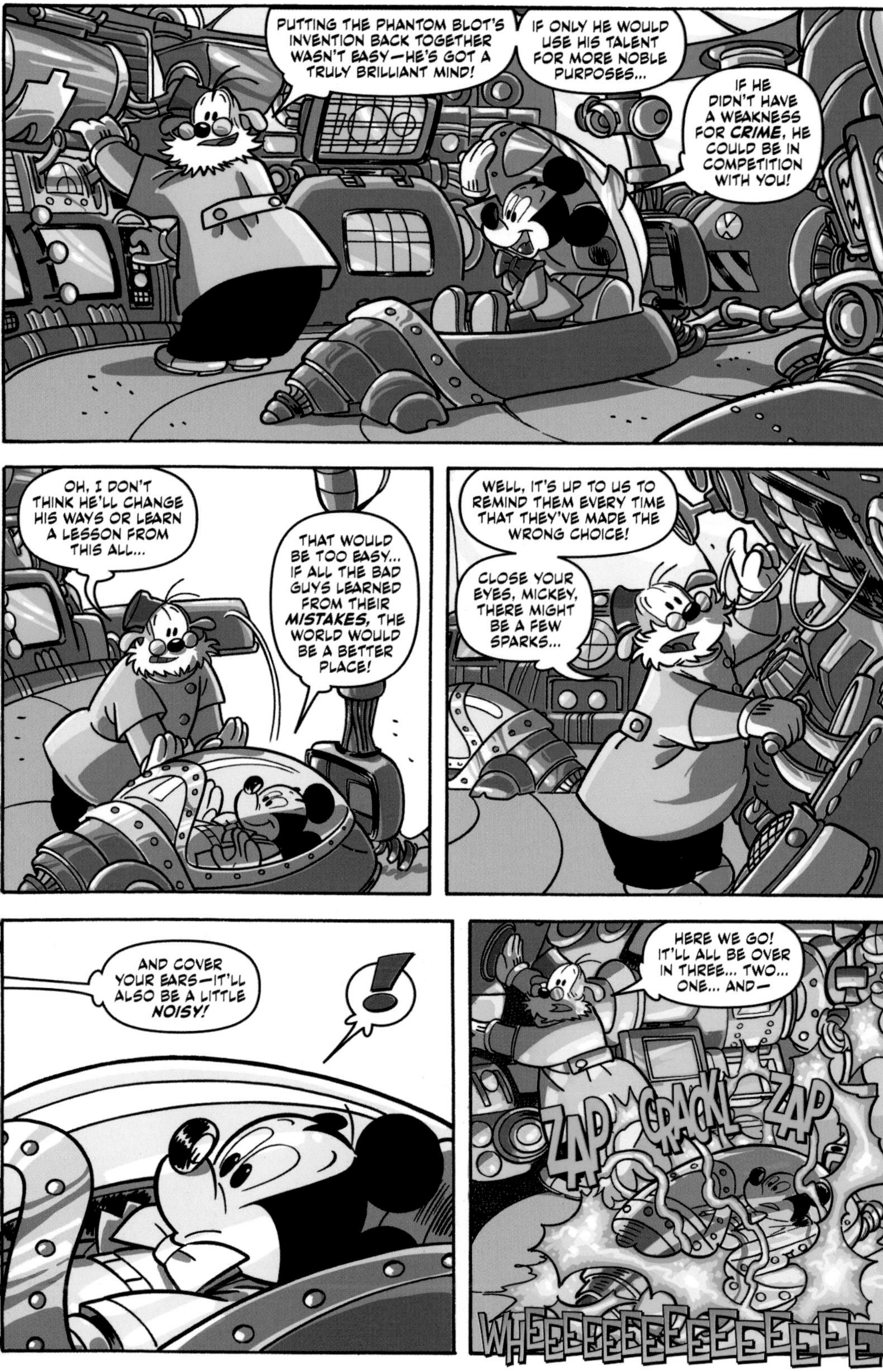

PUTTING THE PHANTOM BLOT'S INVENTION BACK TOGETHER WASN'T EASY—HE'S GOT A TRULY BRILLIANT MIND!
IF ONLY HE WOULD USE HIS TALENT FOR MORE NOBLE PURPOSES...
IF HE DIDN'T HAVE A WEAKNESS FOR **CRIME**, HE COULD BE IN COMPETITION WITH YOU!
OH, I DON'T THINK HE'LL CHANGE HIS WAYS OR LEARN A LESSON FROM THIS ALL...
THAT WOULD BE TOO EASY... IF ALL THE BAD GUYS LEARNED FROM THEIR ***MISTAKES***, THE WORLD WOULD BE A BETTER PLACE!
WELL, IT'S UP TO US TO REMIND THEM EVERY TIME THAT THEY'VE MADE THE WRONG CHOICE!
CLOSE YOUR EYES, MICKEY, THERE MIGHT BE A FEW SPARKS...
AND COVER YOUR EARS—IT'LL ALSO BE A LITTLE ***NOISY!***
!
HERE WE GO! IT'LL ALL BE OVER IN THREE... TWO... ONE... AND—
ZAP
CRACKL
ZAP
WHEEEEEEEEEEEEEEE

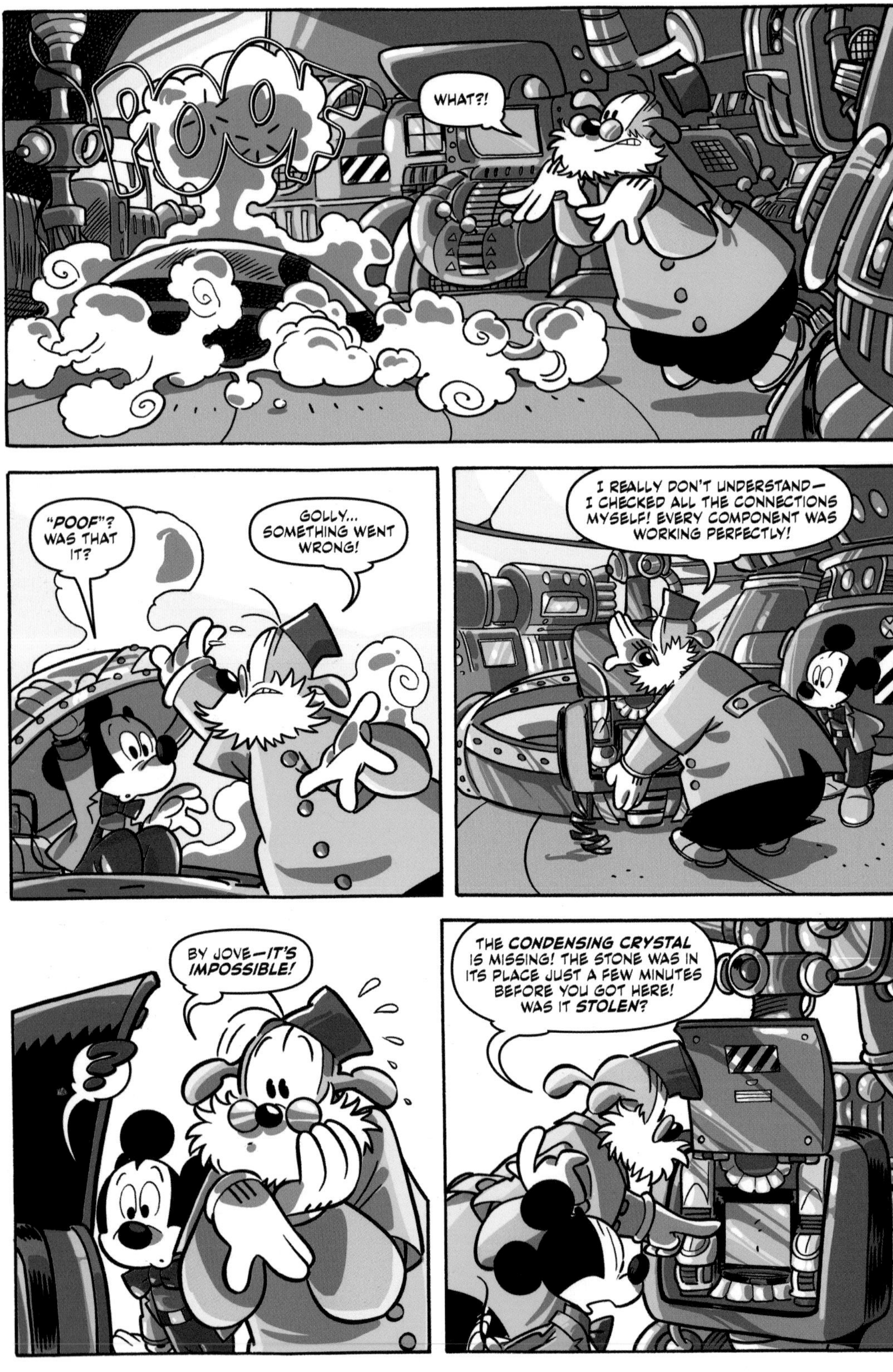
POOF
WHAT?!
"POOF"? WAS THAT IT?
GOLLY... SOMETHING WENT WRONG!
I REALLY DON'T UNDERSTAND— I CHECKED ALL THE CONNECTIONS MYSELF! EVERY COMPONENT WAS WORKING PERFECTLY!
BY JOVE—IT'S IMPOSSIBLE!
THE CONDENSING CRYSTAL IS MISSING! THE STONE WAS IN ITS PLACE JUST A FEW MINUTES BEFORE YOU GOT HERE! WAS IT STOLEN?

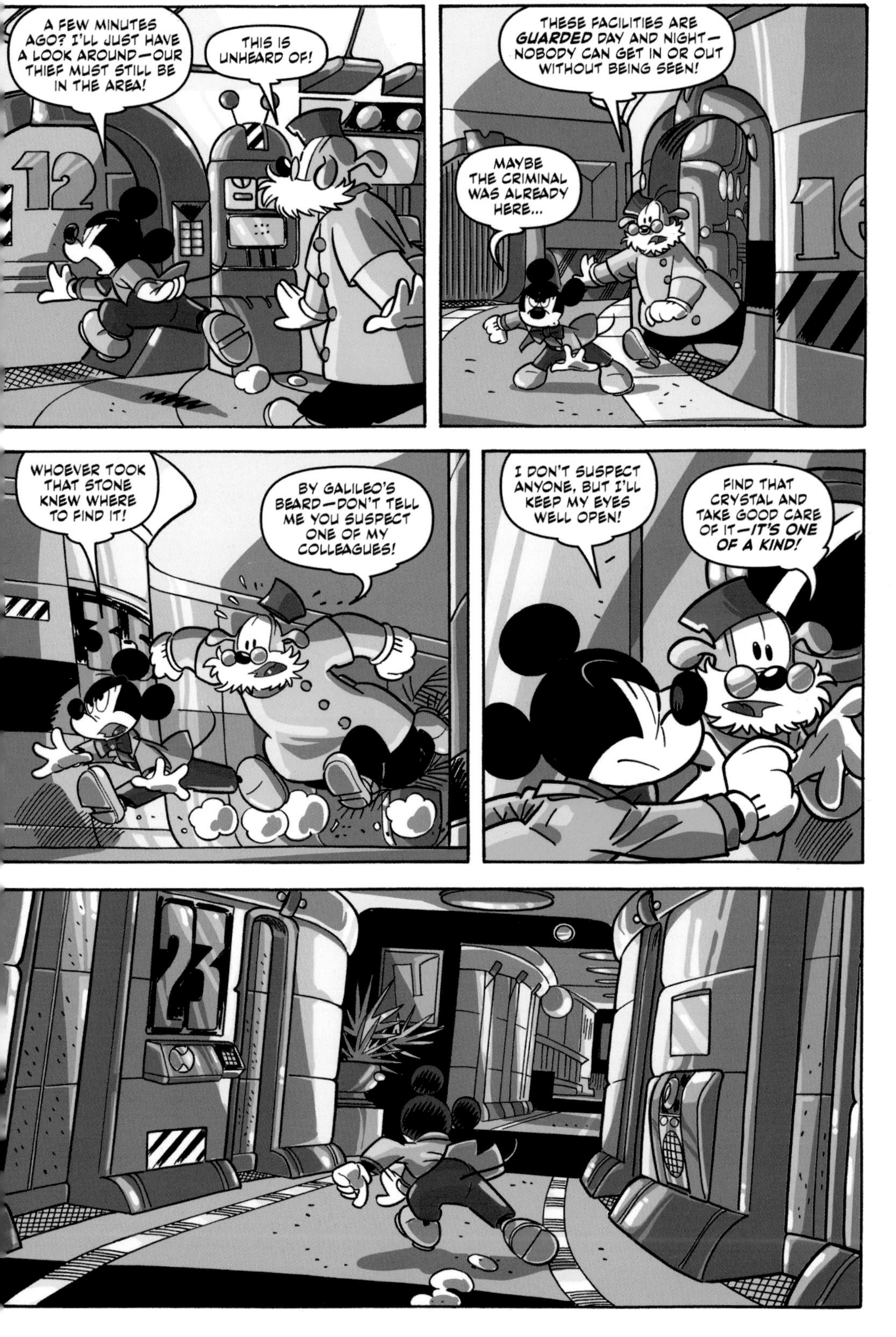
A FEW MINUTES AGO? I'LL JUST HAVE A LOOK AROUND—OUR THIEF MUST STILL BE IN THE AREA!
THIS IS UNHEARD OF!
THESE FACILITIES ARE GUARDED DAY AND NIGHT—NOBODY CAN GET IN OR OUT WITHOUT BEING SEEN!
MAYBE THE CRIMINAL WAS ALREADY HERE...
WHOEVER TOOK THAT STONE KNEW WHERE TO FIND IT!
BY GALILEO'S BEARD—DON'T TELL ME YOU SUSPECT ONE OF MY COLLEAGUES!
I DON'T SUSPECT ANYONE, BUT I'LL KEEP MY EYES WELL OPEN!
FIND THAT CRYSTAL AND TAKE GOOD CARE OF IT—IT'S ONE OF A KIND!

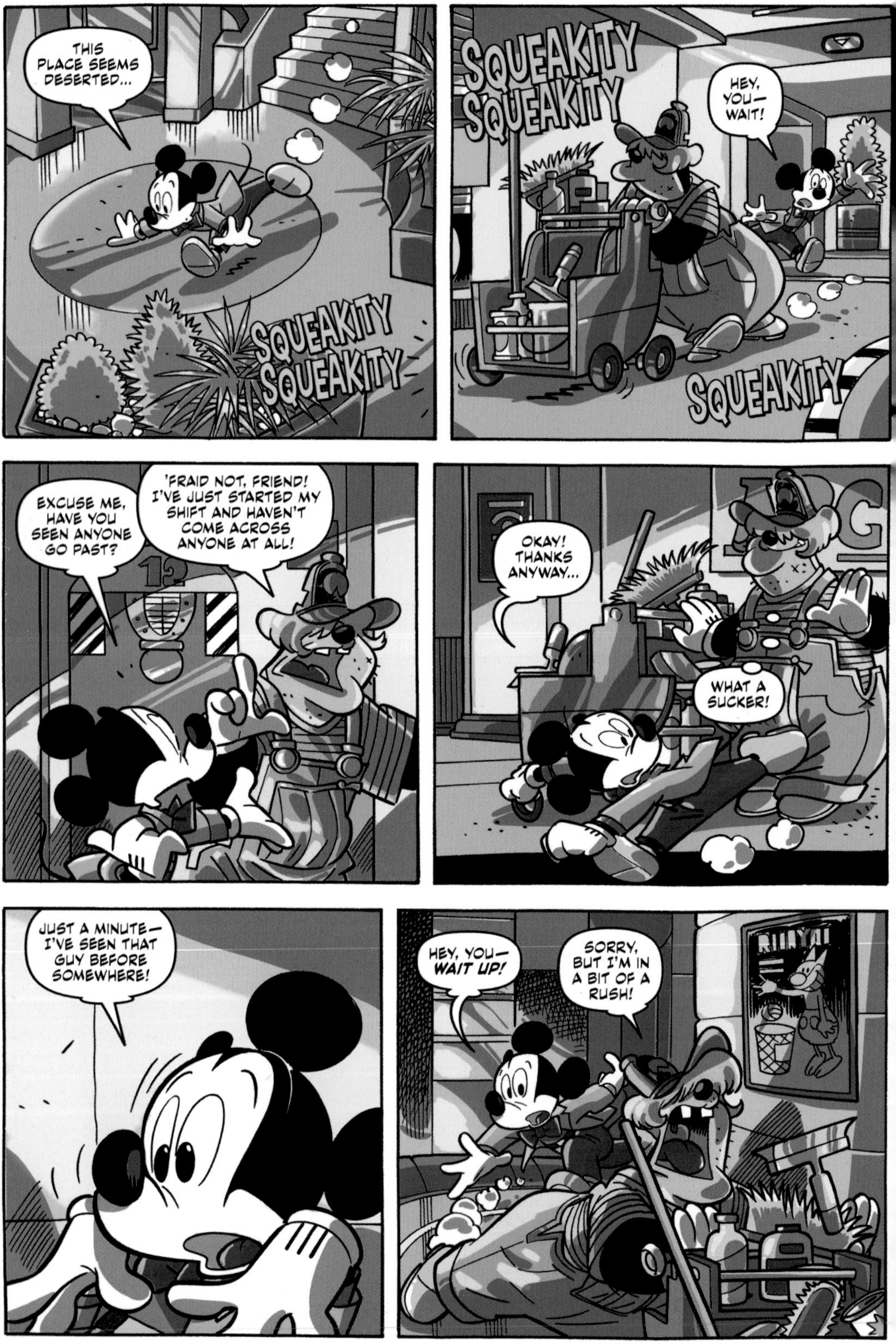
THIS PLACE SEEMS DESERTED...
SQUEAKITY SQUEAKITY
SQUEAKITY SQUEAKITY
HEY, YOU— WAIT!
SQUEAKITY
EXCUSE ME, HAVE YOU SEEN ANYONE GO PAST?
'FRAID NOT, FRIEND! I'VE JUST STARTED MY SHIFT AND HAVEN'T COME ACROSS ANYONE AT ALL!
OKAY! THANKS ANYWAY...
WHAT A SUCKER!
JUST A MINUTE— I'VE SEEN THAT GUY BEFORE SOMEWHERE!
HEY, YOU— WAIT UP!
SORRY, BUT I'M IN A BIT OF A RUSH!

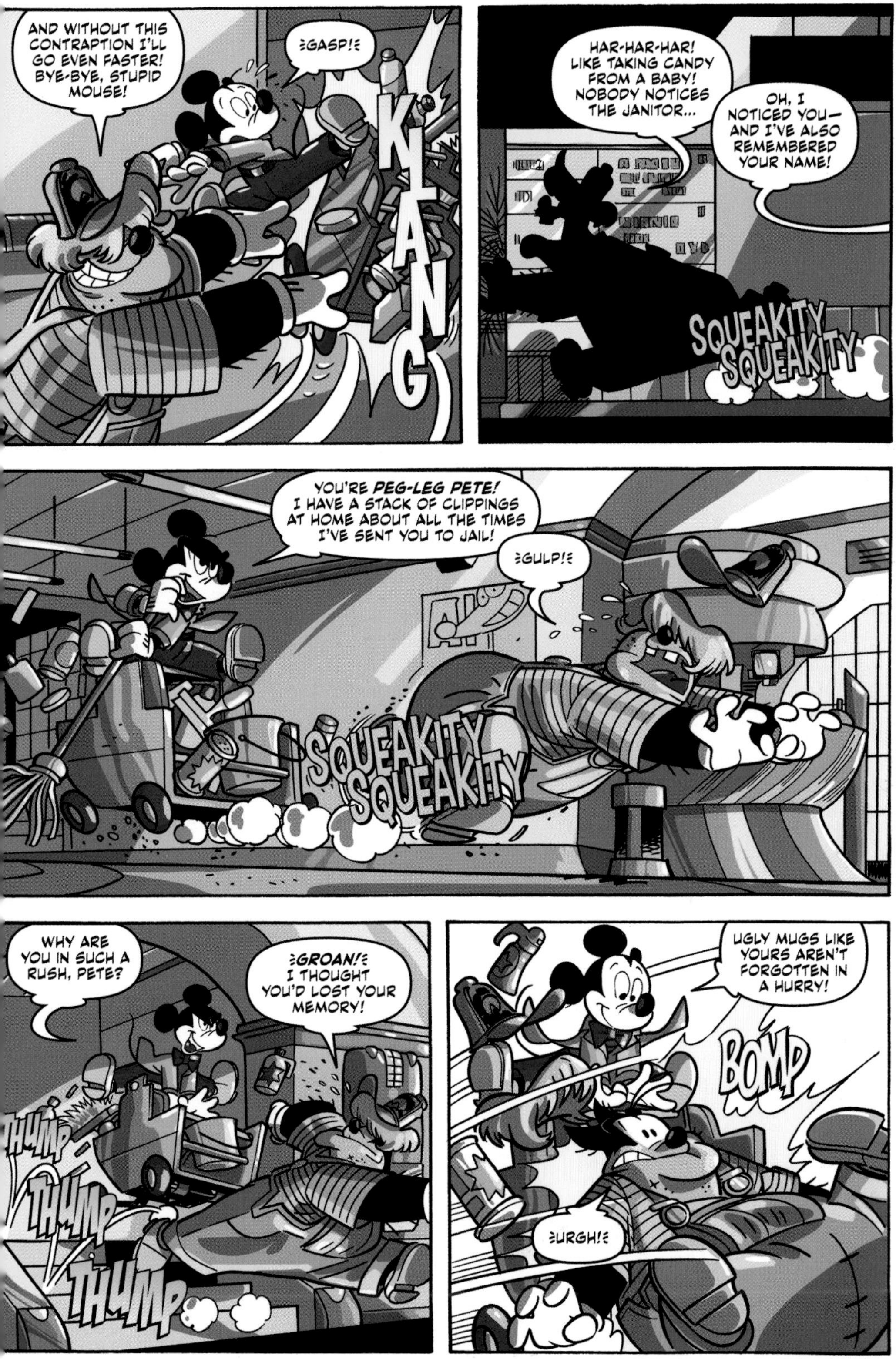
AND WITHOUT THIS CONTRAPTION I'LL GO EVEN FASTER! BYE-BYE, STUPID MOUSE!
GASP!
KLANG
HAR-HAR-HAR! LIKE TAKING CANDY FROM A BABY! NOBODY NOTICES THE JANITOR...
OH, I NOTICED YOU— AND I'VE ALSO REMEMBERED YOUR NAME!
SQUEAKITY SQUEAKITY
YOU'RE PEG-LEG PETE! I HAVE A STACK OF CLIPPINGS AT HOME ABOUT ALL THE TIMES I'VE SENT YOU TO JAIL!
GULP!
SQUEAKITY SQUEAKITY
WHY ARE YOU IN SUCH A RUSH, PETE?
GROAN! I THOUGHT YOU'D LOST YOUR MEMORY!
THUMP THUMP THUMP
UGLY MUGS LIKE YOURS AREN'T FORGOTTEN IN A HURRY!
BOMP
URGH!

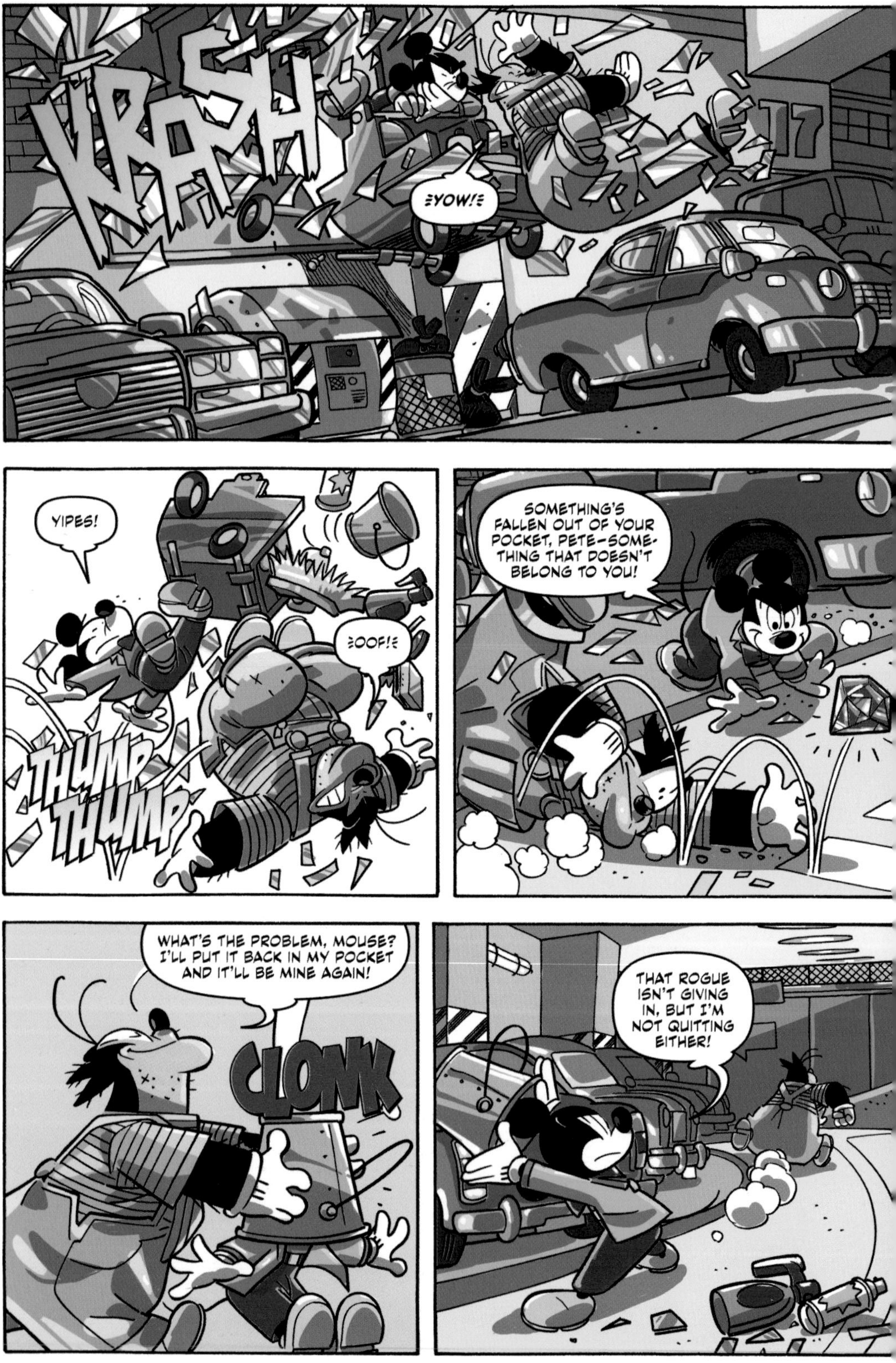
KRASH
YOW!
YIPES!
OOF!
THUMP THUMP
SOMETHING'S FALLEN OUT OF YOUR POCKET, PETE—SOMETHING THAT DOESN'T BELONG TO YOU!
WHAT'S THE PROBLEM, MOUSE? I'LL PUT IT BACK IN MY POCKET AND IT'LL BE MINE AGAIN!
CLONK
THAT ROGUE ISN'T GIVING IN, BUT I'M NOT QUITTING EITHER!

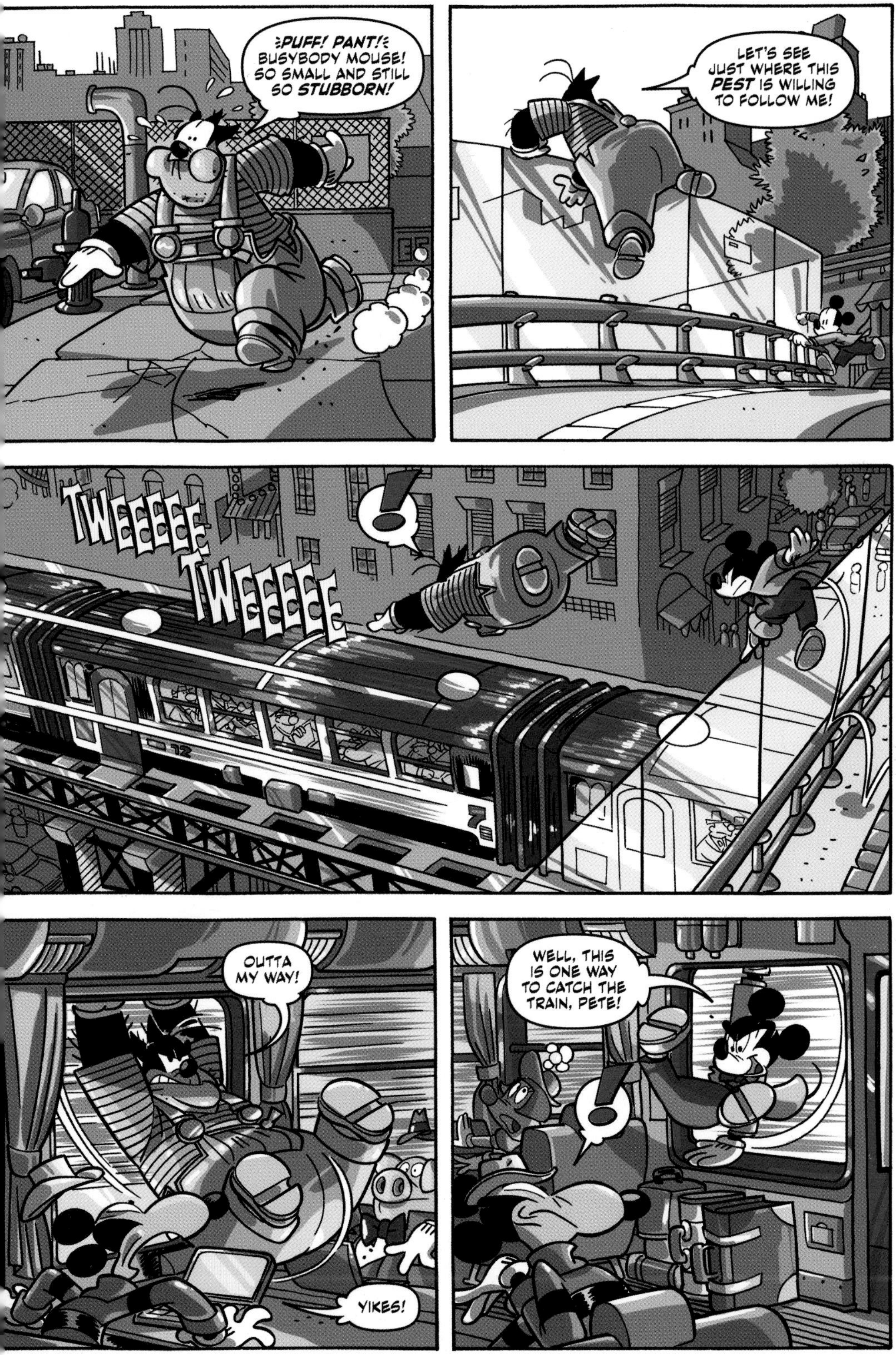
PUFF! PANT! BUSYBODY MOUSE! SO SMALL AND STILL SO *STUBBORN!*
LET'S SEE JUST WHERE THIS *PEST* IS WILLING TO FOLLOW ME!
TWEEEEE
TWEEEEE
!
OUTTA MY WAY!
YIKES!
WELL, THIS IS ONE WAY TO CATCH THE TRAIN, PETE!
!

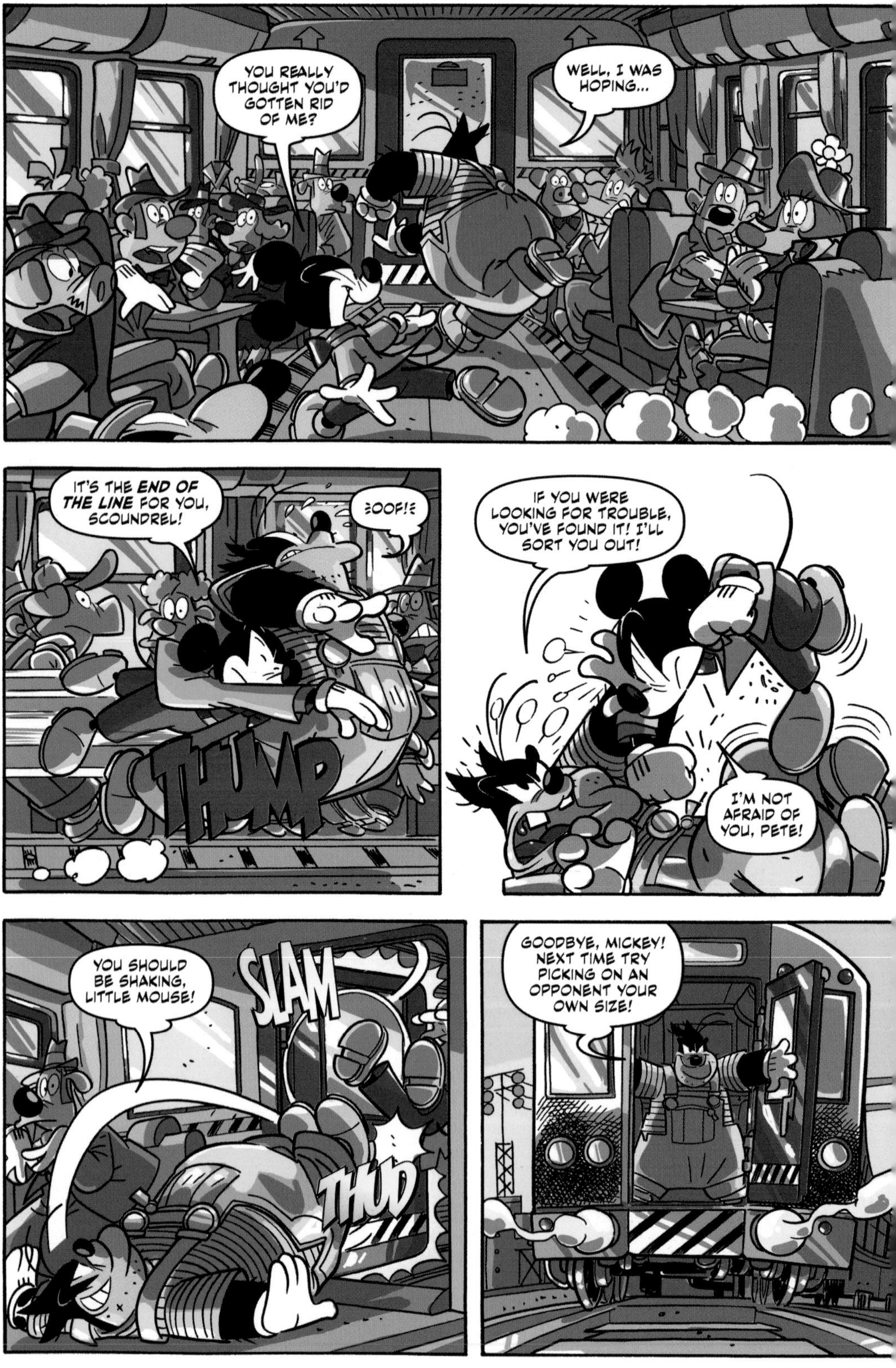
YOU REALLY THOUGHT YOU'D GOTTEN RID OF ME?
WELL, I WAS HOPING...
IT'S THE ***END OF THE LINE*** FOR YOU, SCOUNDREL!
OOF!
THUMP
IF YOU WERE LOOKING FOR TROUBLE, YOU'VE FOUND IT! I'LL SORT YOU OUT!
I'M NOT AFRAID OF YOU, PETE!
YOU SHOULD BE SHAKING, LITTLE MOUSE!
SLAM
THUD
GOODBYE, MICKEY! NEXT TIME TRY PICKING ON AN OPPONENT YOUR OWN SIZE!

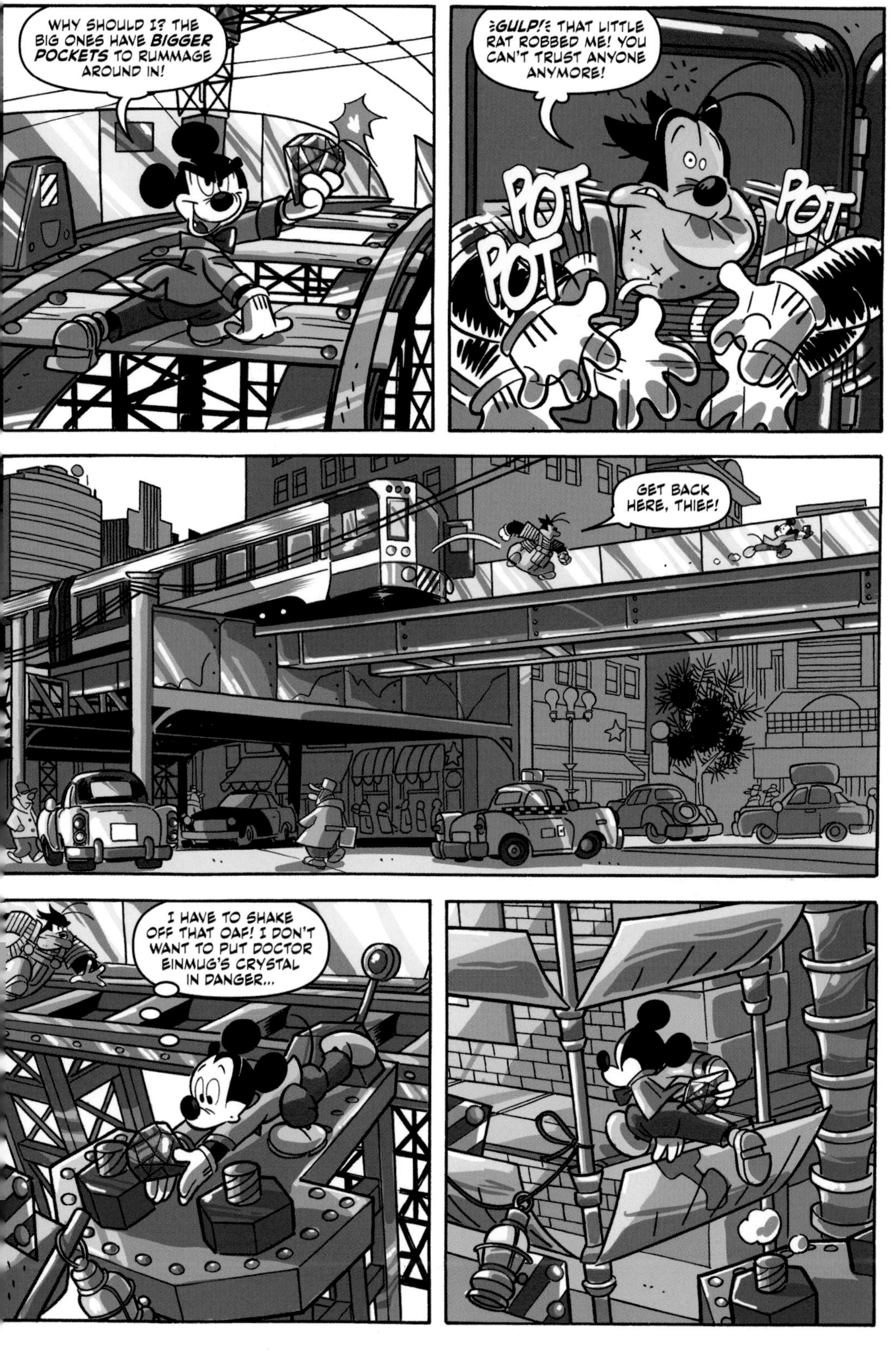
WHY SHOULD I? THE BIG ONES HAVE BIGGER POCKETS TO RUMMAGE AROUND IN!
GULP! THAT LITTLE RAT ROBBED ME! YOU CAN'T TRUST ANYONE ANYMORE!
POT POT POT
GET BACK HERE, THIEF!
I HAVE TO SHAKE OFF THAT OAF! I DON'T WANT TO PUT DOCTOR EINMUG'S CRYSTAL IN DANGER...

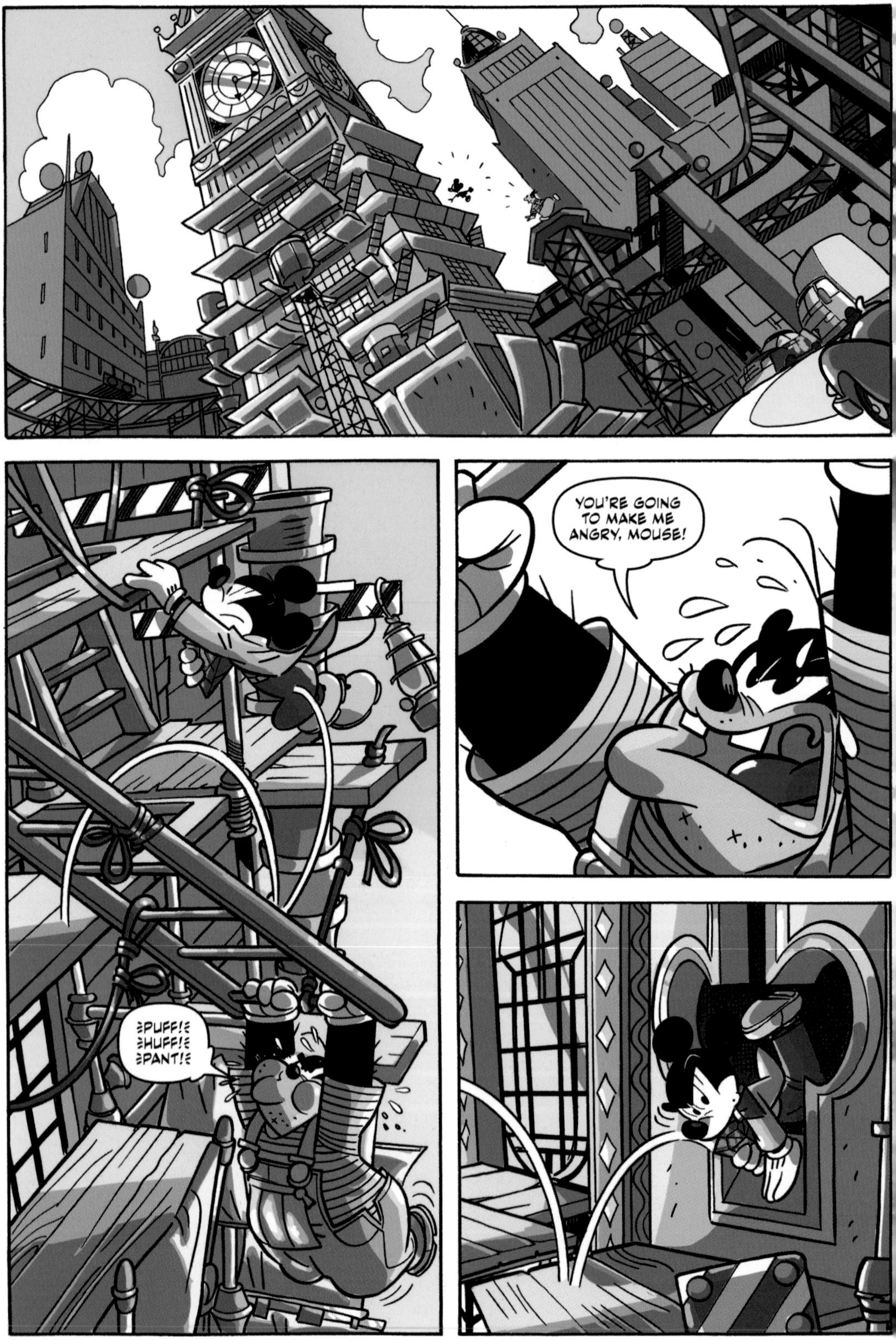
PUFF! HUFF! PANT!
YOU'RE GOING TO MAKE ME ANGRY, MOUSE!

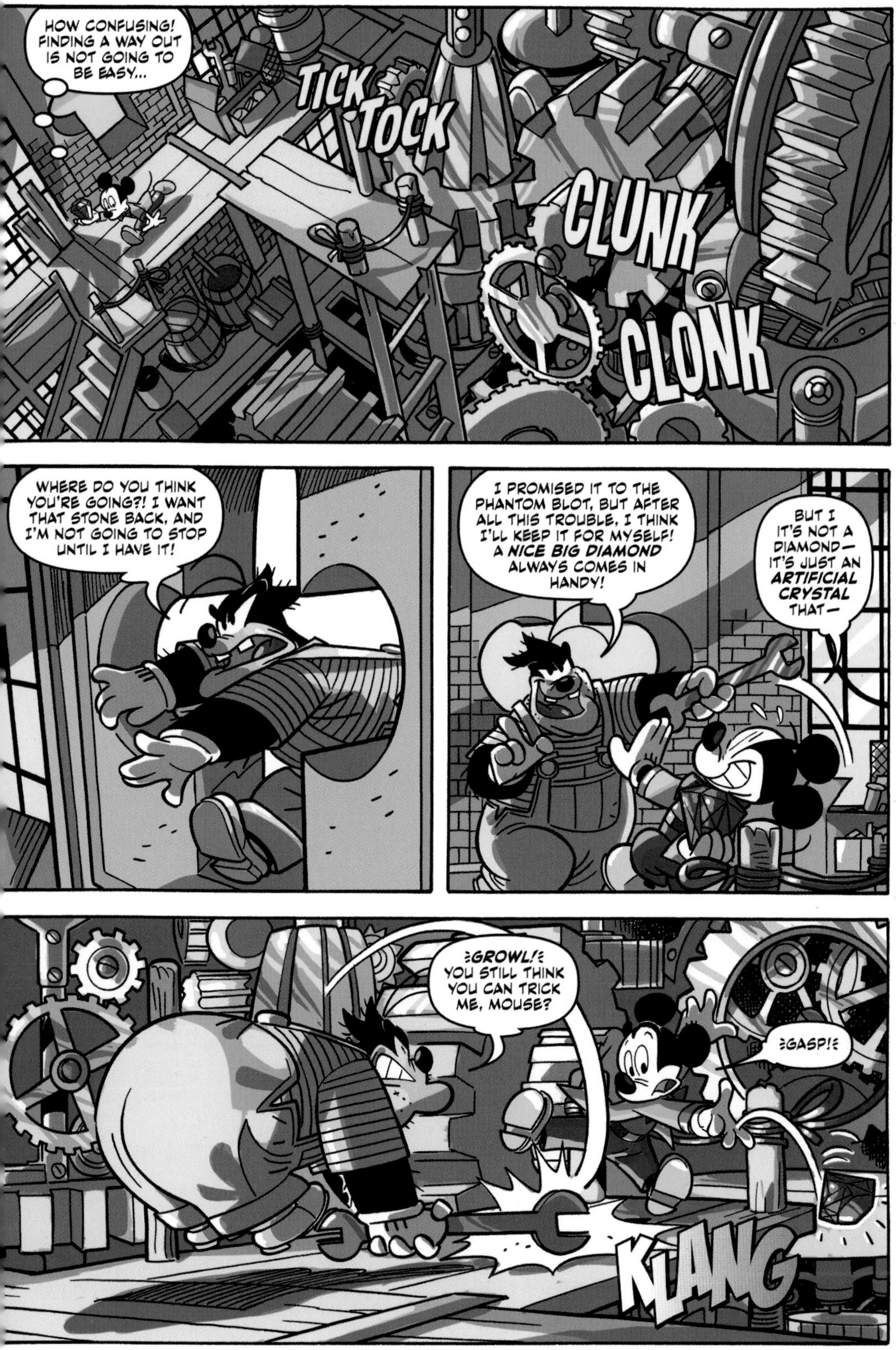
HOW CONFUSING! FINDING A WAY OUT IS NOT GOING TO BE EASY...
TICK TOCK
CLUNK
CLONK
WHERE DO YOU THINK YOU'RE GOING?! I WANT THAT STONE BACK, AND I'M NOT GOING TO STOP UNTIL I HAVE IT!
I PROMISED IT TO THE PHANTOM BLOT, BUT AFTER ALL THIS TROUBLE, I THINK I'LL KEEP IT FOR MYSELF! A NICE BIG DIAMOND ALWAYS COMES IN HANDY!
BUT I IT'S NOT A DIAMOND— IT'S JUST AN ARTIFICIAL CRYSTAL THAT—
GROWL! YOU STILL THINK YOU CAN TRICK ME, MOUSE?
GASP!
KLANG

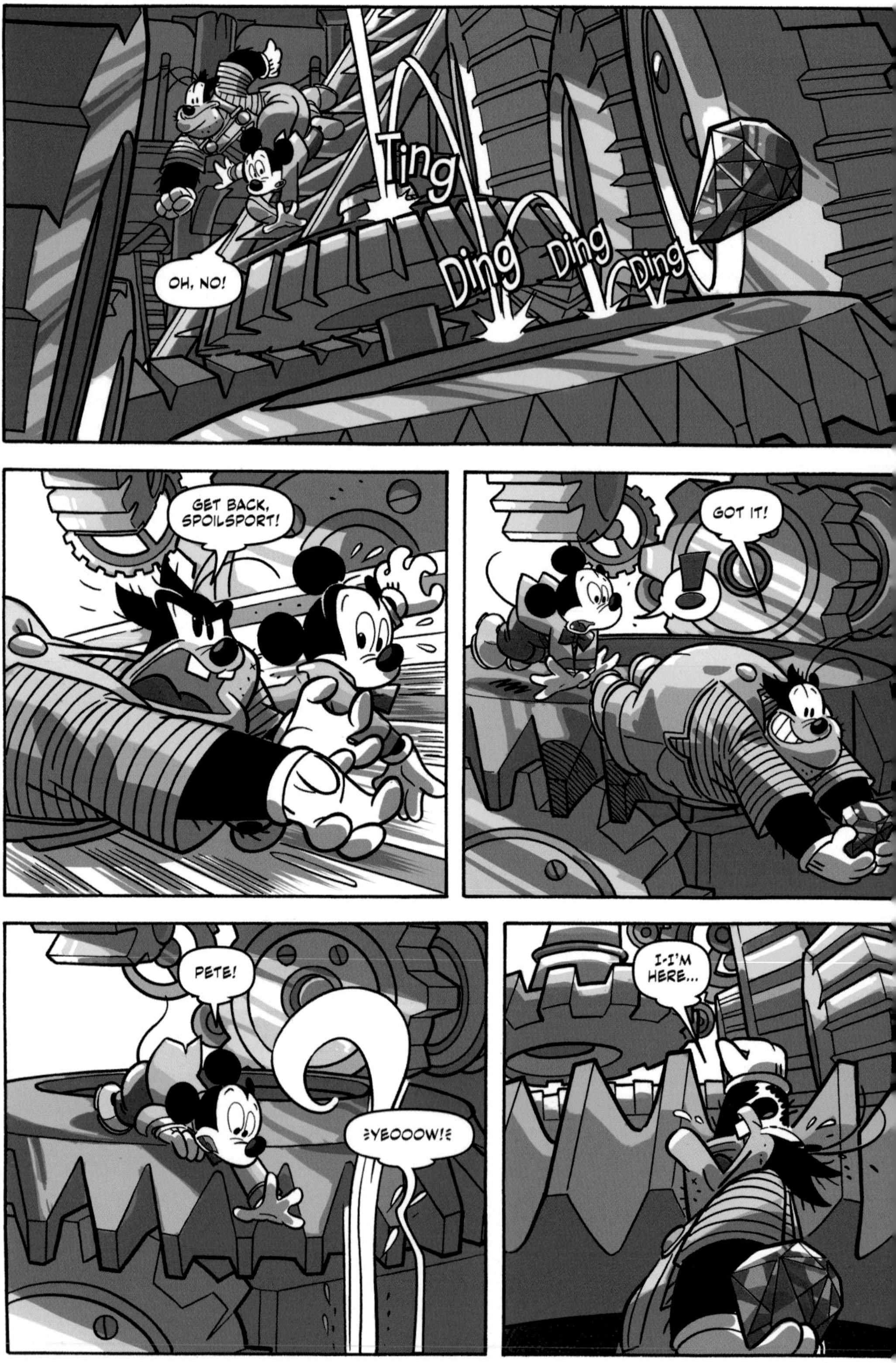
Ting
Ding
Ding
Ding
OH, NO!
GET BACK, SPOILSPORT!
GOT IT!
!
PETE!
YEOOOW!
I-I'M HERE...

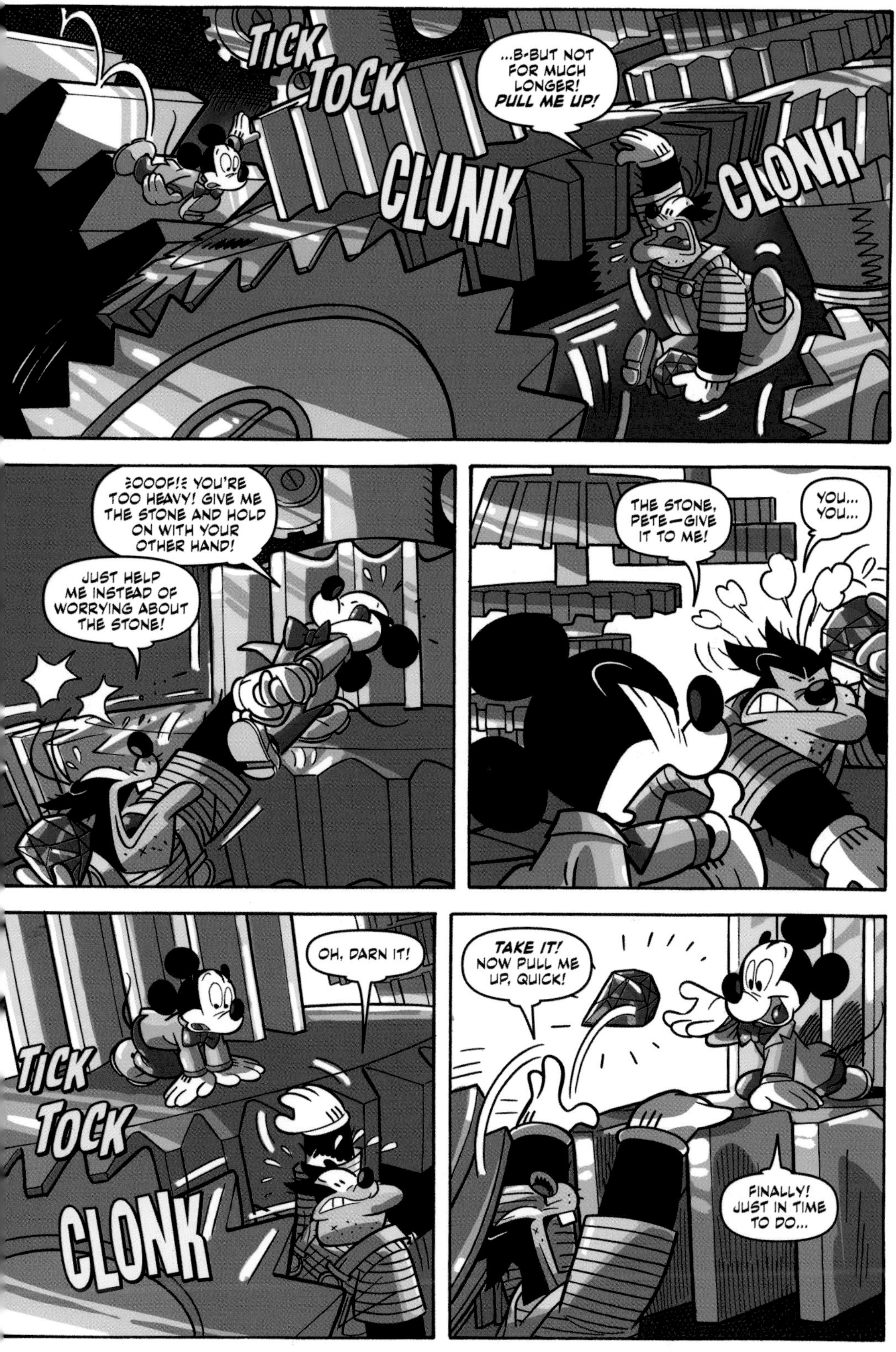
TICK TOCK
...B-BUT NOT FOR MUCH LONGER! PULL ME UP!
CLUNK
CLONK
OOOF! YOU'RE TOO HEAVY! GIVE ME THE STONE AND HOLD ON WITH YOUR OTHER HAND!
JUST HELP ME INSTEAD OF WORRYING ABOUT THE STONE!
THE STONE, PETE—GIVE IT TO ME!
YOU... YOU...
OH, DARN IT!
TICK TOCK
CLONK
TAKE IT! NOW PULL ME UP, QUICK!
FINALLY! JUST IN TIME TO DO...

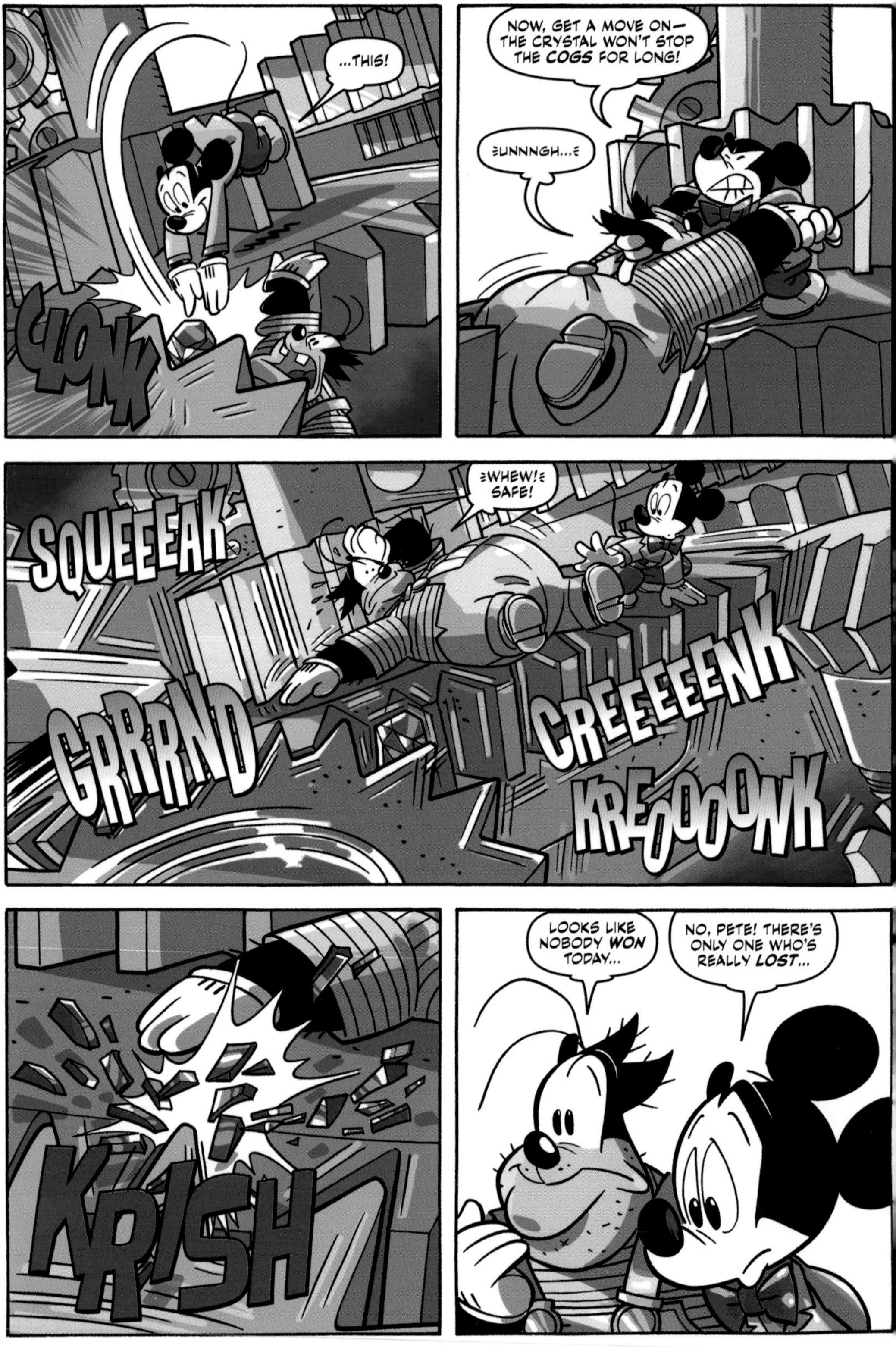
...THIS!
CLONK
NOW, GET A MOVE ON—THE CRYSTAL WON'T STOP THE COGS FOR LONG!
UNNNGH...
SQUEEEAK
WHEW! SAFE!
GRRRND
CREEEEENK
KREOOOONK
KRISH
LOOKS LIKE NOBODY WON TODAY...
NO, PETE! THERE'S ONLY ONE WHO'S REALLY LOST...

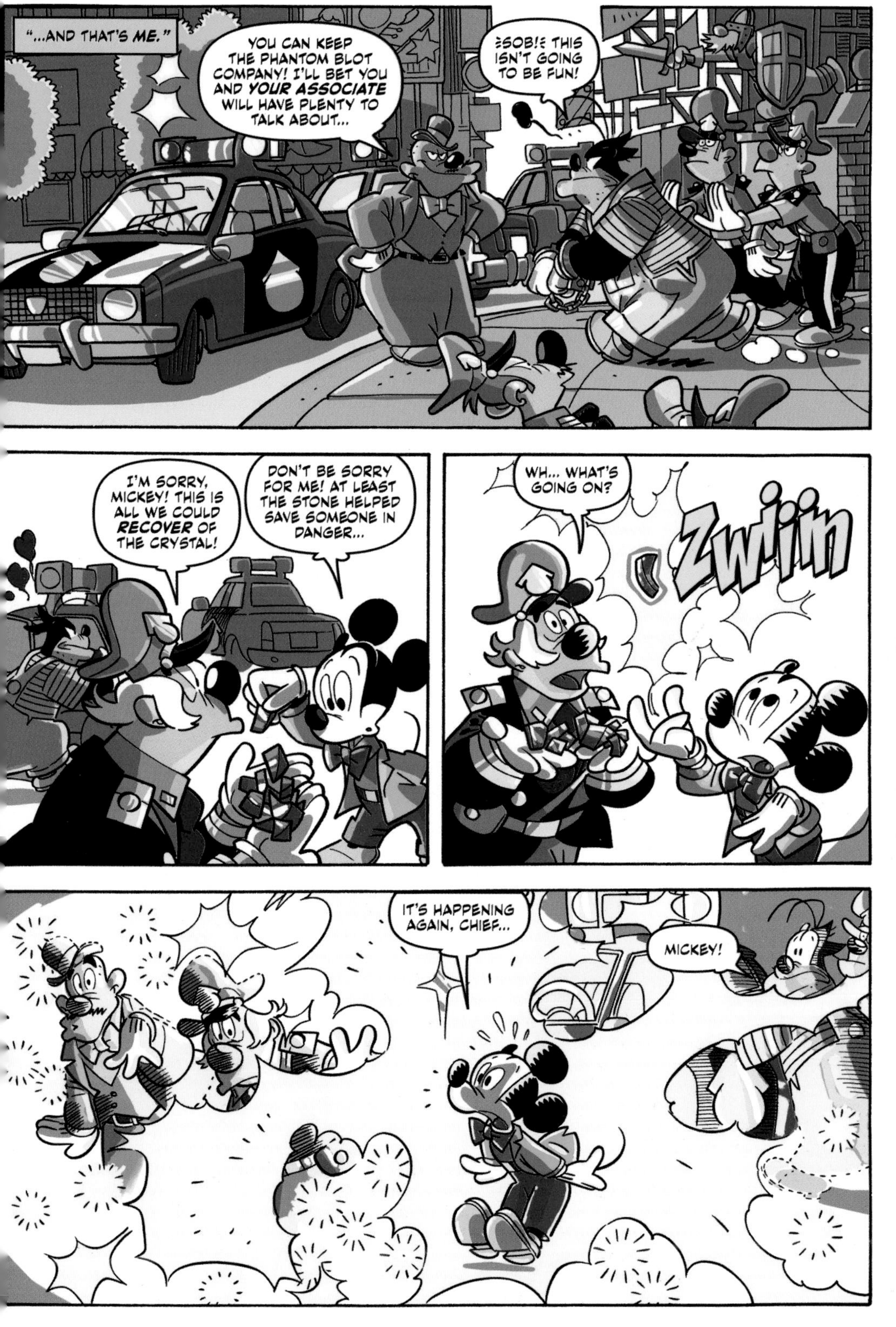
"...AND THAT'S ME."
YOU CAN KEEP THE PHANTOM BLOT COMPANY! I'LL BET YOU AND YOUR ASSOCIATE WILL HAVE PLENTY TO TALK ABOUT...
SOB! THIS ISN'T GOING TO BE FUN!
I'M SORRY, MICKEY! THIS IS ALL WE COULD RECOVER OF THE CRYSTAL!
DON'T BE SORRY FOR ME! AT LEAST THE STONE HELPED SAVE SOMEONE IN DANGER...
WH... WHAT'S GOING ON?
ZWIIM
IT'S HAPPENING AGAIN, CHIEF...
MICKEY!

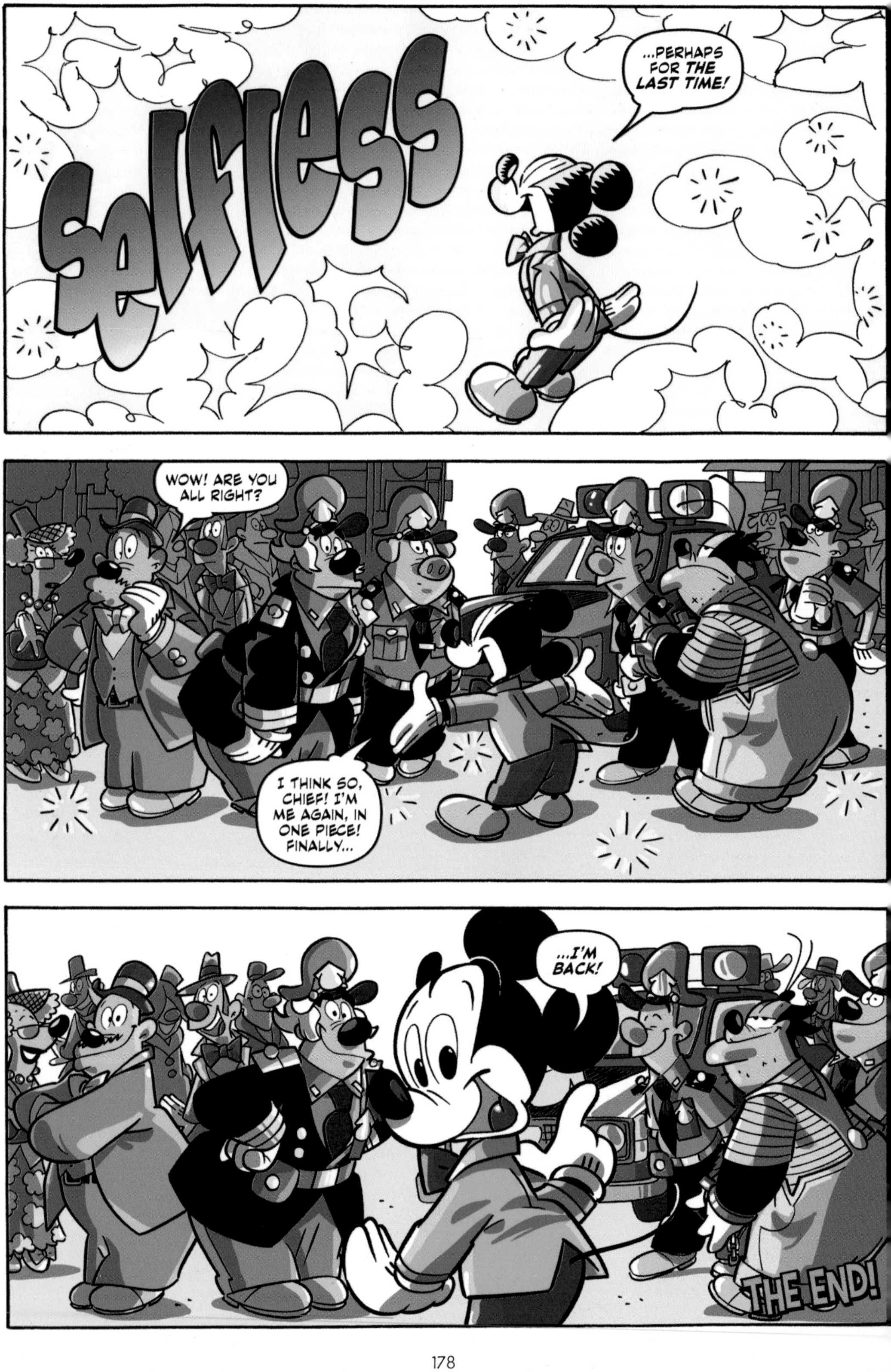
...PERHAPS FOR THE LAST TIME!
SELFLESS
WOW! ARE YOU ALL RIGHT?
I THINK SO, CHIEF! I'M ME AGAIN, IN ONE PIECE! FINALLY...
...I'M BACK!
THE END!

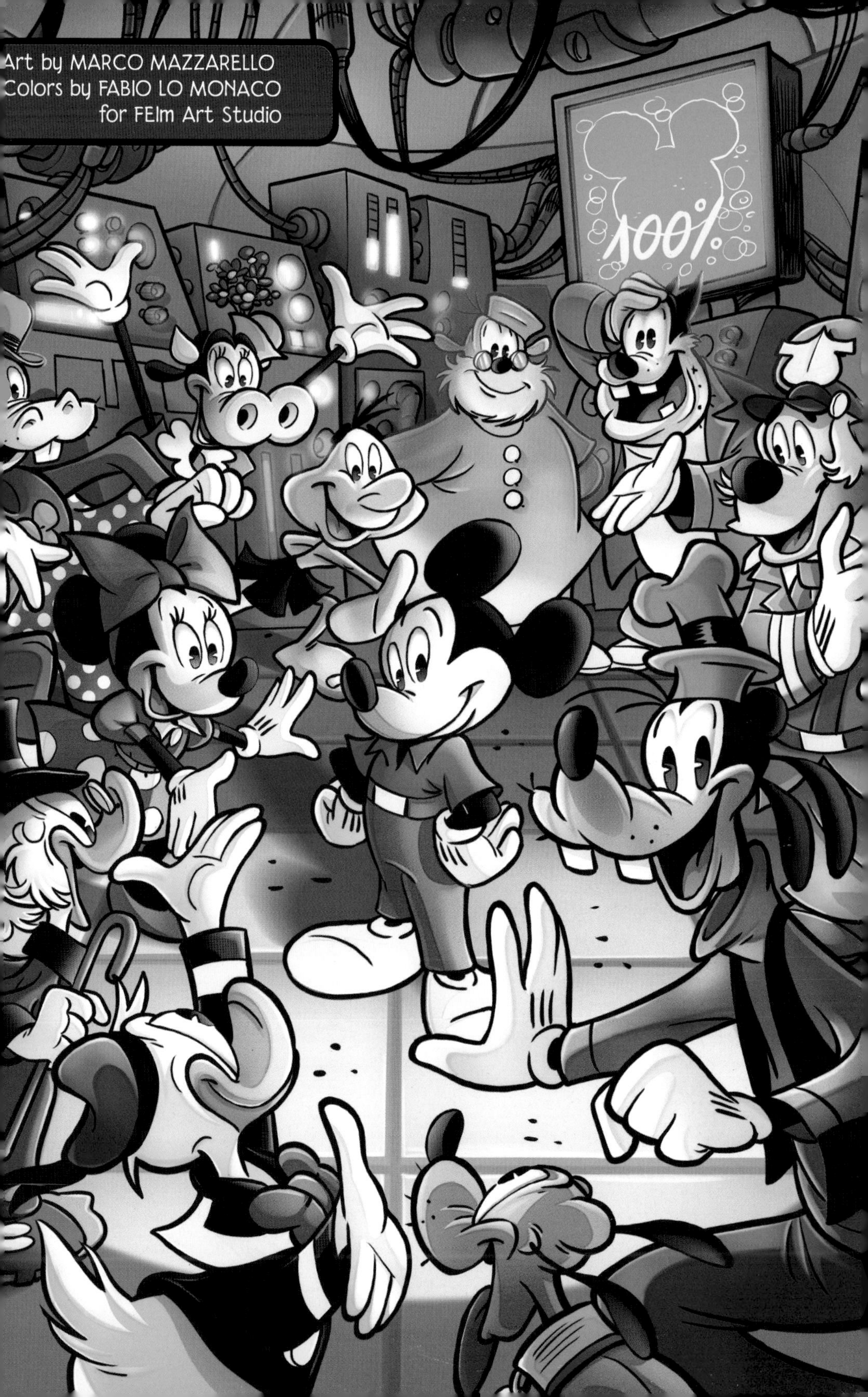
Art by MARCO MAZZARELLO
Colors by FABIO LO MONACO
for FElm Art Studio
100%

Art by MARCO MAZZARELLO

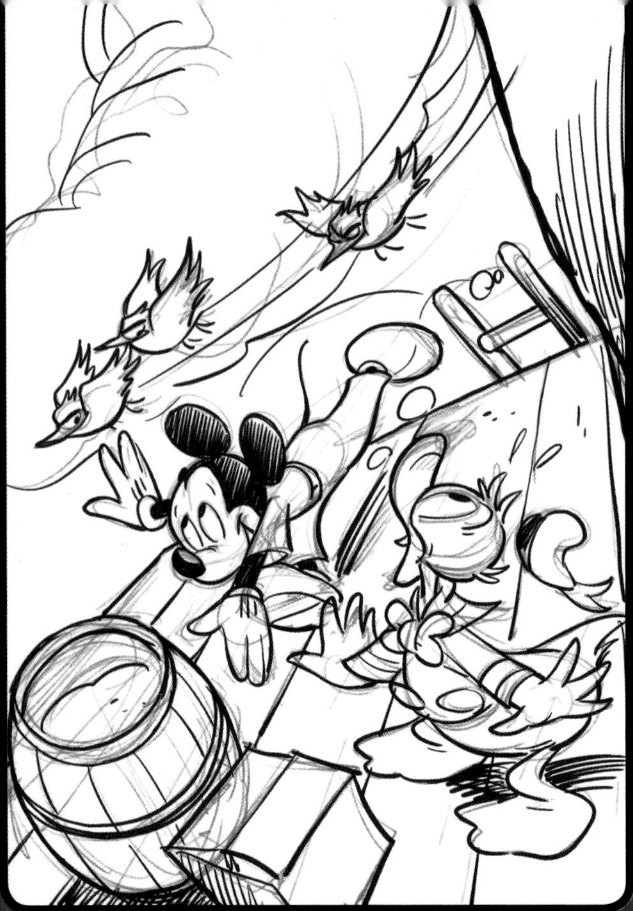

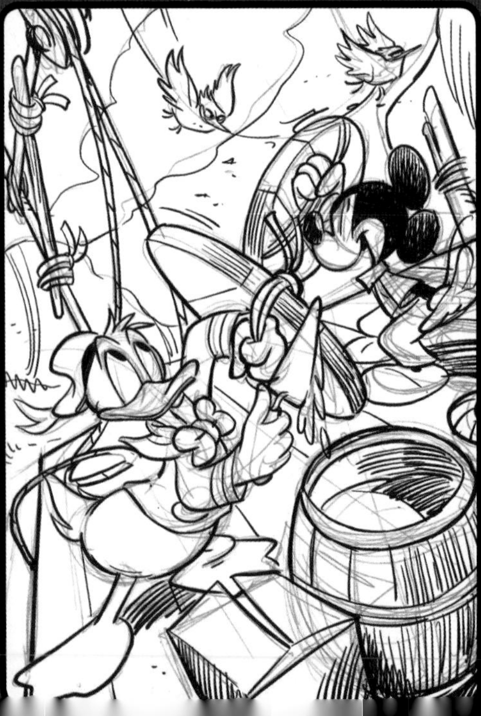

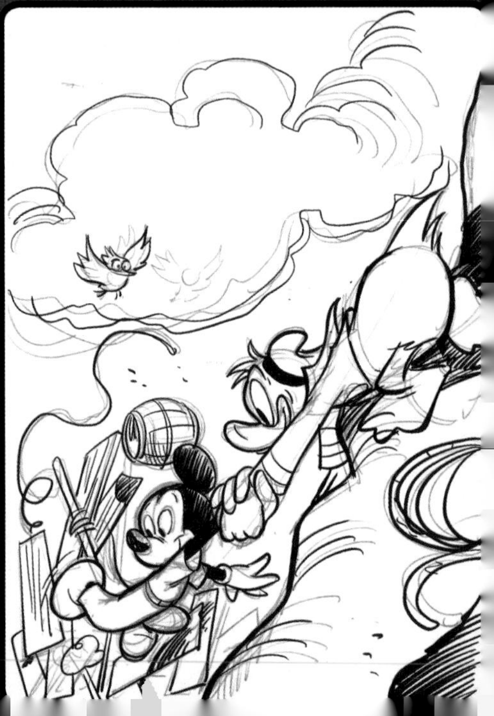

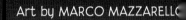

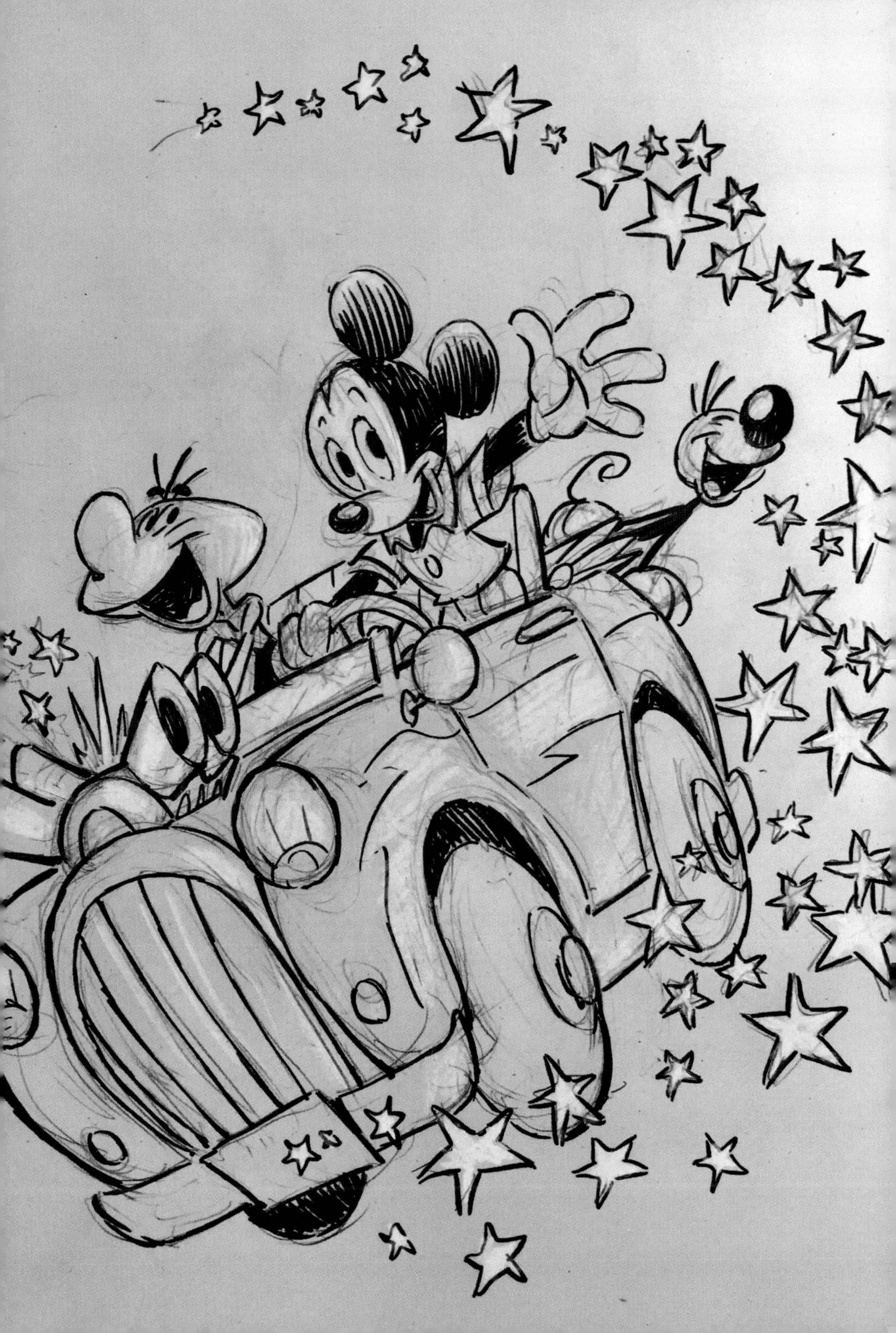

Art by LORENZO PASTROVICCHIO

Art by STEFANO INTINI

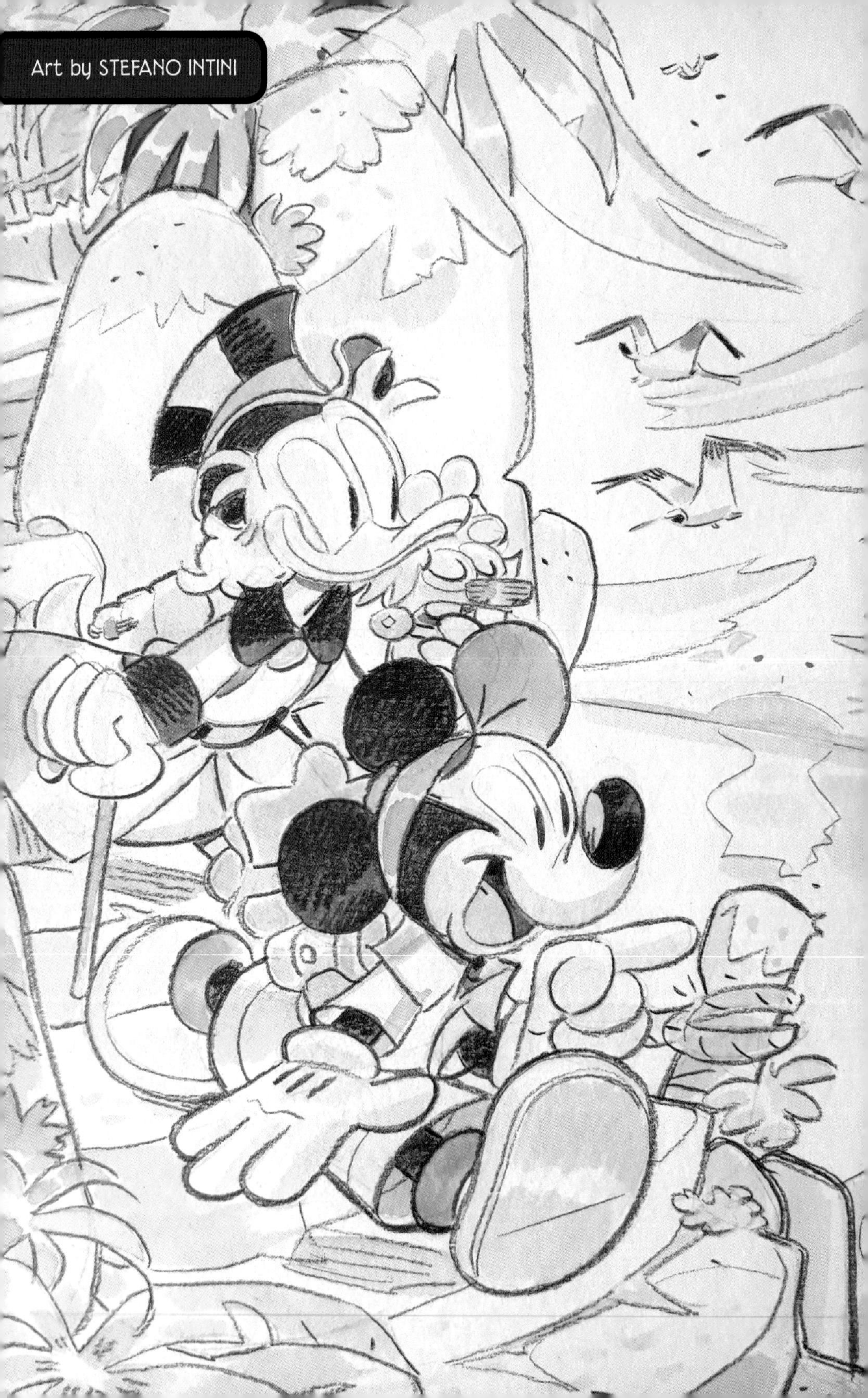

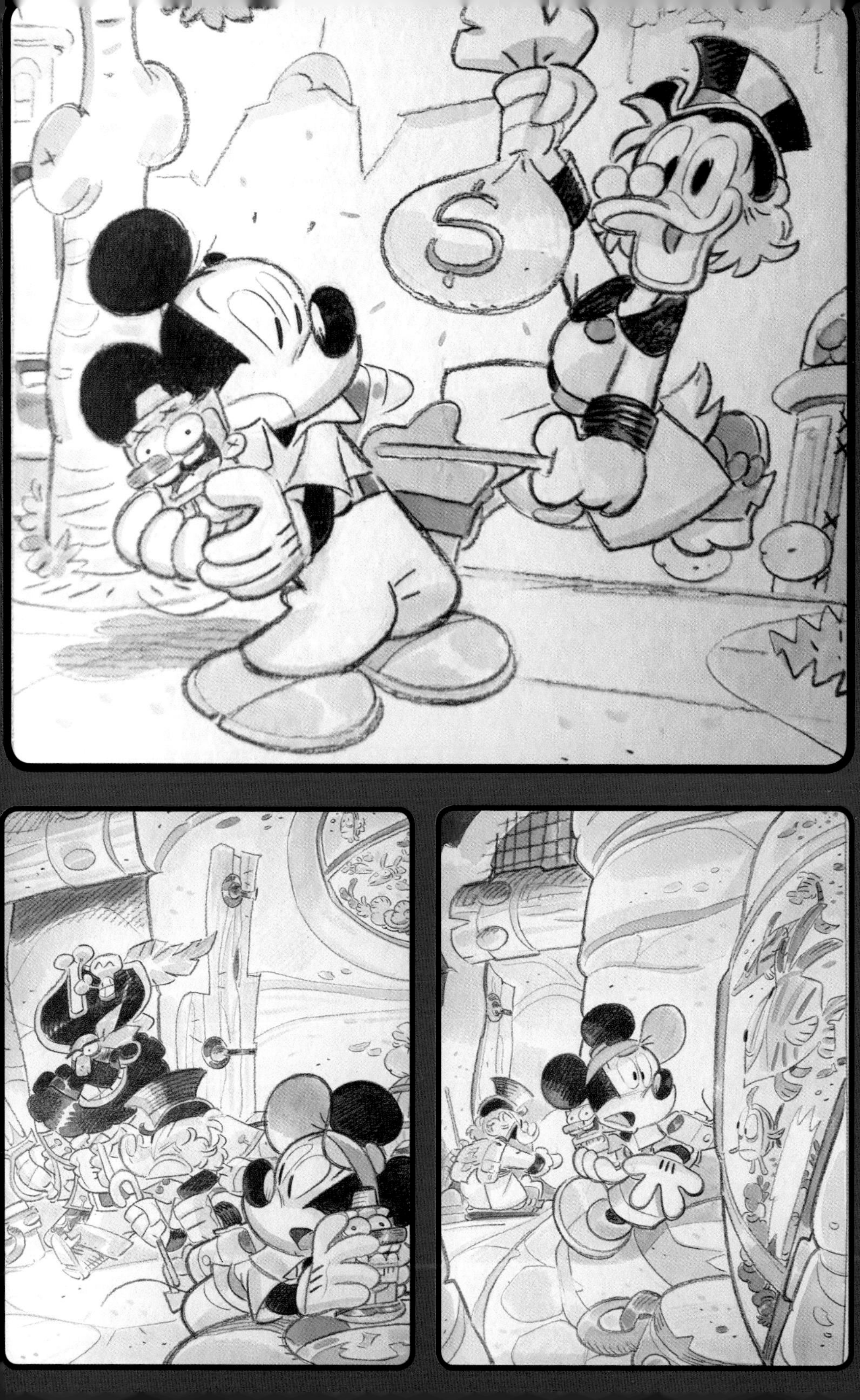

Art by STEFANO INTINI

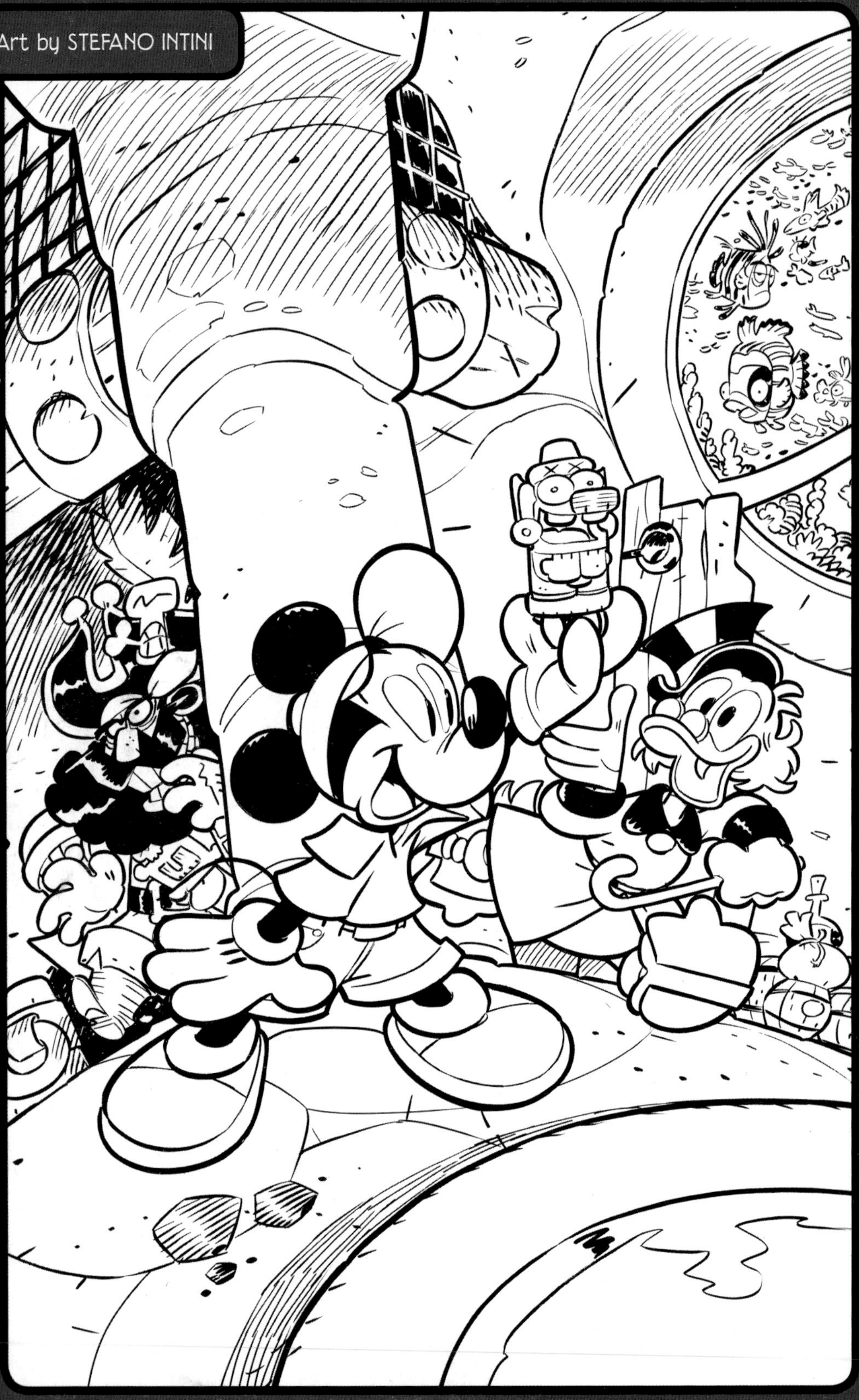